THE LONELY KINGDOM

KATHRYN OSCAR

 Formatted with Vellum

For my dad who told me I could be anything I wanted to be when I grew up. I doubt you had this in mind, but thank you for teaching me to believe in myself.

&

For those who walk this world hand in hand with grief. Love with nowhere to go can be painful, even on the best of days. Way to keep going anyway.

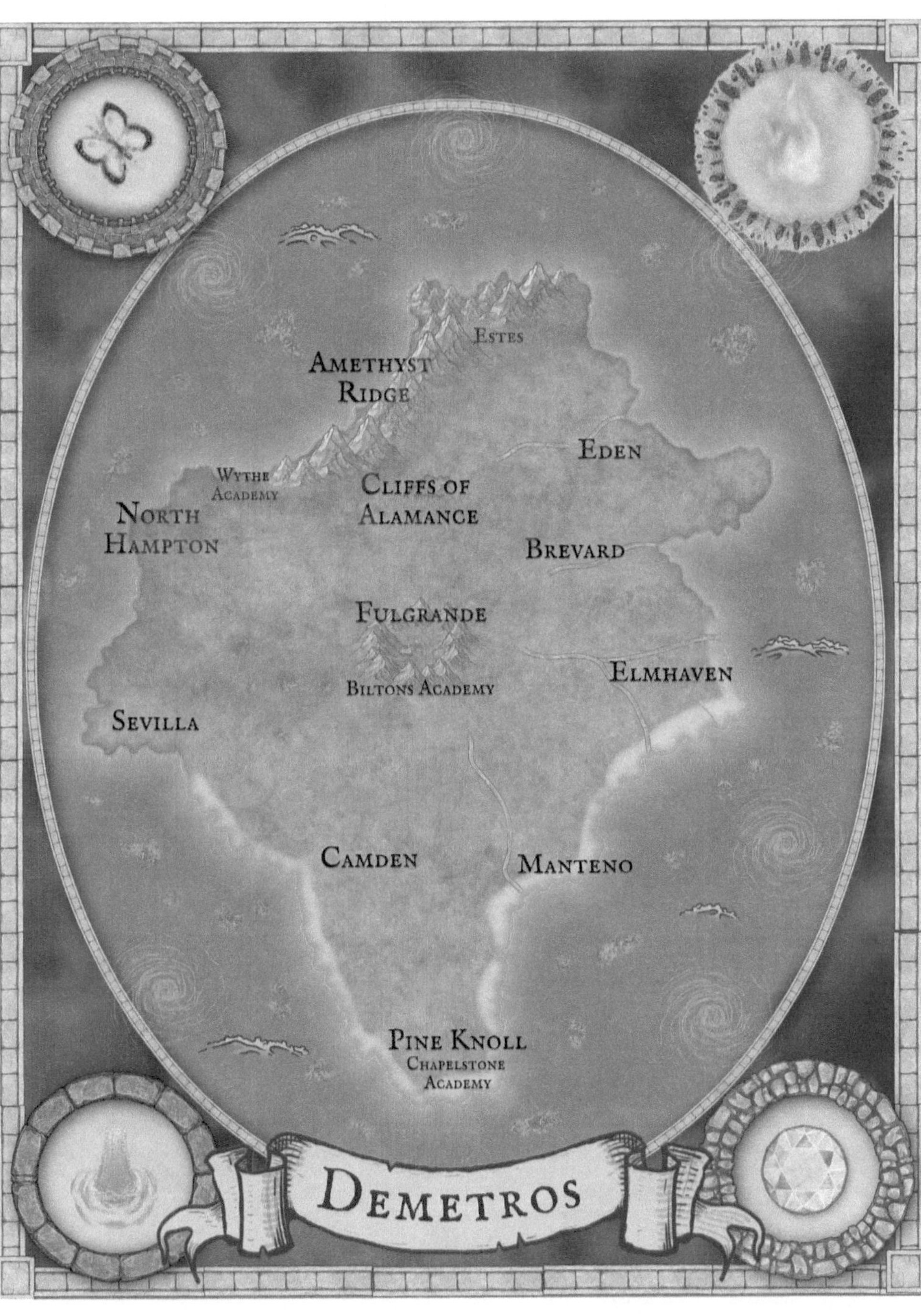

Estes
Amethyst Ridge
Eden
Wythe Academy
Cliffs of Alamance
North Hampton
Brevard
Fulgrande
Elmhaven
Biltons Academy
Sevilla
Camden
Manteno
Pine Knoll
Chapelstone Academy
Demetros

One

THE NAMELESS

She caught the weight of the woman's gaze from across the battlefield. Assessing eyes that were more white than blue stared back at her. The stranger's appearance matched the toll of days spent fighting. She knew this was a mirror to her own state. Covered in dirt and blood, both of them looked wild, far too removed from the cleansing properties of a bath.

That was where their similarities ended, though. The color of their eyes, the haggard state of their dress. They stood firmly on opposite sides of the war, but she had not found hatred in the woman's gaze. Only a deep-rooted, unsettling concern.

That pause, the brief hesitation that they had both allowed themselves, was enough to distract them from deflecting what came next.

A man emerged from the shadows, from her periphery. Had he been standing there all along?

A blast of frost raced from the figure's palm to the woman's chest, and within an instant, her form was nothing more than a shimmering, distorted statue.

From this distance, she could only gauge an expression of twisted terror on the stranger's face. A horrifying reflection of the pain that the woman *must have endured as a glacial prison grew around her, encasing her within the ice.*

She panicked, crying out to the woman, screaming something unintelligible to the figure that no one bothered to acknowledge. She wasn't sure why that woman's fate seemed to be entwined with her own.

Another hooded figure, shrouded in darkness and shadows, approached the woman's form. A broadsword extended above their head, glinting in the evening sun.

What a strange thing for her to experience such a horrible memory, illuminated by the beaming rays from that distant star, when everything around her should have been blanketed in clouds and drenched in the rain.

She willed herself to do something, anything, but all she could muster was the energy it took to keep her eyes trained on the stranger on the other side of the battlefield. She watched as the steel collided with the edge of the glittering brittle body before her, shattering the woman into a million pieces, the sight somehow thrusting her own world into utter darkness.

Memories flooded her heart with adrenaline, forcing gasps across her lips. She hadn't exactly been asleep, just trapped within the confines of the recollection. A waking recurring nightmare that she remained powerless to avoid. She was sure that it was more than a simple figment of her imagination.

Her memories had been stripped from her, including her identity, so there was nothing that supported this knowledge except a gut feeling. She was nameless, adrift in a sea of confusion in her haze-like existence, forever just below the cusp of knowing enough to feel satisfied.

Whenever she attempted to reach for a time before that moment, the nightmare was like a vortex in her mind, and she was met with nothingness. The genesis of her recollection of her former life and *nearly* everything that had happened since was crystal clear, but the names and places remained frustratingly out of reach. Without her identity, her experiences and the knowledge built up over a lifetime, the best she could do was recognize that she should have known the faces that plagued her thoughts.

Her arm stretched over to the side table where she knew there would be a glass of water waiting for her. She drew in tentative sips of the lukewarm liquid as she glanced around the room. Beams of moonlight illuminated the small space, casting a hazy brightness through the gauzy curtains beside her.

The fingertips of her free hand curled around the velvet cushion of the teal settee that she had fallen asleep on. More often than not, she woke on this particular piece of furniture, although she couldn't explain why she clearly preferred it to her bed, which had remained untouched for weeks.

Her chest expanded with another deep breath as she scanned the surrounding room. Nothing had changed since her arrival, not even her wardrobe, threadbare and showing signs of age that spoke of unsettling amounts of passing time.

There was a small wooden bed pushed against the opposite wall, framed in a canopy of fuchsia fabric. The mattress was still made up and covered in fluffy pillows, with an embroidered lilac quilt draped across it.

Plush floral rugs with intricate designs in shades of mint, emerald, peony, and lavender sprawled across the worn wooden floorboards. The room was opulent and yet devoid of any personal touches. From the décor alone, she could deduce that it had once belonged to a young girl, but whoever had dwelled in this place had never come back to reclaim it.

She set her glass down on the table, and a shiver raced up her spine. Pulling a blanket on top of her, she stared across the room at the white marble fireplace resentfully.

A heavy iron screen covered the hearth, complete with curling scrollwork that had reminded her of a vine climbing up a trellis. It was lovely, but instead of bringing her joy, it loomed there, cold and silent, just like everything else in this room. For as long as she could remember, this place had never held the tools necessary to stoke flames. The one thing that might have brought her light and warmth mocked her with the same emptiness she felt inside. Unyielding and unending.

Time was a strange concept when she only held a few definable memories. She was unaware of the duration of her confinement in this strange prison. It could have been weeks, months, years, or even decades; her days were monotonous and lonely. She rarely saw the people who had brought her there. Her food simply appeared on silver trays by the settee, only to be vanished by the same strange magic.

Most of the time, her only visitors were the images of those shadowy forms and that woman. The stranger's hair discolored by the grime; the face staring back at her, familiar in the memory, but everything specific —everything that made the stranger who she was—had been lost to the void that was her mind. However, the flashbacks were so vivid that she knew that the unknown, yet utterly known, person had somehow been an anchor to her own happiness. In the memory, and with every replaying of it, each time the stranger's body shattered, she shattered with her.

She didn't need to learn the stranger's name to understand that, at a deeper level, they had been familiar. The feelings of loss and hopelessness that the memory dredged up told her as much. Like a heartbeat, she could still sense it in her very soul that a part of her had died with the woman on the battlefield.

Maybe their bond had been so resilient that the magic used to rid her of her memories and her identity hadn't had enough fortitude to completely sever their ties. She didn't think that she needed her awareness of her past to comprehend with certainty that she had loved that stranger, that the woman hadn't really been a stranger at all.

The flashbacks and accompanying remorse only elicited a string of questions, rather than any answers.

Why had they been fighting on the opposite sides of what had clearly been a gruesome battle?

Who had they been before that moment, and how had their lives been threaded together and then so obviously ripped apart?

Not that it mattered now. This new reality was the only existence that she knew anymore.

In this room, day after day, her worst nightmare served as a reminder that, once upon a time, she had been fiercely loved.

She had once loved with everything she had.

Now, she was no one, and she had no one.

Nameless and alone.

Two

"**A**gain, Ashton!" my father called from several paces away. His chest rose and fell with his exertion, a match to my own, but he held his wooden sword aloft in a stance that told me he was prepared for my next charge.

My skin shone with sweat from our grueling exercise, making it difficult to palm my own wooden blade. The one he had crafted for me to practice with.

Eyeing him warily, I searched for those tell-tale signs of his fatigue that I had seen all too often as of late. It was getting worse, evidenced by the number of days that he had lain in bed rather than gone to work. Not that he would admit to such things being symptoms of his failing health.

With an eye roll, I stabbed my sword into the ground. "Don't you need to get back to the cottage for something?" The something was the rest that he continued to argue with me over the merits of, claiming there was nothing wrong with him.

"Aren't you supposed to be the child here?" He replied, rather than admit that he was tired.

My brows raised high on my forehead as I offered him a pointed look. "If you're going to continue to wear yourself down in the name of helping me, then I am going to relinquish my title as daughter and continue to mother you all I like." What I left unspoken between us was that he was all I had, and I couldn't bear the thought of losing him too.

My mother had died giving birth to me, their first child, and I had never been told of grandparents lingering in some far-off town waiting to meet me. That left my dad and me, and I owed him everything. There was no way I'd let him run himself ragged for my benefit. "I'm sure we've trained enough," I added when he didn't drop his stance.

With a smirk, Dad outstretched his free palm, blasting a sphere of water straight for my head, followed in quick succession by four more.

Instinct had my feet moving before the gasp even left my throat, my body curling and dodging his attack with expert precision. By the time I stood upright again, my knees were covered in mud, but I was otherwise dry. A wry smile curved my lips. "Don't think this gets you off the hook."

He grinned at me, bright green eyes flashing with amusement. "I just want you to be prepared."

From the time I was a small child and heard of the tales of my mother's time in the Select Guard, it was all I had ever wanted. Joining the prestigious group of soldiers who worked directly with the Elemental Queen was the best way I had found to honor the sacrifice she made in bringing me into the world.

My father had always supported my endeavor—even though we rarely spoke of her directly—by training me to the best of his abilities. This included making me the hand-crafted practice blades we were currently using and teaching me to wield them. Dad was a part of the Flumen class of wielders, meaning he had water power, and he had found creative ways over the years to interject that into my regimen.

I often wondered about my mother's time at Biltons Academy. Did she train like I had? Had she been a natural with the sword or some other weapon? Those thoughts were kept firmly in my mind, though. My father had done so much for me, and I had taken the love of his life away from him, so I assumed that the least I could do was respect his desire to avoid the topic of his late wife. Instead of bugging him over her memory, I put every ounce of my focus into making this dream a reality.

There were three academies in the Kingdom of Demetros. After attending basic education at local schools, from the time we were five until around twenty, all citizens were expected to enroll in one of these to get our required foundational and elemental education.

Foundational education, which began in mid-August, consisted of army-like courses and physical training that prepared us to be called into war if need arose. It ended in December when our brands were given to us, sorting us into one of five elemental classes. After that, the last almost five months were dedicated to specialized elemental training, where each person was taught how to wield their element for everything from general tasks to self-defense.

Every single person born on Demetros' soil was born with a bind on their powers, which had to be released in a ceremony that occurred once per year around the winter solstice and only at one of the three academies. In a ceremony that was largely secretive, considering that no one had a memory of the event at all after it occurred, brands were placed on the forearm of each person that represented the class they belonged to. Something about the brand allowed the binds to be released and gave us each the ability to channel our power.

Each citizen only had access to one elemental power, if any at all. The only exception to this was the Elemental Queen, which was where she got her name. Our ruler had access to all four elements. Water, fire, air, and earth.

Her five advisors, the Guides, had the capability of accessing natural magic somehow, which was why they performed their bind-releasing ceremony around the winter solstice when all magic was heightened. However, even the esteemed advisors could only wield one element each. One Guide for each class. Even the powerless designation, the fifth class, had a representative who would administer the brand for that group.

In theory, I could have attended Biltons, Wythe, or Chapelstone Academy, had my powers relinquished to me, and returned home to live out the rest of my days with whatever elemental magic I obtained. However, only one of the three accepted recruits into the Select Guard, and that was Biltons Academy, located in the capital city of Fulgrande.

My face twisted into a frown as I thought about my uncertain future there.

Catching the shift in my emotions, my father took several steps towards me, clapping his hand over my shoulder. "Have you heard anything yet?"

My throat burned with the desire to cry, but I shook my head and, with it, shed the misplaced emotions. "No. I should know by the end of the week if I got the scholarship. It's still early." The last sentence was more for me than my father, as I kept reminding myself that there was still time.

My father grimaced as his palm squeezed. He owned his own business, doing construction and odd jobs with his water power and a small crew who only worked for him part-time. He traveled all over the kingdom, aiding those who did not have the riches of the upper class that dwelled in the bigger cities, but he so often returned from jobs with goods in exchange for his services rather than coin.

We were not poor in the sense that we had a roof over our heads and food for our bellies, but we did not have excess. Certainly not enough to attend the only academy that required a tuition.

I forced a fake smile on my face. "Dad, I'm sure I'm going to get the scholarship. I got top marks in basic education, and you are documented as having high levels of your elemental power. They're going to accept me."

This seemed to placate him even as my gut clenched with my own doubt. He grinned, swiping his dirt-crusted hand through his greying hair. Once, we had shared the same shade of light brown, but his showed his age in ways that worried me. It seemed that every day, he had a new strand of silvery grey take the place of his youthful hues. Another reminder that time was passing far too quickly.

That was the thing about my dream of being in the Select Guard. It had started as a way to be worthy of taking my mother's place in the world. An ode to her that could make me feel a tiny bit better about being here instead of her. But as my father's health deteriorated, it became something else too. It transformed into a way to keep him alive because the Select Guard had access to the kingdom's best healers and the income to pay for them.

My father might not admit to his declining health, but I noticed the steady descent, kept track of the bad days like he was my patient rather than just my parent.

Dad hummed his consideration of my statement as he dropped his hand, eyes already trained on the little stone fence that ran the perimeter of our cottage. "Well, if you're sure... I could use some time in my garden."

Annoyance flared my nostrils, but I knew it would do no good to force him to bed. If he didn't want to go, the stubborn man would not listen to me simply because I was the self-proclaimed *light of his life*.

"I'll run laps," I offered, so that he would know I wasn't going to give up training just because he was tired. He could rest, and it wouldn't keep me from my goals. Maybe if I reminded him one more time, he'd consider humoring me for once.

His brows came together in a furrowed mass. "Isn't Jemma coming home soon?"

Despite my worry over him, the reminder of my best friend's return to our hometown lifted the corners of my mouth. "Tomorrow," I replied. "Why? Are you thinking of making something special for her and Marjorie?"

Marjorie was Jemma's mother, and both of them left for a month every summer to visit family in the South. The two of them were like family to us, even if my father and Jemma's mother had never been anything but friends. Even if wishing for such a thing made my stomach clench with guilt at the idea that I could picture him with anyone but the woman who had birthed me.

A laugh rolled from my father's lips. "I'm assuming that she will come snooping around soon enough after her return to eat whatever is in sight. I was actually considering harvesting what I could and hiding it."

Jemma had the appetite of a teenage boy, and my father's prediction of her behavior when she returned wasn't too far off. I snorted as my hands waved in the direction of our cottage. "Go ahead then, better hurry up while there is still daylight."

He grinned as he started to make his way down the path that led to our gate. The only thing that gave his intention away was the slight tension that gathered along his shoulders.

Just in time, I dropped low as he wheeled around to shoot two more of his water balls at my head. "Dad!" I called out.

A smirk twitched in and out of view along his face. "Just making sure you're on your toes. Can't have you botching your entrance into the Select Guard over slow reflexes."

Part of me believed that he was truly using every bit of time we had to prepare me for the guard, but another nagging sliver of my subconscious told me that he was trying to show me that he wasn't sick. Even now, as I took in his features, I could see a grey hue to his skin. The dark circles under his eyes were more pronounced than even a month ago, and it looked like he had lost another few pounds.

On the inside, I scrawled all those observations down as a mental note in my mind. A benchmark for exactly how quickly things were devolving for him. Outwardly, I grinned. "I was trained by the very best. There's no way they wouldn't accept me."

There were several reasons they wouldn't accept me, the main one being that I might not be able to afford to go to Biltons Academy, and all of this would have been for nothing. Still, I held my grin even as my father turned away and trudged to our home.

It took everything in me to hold that expression as I watched him visibly limp away from the little clearing in the woods that we practiced in. I didn't take my gaze from him until he was completely out of sight, and only then did I let my guard fall.

My knees hit the dirt as I looked up at the sky, begging all the gods— even the ones who had long since abandoned our world—for anything that could help me save him. Starting with that scholarship.

After a good cry in the solitude of the forest, I made my way back to the cottage, stopping in my tracks at the sight of Mr. Griffin, the man who typically delivered our letters in Elmhaven. He approached me with a smile that instantly set my insides twisting, and my eyes darted to my father's garden to find it blessedly empty.

"Good evening, Miss Blake. How are you today?" His nimble fingers sorted out a few envelopes and then stilled on a large cream-colored parcel. When he plucked it from his pile, I caught the image of the Bilton's Academy logo on the front.

Pleasantries were nearly impossible as I resisted the urge to snatch the letter from his hand and open it right then and there. The smile that curled my lips was anything but warm, although Mr. Griffin didn't seem to notice. He continued to sift through his pile with his usual jolly expression.

"I'm doing well, sir. How have you been? How are the twins?"

At the mention of his youngest children, he beamed. "They're keeping the missus up all night, but I'm about as happy as a peach in pie."

My hand clamped over my mouth as I attempted to transform my sniffed laugh into a cough instead because I was certain that a peach with any sentience wouldn't enjoy being made into a delicacy, but I wasn't going to correct him. My attention had already moved back to the letter. "Glad to hear it. You let us know if you need anything, alright?" Despite my distraction, I meant it. Dad and I were kind of in the business of helping people, and it didn't always require the use of his magic.

"You're too kind. Tell your dad I said hello. Have a nice day." He passed me the envelope, and it felt like the entire weight of the world fit inside that one piece of paper. Either I got the scholarship and had a chance at saving my father, or I was going to need to get comfortable with the idea of saying goodbye.

My fingers trembled as I tore open the seal, making myself take in large gulps of air to slow down my heart rate. It took great effort to blink away the nerves well enough to focus on the words on the parchment before me.

Dear Miss Ashton Elizabeth Blake,

It is with our deepest regret that we must inform you that you did not receive the Venus scholarship for financial aid at Biltons Academy. Please accept our sincerest condolences. Don't forget to let the admissions office know if you need to withdraw from the upcoming semester.

Best wishes,
Stewart Higgins
Chairman of The Scholarship Funding Committee

For what felt like several minutes, I didn't breathe. Sure, I had been worried about what the letter might say, but I hadn't actually thought I wouldn't be considered. In basic education, I had excelled in every class. The only thing I didn't have going for me was the prestige or money that typically accompanied those who were accepted into the academy. A numbness spread over my body as I tucked the letter into my pants pocket and slowly walked inside the house.

Dad was in the kitchen humming a tune, something a bit upbeat that clashed against the heavy emotions settling in my chest. Lost to his preparations, he didn't look up, and I slipped into my room before the tears could fall.

Three

A heavy sigh shuddered through my body as I did my best to expel the thoughts of dread swirling in my gut. As much as I had been looking forward to Jemma's return, I was terrified of telling her about my rejection letter. Worried that if I spoke it aloud, it would somehow make it more true.

With steady steps, I made my way to a patch of the dense emerald forest. The path I took sliced its way through the grass, worn from years of meeting with Jemma at this exact spot, and possibly from the people who had come before us and had found this hidden sanctuary to be a safe haven for their own sacred friendships.

Elmhaven, the place I had been born and subsequently raised, was a coastal town nestled in the cross-section of a mass of winding waterways. Its borders didn't greet the sea itself, but the marshy grasses that thrived in those brackish waters covered our soil like a heavy blanket. In the heat of the summer, the briny scent of the salty water weaved its way through the breeze in a gentle caress.

It took less than an hour's brisk walk to make it to the beaches, faster if you had a horse. I had spent my childhood collecting seashells along the shores, my dad's garden decorated with the proof of my bounty. As much time as I had lingered and explored by the sea, I had spent infinitely more moments on the banks of this creek because of Jemma Kinkaid.

My fingers gripped the soft edges of the worn maroon blanket as I shook it out and laid it over the grass, smoothing the edges before I placed the picnic basket in the center on top. This was the exact blanket that she had found me wrapped in, in this very spot, crying over a mother I would never meet.

It was something that I had done often as a child, but always alone. Never wanting to burden my dad with any more grief than he already had over her loss. The casualty that I caused.

On that day, over eleven years ago, Jemma had silently peeled the blanket from my body and wrapped her arms around me in its place. She held me—a complete stranger before that moment—until my sobs had subsided. Something like fate had called to me that day, allowing me to let this unknown person embrace me in such a way. It had been nice to let someone else hold that sadness for once.

When the tears were nothing more than salty, crusted lines down my face, she laid the blanket out and stretched her body across it. Then she offered me freshly baked pastries from her satchel. She told me they were chocolate croissants, a delicacy I hadn't tried before, never wanting to spare the coin for something so frivolous. The flaky, chocolatey morsels became my favorite treat after that encounter.

Jemma listened solemnly while I talked about my mother. She shared her experience with losing her own father, who had tragically succumbed to injuries in a boating accident years before. From that day on, we had always met up when we needed to talk about something significant, celebrate accomplishments, or just be right here in our spot with that same blanket and a plethora of snacks.

Jemma wasn't there yet, so I plopped down on the tattered fabric, lying on my back and staring up at the trees. The overlapping canopy of arching branches overhead made the spot mostly shaded, but the subtle shift in the breeze gave the midday sun's rays a chance to dance along my face and body.

I lay there, entranced by the kaleidoscope of greens and blues created by the wind caressing the leaves of the tall oak trees that made just enough gaps in the foliage for the brilliant blue sky to peek through.

My eyes closed as I attempted to ground myself into this feeling, even if, once again, I found my mind racing back to the academy and the choice that had already been made for me.

In an attempt at a coping mechanism, I tried to manifest another letter coming in, stating the committee's mistake. Then, I pictured my body adorned in that emerald-hued uniform, visualizing myself conversing with the greatest healers of our kingdom, forcing my brain to see my father whole and well. In these images, he was livelier than I had seen him in years, but I couldn't hold onto those fabricated visions. They faded like ghosts, like they were never mine to behold in the first place.

"Ashton! Wake up!" Jemma's raised voice brought me crashing back to reality as my eyes blew wide open, my pulse skittering in my chest.

Jemma's dark brown ringlet curls hung in a waterfall around her oval face. A face that was hovering directly over mine. Despite her harsh tone, the crinkle of her amusement bracketed her stare. Her irises were always somewhere in the green family but shifted between the lighter shades. Today, they were the color of fresh spring grass.

She offered me her hand, her tanned skin a contrast to my paler complexion. I braced my palm against hers for a fraction of a second before she yanked me upright and directly into her arms for a tight hug.

"I've missed you," she whispered, her breath a warm dusting along the shell of my ear.

A snort pushed its way through my nose. "It's only been a month." I said it as if I were unbothered by the time that we spent apart every summer. Pulling back, I twisted so that I could nudge her in the ribs with my elbow. Having matured since our initial summer apart, I was no longer petulant about the situation. It didn't mean that those four weeks without her weren't the loneliest days of my year.

Jemma Kinkaid understood me like no one ever had, probably like no one ever could, because we hadn't just been friends, we had grown up together. We had fused as one, like two trees that had taken root too close together, intertwining trunks and branches until it was no longer evident which piece could be attributed to which species. Gemels is what they called that in nature, but if I had to assign a name to us, it would be sisters.

So, it was a little disappointing that I could never join her on her yearly trips away.

According to Jemma, her cousin's house was small, and they couldn't accommodate another body in the cramped quarters. I would have been content to sleep on the floor, but after the first few years of useless tantrums and boycotts surrounding our separations, we just accepted that once a year, we had to be apart for a month.

Jemma slid her hand into her leather pack and produced a compact package wrapped in gauzy blue fabric. She held it to me in the center of her palm. "I brought you back a gift."

Eagerly, I snatched it from her and carefully untied the knot of the leather string, shedding the fabric and revealing a little wooden box inside. Its surface was smooth, hand-sanded, and painstakingly stained in swirling shapes that made no discernible pattern.

"That's not your surprise," Jemma stated, and I could hear the amusement in her tone.

A smile crept up my face as I lifted my eyes to her. "You know I hate surprises."

She released a derisive snort. "No, you don't. Plus, you will love this one." Her arms crossed over her chest as she huffed expectantly.

Rolling my eyes, I gingerly pried open the lid, only to discover a delicate gold chain inside. As I pulled it out, a small charm came with it. I raised the pendant up, level with my gaze, revealing a dainty golden crescent moon. Three tiny glittering green emeralds adorned the surface, each surrounded by etches marking the shape of stars in the shiny metal surface.

"It's beautiful, Jem." My voice cracked with the emotions caught in my throat. It was the nicest thing anyone had ever given me.

Jemma offered me a smug grin in response. "I told you that you'd love it." She snatched the pendant back from my grasp in one quick movement. "But you haven't even seen the best part."

With her free hand, she pulled at a chain around her own neck and, out from under her navy cotton tunic, a charm appeared. It was a golden sun, with a round turquoise opal in the middle. Although at a glance, the stone looked a little off center.

She lifted my moon to the space between us, and with a snap, my crescent fit snugly on top of her necklace around her opal. Her eyes strayed to meet mine, eager to see my reaction. "I found it at the cutest little shop down south during our trip to the beaches. The turquoise reminded me of your eyes, and obviously, your emeralds are for mine."

She looked almost sheepish as she continued. "So, this way, you always have a piece of me with you, and I always have a piece of you with me... no matter what happens next year."

Clumsily, she broke the necklaces back apart, letting her gaze fall to the jewelry in her hand. It shouldn't have comforted me in the slightest, hearing her trepidation at our potential separation, but it made me feel somewhat better to know that she was worried about it too. Especially considering I already knew I wouldn't be joining her at Biltons Academy.

"Have you heard anything yet?" She asked, focus still stuck to the necklaces she fidgeted with between her fingertips.

A rough swallow bobbed my throat. "No, not yet. But there's still time." The lie slipped out before I could stop it. I just couldn't bring myself to drag down the moment with my own failure. Not today.

Her head shook, and with it, she dislodged her frown, replacing it with a warm smile. "You're going to get it. I know it."

Her misplaced confidence in me was hardly a balm to my tattered nerves, but I pushed a smile to my face anyway.

"Turn around," she commanded, and I listened, lifting my hair as I did so. Without further instruction, she wordlessly clasped the chain around my throat.

Jemma was one to wear her emotions on her sleeve. She was blunt, but that was something I appreciated about her. So, I knew, without a shadow of a doubt, that no matter what happened next year, we would always be in each other's lives. The crescent moon that dangled between my collarbones seemed like a promise of that expectation, a tangible reminder of our bond.

The mandated education at the academies, no matter which one you chose, took nine months. Then, we'd be sent into the world to begin our lives.

Even though my dreams of the academy were dashed, and with it, my hope of being in the Select Guard, our paths had always been destined to fork. I'd probably come back to Elmhaven to spend whatever time he had left with my dad, and she longed to travel the kingdom, making the road her home rather than any specific place.

Tears that weren't entirely because of the kindness of the gift welled along my lash line. My arms snaked around Jemma's frame as I pulled her into a tight embrace. "Thank you. I love you."

She giggled, squeezing me tighter as she nuzzled her nose against my neck. "I love you too." Then, she gripped along my upper arms and pushed back from my hold, grinning. "Tell me all about what you've been up to without me."

A scoff rustled itself from my chest as I quickly redirected the topic back to her and away from my lie. "I believe it would be far more entertaining for you to tell me about *your* summer."

She pulled me to the blanket, dragging me to its surface so that I was seated beside her. "Okay, so there was this guy..."

I shook my head as I hung on her every word, so grateful that we were reunited once more. Hopefully, at least for the next nine months.

Four

Sugar, the horse that my dad had, unfortunately, let me name as a child, blew a huff of air as he pulled my father's construction carriage down the dirt roads that led away from Brevard, where we had just completed our latest job. He was big, even for his breed, with soft brown fur and a thick black mane and tail that swished with irritation any time I got too close. Personally, I always assumed that he had a vendetta against me for naming him after something sweet when he probably should have been a Magnus. Maybe even a Tarynd, after the god of sunlight, who, like all the old deities, was depicted as tall and broad.

My dad nudged me out of those thoughts with a quick bump of his shoulder. "You did good today, Ashton. Thank you for your help."

"I didn't really do anything," I admitted, "I just talked to Mrs. Stevenson the entire time. You did all the work."

Any time I got the opportunity to ride with my father on his solo jobs, I did. Not just because we could use the coin, but because I liked to keep an eye on him and his declining health. But, without magic, my help usually came in the form of distracting the more chatty patrons. It didn't feel like a lot.

Guilt stacked itself like stones in my stomach, knowing that he'd probably need several more days of rest after this task. Mrs. Stevenson had hired him on behalf of the town to divert a stream to the water mill they had just built. Typically, Saxum power was used to perform such tasks as it was simpler to manipulate the ground than to utilize water to bore through the soil as my father had done. Unfortunately for Brevard, they weren't a wealthy settlement, and my dad was the only person with his power level who would accept payment in the form of tradable items rather than coin.

"Distracting Mrs. Stevenson is a job all on its own," he quipped as he shot me another smile.

Glancing behind us, I caught the sight of his latest barter, a plant with no blooms and no edible features, just waxy green leaves in the shape of teardrops. At least the woman had included a few bolts of fabric and a well-made leather bag that I was certain we could exchange for grain or meat at the markets in Elmhaven. Even if I selfishly longed to keep the fabric for a nice tunic or dress for myself.

A frown twisted my features again. Since I wasn't going to Biltons Academy, I'd have no need for fancy attire.

My dad knocked into me with his elbow. "What's on your mind, little girl."

Making a show of it all, I scowled. "You know I'm not a little girl anymore." My tone remained serious, but a smile crested my features as we finished our age-old routine of me pretending that I was too mature for such titles.

He chuckled as his green-hazel eyes met mine for the fraction of a second that he allowed himself to tear them off the road ahead. "I suppose you're almost officially an adult in the eyes of the law." He moved his free hand about in a swirling motion in the air as he kept hold of the reins in the other. The merriment on his face retreated to make way for affection. "But you will always be my little girl."

My heart faltered for a moment, thrashing heavily against the confines of my chest. How much time did we have left now that I didn't get that scholarship? Could I go to Chapelstone and join their healer program? Would that be enough?

He raised his eyebrows expectantly. "Are you going to talk to me about it?"

I couldn't bear the thought of adding any more worry to his shoulders, but I also knew that he wouldn't believe me if I said nothing was wrong. "I'm nervous about the scholarship." A half-truth.

His brows pinched, and his mouth followed. "You know, Wythe is a completely acceptable school, or even Chapelstone. You like the beach, right?"

Chapelstone Academy was nestled in the southern tip of our kingdom in a town called Pine Knoll. Apparently, the dorm rooms of that school looked out over the ocean, and if I hadn't wanted to be in the guard so badly, I would have been happy to go there. "I want to be in the Select Guard like Mom."

My jaw slammed shut the moment I realized my mistake because we didn't do that. Not that he was ever angry about my questions about my mother. He always answered me when I was brave enough to ask, I just hated seeing the desolation in his eyes whenever I did. Even if it was unintentional, I had caused that look, which made it my responsibility to limit his pain on the subject.

His hand tightened along the reins as the other reached out to pat me on the knee. "She would be proud of you no matter what path you chose. If it doesn't work out, there is so much more out there for you than that green uniform."

I understood that he was trying to be kind and let me know that he would be happy no matter what happened when it came to Biltons, but he also didn't know that my motivations for why I needed to be accepted into the guard had shifted. At some point, my need to save him had overshadowed my desire to honor her.

"Thanks, Dad," I replied in a soft tone. "You know I'd love to work with you if it doesn't pan out."

"You'll make the guard," he said, confidently and I wished that I could share the sentiment but I already knew that dream was over. It had been foolish to ever think I'd be worthy of taking my mother's place.

She had been such a powerful fire wielder that some had even accused her of being a witch. Others had thought she was descended from the Fae. All of it was ridiculous, as neither entity existed in Demetros outside of our childhood fairytales.

Most of those stories were used as warnings about using our magic for good rather than evil as witches were depicted as people who could manipulate the natural magic to bring forth great peril and Fae were considered tricky beings with no moral compass. Both were excellent metaphors for those choosing to do bad deeds with their power, but neither were real. At least not in our kingdom.

Demetros was a continent, haloed by a series of barrier islands, and encased in waters so violent that no one could cross in either direction. We were a lonely kingdom in a sea of unknown allies and potential enemies. I had always wondered if part of our mandatory military-like training at the academy was due in part to preparing for a potential invasion, but we had been reassured time and time again that no one could reach us. Thus far, no one ever had.

Most of the people in Demetros had accepted this information as fact, but a part of me wondered if there was more to all of this than any of us could possibly know. Unknown dangers that perhaps weren't unknown to all.

Out of experience, I knew that speaking about any of these theories and concerns would do me no good, so I kept my lips sealed and willed my mind to look to other avenues. My father and I rode in a comfortable silence, with him none the wiser of my inner thoughts and turmoil, until we crossed the bridge that led to Elmhaven, and Dad cleared his throat. "I've got some things to harvest in the garden when we get back. Do you mind putting Sugar in his stall?"

We shared a barn with a few of the families in town, taking turns with the feeding and chores in a rotation so that no one had to tend to the animals daily. It was how I had met Farren, the boy I had been with the longest. The one I used to meet in the loft to kiss... and eventually other things. I had given so much of myself to the boy I had thought I could grow to love. Up until he went to Biltons Academy the previous year and promptly broke up with me in a letter. He never returned to Elmhaven, having gotten assigned to a position on the western coast of Demetros, and we never spoke again.

Even thinking about heading towards that barn made my fists ball at my sides. My father knew at least part of the story, and he typically handled anything involving that structure. So, if he was asking for my aid in regard to it, then he likely had a good reason.

It wasn't like Farren was just going to show up and taunt me, and despite my lingering anger, I didn't care about him anymore. If anything, I was just mad at myself for falling for his games. Given the amount of time that had passed, I could acknowledge that I had carried my disdain for the building on long enough. "I'll take him back, if you think he will let me."

My eyes narrowed at the back of Sugar's head, and I swore his ears were pinned until the moment my father laughed. "It's a horse, Ashton. Just lead him to his stall and give him an apple, and he will be fine."

My molars grazed along the inside of my mouth, rather than make a retort that would make me sound a bit crazy. It was going to take more than an apple to win Sugar over to my side but that wasn't really my dad's problem tonight.

He pulled back on the reins, bringing the cart to a stop as we both disembarked from the driver's seat of the carriage. Before a minute had even passed, Dad had released Sugar from his harness, and I tugged along the leather lines to guide him to the barn. After brushing him down, placing him in his stall, and giving him an apple—and another slew of halfhearted apologies for his name—I walked back to our cottage.

The sound of his humming reached me before my dad even came into view, the melody floating across the sea of foliage between us. I pushed through the gate and down the short cobblestone path when the light breeze carried with it the smells of night blooming jasmine from the edge of the house and honeysuckle from the outer fencing, blending them together in the familiar aroma of home. Drawing in another deep breath through my nose, I caught the slightest hint of salt. The scent of summer on the coast.

The roses to the right of the path were in full bloom, wild thorny bushes covered in hundreds of red, pink, white, and orange buds. The purple ones were my favorite, but they flowered the least often, and I pouted slightly as I realized that none were available for collection this afternoon.

Another peppy hum came from the left of the cottage, where Dad maintained a much more practical vegetable garden, which was currently playing host to tomatoes, cucumbers, watermelons, and the start of pumpkins. My mouth watered at the thought of all the dishes that he would concoct with those ingredients, my most cherished being pumpkin pie.

Whenever he wasn't working, he could be found tending to the garden. Knees dropped to the earth and hands covered in soil, combing through the plants, and diligently removing the weeds. It was one of the few places he appeared to have no pain.

He cared for the garden like it was his second child. It had always surprised me that he went into construction when gardening was so obviously his passion and not an atypical choice for someone with Flumen powers like his. Not every water wielder could summon the element, which made his gifts rarer and more valuable for such tasks. I supposed that it also would have made him even less coin, with far less flexibility, and raising a daughter alone hadn't been a cheap or convenient endeavor.

With a forced smile, I called out to him. "Where are you?"

He popped up behind a tomato plant, hands curled around two enormous red spheres, a wide grin splitting his face. "I'm thinking tonight it's sliced tomatoes and the rest of that cheese." Tossing the bounty into a basket, he pointed to his right. "Grab some basil, and we can drizzle that balsamic over it. The one that Mr. Gilleske gave us."

Mr. Gilleske had been another client that could only pay in goods. At least his, unlike Mrs. Stevenson's, had been edible. Not only that but was absolutely delicious.

I moseyed to the section of the garden reserved for herbs, plucking a few of the leaves as requested. When I turned to pass them to him, my dad was already standing next to me with his basket held out.

He had that look in his eye that told me he was about to get distracted with creating a new recipe. My dad loved his garden, and as a side effect, it brought him great joy to cook. There had been no choice but to be creative when he had been forced to choose between meat at the market or new clothing items for his ever-growing daughter. We had never gone hungry, but we didn't always eat the most balanced diets, relying heavily on the seasonally fluctuating bounty from his garden for the majority of our meals. Meat was a luxury we sometimes had to forego.

Without any more fuss, he stepped past me, already walking towards the door to our cottage. "See you inside." He hadn't even turned around to call out the words as I stifled a blooming grin.

"Be in in a minute," I replied, knowing that even if he heard me, he was already lost to his next creation.

It wasn't yet late afternoon; the midday sun still beat down across the bridge of my nose as I tilted it upward to survey my surroundings. In the distance, a butterfly landed on a butter yellow rose, and overhead, birds tweeted happily as they flew through the air, a melody as familiar as my childhood bedroom.

My eyes closed, and I forced myself to consider that this life wouldn't be so bad. Maybe Chapelstone could provide the training I needed to save my father myself. Maybe I could be happy here, in the mundane. I was proud of all that my father did for our community, surely I could shift that same pride to myself for doing the work by his side. Unless my absence at Biltons cost him his life...

"Ashton, you're a popular one this week." Mr. Griffin's words jolted me from my downward spiral, and my eyes flew open to greet the deliveryman with a forced smile.

"Good afternoon, Mr. Griffin." My vision narrowed on the cream envelope in his hand. It held none of the markings of Bilton's Academy, but it looked official, and my heart stuttered all the same. This was it, their retraction of my rejection.

It was everything I could do not to lunge at Mr. Griffin, and my pulse fluttered as I held myself back. When he offered it, I delicately plucked the envelope from his grasp, tucking it under my arm in an attempt to rein in my anxiety and be polite. "Getting any more sleep these days?"

Mr. Griffin chuckled. "No miracles have happened in the last few days, but the tea leaves your father sent have helped the missus relax. Give him my thanks." With that, the man had already started walking away, and I scarcely waited for him to disappear from view before I tore into the letter.

Dear Miss Blake,

It has come to my attention that you were not given finan-cial aid for your education at Biltons Academy. I happen to be in the business of investments, and after reviewing your paperwork, I have decided that you would be an excellent candidate for my sponsorship. Please write back if this appeals to you and drop your letter in the hollow of the split elm at the western edge of town.
Keep this to yourself, as spots are very limited.

Anonymously yours, your (potential) gracious donor.

It wasn't the letter I had been expecting, but it was a glimmer of hope that I needed. Even as apprehension prickled my spine, I ignored any worries about how the person had gotten my information in favor of being grateful. Because if this was a chance to achieve my dreams and save my father, I had to write back.

Five

My father had spent two of the last three days in bed, recovering from the job Mrs. Stevenson had hired him for. It wasn't altogether unexpected, considering the energy he exerted to divert the stream, but it served as a stark reminder of just how much his health was declining. A year ago, he wouldn't have needed rest at all.

He needed professional help. But now, even if my father would agree to go, we couldn't afford to send him to the healers in the capital. Not without the salary I would make in the Select Guard. Not without access to the very best in the profession, who tended to the members of the guard and their families exclusively.

The only silver lining to my father's predicament was that he hadn't noticed my shifty moods. Hadn't been aware of just how nervous I had become since receiving the anonymous donor's initial letter. I had written back immediately, and today I retrieved the second letter only minutes earlier from the elm's hollow.

Knowing the secretive nature of the contents, I waited until I was in the solitude of my bedroom to open it this time.

Dear Miss Blake,

I am pleased to hear that you are interested in the opportunity for financial aid. I would be happy to cover all costs of tuition, room, and board. In exchange, all I require of you is to be inducted into the Select Guard. Failure to hold up your end of the bargain will result in immediate repayment of the loan by way of ten years of servitude in my employ.

You have until tomorrow evening to respond, or the deal is off, and I will move on to the next candidate.

The letter went on to give instructions about how to agree to the terms but my mind was stuck on the ten years. It was startling to read the number but not altogether unfair. Biltons Academy tuition was egregious and under normal circumstances I'd consider the offer almost reasonable. Except my father didn't have ten years. He'd be dead before I could return home.

Past that, the request was puzzling for a multitude of reasons. My goal had always been to make it into the Select Guard, but something about that being a requirement for such an exorbitant amount of money didn't sit right with me. It was entirely possible that this anonymous person just wanted someone in their debt on the inside, but why?

Everyone knew that the Select Guard, as Her Majesty's most trusted security personnel, worked in close proximity to the Elemental Queen. Most of them were posted inside the heavily guarded castle and presumably had access to records and history that no one else had even dreamed of seeing. It seemed more than plausible that this stranger wanted someone on the inside for nefarious purposes.

Then again, the letter didn't specify that I had to do anything once appointed a position in the guard, and I knew myself well enough to be certain that I couldn't be so easily corrupted.

My lungs rose and fell in slow, steady breaths. In most regards, I considered myself intelligent, and this bargain, with so many unknown variables, was quite the risk. But, despite whatever intellect I had, I was also desperate. Desperate to save my father and the last remaining familial line that separated me from being utterly alone in the world. An orphan without any ties left. I had Jemma and Marjorie, so I would never truly be by myself, but the idea of being the eldest in my family—the only person left of my blood—was excruciatingly painful to even consider.

There was very little chance that my father had ten years left in him if he continued the way he was. The other day during our training session, he had been in good spirits and health. The exertion had cost him half a day laid up in bed and I loathed to see him like that.

In the very marrow of my bones, I knew that with access to my Select Guard pay, and the benefits and connections that came with the position, my father could have decades rather than years. For that, I was going to do everything in my power to make it into the guard.

Yesterday, I had tried to get my dad to open up about his ailment. Any bit of information so that I could decide if drastic measures were necessary.

"It's just fatigue due to the passage of time," he reassured me. "One day, when you're my age, you won't have so much energy either." It was the same repeat of excuses he gave time and time again, as if it was a normal occurrence to be sporadically bedridden in your forties. "There's nothing that can be done for it, a healer would just send me away."

My father was selfless to the point of damnation of himself. It was evidenced in the way that he trained with me, despite his discomfort and the resulting fatigue that left him incapacitated for hours, if not days. Nothing he said placated my worry for him. He wouldn't even admit that it was a sickness, so I had no choice but to make assumptions and decisions based on what I could see.

As much as I longed to talk to someone about this decision, he was the last person I felt I could confide in. Knowing him, he'd mortgage off the entire house—the home he had built with my mother—just to grant me the chance to achieve my dreams, and I couldn't allow that either. Even if both letters hadn't expressed some warning about speaking of the terms to others, I didn't trust Marjorie not to tell my father, and I wouldn't ask Jemma to lie to her own mother. That left me making the choice all on my own.

Bruise-like smudges popped beneath my eyes from my lack of sleep, and I had bitten my nails down to the quick. This was my one shot, and I held the key to making it happen. I just needed to believe in myself and all that I had worked for. All that my father had helped me work for. It was the very least I could do for him.

Even with all my preparations I stared at that page, heart pulsing rapidly with a wave of nerves. It wasn't the training that concerned me, I had been working up to this my entire life and knew beyond a shadow of a doubt that I was physically capable of being inducted into the Select Guard. There was only one problem.

When the binds that constricted our magic were removed in the solstice ceremonies, we would be sorted into one of five classes determined entirely by nature. We weren't given our magic; it was simply released by the Elemental Queen's Guides.

Saxum, Caelum, Flumen, Ignus. These were the elemental powers we could transition into, the names given to the four magical elemental classes.

The Saxum could manipulate the earth into any form in order to shape the buildings of the kingdom or mine precious metals from the mountains.

Caelum wielders could control air and were typically hired to create winds that pushed the sails of the vessels carrying goods from the Southern tip of Demetros to the North and back.

The Flumen class—the water wielders—were most commonly hired to water the crops that grew in the South but were also found manning the smaller boats along the vast riverways as ferry workers.

Perhaps what I found most alluring about the Flumen class, besides the fact that my father belonged to it, was that someone from the group had figured out they could manipulate ink to mass produce books in typed print to disseminate across the kingdom. Not that I wanted to do that with my magic if I was discovered to be a water wielder, but I found it fascinating that it was their magic that made knowledge so readily available to the masses.

The ability to wield fire put you in the Ignus class, but a small portion of those people could also control the temperature. Individuals who could manipulate fire might opt for a career in a kitchen or with a blacksmith, but those with a higher power level gained reverence for their ability to create ice when around water or in conjunction with a member of the Flumen class. This skill also gave one a higher chance of being inducted into the Select Guard, as fire and ice were revered for fighting, as both, when wielded expertly, could be instantaneously deadly to an opponent of the Queen.

The most powerful of the classes were typically asked to join councils of their respective element which governed and upheld the laws for each group's magic. All of them held prestigious, lifelong positions, which they ensured passed down familial lines by strategic marriages and possibly a bit of bribing. Not that I had any hope of attaining one of those treasured seats.

The only thing worse to me than being a weak wielder was being assigned to the fifth class: Operarius. The Operarius class consisted of citizens with no magical gifts. While there was no official nickname for the people within this grouping, they were collectively known as the working class. Given jobs considered to be of the lowest prestige. Most consequentially, in my case, at least, those found to be powerless were never inducted into the Select Guard.

My muscles tensed at the thought as if it were an ember singing the inside of my mind. It was improbable that I would wind up being powerless, not with two incredibly gifted parents. Not when elemental magic was largely genetic.

Still, the thought snagged against my subconscious like a chipped fingernail against a soft-knit sweater. It wasn't an impossible outcome, and I would be remiss not to at least consider it before potentially signing my life away.

Closing my eyes, I drew in a deep breath, refocusing my attention on the obstacles that I could control. My ability was sound. If I chose to go to Biltons Academy, my ability to join the guard would be judged based on the Ice Games, a series of three challenges that occurred at monthly intervals.

The first challenge historically centered around survival courses, the second built upon that and a mixture of geography and weapons, and the final segment was always a measure of the student's physical strength.

The first two challenges varied slightly with each rendition, but the third was always the same. A single day to show prowess with various weapons followed by several days of hand-to-hand combat, which culminated in a singular winner. Whoever came out on top of that challenge was almost always asked to join the guard.

I was prepared for all of it. Thanks to my dad and his love of his garden I could recognize a plethora of plant life. Traveling with him across the continent, gave me a reasonable grasp on the geography of the land. My top marks had shown my propensity to learn and any gaps in my education from my small-town school, my father had filled with his own knowledge learned during his time at Wythe Academy.

I knew how to wield a sword, at least a practice one, since only police were permitted to carry steel weapons, and I could hold my own in hand-to-hand combat even if my only experience was with my father. He was easily six inches and fifty pounds heavier than me, so I took that as an accomplishment, even if I believed that he went easy on me at times. Either from kindness or his own weakness, I wasn't sure.

So, for the number of things I could control, I was as ready as I could be, and that would have to be enough for now.

My throat was dry, and I had to force down my next swallow as I reached for the mostly blank sheet of parchment the sponsor had included. At the top, it read:

Contracts written on this paper will be magically binding. Failure to adhere to the terms of this agreement will be met with lethal consequences.

As it would require a Guide to utilize the natural magic required to indue paper with such a spell, I didn't think it was likely a true sentiment. However, there was a lot about the world I didn't understand. So much of our history had been erased in the fires that blazed two hundred years ago, and I had heard enough rumors about magical objects that I couldn't discount the validity of the words of warning.

So, with only a deep breath to steady my thoughts, I procured my quill to sign away my future. The sharp tip dipped into the black abyss of the ink, then scratched along the page as I repeated the words outlined in the donor's last letter.

I, Ashton, agree to the terms and conditions laid out by the contract. I hereby acknowledge that I will receive full Biltons Academy tuition, including room and board for the 232nd year of the Elemental Queen's rule. In exchange, I pledge to be inducted into the Select Guard of Her Majesty's royal army. If I am incapable of fulfilling my end of the bargain, I will provide the grantor ten years of my life in servitude to tasks of their choosing.

Ashton Elizabeth Blake
July 31st Year 232 of the Elemental Queen's rule

Gently, I blew against the paper, drying the ink and sealing my fate before I gingerly folded the document into thirds, placing it back inside the prepared envelope. Hot wax dripped against the flap from my bedroom candle, and I sealed it shut with the press of a kitchen spoon.

With some resignation, I pushed myself up from my bedroom floor, walked out of the cottage's front door and down the short path to the tree, slipping the envelope into the hollow space created by the rotting bark.

My heart skipped beats as I walked away, refusing to look back, resisting the urge to grab the document and shred it before I could make a horrible, permanent mistake.

Lifting my chin, I took in the streaks of pastel watercolor that appeared to be painted across the evening sky. Was it a good omen to see such beauty overhead in the wake of such a monumental decision? As much as I tried to convince myself that it was, my trepidation had already turned leaden in my stomach.

Six

My legs were crossed as I sat in the center of Jemma's room, surrounded by a torrent of clothing and shoes. With my thumb and forefinger, I gingerly picked up a vibrant pink tunic, squinting as I tried to remember if she had ever worn this before. "Are you sure you need to bring so much stuff? The welcome letter clearly stated that there was limited storage space."

It had been weeks since I sent that letter, agreeing to the terms my anonymous donor put forth and since then, I hadn't heard a word from them. Mr. Griffin had delivered a welcome packet from the academy shortly thereafter, the only indication I had that Biltons had received some form of payment. Which meant I was formally entered into a potentially magically binding deal.

Jemma emerged from around the open doors of her armoire, hefting another pile of garments onto the floor in front of me. "I'm not taking all of it, I just need to narrow it down to my favorites."

Surveying the mounds of fabric around us made me skeptical that there was enough time left in the evening to subdue the pile into anything that would fit within limited storage space. We were leaving for the academy tomorrow, and per usual, Jemma had waited to do all of her packing until the very last minute.

Spying my favorite lilac top, I hoisted myself to my hands and knees and reached for the soft material. "Can I borrow this? I don't have anything I'd consider nice." What I had already packed consisted of undergarments, practical layers, and the few items of clothing I owned that weren't dotted with stains on them from the jobs I'd helped my dad with. Or sparring practice. His water magic didn't stain, but the mud it created certainly did.

Jemma waved her hand at me, not even looking at the shirt, as she continued to consider the options before her. "Yeah, sure. Take whatever you want. My closet is your closet."

"Thanks, Jem." I clutched the top to my chest as I rose to a standing position. "I should probably go anyway. Dad is making dinner."

Jemma offered me a knowing grin. "Tell Papa Blake that I said hello, and I'll see him bright and early in the morning."

My eyes rolled at her nickname for my dad, even if I found it a bit endearing that she saw him that way. "See you tomorrow!"

Guilt gnawed at my insides as I left. In a bit of a fib, I had already told her and Marjorie that I had gotten the scholarship, after I had offered my dad the same lie, and something about keeping the truth from all of them put a damper on my excitement about what tomorrow would bring. That and the never dwindling feeling that I had somehow made a massive mistake.

Those thoughts simmered in my subconscious, where I shoved them, until I opened the gate that led to our cottage's garden and walked those cobblestones straight to the front door. For once, Dad wasn't in his garden, but based on the smell of warm butter and rosemary wafting through the open window, I could tell that he was already hard at work preparing tonight's meal.

Pushing through the doorway, I grinned as I found him in our cramped kitchen. "Hi, Dad," I called, slipping into my usual chair at the well-worn oak table that held residence just beside the kitchen. Although one might refer to it as a dining room, there wasn't a partition between them. Or any of the main rooms in our cottage.

"Almost done!" Dad called, his focus trained on something he was slicing on the board in front of him.

My eyes scanned my surroundings as I tried to commit every detail of this moment to memory. Everything about the interior of our home was still a shrine to the woman who had once lived here.

The shabby cabinets were white, chipping to show the time that had passed since their last thorough painting. Resting in the corners of each door, there were tiny red roses with tendrils of dark green thorny vines swirling away from every bud. My mother had drawn them when she was pregnant with me and dreaming of the life that she hoped we would all share within these walls. With all three of us.

Scattered across the house were a million more reminders of her. The dark wooden hutch in between the kitchen and sitting area contained a handful of my parent's special dishes, a bone white plate with raised colorless floral designs around the edge and a rim hand painted in gold.

My parents had moved here together from somewhere in the north, but my dad never liked to talk about it. Considering I knew nothing about either of my grandparents, I had to assume something had broken the family apart, severing those ties and causing my parents to flee here. Even years ago, when I had gained enough bravado to ask, he had sharply refused to explain. It was so unlike him that it was not something I attempted to discuss again.

I was happy with it being just me and Dad, so I never thought to seek the rest of my blood relatives, even in secret. He, Jemma, and Jemma's mother, Marjorie, were all the family I needed.

"How was Jemma tonight?" he asked, as if sensing that my thoughts had shifted to them. His tone still sounded kind of far away, like he was engaging in the conversation technically, but not entirely.

My gaze shifted to the living room next, my attention snagging on the cream and brown speckled crocheted blanket that my mother had made. "She was good. Still packing."

My dad chuckled, and I turned to catch him shaking his head as he transferred the potatoes from the wood-burning stove to a stone slab so that they could cool. His attention on the meal allowed me to return to my quiet perusal of the house.

Our sky-blue couch had been placed as a divider between the dining area and living room, dingier and more faded now than I supposed it had been when my mother had picked it out. Something about the combination of that light blue and the cream blanket draped over it reminded me of the coast. Of salty, crusted waves gliding over sandy banks.

A long breath filled my lungs as I attempted to breathe in the briny aroma that I couldn't scent over the smell of the roasting chicken.

On the opposite wall, a painting depicting a stunning garden, overrun with purple plants, flowers, and even trees, perched where it had always been since my father had hung it all those years ago. It was the only item my mother had brought with her from wherever she came from in the north. No matter where we traveled in Demetros, I had never seen such a place, but I loved it all the same.

Her brown leather boots still lived under the small wooden stool next to the door, unlaced and waiting for her as if she would walk back through the threshold one day and resume her life. Although I used to wear them as a small child, no one had touched them in years, and I was certain they had dry-rotted by now. Or were, more than likely, home to some type of vermin.

We never outright discussed them, and neither of us could bring ourselves to toss them. It was another piece of her that we both illogically held onto, as if throwing out a pair of old shoes would somehow make her more dead.

To further drive home that point, Dad had changed very little inside these walls since my birth. She was everywhere, even though she was nowhere.

"Here you go." Dad placed a familiar white plate in front of me, breaking me from my trance. "Tonight's a special occasion. It's our last meal together for a while."

In the corner of his eyes, I saw the start of cresting silver forming. He typically only made this dish for my birthday, as it required purchasing a whole chicken and extra butter from the market, but it wasn't entirely surprising that he had splurged for tonight's meal.

A lump formed in my throat as I was forced to face the significance of this moment, something I had been vehemently trying to block from my consciousness. I wanted to go to Biltons more than I had ever wanted anything, but I was still reluctant to leave. It felt like I was leaving more than a small piece of myself behind. A past I could never return to in exchange for a future full of endless possibilities. One of which was damnation.

Blinking back the thoughts that threatened to spill over, my eyelashes fluttered, heavy with the tumultuous emotions. Dad took to the seat directly across from me with his own dish. In the confines of my mind, I gave silent thanks to Merè, the goddess of life, for providing the chicken and boosting the fertility of the land that gave us the potatoes. The gods and goddesses hadn't roamed these lands for thousands of years, but I was too superstitious not to acknowledge them from time to time. Dad did not have the same inclinations.

It took no effort to fall into simple conversation about everything except Biltons Academy. Internally, I was grateful for what I believed to be his purposeful willingness to avoid the topic so that we could keep some semblance of normalcy to our night. *My last night.*

My bite of chicken had just reached my tongue when Dad spoke up. "Have I ever told you the story behind those dishes?"

I looked up just in time to see him pointing his own utensil towards my plate. Shaking my head, I hummed something resembling *no* around the mouthful of food I had just taken.

He smiled, a far-off kind of twinkle in his eyes. "When your mother and I moved here, we had very little. My family wasn't wealthy, so most of the belongings we had came from her."

Inside my mind, I was warring with where to place my gaze. I couldn't remember a time when he had initiated a story about his past, about their life before me. Was he going to finally explain where that painting came from? Who my grandparents were?

With quiet anticipation, I watched his expression, waiting for what he might say next.

His stare dropped to the plate as his fingers traced the outer rim of the dish. "She saw them in the market and had to have them." A chuckle jostled his chest, but he did not lift his eyes from the porcelain.

"I saved up for months to buy a set." He sniffed another laugh that I failed to decipher. "Of three."

My gaze drifted to the third plate; the one placed in front of the empty chair. "That's why you leave a dish for her?"

When I turned back to him, I found a quarter smile lifting the corners of his mouth. Dad had only ever pulled these out for special occasions, and I had always considered the place setting at the empty chair a sweet gesture. It was also a sharp knife to the chest, reminding me of what would never be. Now, knowing the entire story behind the dishes, the sting of that visual was more acute.

"I always wanted her to be here for this." He glanced towards the door as if she might walk in at any moment, collect her boots, and join us for the meal.

My hand slid across the table, resting over his with a gentle squeeze. "Me too, Dad."

His smile was pained, but there was something beautiful about sharing our grief. With having someone to unload it on who understood with near exact precision what shape the loss took inside my heart.

He cleared his throat, and I could already tell that the moment had dissolved. Whatever questions I might have about my mother and her belongings would have to wait for another opening.

Disappointedly, I retracted my hand from his and continued eating my meal as he asked, "How many bags do you suspect Jemma will bring?"

A snort expelled from my nose. "I just have to hope you've reinforced the wheels on the cart."

Dad shook his head, an ear-to-ear smile splitting his face. "That girl."

The rest of the meal and even beyond was spent in companionable conversation. Hours later, with our bellies still bloated from the delicious meal, the frequency of our yawns increased to a point that we had to acknowledge them. We had both put off the inevitable for as long as our bodies could bear it, and our systems were giving us no choice but to give in to the exhaustion.

"Well, I'm going to hit the hay," Dad remarked with a soft smile directed at me. He looked somber, and I could tell there was something bittersweet about this moment for him, too, even if he didn't know the full weight of my decision. The stakes for my choice.

For my whole life, all twenty years, we had each other, just the two of us. I rarely spent the night away from him, and then it was only down the road with Jemma. While most children probably would have been upset by that, I always cherished our time together. It had been my choice to be with him instead of in the company of other kids my age.

Maybe because I had already lost one parent, I truly appreciated these mundane moments we shared. I never got to have a meal with my mother or carry conversations about the ordinary parts of my life. It made me treasure what I had with my dad more.

Tonight was the last "goodnight" I'd get from him for months while I was away at the academy. After the solstice ceremony in December, I would be permitted to return during the rest period that the entire academy was given after our binds were removed. A time used to wait for our magic to come in. But, past that...

If—*no, when*—I made the Select Guard, my specialized training would start almost immediately at the conclusion of the academic year at Biltons. Even if I returned after that, this place would never be my full-time home again. Members of the Queen's personal guard resided in bunkhouses for the duration of their training and were expected to stay in the capital city, Fulgrande, for the remainder of their employment.

The thought made me feel instantly unmoored. A ship with nowhere to dock. A sailor with no port to return to.

Suddenly, I wanted nothing more than to confess to him about the anonymous sponsor and beg that he help me find a way out of the magically binding contract. But, as I took him in and noted the dark circles beneath his eyes, I reminded myself that this was my only option.

Holding back the tears was an almost insurmountable challenge. Somehow, I managed it, but my voice wasn't as easy to rein in, cracking even within the confines of my whisper. "Goodnight, Dad."

He walked down the hall to his room, his eyes catching mine one last time before he spoke. "Goodnight, little girl," he breathed, just before he stepped across the threshold.

Seven

Lightning crackled across a midnight sky streaked with stars despite the storm raging below. The flash of brightness was enough to illuminate the shadowy shapes that roamed the ground, a field of faceless soldiers. At the far edge of the expanse of grass were beings that could only be described as creatures. With wings that spread wide and teeth that glinted in the storm's onslaught, the shapes were nothing short of nightmarish.

Except... there wasn't a storm per se. There was no rain, no precipitation to bring on the flashes of electricity racing for the ground. Just streaks of white lights slashing across a night sky and bringing awareness to the beasts that watched me through reptilian eyes.

One of them canted its head to me and studied me for a fraction of a second before its jaws unhinged and a raging fire shot from its teeth adorned maw. The fire was so hot that I felt its inferno before it even touched me.

Shooting upright before I even registered the movement, I awoke with my mouth agape on a scream. My heart threatened to claw its way from my chest, leaving me dizzy and disoriented for several extended moments. Thanks in no small part to my ever-increasing anxiety, my nightmares had been growing worse with the approach to this day, but this one had been the most vivid of them all.

With my palms pressed against my eyes, I rubbed feverishly to bring myself back to the present. I felt as if I hadn't slept a single minute, plagued by shadows and dread even as I rested. Despite those steadfast feelings of fear from the dream, something else entirely began to creep to the surface like the glowing red rays of dawn's early light cresting the horizon. It was hope. Today, I was going to Biltons Academy, where I was being given the opportunity to realize my dreams and save my father.

As if my thoughts had summoned him, I heard my dad's steps draw closer to my room. The floorboards creaked beneath his feet as he settled into his position in the hallway. "Knock, knock," he called from the other side of the door, saying the words but not actually completing the action.

A little huff of a laugh tumbled from me, letting me shed those final remnants of trepidation. "Come in, Dad," I called, lifting myself the rest of the way off the bed and brushing out my tangled hair with my fingers in an effort to seem like I hadn't spent the entirety of the night tossing and turning.

The door swung open, and my dad walked in slowly, clearly unsure how deep in the dregs of sleep I still might be, as his eyes cautiously took me in. From experience, he knew I wasn't always pleasant in the mornings.

Upon a brief assessment of my condition, he deemed it safe to continue speaking. "Jemma and Marjorie are in the kitchen; I think it's time to go." His gaze swept over the room, assessing my packing job. His expression did little to hide his delight that I had only chosen to bring one trunk and one smaller leather backpack. If the previous evening had been any indication, I doubted Jemma's packing had been so light.

"I'll just grab this stuff and load it into the carriage," he stated. "Coffee and pastries are in the kitchen if Jemma hasn't consumed it all by now," he paused briefly, shaking his head. His eyes cut toward the room she was in, and his voice lowered to a whisper. "It's a bit alarming how much she can eat."

His chuckle over Jemma's eating habits died when he walked to my luggage and proceeded to pick up my traveling trunk. A grimace replaced his grin, and my shoulders sagged with sudden regret. I should have considered that he was in no condition to handle its weight.

Hustling to get to the trunk, I reached for one of the handles before he swatted me away with a pinched expression. "It's heavier than it looked, but I have it."

He grabbed the leather straps on either end before I could protest again, he was already making his way out of my room. My grimace remained.

Clothing items made up the bulk of the trunk's contents, but I knew the books weighed it down the most. It wasn't as if any of the tomes I was bringing were assigned reading. Those were to be provided by the academy. I had been incapable of leaving behind my favorite storybooks. Watching my father struggle with the weight of it had me reconsidering my choices, even if I really wanted them there.

I preferred fantasy to the dull history books of basic education. Living in other worlds, places full of magic and quests, was so much better than reality and provided a much-needed form of escape when life became too heavy.

Stories of Fae with pointed ears and people who could shift into animals were exhilarating in a way I knew real life could never be.

In each of the stories that I had picked to bring with me, I had seen fragments of a mirror reflecting pieces of myself. A woman grappling with loss. A girl, assumed to be weak, who bested her opponents. Main characters who loved to read and who always second guessed the world around them, never quite trusting the information they were given as truth.

Some stories I had read so many times that I could likely recite them from memory, but they brought me a level of contentment that felt a lot like coming home. My assumption was that I may need a lot of that type of comfort in the coming months.

With haste, I dressed in plain attire, lacing up the boots my father had given me last solstice. Then, I reached around my neck, clasping the moon necklace together, patting the crescent shape that sat just below my collarbone before sparing a glance around the room.

My small bed still had touches from my girlhood when my father had let me pick out the décor from items we got through trades.

Like my faded purple and pink floral quilt, which I pulled up the bed, making it for the last time until December. We had received the blanket through an exchange in Estes for my dad's services long ago. It was another representation of the gracious nature of my father, but for me, it was a testament to the community coming together to support one another. Before this, I'd had nothing in the space that felt like me, and while I wasn't confident that I still identified with the dainty flowery print, it was still a piece of me. A portrait of a sliver of time when it had very much been a representation of my preferences.

Modest curtains, made from white linen fabric that Marjorie had sewn for me, hung from the small window over the headboard. She had embroidered tiny daisies onto the corners, only visible when you were up close. I liked to imagine that my mother would have done the same if she had been alive, so the maternal gesture warmed my heart.

The dresser was simple and left in a natural finish to match the wood of the bed, although they were procured at different times. What should have been used for clothing storage held the majority of my library—more examples of items gained through trade rather than coin. What my dad couldn't buy me directly, he always found a way to procure through these exchanges.

The white-painted armoire in the corner held my entire wardrobe, which was sparse but adequate. The perfect way to describe our home and its contents.

It was the opposite of opulence, but I remembered where each piece had been obtained, the village it came from, and the people who traded it to us for work. It was a humble room in a small cottage, but I loved it. Smiling faintly, I closed the door behind me, even as the reality of my situation brought moisture to my eyes and constricted my throat.

Jemma and Marjorie were waiting for me at the kitchen table, enjoying steaming cups of coffee and an assortment of pastries that one of them must have secured this morning from the town bakery.

Jemma's voice practically accosted me as I entered the space. "I cannot believe it is finally *the* day."

It was only because I had expected the intensity of her greeting that I hadn't flinched. "Yeah, me either." My voice squeaked, still laden with those weighted emotions, as I dropped myself into a free chair.

Jemma reached over the table to grab another pastry. Crumbs gathered along the hem of her top from the food she had already consumed. She had the appetite of a teenage boy, with none of the excuses of growing taller.

Jemma paused her gorging to narrow her celery green eyes at me and speak to the expression she must have found on my face. "Ash, you come from two powerful lines of wielders. You have trained for this. There is absolutely nothing to worry about." She threw out the statement as if it were fact, something learned during our basic education that was not to be argued over. Then, she immediately resumed stuffing her face with a large chocolate croissant.

My eyes roamed over the plate of treats until my vision narrowed in on a second one, which I eagerly snatched up before she could consume it.

"You really have the energy of a powerful wielder," her mother, Marjorie, said, giving me a kind smile before picking up her coffee and taking a long sip. Her raven hair twisted into a long braid that began along the base of her skull, and a pair of green eyes that mirrored her daughters were twinkling with the mischief that always accompanied her stare.

Marjorie was a Saxum with a moderate level of earth power, but she was also skilled in making salves and healing remedies for generalized pain and burns. Unfortunately, none of her goods could help my father. We had already tried everything, and she graciously hadn't charged me for any of it.

She claimed that via a palm reading, she could sense someone's character based on how their energy felt and the color of their aura, or something like that. She was certainly quirky, but no one would consider her mentally unwell. Most of the time, her assessments and predictions were correct, garnering her the skeptical attention of the older generation, who whispered about her being a witch, just like they had my mother. Ever since the gods and goddesses abandoned our world, only elemental magic remained with the people. So, anything outside of the norm was regarded with suspicion.

In Marjorie's case, it wasn't some undiscovered or fabled magic that made this possible. She carefully observed those around her before making her readings. It did not take a genius—and certainly not a witch—to determine that a child born from two Caelum parents would almost always find themselves assigned to the class with abilities to wield the air.

Marjorie jerked her head towards her daughter with an expression that held amused annoyance. "This one has been up for hours, begging us to just go ahead and leave."

A chuckle broke around my bite of croissant, which I hastily swallowed as I grinned at Marjorie. "Then I suppose my father and I owe you a debt for keeping her contained until a reasonable hour." Jemma was like that, always eager to start the next adventure. In all honesty, I couldn't decide if Jemma was more interested in the magical aspects of the academy, her access to the capital shops when we were allowed to leave, or the wave of new men that she would meet. Knowing her, the latter was at the top of her list.

Jemma and I had both had our fair share of boyfriends and harmless crushes over the years, but my best friend had never opened herself up to anything outside of platonic love. She liked to have fun and had amassed quite the list of past lovers.

Jemma was a free spirit in every sense of the word. The affection of those who inevitably ended up lusting after her, long after she left them in the dust, only increased her confidence. She had been with multiple partners, an exact number I did not dare count, and none of them had lasted longer than a few weeks before she tossed them to the side.

We were not alike in that. Not that I hadn't been physical with the boys I had courted, I just hadn't viewed relationships in the same way that she did. If I was careless with my affections, it never went past kissing unless there were feelings. While Jemma seemed to be repelled by attachment, I craved it.

Plus, there were more ways to feel love than romantically. Love to me would always be Jemma. Unfailing, strong, and consistently there for me through everything. If she was the only love I ever had, I was content with that. Even if I never stopped wondering if there was someone else out there for me. Someone to have a family with. Someone to grow into old age with.

Maybe, after I secured my place with the Select Guard, and cured whatever ailed my father, I would find out.

My dad's voice brought me out of my thoughts. "Time to hit the road, girls." He dusted his hands off on his pants before stretching his back in a way that spoke of hours of manual labor. To Jemma and Marjorie, they probably saw it as a dig at me, a joke about the weight of our bags, but I saw the underlying soreness. I saw the calm before the storm, the period of mobility before the inevitable crash.

Blinking away the notion of my sadness before it could take root, I turned my attention to the women gathered around my kitchen table instead. For as long as I could remember, we had planned to take this trip together, the four of us. Even when Biltons had been a distant dream to me, we had discussed traveling as much of the road together before we had to veer off to whatever academy I had chosen. I was grateful, if for nothing else, that my choice had kept us taking that path together, at least for today.

Jemma snatched a few more pastries from the plate before resigning herself to scooping up the entire dish and carrying it with her out the front door. Marjorie followed her, chuckling over the lip of her coffee mug. My pace dwindled as I approached the entrance to the cottage, pausing just before I reached it.

A smile curled the edges of my lips as I released a drawn-out exhale, reflecting on all the memories that my father and I had shared in this cottage, eternally grateful that my dad had knowingly shuffled the others out of the house so that I might have this last quiet moment to bid farewell to the only home I had ever known.

With a hand braced on the doorframe, I took one more heartbeat to linger at the threshold, allowing myself one final sweep dedicated to committing every nook and cranny of this place to memory. With the final twist of my neck, I turned around and stepped outside.

I wondered who I would be when I crossed this doorway again.

Eight

A bright light filtered on us as we emerged from the eastern tunnel that led to the capital. Fulgrande was completely surrounded by an otherwise perilous mountain range. So, long ago, Saxum wielders had formed four tunnels, each aligned with a direction on a compass, through the rock and dirt so that travel and trade with the city would be possible. Or so the stories go. Much of the specifics of our kingdom's history had been lost over time.

My hand created a shadow over my eyes as I took in our surroundings. There were sections clearly designated for homes, others for storefronts, and some larger pockets where trees and foliage reigned supreme, purposeful little parks that allowed a sprinkling of nature to still exist within the bustling community.

We passed by a bakery that stood proudly next to a jewelry store that held cases of sparkling diamonds pressed up against the window for potential patrons. We meandered past townhomes that circled around a small park, encased by a wrought iron fence that told me it was a private area for those specific residences.

Based on previous trips and a rather embarrassing question to my father, I knew that several streets over, one could find an establishment where men and women alike sold their flesh willingly for coin.

According to Jemma, fire and water wielders made the most money in such places, and she hadn't been shy about telling me why or how she had come to know that information.

Jemma squeezed my hand from her spot next to me, drawing my attention to our destination. A panic pulsed in my bloodstream, and I hoped that if she could feel that uptick in my heart rate through our joined palms, she would attribute it to regular nerves.

Even from a distance, I had seen the flags flapping from the tallest peaks of our destination, overtop the buildings we had passed. I had memorized the crest of Biltons Academy already, an ode to the five classes and the Elemental Queen herself. That symbol snapped in the sharp breeze beneath the flag of Demetros, which boasted a golden flower atop a background of equal parts blue and green to symbolize the fertility of the land and the water that surrounded our entire kingdom.

Jemma's knee began to bounce up and down with her excitement, and she leaned in to whisper so that our parents wouldn't hear. "How long until I find the sexiest man?"

I flashed her a conspiratorial grin as my eyes darted back to the road. "I'd bet just about anything you find a boy to lay claim to before you even step foot in the gates."

As if I had summoned them, the elegantly scrolling wrought iron gates came into view, wide open and already welcoming a mass of students within the academy walls.

My breath caught in my throat as Jemma's resounding laugh faded to a dull thrum in the back of my mind. No one was permitted within the walls of the academy outside of faculty and students, and this was as close as I had ever come to seeing the property up close that I was about to call home.

Four turrets in speckled shades of gray and tan reached high into the sky, like outstretched hands begging for rain from the clouds. Intimidating stacked rock walls connected each tower. The stones to construct the academy had come from across the kingdom, so some matched the gray rock mined from the north, while others looked more reminiscent of the sand-colored materials brought in from the south, blending together seamlessly.

The highest peak of the central building stood over double the height of even the tallest of the outer towers, with one long spire resting on top. The flags seemed to snap to attention, flashing me another glimpse of the crest of this magnificent school and the symbol of our great nation.

My gaze slid back down the main structure, over the cerulean roofs of the buildings—that had once been a shiny copper but had transitioned to a light green hue after centuries in the elements—and back to the open front gates.

Jemma's grip became vise-like, and I followed her gaze as our carriage came to a stop. Her attention wasn't on the impressive architecture of the building, but rather the gathering students, some already bidding farewell to their families and friends. She hardly waited for my father to bring the transport to a complete stop before she leaped to her feet, releasing my hand just as she jumped from the opening.

In the process of her escape, she nearly toppled into another person who had been walking past on the sidewalk. The stranger righted himself instantly, but Jemma fell helplessly to the ground with a loud thud.

"I'm so sorry, are you hurt?" The voice belonged to a man who was already extending a hand to help her up. I could only see the back of his head, so I couldn't discern if he was a student, one of our instructors, or just an innocent bystander.

Jemma's face pulled into a smirk. "You are totally fine..." She allowed the man to pull her to her feet, not once taking her gaze from his face. "I mean, I am fine," she corrected, batting her eyelashes and tucking a loose curl behind her ear. I knew my best friend well enough to determine that the stranger before us must have been attractive in some capacity to garner such a response. It left me to wonder if the collision had been an accident at all.

In a bid to save her, or perhaps him, from her plotting, I departed the carriage and joined them on the sidewalk. As I reached level ground, I noted the way my vision aligned with the stranger's shoulder blades.

"My name is Caden, but most of my friends just call me Cade," he stated, still holding onto Jemma's hands.

She flashed him a dazzling smile, finally releasing the hold she had on him. "I'm Jemma." She jerked her head in my direction. "And this is my best friend, Ashton."

The man turned around to face me and it was a conscious effort to keep my jaw from hitting the floor. Caden, or Cade, was perhaps the most beautiful man that I had ever seen.

By my estimate, based on my height of approximately five foot seven, he was over six feet tall. My gaze scraped over his physique, collecting the distinct impression that the muscles that strained against his tunic were born from labor, even if the quality of his garments spoke of affluence. I allowed my attention to languidly drift across his body, catching on the sight of his hair, a warm chocolate brown that fell in thick waves across his broad shoulders.

His skin had the kind of flawless tawny sheen that only came from the bronzing rays of the sun, and his features were an amalgamation of feminine and masculine that shouldn't have been appealing but somehow made him both handsome and beautiful. Despite all of that, perhaps the most captivating part of the man before me was his deep blue eyes, dark and dynamic as the evening sky just before it succumbs to nightfall, speckled with flecks of violet that almost made them seem iridescent.

My own eyes came into focus about that time, realizing that I had been silently staring at this man instead of introducing myself. Warmth crept into my cheeks. "Hello." The words came out as a stammer as I thrust my hand between us.

Cade grinned, flashing me another hypnotic smile that spoke of his awareness of his attractiveness but wasn't outwardly rude. He took my hand in his, calloused palms sliding against my own.

His proximity invaded my senses and somewhere in some far reaches of my brain I knew I was acting like I had never seen a man before in all my life and yet I was powerless to stop the behavior. Incapable of forcing myself into normalcy as his heat cascaded over me in waves.

My inhale, which was meant to be steadying, drug in the scent of salt air, cedarwood, and honeysuckles into my lungs. It was familiar but blended in a new configuration. A comforting thing and yet somehow exhilarating.

"It's nice to meet you," he said through his amused grin, like maybe he was used to girls stammering over him.

In my stupor, I assumed he was pausing at the end of that sentence to ask for my name again. "Ashton." The word was blurted like a cough or hiccup I hadn't been expecting. The heat gathering along my cheeks burned as my skin turned a deep shade of crimson.

Cade chuckled, a rich, warm sound that made butterflies swarm and somersault in my stomach. "Well, it was nice to meet you, Ashton and Jemma." He turned to my friend with a nod. "I'm sure I will see you around." He punctuated his sentence with a wink before running off to meet a group of guys who were lingering just outside of the gates.

I looked around to see if my dad and Marjorie had witnessed that awkward moment, but they were thankfully on the other side of the carriage, preoccupied with unloading our things. Jemma was still laughing as she slung her canvas backpack over her shoulder. She put her arm around me and guided my body towards our parents.

They had already loaded all our belongings onto carts that they must have procured while I was embarrassing myself with Cade. Marjorie's cart with Jemma's traveling luggage and bags towered over my one trunk and leather backpack by my dad's side.

With a sideways glance, I eyed Jemma's belongings with skepticism. It would be a miracle if less than half of this stuff wasn't sent back to Elmhaven before the week's end.

Tearing my gaze from her mountain of things, I found my dad. His eyes crinkled with a melancholy smile as my eyes met his. "Well, this is where we say goodbye."

Instead of spreading his arms wide, he fidgeted around in his coat pocket. He produced a small wooden box, about half the size of the palm of his hand. "I was waiting to give this to you until you got here. Your mom would have wanted you to have it."

Silver threaded through his eyes, and I forced my stare to the box, grabbing it and opening it quickly, grateful to have something to focus on and distract me from the swelling emotion in my chest.

A rich blue velvet lined the inside of the box, and on top of the plush pad of fabric sat a single golden ring that I had never seen before. At the center was a brilliant blood orange cushion cut stone surrounded by three metallic wheat shapes on either side, reminiscent of the shapes that clustered around the kingdom's flower on their official flag. In these leaves, tiny white diamonds filled up the curves of the foliage in a sparkling display.

My dad's voice dropped to a whisper. "It was her wedding ring." He cleared his throat as if to banish the emotions surrounding his words. "She wanted you to have it when you came of age."

Determined not to cry in front of all my future classmates, I stepped toward him and hooked my arms around his back, pulling him into a full-body embrace. Of all people, I was painfully aware of what it meant to give away a piece of her like this. After someone's death, these physical reminders of them were finite, and this gift meant that he had one less memento for himself from their time together.

My dad hugged me back, fiercely, as if he thought he would never see me again and we stayed like that for several moments before I ultimately pulled away.

"Thank you," I muttered the words as if I was afraid if I spoke much louder, the cork holding back my tumultuous emotions would come blasting off. Being known as the blubbering mess of a girl being dropped off by her dad was not the way I wanted to be remembered, even if I could hardly fight back the burn in my throat and the sting in my eyes.

Suddenly I was being pulled into another embrace as Marjorie's arms wrapped around me. She smelled like cinnamon, vanilla and incense, a product of concocting her healing remedies. I buried my face against the plait of her braid as I returned the gesture.

"Your mother would be so proud of you, Ash." She breathed the words into my ear, low enough for only me to hear. "I am, too, for what it's worth."

It was worth everything, but instead of simply saying that, I squeezed her tighter, hoping she felt the meaning between the press of my arms around her. Behind us, I heard my dad whisper a similar senti-ment to Jemma in their hug, and my chest tightened with the outpouring of love.

Jemma and I stepped back towards our belongings, and our parents moved closer to the carriage. A line seemed to form between us, something signifying the present moment was about to be wrapped up in the before chapter of our lives.

My eyes caught on my dad's bittersweet smile. "This is where we have to leave you."

Looking hopeful, Marjorie followed that up with, "Unless the rules have changed, and we can go inside to walk you to your dorms?"

While I had known Marjorie had only been teasing, Jemma clenched her jaw, pointing directly at our parents. "Mom, no!" Her finger wagged between them. "You two cannot come in."

Dad huffed a laugh to alleviate the tension. "Then this is goodbye." He beamed at both of us, pulling Marjorie into a side hug so that they could share the view of their only children standing at the gates of the magical academy.

Marjorie glanced up at my father, staring up at him with a tender-hearted expression. "Look at our girls, Christian; they're all grown up." She swiped along the edges of her eyes in a sort of sentimental daze.

Crossing the line between us once more, I doled out another round of hugs before Jemma dragged me by my elbows towards my cart. "Come on, Ash, we have things to do and boys to meet."

With a white-knuckled grip, Jemma pushed her cart forward, eyes trained on the thick iron gates that reached for us, calling us into its depths with wide-open arms.

My head swiveled to steal one more glimpse of my dad. He looked healthy today despite the strain of packing my belongings, and I only hoped that he would stay that way until I returned. "Bye, Dad!" I yelled over my shoulder, trying to keep up with Jemma as she practically ran to the entrance, undeterred by the weight of her heavy cart.

Bye, little girl, he mouthed, making sure my eyes were locked with his when he did. This time, one tiny tear rolled down my cheek, and I felt his magic wash over me as he banished it from my face with his water magic before I could swipe it away. Blinking, I glanced back to meet his comforting gaze, but the crowd had swallowed us up, and all I could see were the faces of my classmates lining up behind me, eager to start their adventure too.

A disappointed sigh fell from my lips, but I turned to join the crowd. At the head of the line, a woman, holding a wooden clipboard, was clearly directing students to their houses. She stood about my height with medium length blonde hair. The ends dyed in various shades of blue. Her hair color seemed whimsical, but out of place connected to her face, which was set in a stern scowl.

"Name?" she barked when it was my turn, only briefly glancing up at me before returning her gaze to the paperwork resting on the clipboard.

This was my last chance to turn around and run as far away from my fate as possible. Once I gave my name and started the semester, there would be no refund on the donor's money and no way to get out of the contract. If I even still could with whatever magic laced the parchment.

My heart thundered in my chest as the woman before me stamped her foot in annoyance.

It was now or never.

I lifted my chin as I made my final decision. "Ashton Elizabeth Blake," I stated, enunciating every word to ensure she got it right.

She flipped a couple of pages and checked my name off her list, but she didn't lift her eyes as she spoke. "You're in house one. Please head to the yellow flag and meet your team."

Worry pulsed through my veins, but at this point, I couldn't turn back. Officially, I had been registered, and the only thing to do was to move forward and do what I had spent my life training to do.

"Thanks," I muttered, pushing past the woman who had already moved her focus to the next in line.

Jemma was waiting for me right past the clipboard girl, looking up to smile at me as I approached her. "This is where we part ways too."

This was expected. Houses were assigned based on birthdates, and while I was born in October, Jemma would be assigned to house three, where the other March birthdays would be sorted.

Wincing, I echoed her statement. "Yeah, this is where we part ways."

Jemma was practically vibrating with excitement, and I knew it was more over the new possibilities and not about our separation, but I still felt a pang of hurt as I watched her eyes dart over to a cluster of people that I assumed belonged to her new house.

Somewhat unexpectedly, the vision made me nervous all over again. "I'll see you at dinner, right?"

Jemma grinned, oblivious to my strife. "Of course, sis. I'll see you in a couple hours." She rested her hand on my forearm for only a second before retracting her touch and committing fully to wrapping her arms around me.

"I love you," I whispered into her long, curly hair, trying and failing not to clutch onto her like she was my only friend in the world.

"Always and forever," she replied. With that simple exchange, we let go of each other, and I forced myself to turn around, grabbing my cart and pushing it towards the crowd surrounding the yellow flag that signified the muster point for my house.

Jemma walked the opposite way towards the gathering at a green flag. When I looked over my shoulder to give her one last goodbye, she was already mid-conversation with a pretty blonde girl, no doubt well on their way to becoming fast friends.

A reluctant smile curled my lips, even if the sight made me a tad jealous, and I pushed on towards that yellow flag.

Nine

A dainty yellow triangle of fabric flapped in the breeze at the edge of one of the two copper-plated fountains that took residence in the front part of the courtyard. The features were circular, each boasting a single plume of water sprayed into the air by what appeared to be a swan. A perimeter of thick slabs of stone, about knee high, encased the water within, wide enough to sit on.

Pushing my cart to a spot along the fountain's edge, I took a seat that seemed relatively dry and close enough to the growing crowd that I'd be able to hear anything important. A fine mist collected along my cheeks, and I closed my eyes to concentrate on the sound of rushing water rather than the seriousness of my predicament. Deep breaths expanded my lungs as I waited for my heart to steady itself, and when my lashes fluttered open again, a woman was perched on the lip of the fountain, not even two feet beside me.

She was petite, probably more than a couple of inches shorter than me, clad in a simple navy dress that gave me no indication of her social standing. Her milky white skin was completely unblemished, creamy, and soft, like maybe she had never been plagued by an ounce of acne in her entire life.

Her head canted as she took in the sight of me with a sweep of her mottled brown eyes, clearly unperturbed that I had just caught her staring. As she blinked, I noted the reflective quality of her chocolate-hued irises, shining with fragments of amber and honey.

She tucked a strand of her dark, cropped locks behind her ear, the color popping violet beneath the rays of the afternoon sun. The woman offered her hand to the space between us. "Hi. My name is Ryana; it is nice to meet you."

There was something inviting about this person, a quality about her nonjudgmental stares that had me contemplating if she had just been sizing me up. Not maliciously, but to determine if I would make an agreeable companion to her. She seemed just as nervous as I was to be here, although it was possible I was projecting.

Our palms pressed together as I curled my fingertips around hers, shaking once before releasing her. "I'm Ashton," I replied. "You're in house one, too?"

It was a ridiculous thing to ask. Everyone assigned to house one had been told to stand by the yellow flag. So, unless she was incapable of following directions, it was a safe assumption that we had been grouped together. Either way, the bumbling question had come from an urge to engage in small talk with this new person, and I hoped she gathered that instead of writing me off.

If she had found the question stupid, she didn't let on. "Yep." Her grin widened. "My birthday is November 20th, I just barely made the cut."

At Biltons Academy, our birthdays placed us in one of four houses. August 23rd to November 21st was house one, November 22nd to February 18th was house two, February 19th to May 20th made up house three, and May 21st to August 22nd rounded out house four.

Despite the criteria relating heavily to the old religious observations about sun locations during the birth of a child, there was no magical reason we were split this way. At one point, people believed that the sun god Tarynd bestowed specific personality traits to those born during certain times of year, but those ideals had largely been abandoned with the disappearance of that same god.

Even now, there were only vestiges of the old religion, like this one, that popped up in official capacities for no particular reason, as there was no correlation between a birthday and the assignment of an elemental class or power levels. Which was fortuitous for me because I didn't like to linger on my birthday at all, and other than it being the criteria used for sorting me into a house, I wouldn't have to consider it at all.

Blinking my eyes, I cleared away those thoughts as I brought my focus back to Ryana. "Where are you from?"

Most people had likely hailed from bigger cities, ripe with trade and bustling markets. I assumed there were very few, like me, who were here on a scholarship. Or, in my case, a sponsorship. Not that I could outright ask, the donor's rules were clear-cut enough. I wasn't to speak a word about this to anyone.

Ryana's smile was friendly, even if her expression was guarded. "Eden. It's north of here. You?"

My chin dipped with my nod. "I know of Eden," I admitted. "I'm from Elmhaven. I live there with my dad."

The confession seemed to draw realization to her expression. "I'm an only child too."

A nervous laugh rippled from my mouth. "So, you don't know what kind of element you might get out of this either?" A sibling was just as good of an indication, if not a better one, as to what elemental gift might be inherited.

She shrugged, twisting her lips nonchalantly like it didn't bother her. "Both of my parents are gifted with the fire element. I assume I will be much the same." She explained it with an air of disappointment, but I didn't have time to linger on that expression before another came to join us by the fountain.

A man with platinum blonde hair that fell to his shoulders cast a shadow over my face as he approached. His bright green eyes darted between us. He was attractive—nothing breathtaking in the way that Cade had been—but it had me wondering if anyone was permitted into this school who fell below the line of average looks.

"Do you guys mind if I join you?" he asked, and it was almost endearing how unsure he seemed about the interaction. "I'm Grethe, by the way." He held his hand out for me to shake first, only turning to Ryana after that initial introduction was out of the way.

He joined our conversation effortlessly, offering that his parents were Flumen and that he lived near Eden, traveling there often.

I watched their interaction for a moment after Grethe's confession but didn't sense any familiarity. "Do you two know each other?"

Ryana shook her head and looked like she was about to say no when another man walked to our group, cutting off her response. "This is house one, right?"

The guy had brown hair, dark like coffee without creamer, and equally rich eyes that assessed us like competition and not classmates. "She wasn't very articulate," he added, jerking his head towards the girl with the clipboard.

Whatever awkwardness I had sensed evaporated with the mention of the stern woman who had practically scolded me for not already knowing what to do, even though it was her sole purpose. "Yeah, she's really chatty and overly helpful. Which is how I already knew everyone's names and where they were from."

The newest addition to our group seemed unimpressed by my attempt at sarcasm, but he didn't leave us. His tone was neutral as he spoke. "My name is Nielsen, and I am from Fulgrande."

At least he recognized that my words had been in jest. Although between his impeccable attire and posh accent, I should have guessed that he was raised in the capital city.

Another girl stepped towards us before I could say anything further to Nielsen. Her almond eyes caught mine as she plastered on what was clearly an apprehensive smile. "At the risk of sounding like an idiot... the yellow flag is for house one, right? I'm afraid to ask for clarification."

We all laughed, even Nielsen, as we accepted her into the fold.

She lifted a single hand in the air, curling her fingers in an approximation of a wave. "I'm Ingrid, I'm from the west coast."

It was interesting that she left off the name of her hometown. I couldn't determine if she was from a smaller town she thought no one would recognize, or just not overly eager to share too many personal details. Just as I was planning to ask her more, Nielsen spoke up. "What element do you think you will be?"

The question was posed to no one in particular, but Ingrid answered first. "My adoptive dads are both Caelum, and I would love to share that with them, but I believe at least one of my biological parents is Flumen, so I'm not sure it's in the cards for me."

Nielsen ran a hand through his brown hair. "I get it. My parents aren't Saxum, but I know that I am. I can feel it."

My eyebrows climbed towards my hairline. As far as I could tell, there were no definitive ways to sense the element outside of whatever testing the Guides performed prior to the ceremony. Even the particulars of that remained a mystery to everyone.

"I'm pretty sure I'll have fire magic," Ryana said, interrupting my thoughts and mirroring what she had already told me.

Grethe grinned, his smile almost lopsided. "Air."

All eyes turned to me, and I wasn't sure how to respond. I'd be honored to be Flumen, but a part of me wanted to share the ability to wield fire with my mother as if that was another piece of her that I could cling to. My shoulders bounced on a shrug. "My parents are Flumen and Ignus, so I think it's a toss-up."

Nielsen regarded me with skepticism as if it were preposterous that I didn't have an inclination either way. "So, are you here for the games or the education?"

Those who wanted to be inducted into the Elemental Queen's Guard knew that the three challenges that made up the Ice Games were the surest way to be noticed by the Guides who hand-picked the newest recruits to the guard. However, the majority of the student body was likely only here for the prestige of attending the notable academy and nothing more.

My eyes sliced across the group, wondering if these people would be my competition now.

Nielsen might have been speaking to me when he posed the question, but Ingrid replied first, sighing out some undetermined emotion. "My fathers believe that Biltons Academy is the best education the continent offers. I was going to be sent here regardless of the rumors."

My focus narrowed in on that word. "What rumors?"

Nielsen scoffed as if my question was some yearlong subject studied within our basic education that I had just ignored for the hell of it. "The Queen is to name an heir," he remarked. "It's the reason that they had a record number of applications this year. The Ice Games are going to be a bloodbath."

It felt like the earth beneath my feet had been swiped away by a Saxum wielder as my stomach twisted. The Games were supposed to be fun. Lighthearted, almost. Not dangerous.

Why would she choose to pick an heir now? The Elemental Queen had never been married or entertained suitors. She had no children of her own and no remaining family, but the topic of an heir had never been discussed before.

Not once in her two hundred and thirty-two years of being a monarch had her line of succession, or lack thereof, been questioned. Interestingly, her exact age was not recorded anywhere that I knew of, but the fact that she had lived well beyond the average life expectancy of most residents of Demetros made many people assume she was immortal. She and her Guides, whom she had gifted with the same extended lifespan, were the only people who could survive much past the age of one hundred, but given that there seemed to be no end in sight for her reign, the somewhat sudden rumored proclamation of her choosing an heir had me questioning that.

Was she sick? Dying?

And, more importantly, how was this going to impact my chances of fulfilling my part of the bargain?

My pulse was nearly frantic as I opened my mouth to speak, knowing fear laced my every word. "What does that have to do with the Ice Games?"

Nielsen pinned me with another disbelieving look. "They are determining the heir based on the Ice Games, the same way that they choose Select Guard candidates."

My neck swiveled so that I was facing Ryana, hoping that out of all of them, she was just as clueless as I had been about the announcement. How was this the first time I had heard something so pivotal?

Her eyes held uncertainty, maybe a pinch of pity. "The situation surrounding the selection of an heir was the main reason I was sent here. I have no intention of joining the Select Guard."

"Me too," Grethe added, pulling his curly hair into a tie behind his nape. His face scrunched. "Or me either?"

A panic rose within me, twisting my stomach in knots that I wasn't sure I'd ever be able to untie. "How do you know this? I haven't heard these rumors at all."

Nielsen's returned gaze was saturated with condescension. "It's all anyone in the capital has been talking about for months."

The insinuation was there. He could probably look at me and decipher that I was from a small town on the outskirts of the kingdom. Whatever valuable information came to us trickled slowly through trade or travelers.

We had a market whose traffic ebbed and flowed with the seasons, but was predominantly visited by those residing in other equally small neighboring towns. News sometimes took months to be dispersed to us unless it was by official royal proclamation. There had been no such announcement.

Ryana laid a hand on my shoulder. "Are you okay?"

No, I thought. The word echoed within my mind, longing to be set free from the cage of my lips. I had put my freedom on the line to become a member of the Select Guard. It was a risk I had thought to be low because it was something I had been preparing for my whole life. Real danger as a part of my trials in the Ice Games had not been a consideration, but Nielsen was certainly making it sound like the challenges might turn deadly now.

Signing that document had largely been a testament to how well-prepared I had assumed I was. Now—if the rumors were true—I wasn't just going to be competing against the small fraction of people who wanted to be inducted into the Select Guard, I'd be up against anyone who wanted an opportunity to be a monarch.

My throat was dry, and my voice cracked as I spoke. "I've wanted to be in the Select Guard my entire life." There was no decent way to articulate how deep my fears went and the stakes that no one here was allowed to know about. "I didn't realize that the competition would be so fierce."

"If you've prepared, I don't see the problem," Nielsen commented. Of course, he couldn't understand. He didn't know me, and he had no idea of what would happen if I failed.

Ryana's palm rubbed against my upper arm, squeezing when it

reached my shoulder again in a gesture that was too intimate between practical strangers but somehow welcomed all the same. She locked her gaze with mine, the honey stripes that slashed her irises flashing with her concern. "You'll be fine. Most people will not take this seriously. It will be no different from the previous years."

I felt a wave of embarrassment wash over me. These people were circled around me, watching me absolutely lose it over something that should not be of this much consequence. My throat bobbed on a swallow that did little to banish the prickly feeling at the base of my neck.

"Of course." I straightened my spine, forcing my lips into a smile. "I was just surprised." This was not how I expected to learn that my goal had just gotten much harder to achieve.

Ten

A shrill whistle echoed across the stone structures that surrounded us, snapping my attention to the girl holding the clipboard from earlier. "Hello House One!" Her voice boomed over the crowd as her eyes scanned over our group, landing on no one in particular.

With our stares firmly in place, her voice lowered to a normal volume. "If you are not assigned to house one, leave. Everyone else, follow me."

She didn't even wait a fraction of a second before she plucked the yellow flag from the ground, lifting it above her head, apparently as a gesture to follow the leader.

Scrambling to my feet, I located my cart with haste so I wouldn't get lost in the chaos in the courtyard as all four clusters of houses moved at the same time. With my proximity to the woman leading us, I was able to catch a glimpse of the tattoo-like brand on her forearm. Two water droplets inside of an upside-down triangle. Hers matched the design on my father's arm, meaning she belonged to the Flumen class as well.

The crest for Biltons Academy boasted all four elemental symbols, including illustrations for the Operarius and the Queen herself. Each of them rested in a way so that when all six shapes were pushed together, it formed a larger, piecemealed diamond.

The Ignus brand was an upright triangle with a flame inside, and directly below that sat the Flumen symbol; the one on clipboard girl's forearm.

In a mirror to this setup, the diamond to the right was halved in much the same way. The top held a feather that represented Caelum class, and the bottom boasted a glittering red gemstone for the Saxum wielders.

The diamonds at the peak and valley of the crest were unbroken, with the upper portion filled with the three-pointed crown that was worn by the Elemental Queen and represented the monarchy. In the bottom sat the golden rose. The flower, and its position on the crest, was said to embody those of the Operarius class as the foundation of the community.

The symbols were typically nestled on a shield, surrounded by a ring of golden leaves as an ode to the flag of Demetros, which usually showed the flourish around the golden flower. Even the academy crest and its depiction of all five possible classes was another reminder that we were all a part of the bigger picture, serving the greater good of the kingdom.

Although various depictions of the crest existed, some more creative than others, all of them had the same slogan, the one that also belonged to the kingdom itself: *Ad Maius Bonum,* which translated into *for the greater good*, a mantra that was drilled into us from an early age. Everything we did, everything that we should be striving to do, was to support the betterment of our kingdom.

My focus returned to the woman marching ahead, her blue ponytail swishing with the same sways as the yellow flag she held in the air. She led us through the enormous double doors of the largest building before us. "This is Biltons Hall. It is home to your library, classrooms, and the dining area." She vaguely pointed to her right. "It connects through a small hallway to the dormitories and faculty apartments." Her pace didn't even slow as she yelled the facts over her shoulder.

As I crossed the entryway, my eye caught on the stained-glass panels that stretched the full height of the towering doors, boasting four distinct scenes. The one closest to my periphery seemed to show two young girls, both with pointed ears: one white-haired and one with fiery red strands, standing side by side and holding hands as they stared up into a star-studded skyline.

Maybe the girls were an ode to the fairytale that explained the origins of all magic—powers extending from Fae ancestors long ago—but my gaze didn't linger on their pointed ears for long. Rather, it was drawn to the same starburst shapes they stared at. The unusual material, winking in the backdrop of a cornflower blue sky, reminded me of the way the Ice Trophy, the prize for winning Biltons' famous Ice Games, had been described. If rumors were to be believed.

Just like that, my thoughts were back on the challenges that would define my future in the Select Guard. Excelling in those trials acted as a minimum for induction into the prestigious group.

My stomach tied itself in knots as I tore my gaze off the image of the two girls and lengthened my strides to catch back up with the rest of the group. It took all my energy to attempt to listen to the short descriptions of the corridors and rooms we passed over the squeak of the wheels of fifty or more carts. Eventually, I gave up in favor of just ingesting the visuals around me.

We wound through stone corridors, and every sight reminded me how far from my quaint cottage I had come. Before long, stone floors had given way to oak planks, covered in part by ornate rugs depicting scenes from a forest. Grey wolves chased reindeer in the intricate patterns, and I even caught sight of a bear or two before my attention was pulled to the tapestries on the wall where men on horseback hunted fluffy white foxes alongside a pack of dogs.

Marble busts stood atop thick wooden pillars with no indication of who they honored. Any single item in this hallway could have fed my entire town for a week or more. The feeling of just how little I belonged here washed over me all at once, and I smoothed down the edges of my tunic with my free hand to wipe the sweat from my palm.

The disparity in wealth had been expected, I just hadn't anticipated how truly out of place it would make me feel once I was here. My only focus had been getting into the Select Guard and securing payment for my tuition. Considerations had not been made for anything else.

Abruptly, clipboard girl halted at a set of double doors, which were painted a fresh white that was almost too bright and clinical for the textured grandeur around us. With a jerking movement, I barely stopped my cart before it slammed into the back of Ryana, then urgently snapped my attention to the woman who had been leading us just in time to hear her next round of instructions. "This is the most important room in the entire campus!" Again, her gaze swept the growing crowd as the people in the back of our snaking line finally caught up.

There was no further instruction as to what the room was, but it became entirely unnecessary as she pushed forward, palms braced against the doors, which gave way to reveal the answer. The comforting smell of paper and leather that had become one of my favorite scents wafted gently to my nose, welcoming me in as the entirety of what could only be a library came into view.

In all my days, I had never seen—and certainly could have never conjured up—anything like the image before me. Of course, I had heard the rumblings that the academy archive at Biltons was the largest in Demetros. But until I was standing in its center, seeing its majesty for myself, I hadn't truly believed it.

"It's bigger than I thought it would be," Ryana whispered from my side, and it made me feel a smidge better that even her expression contained wonder.

My eyes struggled with where to land first as I responded with a breathy "Yeah."

Grand marble flooring, orchestrated in a diamond pattern, covered the floor. Evenly spaced sumptuous, fern-colored rugs were spread out in the middle of the room with long, sturdy oak tables on top of each one. I counted twelve leather-covered chairs at the first table. Assuming the others followed suit, there had to be over a hundred seats in this part of the room alone.

The library was at least three stories high, and my neck strained backwards to take in the cornflower blue coffered ceilings and ornate crown molding at its edges. From the bottom of the embellished border to the marble floors were rows and rows of books, their multicolored spines filling every available space on the shelves.

"I didn't realize this many books even existed in Demetros," I offered offhandedly to Ryana. With so much of the kingdom's written history destroyed in the battle that had raged across the continent over two hundred years ago, I couldn't fathom how so many tomes remained. What had the collection been like before if this was what survived?

Ryana declined to respond, and I hardly noticed as I continued to take in the majesty of the room and the sheer enormity of the collection before me.

In two equally spaced segments along the towering shelves, narrow walkways with dark wooden handrails snaked the perimeter of each level. An almost monstrous white marble fireplace loomed like a god in the middle of the soaring shelves, surrounded by a collection of tufted sofas. Halfway to the fireplace, on either side of the room, two spiraling staircases reached for the upper floors, trimmed in matching ebony wood just like the walkways and handrails that wound around the room like a vine climbing a great oak.

Clipboard girl's fingers snapped in the air, and I jerked my head towards her again, clearly having missed something important while I gawked. "My name is Katarina Evans, and I will be your house leader for the year."

She waited a beat while silence settled across us.

"In case you couldn't tell," she said, sweeping her hand behind her in a grand gesture. "This is the library."

Her hand came to rest on the clipboard again as her gaze danced along our faces. "I know once you've made it to foundational training, you might think you won't need a library because this segment of your education is more physically inclined than your previous learning situations. But you would be wrong."

Katarina pointed a finger toward the very top of the book-filled shelves to her left to emphasize her point. "In these walls, you will find books on natural remedies for wounds incurred on the battlefield. You might discover texts on plant species that are edible."

She raised a golden brow. "You could also be interested in various illustrated guides to hunting and preparing wild game for consumption. Never underestimate the value of the written word, especially not in my house." Her eyelids narrowed to slits as her gaze raked over each and every person in the room. "Not when we plan to win the Ice Trophy this year."

Murmurs littered the quiet of the room, rippling across the crowd like a stone being thrown into a still lake.

"As is tradition," Katarina stated, raising her voice to dominate the conversation over the sound of the mumbling. "We won't be calling ourselves house one forever. You have until dinner tonight to come up with a house name to present to the academy."

The act itself was no surprise, as many alumni still regularly identified with the animal chosen to be their team's mascot even long after their graduation from the program. Still, I frowned at the mention of it. There was something so ridiculous about picking our house name in the wake of why I was even here.

A scoff attempted to slide its way out of my throat, but I held it back, knowing that I was alone in my feelings. Forcing neutrality back to my stare, I returned my attention to Katarina once more.

There was no excitement on her face as she watched our reactions, no hint that this was in any way amusing to her either. "I will show you to the dormitories, and after that, I expect you to meet amongst yourselves and agree on the house's name. This is your first task."

She wheeled around to me, her hazel-green eyes pinning me to the spot before contracting to slits. "Congratulations," she deadpanned, pointing directly at me. "You are the house captain. Find me at dinner."

My eyes widened, but I mustered just enough wherewithal to nod lamely before she turned on her heels and embarked on her quest to show us to our rooms. There were no further instructions, just a waving yellow flag and a swishing blue ponytail.

Eleven

The room I landed on, designated as "Suite C" by the plaque outside the door, was nothing special, but it was empty when I found it. There were only two windows on one wall and bunks and armoires made from the same yellow oak spaced evenly across several sprawling rugs. Each bed was wide enough for a pillow, topped with a standard issue navy covering. The very edges of crisp white sheets peeked out from beneath every mattress. It was so impersonal.

Ryana gestured to the stack of beds in the far corner of the room. "You want to be my top bunkmate?"

The suggestion filled me with a kind of immense relief that seemed out of place, given the longevity of our acquaintance. Maybe I was simply grateful that my earlier panic hadn't deterred her from wanting to talk to me.

Attempting not to show all my teeth, I offered her what I hoped was a normal smile. "I'd love that."

Immediately, I got to work dragging my trunk across the room to the bed she had claimed. When my hand reached out for the parchment and ink that I had brought, I stalled, filled with the sudden urge to contact my dad and tell him everything. Beg him to help me out of this mess. With the news of heir selection, my odds were diminishing before my eyes.

Except, I couldn't do that.

My palms were clammy as I set the items neatly in the drawer of the nearest dresser.

"Are you sure that you're okay?" When I turned to face her, Ryana was watching me with concern. "You seem…" Her lips pursed in an expression that relayed her careful consideration of her word choice as she mulled options over in her mind. Finally, those amber eyes slid back up to meet mine. "It feels like there is more than first-day jitters."

You mean like how I lost my shit over the mention of the Queen choosing an heir? I thought to myself. Instead, I voiced, "I don't have a backup plan. If I don't make the Select Guard, I don't know what I will do."

Sympathy that I took as a kindness washed over her features. She opened her mouth to speak just as a shrill shriek split the surrounding air. My head snapped to the doorway, where I found Jemma, eyes wide and mouth agape with excitement as if this was our first reunion after years of separation.

Beside her, the light-haired woman from before grimaced, drawing my attention to her face. She was even more lovely than I had noticed the first time around. Her skin was sun-kissed, appearing to almost shimmer, even in the dimly lit room. Waves of fluffy blonde curls cascaded down her back. Warm brown eyes, the color of honey, caught my gaze just before they narrowed in my direction.

Jemma pushed past her new friend to barrel into my body, arms wrapping firmly around my neck. "I was hoping I'd find you before your room filled up."

She released me from her hold long enough to nod towards the girl in the doorway, still assessing me with squinted apprehension. "This is Connally Owens. Her parents are both Ignus, and she's in my house and now your third roommate."

With a resigned expression, the blonde, Connally, crossed the room, leaving the trunk behind her as if it was of no consequence to abandon it altogether. Her dusty blue dress, while plain in design, hugged her curves in an expensively tailored fabric, almost as if the garment had been hand-made specifically for her.

A delicate chain fell from her shoulders, the charm dipping below the edge of her collar, hiding all but the tips of a pair of matching silvery wings. It drew my attention enough to make me wonder if it was an angel or something else equally divine that she wore beneath that fabric. I hadn't meant to stare for so long, but there was something alluring about her, in almost the same way that I found myself drawn to Cade, but without the attraction.

She cleared her throat, raising a single pale brow. "And your name is?" Her words were not harsh, but not altogether warm, snapping me from my trance at her beauty.

Clasping her waiting hand, I hurried to reply. "I'm Ashton. It's nice to meet you."

A sugary smile that appeared genuine stretched across Connally's face. "It's a pleasure to meet you too. I've already heard so much about you."

Her eyes took on a mesmerizing quality as they crinkled through her grin.

"We are taking the bunk next to Ash," Jemma called, already throwing her bag to the top bunk before sighing heavily, as if burdened by some monumental tasks. Her eyes flickered to the open doorway behind us. "Some of the staff offered to bring the rest of my bags up. I was hoping they would be here already."

Recalling the look of the cart holding Jemma's things, already nearing toppling before it was in motion, I snickered. Leave it to her to have already enamored a member of the staff to tote her explicitly over-packed bags to her room rather than force her to send them home as we were directed.

Jemma wheeled back to me, excitement already blossoming across her features. "You will never guess who our house leader is!" She gave me no time before she answered her own evidently rhetorical question. Her lips curled up, that hint of mischief glittering in her rounded eyes. "Cade!"

Disappointment that wasn't entirely acceptable settled in my stomach. House Leaders were appointed from the previous year's top-performing students. Those invited back to the esteemed positions considered it an immense honor. They were assigned as instructors on topics of their own choosing and, therefore, considered to be staff. Some even stayed on full-time once the semester of training was over to aid with elemental education, making them an official part of the faculty.

The infatuation I had felt for Cade would have to be snuffed out because his position meant that he was strictly off limits.

That didn't seem to deter Jemma, though, and she continued to ramble. "He's also Ignus, which makes sense, right? He's so hot." She fanned herself as if she were feeling the effects of his flames right now. Of course, she hadn't seen them. Elemental magic was prohibited by staff until the second half of our year commenced.

Even if the horrible joke brought about a groan, I found myself smiling through the letdown. It wasn't as if I had the time to focus on boys while I was here. Not when I needed to keep the entirety of my attention on making it to the Select Guard. Plus, I had made an absolute fool of myself during our introduction. I was certain that a budding romance between us wasn't even an option.

"Fuck," Jemma called out, making me nearly dizzy with her series of outbursts. "We have to go meet with our house on the practice fields to come up with a name."

She looped her arm around Connally's, dragging both of them towards me so that she could plant a quick peck against the side of my cheek before swirling out of the room nearly as quickly as she had entered.

"She's..." Ryana paused as she considered her next words carefully. "Interesting?"

I sniffed a laugh. My best friend was interesting. She was outgoing, brave, daring, talkative, and all things happy and sunny in the world. For me, she pushed me out of my shell and brought me joy on the darkest of days. Just like with our interlocking necklaces, she was the sunshine to my moon. That didn't mean I couldn't understand how her bold personality might take some getting used to.

My shoulders rose and fell in quick succession. "Jemma is a lot, but if you give it some time, I promise you will love her. She's just got loads of energy. Like a wild squirrel or a very lively, untrained puppy."

Something crossed Ryana's face so briefly I almost missed it, vanishing like smoke on a breeze before I could fully pinpoint it. Her features abruptly softened into a light smile. "Of course, I'm just not used to it. That's all. We have birds at home."

A grin split my face as I turned my attention back to unpacking my things, my fingertips trailing over that parchment, my heart longing for some better option than this.

With a heavy sigh of resignation, I pulled the last of my items from my trunk, placing my books atop the paper for now. There was no use in leaving when I was warned that the bargain that I had struck would follow me wherever I ran. Even though I didn't understand its logistics, I wasn't going to risk an unfavorable outcome by breaking the deal.

Even if I could, pulling out of the bargain now would be the final nail in the coffin of my dreams, and if I buried my chances of joining the Select Guard and gaining access to the healers that trained them, I'd be burying my father soon too.

"Are you ready?" Ryana's cheerful voice sounded beside me.

Mentally, I placed my troubles into the drawer next to the parchment and books, shutting it firmly and agreeing to reassess it at a later date. Pushing what I hoped was excitement into my tone, I replied. "Yeah."

Ryana lifted her fist in a mockery of a cheer. "Then let's go name our house!"

A few hours later, I entered the dining hall beside Ryana. The room was massive, and I found it difficult to keep my attention pinned to any singular location. It was larger than the library, the ceilings nearly as tall, which made sense because it was the one place where the entire student body could fit.

That rationale was the precise reason that we had already been informed that any important announcement would be given here, rather than distributed across our various classrooms. The only other place large enough to accommodate that many people were the expansive practice fields that spanned most of the acreage dedicated to the academy.

My gaze trailed over the bodies already gathered within the dining hall, estimating nearly three hundred so far. Instead of focusing on any of the people around me, I let my eyes scan the décor instead. It wasn't nearly as regally decorated as I had expected, especially considering the opulence of the rest of the wing.

The floors were a modest stone, roughly cut and patched together with a sand-hued mortar. There was an obvious lack of rugs, causing the sounds of the gathering of people to ricochet across the rock-lined walls.

The only item that served to dampen the noise in this space was the floor to ceiling curtains that framed the multi-storied windows towards the back of the room. My attention snagged on who I believed to be the instructors, framed by the panes, sitting neatly on a raised platform at a considerably sized sturdy wooden table running perpendicular to the cluster of furniture assigned to the students.

They were called instructors, or educators, but not considered professors because the latter implied a certain passive education. The lessons taught here were physical in nature, requiring active participation in many cases. What we absorbed would be tested in a very real manner during the challenges of the Ice Games.

Katarina's stern face immediately came into my line of sight. She was occupying a seat at the table with the other House Leaders, wearing a scowl that twisted her features and a glare aimed right at me. With an outstretched hand, she beckoned for me to join her.

"Good luck with that," Ryana offered as I bid her farewell, bobbing and weaving through the crowd to meet Katarina's unspoken demand. I came to a stop just in front of the instructors at the same time as Jemma. My green-eyed friend only wiggled her eyebrows up and down, dragging her lip between her teeth as she jerked her head towards the leader directly in front of her chair.

When I followed the direction of her gesturing, I found Cade. For some unknown and certainly unspeakable reason, the butterflies in my stomach became aloft again.

He was lost in conversation with the house leader to his left. She had ebony skin and even darker hair, cropped short to her head. Thick gold hoops, about two inches in diameter, fell from her delicate ears. A forest green, narrow-strapped top showed off toned arms. She was petite, but with all the muscles of an elite soldier. She met Cade's stare with a warm smile as she spoke, her brown eyes alight with kindness.

It was official; everyone here was stunning.

"Sit in front of me," Katarina commanded. My attention dutifully returned to her as she gestured to the seat across from hers. My assumption was that the leaders were assigned spots in numerical order, based solely on the fact that Katarina was first, and Cade—with Jemma seated in front of him—was third.

Between them, a mountain of a man diligently focused on cleaning the remaining meat from a smoked chicken carcass with his teeth. His broad chest completely covered the back of the chair he was sitting in, and his shoulders were far outspanning the confines of his allotted area, spreading into Katarina and Cade's spaces as well, although neither seemed to mind.

Dark, bushy eyebrows arched upward as if he were consistently expressing his intent for mischief. His hair fell in loose curls to his chest, the dark brown locks turning slightly golden towards the ends as if they had been slowly bleached by the sun.

He had a thick beard framing full lips and probably hiding a strong jawline to match the masculinity of his nose. His green eyes—dark like the shades of a dense forest or seaweed that grew along the ocean floor—remained locked on the meal in front of him as he nipped away at the scraps of meat that clung to the bone.

Maybe it was wealth that bred such beauty amongst the students at Biltons Academy.

A throat cleared in front of me, dragging my attention back to Katarina's icy scowl. "Any time now," she said, glancing pointedly at the still-empty chair in front of her.

Scrambling a bit more than necessary, I dropped into the seat, muttering a quick "Sorry."

In the space beside me, a gangly girl with mousy brown hair had already taken her place in front of her House Leader. On the other side of her, Jemma sat with her attention firmly on Cade, and in the last seat, a guy about my height, with sandy brown hair piled atop his head in a bun, filled the final space. *Had they all been chosen in a similar manner to me?* It felt like there had been zero contemplation on Katarina's part before she had singled me out.

A booming voice stole my attention yet again. Behind the House Leaders at the instructor table, a man with thick charcoal gray hair cropped to just above his shoulders stood to address the hall full of people. "My name is Headmaster Trenton Dracorris. Welcome to Biltons Academy!"

A prominent white streak made its way from the roots just above his left eye all the way to the tips of his gray strands, probably an effect of a birthmark. His cheekbones and chin were sharp, and even his lips were a thin slash across his face. But he didn't appear to be intimidating, despite the severity of his features, as something gentle rested in his gaze.

"You will have plenty of time to get to know your instructors when courses begin tomorrow, so for now, they will simply introduce themselves." He pointed towards the table of house leaders. "Afterwards, our honored returning students will give brief introductions and reveal the names you have chosen for your houses."

Every year, students chose names of ferocious beasts from fairytales. Mythological animals were permitted and therefore the dragon was so frequently chosen that we could only use that creature if we narrowed it down to a particular subspecies.

The school recognized only the breeds of dragons within the *Unofficial Handbook for Magical Creatures*—a collection of fables and stories that were common in Demetros—in order to maintain some semblance of consistency amongst the more fantastical choices.

Even then, it was not uncommon for houses to be sent back to their huddles to choose another name when the same dragon species was chosen by more than one set of students. It had been unanimous amongst our house that we wouldn't even consider dragons or any of the other beasts in the *Unofficial Handbook* in our quest.

In the pause that followed Headmaster Dracorris' introduction, I hastily whispered my group's choice across the table to Katarina. When the task was complete, I leaned back against my chair, pushing my food around as I half-heartedly listened to bits and pieces of the prattling of the introductions. Not everyone perched at the enormous table was an educator. Some were general staff that supported the academy in other ways.

There was a groundskeeper, whose name I did not catch, an instructor named Mr. Higgins, who claimed to be prepared to teach us about plants even though he looked more fit to work at a front desk than anywhere near the outdoors. A librarian introduced herself as Bella, a name that I only retained because I recognized it from the name-plate at her quaint desk from our house's brief stay in the library earlier that evening.

The words droned on until Katarina's chair scraped against the stone floor as she stood, the sound causing me to flinch back into the present with more intent.

Her fingertips rested along the edge of the table as if she were grounding herself to something solid. "My name is Katarina Evans, and for those who do not know me already, I am the leader of House One, who will now be called House Lynx. I belong to the Flumen class, and I will educate you on survival techniques." She sat just as abruptly as she had stood.

Mountain man didn't stand to introduce himself, but he did drop his second chicken carcass to his plate with a great clattering. "I'm Dante Wolfe, also Flumen, and I will teach you everything you need to know about weapons." There was something mischievous in his stare as if the information had been the starting line of a joke, but he proceeded without delivering a punchline. "House two is now House Irontail."

A dragon breed. How unique.

At the completion of his sentence, I let my eyes slide over to Cade, who chose to stand. "My name is Caden. I am part of the Ignus class, and I will be the instructor for one of the hand-to-hand combat sections. We are House Wyvern."

Another mythical creature, although slightly less common.

Cade shared a look with Dante, and I forced my attention to the last woman as she pushed away from the table to bring herself fully upright. "My name is Tamari Cole, and I have Saxum powers. I will instruct you in horseback riding lessons, and I can't wait to meet you all." Her features grew pensive as she drew in a deep breath. With absolutely no emotion, she continued. "We are House Platypus." She sat abruptly, clearly trying to divert attention from her house's chosen name, a feat which didn't work.

"I think you mean platy-pussies," the boy with the bun in front of her said, loud enough to garner several sniggers from tables close enough to hear him. She dutifully ignored his immature outburst; the only evidence she was bothered was the tic in her jaw.

The headmaster cleared his throat, and I couldn't determine if it was annoyance or amusement that dwelled within his stoic stare. "Now that introductions are out of the way, we will bring out the dessert! Enjoy yourselves and get some rest. Your foundational training starts on Monday." With that, headmaster Dracorris sat back down with the rest of the educators and resumed his conversations with his staff.

Sparing a glance at Katarina, I tried to glean if we would be dismissed. Whatever ire the house leader had felt for me had been transferred to her empty plate as she scraped her fork against the barren dish and dutifully ignored me.

Turning to the girl next to me, I struck up a conversation with her to pass the time and drown out the sound of Katarina's fidgeting. It wasn't until we all stood and Jemma linked her arms with mine, dragging me back to our dorms, that I realized I hadn't even gotten the girl's name.

Twelve

Monday began with a warm body pressed against mine and a pair of celery green eyes staring down at me. Jemma had climbed up on my bunk and was currently straddling my waist, her hands planted on either side of my head.

"Good morning, sleepyhead," she cooed, bringing her face down to rub our noses together.

Groaning, I shoved her away, trying and failing to roll over as her hips locked me in place. Her brow scrunched in mock irritation. "Seriously, Ash, it's time to go. Breakfast is almost over, and it's the first day of classes!"

A growl escaped my throat, but with the threat of missing a meal or being late for my first day, I quickly roused myself. When Jemma extracted herself from me, I forced my feet down the ladder of my bunk and hastily pulled the academy-issued clothing from my armoire. Navy skirts that matched the drab blue bedding and a crisp white button-up with the embroidered academy crest stitched into the left breast.

Tossing the more casual attire that we were told would be required for the physical education courses into my leather bag, I eyed my mother's ring, ultimately choosing to leave it within its box safely in the drawer.

Fingers dragged through my tangled hair, weaving it into a braid as we raced to the dining hall. With our plates of food secured, we grabbed seats next to Connally and Ryana. Surprisingly, conversation between the four of us was natural, and before I knew it—and partially due to my tardiness—our time for breakfast had ended, and we separated with hurried goodbyes, scurrying off in separate directions. According to my timetable, none of them shared my first class with me.

At the academy, our days were broken into four sessions with a lunch break in the middle. Our curriculum was identical, but we were intermingled with the other houses during the morning sessions.

The first two blocks were dedicated to a general physical activity, which meant to put us in peak fighting health, as well as generic classes that didn't fit the criteria of military strategy. Courses included running, mind and body, strength training, rock climbing, horseback riding, and various other activities that kept us well-rounded.

After lunch, we rejoined our house to attend sessions dedicated to war education, such as battle studies, weapons, and a combination of botany and survival. On Fridays, we all got reshuffled again for hand-to-hand combat, which spanned the majority of the day. We got the weekends to rest and study, and then it started all over again.

Unfortunately for me, my day wasn't going to start with one of the simple sessions that would allow me to ease into the education. Before me was a man, short in stature but practically bursting at the seams with determination. Not a good sign, considering this class had been referred to as "conditional running" on the parchment that held my agenda.

He assessed us beneath his bushy brows, allowing his gaze to sweep over us once before addressing the group. "As you should already know, I am Mr. Grupert. I like to use this first day as an initial test of sorts. I can't possibly have an indication of how far you have come if I don't know where you've started."

The words were simple but foreboding.

He pointed to the field behind us. "With that being said, I want you to run around the perimeter until you can't or until the bells ring. Come find me when either of those things happen so I can mark the number of laps you complete in your assessment."

A few groans sounded from around me, one coming from Grethe

who I immediately recognized from my house, but this did nothing to deter our instructor. The man placed his pointer and thumb into his mouth and released a shrill noise that seemed to initiate the start of our session long race.

I started slowly, falling into pace next to Grethe, pleasantly surprised to find Ingrid on my other side. Some students opted to take off with a jolt, deciding initial speed was more important than longevity, but the three of us kept a steady rhythm, enough so that we could carry on a conversation.

"I've heard he's the worst instructor for this," Ingrid whined from my right.

Grethe shrugged through his jog. "At least he's allowing us to set our own pace. I'm good with this."

Grethe's words were clearly a jinx because the very second that he uttered them, Mr. Grupert released another high-pitched whistle and then screamed at us to pick up the pace. After that, all conversation died down.

Time passed in agonizing waves until the sound of the tolling bells released us from our torture. My clothes dripped with sweat, and I didn't need to take in a deep whiff to know I reeked.

Glancing down at the academy-issued athletic clothing, I was instantly grateful that the loaned navy pants and plain grey cotton top with the Biltons crest along the left breast could be returned to the facility to be washed. There was no time in my packed schedule, nor coin for frequent laundering, if this was going to become the norm.

Ingrid was panting on her hands and knees in the dirt, Grethe standing over her, as I waved a polite goodbye to the duo, making my way to one of the drinking fountains on the edge of the practice field. Being a little preoccupied with simply breathing, I absentmindedly bumped into a thick wall of muscle on my way. The scent of salt, cedarwood, and honeysuckles hit me before my brain could fully register who it was.

My eyes drifted up to his face, confirming his identity at the same time he grunted his surprise.

"I'm so sorry this keeps happening," I muttered, reaching out to Cade's arm in an attempt to stabilize him.

His face scrunched, and I watched in embarrassed horror as he tried and failed to recognize me. I probably should have been glad that he didn't remember our earlier altercation, but now it was too awkward not to remind him.

Retracting my hand from his skin, I smoothed it against my pants to have anything to do with it other than hold him in place. "I'm Ashton. We met when my friend Jemma ran into you on move-in day."

His expression shifted again, but I wasn't confident that it had clicked for him yet. "Oh, yeah. Hey." He offered me a tiny wave. "How are classes going?"

Again, I should have simply walked away. Let him remember me as the forgettable girl who claimed to know him, but something had me responding against my better judgment. "I have Grupert for running conditioning and I'm really proud of myself for not puking."

Cade's eyes roamed my soggy attire, but his grin deepened. "I had him last year, and I was pissed to learn that the other instructors don't make you run around so much."

Scoffing, I let my eyes roll dramatically. "If I hadn't had a regimen at home, I wouldn't have survived."

With my focus stuck on the House Wyvern leader, I noticed when his head cocked almost imperceptively to the side, eyes surveying me again. "You trained before you came here?"

My chin lifted incrementally higher. "Yes, I plan to be part of the Select Guard when all this is over." This time, the words didn't carry with them the heaviness of all I was risking to be here.

Dashes formed between his eyebrows as he considered it. "That's not a typical choice for most people here. Especially this year. What drew you to that decision?"

Suddenly, I was all too aware of the trail of sweat that ran down my spine, and I crossed my arms over my chest to block out large splotches of dampness on my shirt. "My mother was in the guard, and I wanted to honor her."

There was something contemplative in his gaze then. "She must be a powerful wielder to be inducted into the guard."

It wasn't exactly a question, but I answered him all the same. "She was." For the first time in a long while, thinking about her didn't make me want to cry. I felt proud to call her mine. "She was Ignus, too. Some of the lunatics in my town thought she was powerful enough to be a witch or Fae."

He frowned as if finally catching my use of her in the past tense. "Was?" His voice was soft and gentle.

Keeping our eye contact, I nodded subtly. "She died when I was born."

The frown didn't shift much, but the crease that had formed between his brows loosened. "I'm sorry to hear that."

Wishing that I had steered the conversation anywhere else, I simply shook my head. "It's okay. My dad and I made do, and I'm here so..."

Bells began chiming in the distance, warning me that the second session was starting, and I was on the other side of campus from that room. My eyes widened in alarm as I looked to Cade to bid him a quick farewell. "I'm late, I've got to go!"

As I turned to literally run away, I froze, twisting back to look at him once more. "Any clue where Miss Angela's *mind and body* class is?" I had counted on having plenty of time to find it after my drink of water, and instead, I hadn't had a drop and had stood there talking to a boy who probably wouldn't even remember this conversation.

He pointed towards the closest arched doorway that led into Biltons Hall. "Take a left when you walk in, up the first set of stairs, second door on your right."

"Thank you!" I called over my shoulder, running while my muscles screamed in protest, and the sound of the bells dwindled away.

I wasn't too late when I opened the door to the course. A petite, tawny-skinned woman met me with a wary glare, already crossing her arms.

"I got lost," I muttered, finding the first open mat at the front of the classroom and plopping onto it like everyone else already had.

Her eyes narrowed, but after what seemed to be a forced inhale and a very drawn-out exhale, she simply smiled. "It's the first day, but I do expect promptness in the future."

Heat bled into my cheeks, and I couldn't bring myself to look at anyone else. "Of course. I'm so sorry."

She carried on as if it was truly no bother and before I knew it, I was being forced to bend and contort my body in ways that I never thought possible. We held poses that required the use of steady breathing and concentration to endure.

The instructor, Miss Angela, explained that everything was meant to connect our minds to various points on our bodies. Even though I met her explanations with skepticism, by the end of the session, I realized that my focus had been on my muscles—or the surprisingly difficult job of getting into my positions—rather than the stressors in my life.

There had been few moments I had spent during class beating myself up over my interaction with Cade. Notably, my stomach was absent of the pit of dread it usually summoned whenever my mother's death was mentioned. If anything, it had kind of been nice to be able to talk about her to someone, even if it had only been for a brief moment.

Still, I had to hope that I wouldn't have any more run-ins with the House Wyvern leader after this. Humiliation seemed to hang over me like a dark cloud whenever he was around, and I had no interest in adding to the troubles in my life. I just needed to focus on my studies and make it to Select Guard initiation, and then I could let myself consider the attentions of an attractive male.

Thirteen

It turned out that if I hadn't been so distracted during staff introductions, I would have already known that there were multiple instructors for each subject. Our timetables only gave us the names of courses and locations to muster when there were multiple educators for the course. So, when Ryana and I arrived on the training field at the prescribed time for weapons, I had expected the Irontail House Leader, Dante Wolfe, to be there.

Instead, I was greeted by a middle-aged woman with a stern face.

"I am Helga!" She bellowed to the crowd of nervous students.

She towered over us and likely would have done the same to Dante if he had been in her presence. Her vibrant red hair was pulled into a tight braid that ended in a tidy bun at her nape. As she waited for us to fall into line, her chest—easily twice the width of mine—rose and fell in a calm rhythm under a leather breastplate which seemed like overkill.

Helga pointed towards a stand to her left, showing off biceps that were thicker than my thighs. "Today, we will determine your proficiency with the sword. Grab your blade and wait for further instructions."

Ryana and I wordlessly fell into line behind the others, stepping forward in tiny increments until we each procured a weapon from the stand. Upon further inspection, I discovered that the blades weren't iron at all but rather a dense wood. My palm wrapped around the hilt, and I let my glance fall to our instructor again, flinching when I found her staring at me. A fake cough eased its way from my chest as I slipped behind a cluster of students to avoid her perceived ire.

When everyone had gotten their wooden sword, she began. Her eyes narrowed at a student to my right. "You," she demanded. "Come here."

The person who had been chosen, a woman just about my size in height, eagerly walked to where Helga was standing. Helga said something I couldn't hear to the girl, prompting her to take a stance.

After a brief demonstration, the weapons instructor turned towards the mass of gathering students who had all been drawn closer during the display. "When I give the go-ahead, you may begin your practice swings and blocks. I will assess."

Interestingly, Helga wasn't outwardly aggressive. She seemed stern, but perhaps it was conjecture due to the deep lines etched in her forehead and between her eyebrows which I assumed to be from years of displeasure as she assessed unworthy students for a living. But, as I paired off with Ryana, I could hear Helga encouraging a few of the others into a proper posture for a duel.

"Ready?" Ryana asked, already in her stance.

My chin dipped once as I made sure my feet were positioned properly as I faced her. "I am."

As our practice swords collided, I found the muscles in my shoulders loosening. Granted, I was still using a practice blade, but every move I made—and more importantly, the counter to every move Ryana made—was familiar to my body, thanks to my dad's extra training. Neither of us appeared to be surprised at the other's skill in the subject, which lent itself to a more casual conversation.

Ryana kept her eyes trained on me. "So, how was your day?"

My gaze slipped over my shoulder to catch a glimpse of Helga's location before I deigned to answer. "Good, so far. I had running, which was awful. Then mind and body, which was better."

Our swords came together, the wood splintering from the impact, only just covering up the sound of my growling stomach. "I'm going to have to start packing lunch, though. I decided to shower between sessions two and three, and now I'm starving."

A twinkle of amusement glistened in Ryana's brown eyes. "You must have Mr. Grupert. I've heard about him." She assessed Helga's whereabouts before continuing. "I had horseback riding and strength training today. Tamari is great. You're going to love her."

We picked up the pace a little with a steady thwack of our wooden swords, its rhythmic cadence causing me to drift back into my own thoughts as we continued to spar. My preparedness provided some relief, but looking around, it was evident I'd have to improve to stand out.

After a few more rounds, it became glaringly obvious that at least half of the people here had some sort of weapons training, either because they had also aspired to be members of the Select Guard or because it was something affluent families just did, I wasn't sure.

Based on that alone, I was forced to face the fact that I had severely underestimated my competition. Wrongfully assuming that those who were not set on being inducted into the Select Guard were only here for the prestige of attending the most elite of the academies. The fact that others were so well prepared in all the subjects went against those initial theories.

And honestly, the fact that we were being trained in combat when, by all accounts, Demetros was a peaceful island kingdom had always bothered me.

Sure, those who policed the cities would need specialized training—which they would receive after their stint in the academy if they chose that career—but why did an entire population need swordplay as a skill? Fundamentally, I understood that just because we had never been invaded didn't mean we never could be, but there seemed to be no indication as to why this level of battle education was necessary for the entire kingdom rather than on a voluntary basis.

Jemma often accused me of being too apprehensive. No one else seemed to spend this quantity of time mulling over any of the information that we had been taught during our basic education. In fact, it appeared as though I was the only one who was constantly questioning the foundation of our kingdom's *truths*.

Typically, I was reminded that even if an invasion never occurred, we could use these same skills for other positions throughout the kingdom.

As much as I wanted to find fault in that logic, I couldn't. Although it still nagged at me on occasion. Like right now.

Helga's stern voice jostled me from those harrowing thoughts as she instructed us to switch partners again. My chin dipped in Ryana's direction before I turned to find another match. Almost in a daze, the same routine repeated with each new partner, thwacking the practice swords in whatever cadence my companion set.

At some point, I had been paired with Grethe, and we commiserated about how horrible the first session's running was.

"I had to skip lunch," he admitted with wide green eyes framed under raised platinum blonde eyebrows. "I never skip lunch, Ashton." His tone was jovial and serious at the same time, as if even though the topic was lighthearted, the situation might have disturbed him anyway.

My sword swung out in front of me to block his next advance as a chuckle escaped my lips. "I had to wonder what actually happened to those who stopped, but I was too afraid to even look back to see."

Grethe's brows creased, and his face scrunched in an amusing rendition of Mr. Grupert as his voice deepened to align with the instructor's tenor. "Why did you even come here if this is the best you can do? Go ahead and march yourself home."

A barking laugh tore through me at the accuracy of his depiction, which resulted in another stab of Helga's disapproving stare. Instead of chastising me, she just blew her whistle to inform us we needed to switch off again. With a guilty grin, I bid farewell to Grethe.

Nielsen approached me next, not an ounce of levity apparent in his features. He held his hand out in a practiced motion, as if we were about to duel with steel rather than spar on our first day with these wooden approximations of a weapon.

He was gentlemanly, and while I hadn't been fully taking the lesson seriously, there was a certain graveness to his disposition that had me bracing myself as we backed away to begin.

Nielsen did not go easy on me, nor did he seem to consider this an assessment of abilities. He treated our match like his life depended on it, and for the first time since the session started, I was forced to exert copious amounts of energy to keep up with his movements.

In those moments, I hardly had the wherewithal to consider writing my father a thank-you note for everything he had done to prepare me for this. Because I was holding my own.

"How are you already so good at this?" I asked him between the heavy clashes of our blunt practice blades.

He grunted as he slammed his weapon back into mine with enough force to rattle my teeth. "I've been training for this my entire life. Many members of my family have been Select Guard, an honor that I had wished to accomplish as well."

His answer prompted me to assess him in a different light, considering our previously shared goal. "You don't want to be Select Guard anymore?" My body lunged as I dodged a particularly sharp slash of the wooden blade.

Nielsen's face betrayed no hint of skepticism as he replied. "My family seems to think I have an excellent shot at being named heir. I come from a prestigious bloodline that has always served Her Majesty." Arrogant but not rude.

From all my years of traveling the kingdom, I had never met anyone who truly knew the Queen. My sword shifted in my grip. "What is she like?" The current monarch was such a mystery to me, the question came out before I could stop it.

Nielsen's brows flexed upwards. "They aren't permitted to talk about her outside of the castle walls. Why would you even ask that?" His tone was sharp and incredulous.

Heat flooded my cheeks. Of course, the Elemental Queen's affairs were private. Years of studying the ways of the Select Guard should have kept me from asking such a question because I knew the rules that guided those in her employment.

The flash of embarrassment caused me just enough pause in my defense that Nielsen easily pointed the dull blade to my throat. He gave me a smug smirk before lowering his weapon and bowing, a sign that our match was over and that I had definitively lost. Relief flooded me when Helga immediately called for us to switch again, and I turned from Nielsen with only the mutterings of a goodbye.

For the rest of the session, I was partnered with other members of House Lynx that I didn't recall previously meeting, carrying on the most basic of conversations, my mind still hovering over thoughts of the Elemental Queen.

There wasn't a definable explanation for the range of emotions I felt during this session. Determination to prove myself amongst these people who had also prepared for this very situation. Curiosity about who the Elemental Queen was and what I might uncover in her service. Nerves over how I would stand out amongst my peers. Excitement for the prospect that, based on today alone, I had a real shot.

The sound of Helga's shrill whistle drew my attention to her face like the crack of a whip. "Your forms are all lacking," she exclaimed, raking her eyes over the group with evident discountenance. "Next time, come prepared for more grueling instructions."

Any confidence I had gained during those matches shriveled up and died like the tomato plants of my dad's garden in the winter.

A frown creased my expression as I turned to find Ryana. She was placing her practice blade back on the stand, chatting with Grethe about something that had him smiling crookedly in her direction. A quick observation of the other students showed that none of the rest of them appeared to be deterred by Helga's assessment as I was.

None except Nielsen, who was standing with his arms folded, the muscle beneath his jaw working as he tracked Helga's departure from the field. It was an odd sensation, both pitying the man while recognizing the same hardened resolve lighting up his deep brown eyes.

Because, while it was possible that I had come adequately experienced to make a good impression here, I was not the only one with something to lose if failure was the result. Looking at Nielsen, it was hard not to recognize the desperation seeping from him in waves.

My lip tucked between my teeth as I crossed the field to put my sword away, then joined Grethe and Ryana on our trek back to the academy for battle studies.

Fourteen

"I'm Viggo Wood, and within these walls, you will learn the art of battle." The battle studies instructor in front of us waved his hand about the room, and I expected to find illustrations of such engagements or even maps on the walls that he gestured to. Instead, they were blank and undecorated. Bland grey stone with no adornment.

He stood still for a moment, giving me a chance to take in his appearance. In all honesty, he seemed elderly. To the point that I wondered at what age employees typically retired.

His curved spine forced him into a hunched position, which hadn't deterred him from starting to pace around his podium. A leather tie bound his crisp white hair neatly at his shoulders, and his clean-shaven face did nothing to deter the full view of the lines deeply gouged into his cinnamon-hued skin.

Viggo stalled just right of center, narrowing his eyes at a student in the front row of tables. "Today's topic will be on the Great Conflict." This wasn't completely unexpected considering that the years-long civil war that plagued the kingdom a few centuries ago was Demetros' only evidence of battles.

The instructor hobbled back to his podium, his eyes scanning some prompt on its surface. "In the early years of the Elemental Queen's reign, on year twenty-eight of her rule, a rebellion threatened to overthrow the monarchy. The people complained that only the wealthy could afford the tuition required to attend Biltons Academy and have their magical binds removed. For months, the rebels ransacked Fulgrande, and many lost their lives in defense of the city. Fights broke out across the kingdom between the wealthy and the poor. The entire nation was at war with itself. The death tolls were catastrophic."

Squinted brown eyes slid across the faces seated in his classroom. "Can anyone speak to why they think it was such a deadly war?"

The room was eerily silent, save for the nervous exhales of the student body.

Motion from the corner of my eye drew my attention to Nielsen, hand raised, grooves indenting the space between his dark brows.

The instructor turned to him with a knowing smile as if he halfway anticipated the answer to be incorrect but was looking forward to the segue into his lesson. "Yes?"

Nielsen's hand lowered slowly. "No one was trained in the art of war."

Astonishment filtered across Viggo Wood's features before a smile graced his lips. "And why would that make for a more deadly war?"

Nielsen seemed less assured now that the new question had been posed to him. His eyebrows drew even closer together, nearly forming one singular sweep of hair.

While the Great Conflict was touched on during our basic education, details surrounding it were far and few between, something I never truly understood. It was my father's recount of those times, tales passed down from generation to generation, that gave me the knowledge needed to respond.

Viggo caught my stare as my hand raised slowly into the air. He lifted his brows in a silent acknowledgment to proceed.

"It wasn't battle that killed most of them, it was famine," I replied, cutting my eyes to glance at Nielsen, whose features had hardened.

Viggo smiled, pleased with my response. "Yes. Even those who had access to their elemental gifts had no clue how to defend themselves with it, and none of the population, save for the Select Guard, had been trained in combat."

He sighed on an exhausted exhale, the grin dropping from his face. "Many died, not just because of the physical violence and the wounds that were inflicted, but because the production of food stopped during those dark times."

He limped around his wooden stand at the front of the classroom, no longer needing his notes to continue. "The Elemental Queen used her magic to freeze those attacking the capital without harming them. She and her advisors agreed to meet with the leaders of the rebellion to work out a deal, thus ending the war."

The very same Guides that released our power, had been simply her advisors back then. Now, they were so much more.

The instructor scanned the faces of every single person in attendance. Only when he had made his way around the entire room did he continue. "Because of this, we have two other magical schools, one in the north and one in the south. This gave way to the education and training regimens that every citizen partakes in now."

In Elmhaven, we had been taught that the establishment of Chapel-stone and Wythe academies was a direct outcome of the civil war. When Biltons had been the only academy, as Viggo had already stated, only the wealthy could afford to send their children and have their binds removed. Now, the opportunity was not only available to everyone but required.

His eyes squinted as he gauged our reactions. I wasn't sure what he had been expecting, but the conversation had me thinking about old curiosities.

My hand rose into the air, and he nodded at me to speak again. "If that's the story, why aren't we taught much about it in basic education?" It was possible that it was only Elmhaven's teachings that were inadequate, but the lack of responses from my peers had me thinking otherwise.

Something akin to irritation flashed across Mr. Wood's features as if my question was offensive. He stared down his nose at me, eyes pinching under heavy white brows. "Sensitive material requires a delicate, well-thought-out structure for dissemination."

The answer was too vague, and his simmering anger was not what I had expected in a classroom designed to have us learn of battles. Having only had one civil war on record, I had assumed that majority of the class would center around the Great Conflict.

A voice sounded from my left. "Why train everyone to fight, then? Wouldn't that make everyone more dangerous?"

Viggo Wood visibly flinched before he caught himself and snorted a laugh. "Ah yes, that seems counterintuitive." His pointer finger lifted to the ceiling to illustrate the overexaggerated *ah-ha* moment. "It actually hasn't been the case. Giving people equality has ceased all need for turmoil between those of different social standings." A satisfied grin curled his lips.

To me, the response was wildly unimpressive as it had skirted around a proper answer and hadn't even touched on why training the entire population to be a part of the army had anything to do with the previously unequal access to elemental power.

My face scrunched with confusion. But the instructor moved on quickly before any further questions could be asked of him—questions he clearly did not intend to answer.

He droned on about specifics of the war, including dates and names of battles of consequence, but it all blurred on the fringes of my mind, only allowing me to catch sentences here and there. It didn't matter because it was all a reiteration of our basic education coverage of the topic.

In March of the Year 28 of the Elemental Queen's rule, riots broke out in Fulgrande.

May 6th of the same year signified the shift between protests and the first official battle when a legion from the northern region marched upon the capital, slaughtering most of the unarmed people they met along the way.

"We were never told where the people came from. Can you tell us that now?" A guy a few rows behind me asked.

The town's name had always been stricken from the record to ensure that no ill-will remained between the regions once the war was over.

Viggo only cleared his throat before continuing to skim over the highlights from each year of civil unrest until he made it all the way to the famine that was responsible for the majority of the casualties. All the while, I tried to find any piece of information—hardly any of which was new—that gave an indication of why the monarchy had decided to train the population for war in the wake of a war.

Furthermore, Biltons was no less exclusive, and the monarchy still participated in the same preferential treatment of its students that had occurred before the Great Conflict. No candidates from Wythe or Chapelstone were ever chosen for the Select Guard, and everyone knew it. It was the entire reason I was here. That and someone had seen my vulnerability and offered to help. A stranger who was either going to be my saving grace or my ruin.

"We will go into more detail on each of the prominent battles as the semester continues, but for now, the takeaway is that we persevered through these dark times and are currently more unified than ever." There was no hint of sarcasm in Viggo Wood's voice, and I could tell that he wholeheartedly believed what he was uttering, like he had no clue of the inequality still so blatantly obvious to me.

Then again, most of the people here had never had to trade goods for their clothes or work manual labor to ensure their next meal. Or any meal, for that matter. Did they even know what a luxury it was to walk these hallowed halls, or were they all just imagining themselves as monarchs, picturing their faces set beneath a glittering crown?

My jaw clenched at the thought of it. It made me angry that something that meant so much to me was just a game to them. My father's life hung in the balance, my own freedom as well, and as I scanned the surrounding room, not a single face looked as perturbed as I felt at Viggo's statement. At his casual ignorance.

The bell chimed, and the last dregs of the early morning anticipation I had felt drained from my body. Disappointing, considering it was only day one. Numbly, I packed my things into my satchel, mentally reminding myself that I still had so much more to endure.

Fifteen

Later that evening, Ryana and I caught up to Jemma and Connally in the dining hall for dinner. Over the weekend, we had claimed a table towards the edge of the room, about halfway between the instructor's seats and the entrance to the hall.

My spoon dipped into the bowl in front of me, dredging up a thick chunk of beef with a tiny sliver of sliced carrot, both dripping in broth. Somewhere in the confines of the dish, I knew I would find potatoes, too. Beside the bowl, I had a plate with two warm buttered rolls, steam still drifting from the rounded hunks of bread.

Prior to coming here, I had never had access to such a plethora of food and flavors in such a short amount of time. Dad and I relied on the seasonal harvests from his garden to supply most of our produce, trading or buying meat when necessary. Each meal here consisted of a balance of protein, vegetables, and either bread or pasta, the latter of which I had only recently discovered.

My gaze departed from my delicious stew, rising to find Connally Owens staring at me with those assessing honey-drenched eyes again. She smiled when I met her gaze, but her lids narrowed with something other than fondness. "I heard you had a run-in with Cade today." She shoveled a steaming bite of her own stew into her mouth, nearly smug at the drama that she was about to start, even if there was nothing to tell.

"Excuse me?" Jemma gasped, her vision flickering between Connally and me. "Why am I just now hearing about this?"

A ruddy blush crept up my face. Jemma had demonstrated her intent to be with Cade, and I didn't want her to think I was going after the man she had claimed. We never fought over boys.

Roughly swallowing down my last bite, I offered Jemma an apologetic grin. "I literally ran into him after my running conditioning class, and we talked for two whole seconds."

Jemma eyed me suspiciously, the green in her eyes today pulling slightly more emerald but still bright and fresh like the skin of an apple.

"Talking about what?" Connally inquired in a tone that wasn't exactly kind. It was almost as if she couldn't understand why he'd even wanted to talk to me at all.

Consciously resisting my impulse to glare at her, my spoon dropped to the bowl with a clattering. Against my better judgment, my mouth curled into a forced grin as I attempted to keep from mirroring her attitude. "He asked me about classes, and then the bell rang."

It was a lie, or a partial lie. There was no reason to admit to Connally Owens that I practically spilled my guts to the House Leader, whom I barely knew. Who hadn't even remembered me at first.

If we had been alone, I would have likely made the confession to Jemma, but it felt too vulnerable to say out loud at the table.

My gaze drifted back to my oldest friend, who was grinning from ear to ear. "If you like him, you can have him." That mischievous curl to her lips told me she was up to something. "I have my eyes on Dante Wolfe, anyway."

Her focus darted in his direction. "He looks like he really knows how to handle a weapon, if you know what I mean?" Her eyebrows bounced up and down suggestively as she spoke.

Connally elbowed Jemma square in the ribs, but her amber gaze met mine again. "We might have to fight over him if you're up to the challenge." Her tone and expression were halfway amused but with just enough seriousness mixed in to make me think she might be genuinely ready to go to battle over the Wyvern House leader.

Not that it mattered what Connally thought, because I had already made up my mind. Cade Hudson had distracted me enough for the year, and I could not afford to have him—or thoughts of him—hinder any more of my progress here. It had been pure luck that my instructor hadn't reprimanded me for my tardiness. Plus, he didn't even remember me.

My head shook as I expelled a breath. "I didn't think the house leaders could date students anyway." I let my attention return to my food, practically moaning around the bite of warm buttery bread.

Ryana sniffed a laugh. "Who said anything about dating?"

All eyes shot to her. Jemma pointed her spoon in Ryana's direction. "See that right there? I knew I liked you. I had a feeling."

A chuckle made its way around my bite of food as I chewed. Relief at the idea that the conversation had steered away from Cade had just settled in my stomach when I heard a gruff voice say, "If the joke is that good, someone has to tell it to me."

This time, it took extreme willpower not to choke on my roll as I turned to face him.

Cade's eyes met mine for the briefest of moments before another voice called to him from across the hall. Dante was standing on his chair at the House Leader table—much to the disapproval of the instructors seated behind him—motioning for Cade to join him. At first, Cade only lifted a palm in the air.

His attention turned back to me. "Hello, Jemma and Ashton. It is nice to see you again." At least he recalled my name this time.

The bread still lodged in my throat did not want to budge as I forced out my response. "Hello." Instead of sounding carefree, my voice came out a tad squeaky from the near-choking incident.

A grimace flashed over my features, but in response, Cade winked. Then, he turned back to Dante, mouthing something I couldn't make out. His head swiveled back in the general direction of the table, not quite landing on any of us. "See you ladies around."

"Yeah," I replied lamely, watching as his form disappeared into the crowd of people.

A stifled laugh caught my attention, dragging it back to Jemma, who was practically giddy with anticipation. "You like him," she whisper-shouted across the table.

"I'm not here for that," I replied flatly. "He's just attractive in that initially shocking kind of way." It was the truth. There was no excess energy to throw into a relationship right now. Not until I wore that emerald uniform, and my dad was cured.

A throat cleared towards the instructor's table, and I was glad to shift my attention there. Headmaster Dracorris was standing, eyes slipping over the students, as he waited for a hush to settle.

The man looked weary, too tired for it to be so early in the academic year. He drew in a deep breath that expanded his chest slowly before exhaling and resigning himself to address us. "As most of you are probably aware, the Elemental Queen has sent an official proclamation that an heir will be chosen this year from the students sitting in this room."

Hushed murmurs rippled throughout the seated crowd but did not deter Mr. Dracorris from speaking.

His gray hair had already been tucked behind both ears, which made his features appear younger as he rotated his head to watch the crowd before him. "I know that many of you have heard the rumors, and I am not fond of giving in to those sorts of things, but I believe it is pertinent to inform you of the criteria by which you will be judged."

A pin could have dropped in the hall and echoed throughout the chamber, as silent as it had become, as everyone waited with bated breath to hear the next words. Especially me.

"Selection for heir candidates will be done in much the same way as choosing members of the Select Guard. And also through a combination of your marks in your seated sections, your performance during the Ice Games, and the outcome of the solstice ceremony."

A breath slid between my teeth. This was not exactly fresh information, but it solidified the unease in my gut.

"The Guides may be present in some capacity at all three challenges," the Headmaster continued. "There will be a program that commences a few weeks after the end of the academic year, where the final candidates will compete in a series of trials. Only those invited to this stage will be eligible, and final recommendations for admittance will come from faculty."

Hushed whispers swelled in the room, bouncing off the harsh stone and wooden surfaces.

Mr. Dracorris glanced down the bridge of his nose, his chin lifted into the air. "I expect you to uphold the values of this grand establishment and prove yourselves worthy of such an honor being bestowed upon you. Only those within these walls will be considered for the title of Elemental Heir." Which meant, once again, Wythe and Chapelstone were being excluded, as well as the entire population not currently attending this magical academy.

The man did not wait for any further acknowledgement, and dutifully ignored the growing number of raised hands as he walked from the table and exited through the double doors and into the hallway without another word.

The murmurs turned into a cacophony of frantic speech as conversations erupted around the room.

My appetite was gone, and I dropped my unfinished roll onto my plate, turning to Ryana for clarification. "Why is everyone freaking out if the rumor was the reason most of them came here?"

The question seemed to catch her off guard, causing her to startle at the sound of my voice. Her gaze drew back to me slowly, coming into focus after a round of rapid blinks. "I think everyone believed the Ice Games would be the sole method to determine candidates."

Ryana's nose scrunched as she continued her contemplation. "I think that adding academic standing and faculty recommendations is problematic for some of those hoping to be chosen."

Some pivotal piece of information was missing because I was not following her line of thought. Doing well in the classes predicated success in the challenges, so I couldn't understand why this would bother anyone. "Why?"

Connally scoffed, a grating noise that I dutifully tried to ignore. "Because," she declared in a haughty tone, "instructor loyalty can be purchased by the highest bidder." Then she shrugged and added, "And so can sabotage."

My inhale was shaky, rendering me momentarily incapable of thinking clearly through the jumble of thoughts winding around each other in the confines of my mind. "What does that even mean for someone like me? I don't even want to be an heir."

It was Ryana who replied in a voice that was drenched with concern. "It means that the better you are doing in class and in the challenges, the more likely you are to have a target painted on your back."

The world seemed to shift in a stark horizontal slash. How was I supposed to prove myself in the Ice Games if doing so was going to make it infinitely harder to succeed at my goal? It wasn't like I could pay for my advantage; I couldn't even afford my tuition. My fists formed balls by my side.

It was Jemma whose hand darted across the table to rest on mine. "It's fine, Ashton. I'm sure everyone will leave you alone if they know you don't want to be the heir."

There was only a split second where I felt a modicum of relief before Connally interjected. "It won't matter what she wants. If the instructors deem her the most impressive candidate, they will still nominate her."

The legs of my chair scratched against the stone floor as I stood abruptly from the table. "I need to go," I stammered, crossing my arms over my midsection and running from the room without confirmation that anyone had even heard me.

Theoretically, I knew I couldn't run from my problems, but I needed to get away to think and reason my way through how I was going to proceed. The hallways blurred around me until I made it to Suite C, grateful that it was blessedly empty. It wasn't until I climbed the ladder to my bunk that I discovered the letter resting on my neatly made bed.

It was impossible not to recognize the penmanship as the scrawling handwriting of my anonymous sponsor. Ice-cold dread flooded my veins as I contemplated whether I should tear the letter into bits or open it. My subconscious decided for me as my fingers moved numbly against the wax seal, and before I knew it, my eyes were scanning the words held within.

Dear Miss Blake,

By now, you will have heard that the Elemental Queen is naming an heir. This does not change our agreement. Should you fail to be inducted into the Select Guard, ten years of your life will be forfeit. Do not try to run, I know all the places you would go.

Best Wishes,
Your Gracious Donor

It wasn't just the casual way that they addressed me that spun my stomach into tightly woven knots, but that someone had hand-delivered the message to my bed only moments after the same news had been officially rendered to the student body.

In a panic, my eyes darted around the room, hoping for some sign of who had brought it here. All I found was the glaring emptiness I had walked into.

"Ash?" Ryana's voice sounded from the open doorway.

Quickly, I stuffed the letter beneath my pillow, trying to right myself before she could make out what I had just done. "Yeah?"

Ryana approached on nearly silent feet. "Are you okay?" She looked up at me with such warmth in her gaze that I wanted desperately to admit everything to her right then and there. But if whoever the sponsor was had gotten to me in this room undetected, then nowhere in this entire academy would be safe, and until I got to the bottom of it, I wasn't sure there was a single person I could trust fully.

If that wasn't enough, the terms had been crystal clear; the deal was broken if I told anyone, and I might as well pack up my bags and start my decade of servitude the moment the donor found out.

My jaw clenched against the nerves, doing nothing to deter the heavy trepidation from settling like a boulder on my chest. "I'm good, just tired," I lied. "It's been a long day."

Ryana's eyes glistened with something I couldn't place. "Well, if you change your mind and you need to talk to me about anything, I'm here. I will help you in any way that I can."

Even knowing that Ryana had come here to be named heir, I couldn't detect anything obviously fabricated in her words or the way her brow creased with worry. Although that should have been a comfort, fresh tears prickled along my lash line. It didn't matter that she was being a good friend; I couldn't allow her to be. "Thank you," I muttered, even as my insides churned.

She smiled up at me. "Any time."

Sixteen

The next few days went by in a blur, racked with glances over my shoulder and the anxious assessment of every person around me. Even within my own mind, I couldn't glean if the nerves were due to the impending challenge or the feeling of mistrust that hung in the air like a dense fog.

Now I was forced to grapple with the fact that not only would the faculty, and ultimately The Guides, measure my worth against the typical set of criteria, the ones I had prepared for, but perhaps an unknown variable of favoritism and sabotage that could be purchased by almost everyone here but me.

Unlike with the letters in the tree's hollow in Elmhaven, I had no way to contact that anonymous donor, no way to respond to their threatening words or beg them to release me from the deal. Not that I was ready to abandon the hope that I could cure my dad, but with the risk of failure so much higher, the urge to run had grown tenfold.

Do not try to run.

The warning could not have been clearer. The fact that they had anticipated what the news of the Elemental Queen's heir trials would mean for me and my competition here was unsettling. And now, I was almost positive that being named heir would not satisfy the bargain, or they wouldn't have called it out in such a way in their most recent correspondence.

If it were just a battle of determination and skill, I was confident I could come out triumphant. It was the other parts—the uncertainty of the character of everyone around me and the subsequent inability to distinguish friend from foe—that plagued my every waking thought.

It wasn't all heart-thundering terror, though, as there were a few bright spots to my week. For starters, Ryana had been thoroughly correct in her assessment of Tamari, the Platypus House leader responsible for instructing us on horseback.

Tamari was a natural with the horses, but there was something calming about her that extended past her abilities with the animals. She observed each of us and adapted her behavior and her rhetoric in the same careful way a trainer might work with a foal.

Her affable personality drew me to her, not in the same way Connally's ethereal beauty had, or Cade's surprising attractiveness, but some indefinable pull that had me spending the majority of my session time by her side. Or maybe it was just the fact that I knew she wasn't my competition.

"How did you end up choosing this as your course?" I asked her, after she had given the other students some time to practice saddling their animals. Due to my time around Sugar, and our shared use of the community barn, I had plenty of experience in such matters. Something that my more affluent classmates did not.

The corners of Tamari's eyes crinkled with her grin. "As long as I can remember, I've loved animals." She ran a flattened palm from the horse's forehead to its muzzle. "I just have a special place in my heart for the horses. So, when I was offered the position of House Leader, I suggested this, as many of the students have no experience readying their own steed."

Her gaze flicked over my shoulder, drawing my attention there as well. A gray, dappled mare snorted loudly as a student on her knees attempted to connect the straps underneath the animal's belly.

A smile dusted my lips as I swiveled my head back to Tamari and her horse. "This hasn't always been offered?"

Tamari produced a brush from a nearby bucket and began swiping against her animal's chestnut brown fur, leaving behind streaks that reminded me of rippling waves. "No. Actually, I came up with it because I saw a need."

She shot me a knowing glance before turning her attention back to the horse. "Eventually, we will get to more complex skills where we will build on the knowledge gained in the other courses, but not everyone is ready for that yet."

It almost seemed as if she was warning me that some element of her course may be useful. It wasn't far off to assume that it might be part of any of the three challenges that made up the Ice Games, but my bet was on the final trial that occurred at the end of November, where our battle and combat skills were put to the test.

None of the instructors had given much indication of what to expect, considering the week had primarily been dedicated to deciphering our base aptitude rather than preparation for the Ice Games. Knowing it was possible that they weren't allowed to say much, I still tempted fate, recognizing that any advantage I could gain would be useful. "When would these skills come into play for the games?"

She laughed, and her mare lifted its head briefly to eye her before dropping its muzzle back into the bucket of feed. "Likely not until the end. If even then."

A noncommittal hum vibrated in my throat. My hypothesis had been correct, but I still wasn't sure how a horse would play into the final trial, so I let it go.

The bells interrupted our conversation before I could ask more, and Tamari politely dismissed us, scurrying away from me to ensure that the horses were tied to their respective posts prior to the next session.

After horseback riding, I had survival lessons with Katarina. Initially, I had found her stern mannerisms very unapproachable, but in her course, the succinct way of teaching was effective.

Her hazel eyes narrowed on the gathered students as she cleared her throat. "As most of you know, the first challenge that will occur in less than a month will pull heavily from topics discussed in this course."

Again, her gaze swept over my classmates before landing on me. "It would do you well to take good notes if you want to succeed."

With that, she began her lesson, introducing Mr. Higgins, the botany instructor, to the class before they both led us through the woods along the outer perimeter of campus. They took turns pointing out edible berries and taking meticulous care to explain the difference between the ones that would harm us if we touched or digested them.

Katarina spoke slowly, careful to ensure we had adequate time to take notes, even passing out parchment and writing quills to those who had forgotten theirs in the academy.

While my father had bestowed upon me a great knowledge of the plants that grew in his garden, I was less aware of the species that Katarina and Mr. Higgins pointed out along our walk. Everything shown to us was specific to Fulgrande, or the central region of the kingdom.

"We will eventually branch out to non-local flora, but for the next few classes, we will focus on these *important* species," Katarina stated. I suspected that the House Lynx leader wasn't one to wink, but the statement felt like it should have been punctuated with the gesture.

"Ah yes, for instance, this leaf," Mr. Higgins added, plucking a leaf from a nearby bush, "has some nutritional value. It has a bitter taste, but a bowl of this will give you much-needed energy if you find yourself lost in the woods." To show us his point, he plopped the leaf into his mouth, wincing a little as he chewed.

Stifling a laugh, I wrote down the name of the plant with a small illustration of its three-pointed foliage. Everything that the pair of them offered, I soaked up. Not just because it was obvious that edible plants would be a consideration in the first challenge, but also because this knowledge seemed so useful outside of the competition.

My father was a powerful Flumen who could summon water from nothing, so his garden rarely saw any effect of drought. But there was no magic that thwarted the advance of hungry bugs or particularly devastating rounds of infectious diseases that proved more diabolical than the pests.

It was inevitable that the output of the crop would ebb and flow, so having this knowledge handy gave me one more proficiency to survive with minimal income if the need ever arose. There was something reassuring about a skill that felt so practical, even outside of the confines of serving on the guard or battling in an unlikely war.

The week continued in a good pattern until I returned to Viggo

Wood's battle studies course. Apparently, my questions on that first day had given him an inflated level of skepticism when it came to me. That made two of us, though, because I now regarded his lessons with more apprehension.

He did nothing to prove those assumptions false, as he skipped right over the prominent battles of the Great Conflict to instead discuss the history of the Elemental Queen. It was a topic I was highly interested in, which only made me more frustrated as he continued to give us vague information.

Viggo Wood's fingers rapped against the wooden podium at the front of the room, bushy eyebrows locked on a parchment resting on its surface. "The Elemental Queen's father was from the royal line. Her mother hailed from a wealthy northern family." He paused, and just when I considered that he might be diving deeper into the subject, he said, "She has been the Queen for two hundred and thirty-two years."

It was bad enough that none of this information pertained to the civil war, but it wasn't even educational in the slightest. A huff of aggravation blew a stray strand of hair from my face as I raised my hand.

The motion garnered me a glower from the elderly educator. His mouth pursed as he stared in my direction, considering whether to even acknowledge me.

"Which northern family?" I asked before he formally allowed me to speak.

His nostrils flared with an elongated inhale. "She is not related to any of the current bloodlines in the North." His words were sharp and biting, and he instantaneously returned to his lesson. Not that I kept tabs on the *bloodlines* he casually referred to.

"The Elemental Queen is a monarch by blood right. She—"

"How long did her parents rule before the Elemental Queen?" The words tumbled from my lips as I found myself unable to move away from the topic despite—or perhaps because of—his efforts to evade a real answer. "Are they long-lived like her? Or multi-elemental?"

No one in the Kingdom of Demetros had the lifespan of the Elemental Queen, except her Guides, to who she had gifted the extended years. No one knew where that power originated from or how it was possible for her to bestow it.

I didn't care to know how many years she had been queen; I wanted to know what came before. Why was she the only person with four elemental gifts?

It was yet another incredible piece of information that was never questioned. Allegedly, the proof of her magic resided in the very trophy that the Ice Games were named after. Rumors spoke of a chalice made from the dust of a rare aqua-hued stone, frozen with water and fire magic, and then kept cold with a steady breeze of air flowing over the surface at all times. The Ice Trophy—very imaginatively named—had remained a glittering icy prize for the winners of the games for almost as long as the Elemental Queen had been ruling.

Mr. Wood cut his eyes towards me from across the room, turning to face me with a blooming purple-red pallor. "No one knows the exact information. Much of the history prior to the Queen's reign was lost in the Great Conflict and the fires that destroyed the records building."

It was all too convenient that the most suspicious of our nation's circumstances could be easily waived away under the guise of being lost to the flames of that final battle.

Viggo stomped away, stalking to the opposite side of the room in order to physically evade further questioning.

My mouth opened without a second thought. "Why can't we just ask her?"

The instructor's infuriated gaze arced to my location, never quite focusing on me; his frail attempt at decorum was close to shattering. "How would you like it if people bombarded you with questions about your dead mother? This is the only family her majesty had in the world. Show some respect."

My body recoiled at his words, and my shoulders slumped as if shielding me from the blow. He hadn't said parents; he said *mother*. *Had he read some file on me? Was this an attempt to strike a chord?*

Despite his intent, the statement landed like a tight fist to the gut all the same. It had its desired effect, and my lips snapped shut as I remained silent for the remainder of his lecture.

The problem was, while I was outwardly quiet, on the inside, my mind was still racing, spiraling around ideas and half thoughts that had plagued me for years.

There was so much that was unknown about the Elemental Queen and her family, especially considering that she was still alive to ask. The fires may have consumed the public records of her past, but surely, someone close to her must know more information. The fact that, as a nation, we hadn't thought to restore those gaps in our history by asking any of the six people who had been alive since before the Great Conflict to recount this knowledge was absurd.

Had the people not demanded more from her than her supposed claim to the throne? Had no one posed this question to her as she walked the streets of her kingdom?

Of course, no one had seen the Elemental Queen in years, save for a few carriage rides through the streets. She did not hold court; she never opened the gates of her castle to visitors, with the rare exception of the house invited to view and touch the Ice Trophy at the conclusion of the games. Even those students would not lay eyes upon the elusive monarch. Only the Select Guard and her Guides got that honor.

Wrongfully, I had assumed that I'd have all of my questions answered when I made it to Biltons Academy, but my time here had only welcomed a sinking feeling that whatever we didn't know wasn't an unfortunate lack of knowledge but a purposeful omission of secrets.

Seventeen

With a weary mind and sore muscles, I trudged to the practice field with Ryana by my side. It was pure luck that had placed her in my session of hand-to-hand combat, considering the Friday course had the entire student body randomly shuffled across thirteen or so instructors.

"Want to grab that bench?" Ryana asked as we neared the designated muster location. "We can quiz each other on the poisonous plants."

Mr. Higgins had not so subtly hinted at a quiz coming up in one of our upcoming survival sessions, and both Ryana and I were eager to ace it.

"Definitely," I agreed, finding my seat quickly and facing her so that we could begin.

Although it was nearing the end of the month now, it was still a typically hot August day. The crisp winds of the fall hadn't made their move to push out the summer swelter. Sweat was already beading on my neck and sliding down my spine, making me confident that I would require another shower before the day was over, and it hadn't even started yet.

Ryana's cleared throat was the only thing that alerted me that we were about to begin. "Name a plant found in Fulgrande that has berries that are only edible when cooked."

My mouth opened on a response, but Ryana held her hand up before I could reply. "And... the rest of the plant is poisonous."

I rolled my eyes at her. "I was already going to say elderberry with the first hint."

She grinned in response. "Your turn."

My next question had hardly formed when we were interrupted by a booming voice.

"Alright, group! You have been assigned to me for your combat training, and just because I am new at this does not mean I intend to go easy on you."

Every muscle in my body froze. That voice was familiar in all the best and worst ways.

A few giggles sounded off across the crowd. Cade had gained immense popularity with the females in our year and probably more than a few of the males. It was not uncommon to hear his name come up in the common room at night when the residents of the women's dorm room gathered to discuss crushes and other frivolous gossip.

Initially, I had listened on, eager to hear of the others' intents with the Ice Games and upcoming challenge, but had only heard the continual reiteration of the same rumors and giddy chatter.

Not that I could judge them when the sound of his voice set my nerve endings alight with a tingling sensation.

"For those of you who don't remember, my name is Cade, and today, I am going to focus on self-defense strategies."

With a self-deprecating sigh, I rose from the bench and followed Ryana to the fringes of the gathered students.

Cade looked good today with his fitted navy pants and academy-issued grey top that clung to his muscles like a second skin. His indigo stare swept the crowd, clearly looking for something, only pausing when he landed on me. His brows raised in a show of recognition. "Ashton," he called out.

A completely unnecessary blush climbed its way up my neck. "Yes?"

"Can you come help me with this demonstration?"

A rough swallow cleared my throat enough to reply. "Of course."

Weaving my way around the other students, I pushed my way to stand in front of the House Wyvern leader, squaring my shoulders as I stopped a few feet away from him.

"Can you face the group?"

My toes curled within my boots as I positioned myself to face the group before me. Without additional warning, Cade's arm came to circle around my waist, and the opposite hand wrapped over the front of my chest, his fingers gripping just below my shoulder.

A tiny gasp whooshed through my teeth before I reacted on instinct —just the way my father had taught me—slamming my head back against his nose so hard that I heard him release a quiet curse before he let me go.

Instantly, my face flamed, and I whirled around to apologize, hand held aloft. "I am so sorry. I—"

He pinched the bridge of his nose with one hand while he waved me off with the other. "That was exactly what I was trying to show them."

A grin I hadn't expected lifted the edges of his mouth. "Next time, though, let me explain the move first."

"Right," I muttered, already starting to turn away from him when he grabbed me by the wrist.

"Since you know what you're doing, this makes it even better; come back to the front."

The only thing I wanted to do was crawl in a hole and lie there for the foreseeable future because when I hazarded a glance in his direction again, I noted a fresh line of blood pooling under his right nostril.

Defensively, I held my hands in the air. "I don't think that's a good idea. I could hurt you."

He scoffed at that, crossing his arms over his chest. "I graduated top of my class, and they asked me to teach hand-to-hand combat. I doubt I'll be leaving a simple demonstration in a body bag."

Despite my embarrassment, I laughed and nodded as I stood to face the group rather than him. His voice sounded entirely too close to my ear, sending shivers down my spine as he spoke. "As Ashton has so dutifully demonstrated, one method of deterring an assailant who attacks from behind is a headbutt to the face. If you are much shorter than your attacker, you can throw the back of your skull against their throat for a similar effect."

Cade slid his arm around my chest, letting it rest at my collarbone, rather than my neck, and I could feel his warmth as his front melded with my spine.

A male student whom I couldn't see called out from the gathering mob. "Is there a reason we are learning self-defense like this rather than going into basic stances?"

The arm that had been braced around my front moved away as Cade took one long step back, releasing me from his hold. "Yes. It's the most practical thing that you will learn here."

"I don't understand," the guy replied, confusion evident in his tone.

"Only a few of you will be inducted into the guard," he looked at me when he said that, but only briefly. Enough to give me a strange fluttering in my stomach, like maybe he had remembered more about me than my name. "Probably only a handful will go on to police in the towns across Demetros, so for the most part, none of you will see combat outside of self-defense."

"You really think people are just going to be out there attacking me from behind?" The guy laughed, and I couldn't see his face, but I assumed there was a look of incredulity based on his tone alone.

Turning to face the direction the voice seemed to be originating from, I peered around until I caught sight of the person speaking. It was obvious who it was because the red-haired boy wore a scowl across his face and pale, freckled arms folded over his chest. "This is a waste of all of our time," he muttered, shaking his head.

With a deep breath, I straightened my spine. "Maybe you don't see any merit in it, and that's great for you, that you're a guy who has never had to worry about being attacked for no reason. But, from a female perspective, this is valuable information, and I, personally, would like to continue the lesson."

His dark eyes gleamed as he took me in. Seemingly finding my rebuttal as a sort of challenge, he pushed through the crowd until we were face to face. He was only a few inches taller than me, but he leaned down just enough so we were eye to eye. "Excuse me if I don't need my time wasted on something that doesn't apply to me. I'd never be weak enough to be caught off guard like that."

Every ounce of my being wanted to recoil from his rage-filled attention, but I kept my gaze steady. "I can't imagine there's not a single person out there who would want to knock you down a peg or two with an attitude like that."

"We'll see how tough you think you are after the first challenge," he seethed. His determination reminded me so much of Nielsen but without my housemate's decorum. And a double helping of anger.

Cade pressed a hand against the guy's chest, physically separating us. "Alright, Berit, go back to where you were standing and pay attention. When we are done, you will have plenty of opportunities to prove your self-defense skills."

Berit shrugged his nonchalance. As if he wasn't even concerned with threatening me in front of an instructor. Meanwhile, my pulse was roaring in my veins.

"Anyway," Cade said, brushing off the interaction, "if you would come stand in front again, we might be able to finish this part of the demonstration."

A weak smile lifted the edges of my lips, and I took my place again. This time, I didn't even flinch as he braced against my body with his arm and chest. Instead of lingering any longer on Berit, I let myself relax into the warmth of Cade's embrace, grounding myself on the feeling of his hands on my body.

It had been nearly a year since Farren had broken up with me, and given my father's declining health, I hadn't put any thought into any boy since. Now, I was reminded, with unfortunate timing, how nice it was to have strong hands caressing me.

"Now," Cade stated, lips just a fraction of an inch from my earlobe again, "you've seen what will happen if the headbutt works." I could almost hear the smile in his voice, and I fought against the urge to turn around and see it for myself. "But if that doesn't work, there are other methods to take down an attacker. Does anyone know what to do?"

My spine shifted against his abdomen as I made to turn around and answer him, but his arm tensed and held me in place. "Not you," he laughed so low I was sure only I could hear his playful tone.

"Anyone?" he asked again. "Berit?"

A few people snickered when Berit didn't immediately answer. "Sir, could you just tell us so we can get on with the lesson?" His tone bore the evidence of his irritation, and I couldn't decipher if he just didn't know or if he was too stubborn to say.

"I guess it's up to you again, Blake," Cade stated, and before I could move, I spent an uncomfortable few seconds racking my brain to see if I could find the moment I had given him my last name. Of course, it would be on the class roster, so it was stupid of me to even consider that he had looked me up.

Clearing that thought out quickly, I raised my voice so that the entire class could hear my response. "If that doesn't work, you can bend down and reach between your legs. Grab either their knee or calf and pull towards you as hard as you can."

This time, his lips brushed against my ear when he spoke, sending a shockwave of goosebumps across my flesh. "That's your cue."

It was a miracle that I didn't melt into the ground right there because it honest to gods sounded like he wanted me to demonstrate the move. Whatever evidence of my blush had disappeared from my earlier blunder came back with a raging tidal wave of crimson that splashed across my features as I slowly made to bend at the waist to demonstrate the move.

"For someone significantly larger than you, it's best to try to get their knee to buckle," I said, reaching between my own legs and gripping Cade's knee, refusing to look at him in the process. This was the most mortifying thing I had ever done.

"Then you just grab and yank," I said, doing the gesture I had just explained. Except I had used a bit too much force, and before either of us could brace ourselves, we both toppled over, turning onto a heap of limbs on the ground.

Cade was almost on top of me, and while I scrambled to right myself, he gracefully rolled to the side. He remained seated on the dirt, elbows resting casually on his bent knees as he turned to the class. "Now, pair off and try those two exercises yourselves, and try not to break any noses if you can help it. We don't want to overwhelm the healer's office in the first week."

Berit crossed the short gap between us, coming to stand a surprisingly respectful two feet away from me. "Ready to spar, partner?"

My pulse hammered in my veins again. It wasn't his size that bothered me, it was the cold way in which his gaze raked over my body in emotionless assessment.

"I actually need to speak with Miss Blake, Berit," Cade stated. "Find somebody else today."

At that, I saw a flicker of aggravation flash over Berit's onyx-hued eyes. I couldn't interpret the flicker other than to briefly consider that it was jealousy. Like he thought this was some sort of special treatment, even though it was the worst torture being continually thrust into Cade Hudson's path, just to consistently humiliate myself over and over again.

Berit huffed away, and only when I was certain he wasn't coming back did I turn to my hand-to-hand combat instructor, offering him my hand to help him up. It was the least I could do. "I'm sorry. Again," I mumbled.

He waved off my hand with a shake of his head. "You're not in trouble, Ashton, I just wanted to ask if you would help me with demonstrations for the next few classes."

All I could do for several seconds was blink down at him. "You want me to attack you at a future date?"

A barking laugh fell from his lips, and he offered me the most dazzling grin I had ever seen. "It's clear that you have been trained, and I could use a good demonstration partner. It's difficult to teach moves to a bunch of students without showing them. You know?"

With very little experience teaching anyone anything, I couldn't exactly relate. However, I did understand what he meant to convey. "Okay." My agreement came out like a whisper, regretfully close to a dreamy sigh. Clearing my throat, I straightened my spine. "What does that mean? Do you need to show me the moves outside of the session or..." Those words trailed off as I realized that I had basically just asked my instructor to meet me outside of the professional setting of the course and...

"Yeah, that would be great." Finally, Cade got up, brushing the dirt off his navy academy-issued pants, thigh muscles flexing with the movement. He towered over me as he unfolded himself to his full height, but rather than intimidating me, I was drawn to it.

Remembering where I was and who might be watching, I elongated my spine and smiled as if I wasn't completely melting down inside. "Just let me know when you'd like to go over demonstrations, and I'd be happy to help."

It was reasonable to believe that I could do this without it turning into some sort of distracting infatuation. If anything, it might be an opportunity to have his recommendation for the Select Guard.

Cade pointed to where a girl a few feet away was struggling with her moves against a female who was about her size. "You can start by helping me with them while I go work on Berit's posture."

A laugh escaped his lips as he jogged over to where the redhead was indeed botching his movements, and I moved on to help the woman he had pointed out.

Hazarding one more glance at the House Wyvern leader, I reminded myself that I was in control here. There would be no unfortunate feelings. Just professionalism and tons of physical contact. What could go wrong?

Eighteen

It was lunch before I roused myself out of bed and into the dining hall on the first Saturday after classes began. Before I had even slid into my chair, Ryana had already bombarded me with the first question of the day. "So, do you want to have a study session today?"

Her expression was so eager that I agreed almost instantly. "Can I finish eating first?"

Ryana grinned as she nodded her head. "There's just so much to go over before the challenge, and I want to make sure we are prepared to dominate over the other houses." She hazarded a glance at Jemma and Connally. "No offense," she offered.

"None taken," Jemma replied with a dramatic eye roll. "Although the last thing I'm going to do is spend a weekend studying. So, you two have fun." She gestured dismissively, even if there was amusement in her gaze.

Connally shook her head, blonde curls bouncing with the effort. "I don't think we were invited anyway." Her elbow nudged into Jemma.

Ryana had the good sense to look guilty, even if it might have been for show. "Well, we are supposed to work together with our houses, so..."

Jemma snorted. "Oh no, I won't be able to study on a Saturday."

The back of her hand pressed against her forehead as she feigned a dizzy spell. "Whatever shall I do?"

Before we had come, I had known that Jemma and I didn't share the same goals, but it was still surprising to see her give so little care to her studies. Although it was the first weekend, so maybe I wasn't giving her enough credit.

A pang erupted in my chest as I considered she had only come here for me, knowing Biltons was my only shot at being in the Select Guard. It wasn't that Jemma couldn't be selfless, she just never did so with much fuss. Her kindness was a subtle thing that simmered below the surface, like a fabric you thought was plain, only to get close enough to reveal flecks of gold woven throughout. She did not require fanfare for her actions, most of which were a collection of tiny, unassuming gestures. From the outside, they might even be viewed as insignificant, but to me, they were everything.

The corner of my mouth lifted as I recalled all the ways in which Jemma had become like a sister to me, willfully overlooking her less-than-enthusiastic behavior around my weekend plans.

Jemma stood, grabbing her tray from her spot. "You know, this makes me so distraught, I think I will see if there's anyone that can help me work with their weapon." Her celery green eyes flickered to where Dante was already walking over to the rubbish bin with his own tray, and something mischievous gleamed in her stare.

"See you all later. Enjoy all the heir chaos," Jemma called over her shoulder as she walked away without a backwards glance.

Rolling my eyes, I took my final bite of food, pushing away from the table as I watched Jemma *accidentally* bump into the House Irontail leader. "I'm ready when you are, Ryana."

Without a word, Ryana stood and gripped her tray, already making her way to the bin Jemma and Dante had just left together.

"Bye, Connally," I hastily added in an effort to be polite. Even though she didn't respond. It was all the same to me.

Catching up to Ryana just as she dropped off the scraps of her food, I noted the strange look on her face. She seemed lost in her own thoughts, a scowl dominating her expression.

"Everything okay?" I tilted my head in her direction as we meandered to the hallways, which were mostly empty even at this point in the day. Most students were taking advantage of the warmer weather, gathering along the shores of the lake in the sliver of beach that was encircled by the outer fencing of the academy.

She shook her head as if she was loosening a thought and casting it away. Her brows scrunched as she turned to face me. "I can't seem to figure out why the Elemental Queen has chosen to name an heir now, or why it's only from such a small group of students. She had to know it would create a frenzy."

Her words echoed my thoughts on the matter, adding to the ever-growing list of ideas that were parceled off as fact by the monarchy, only to be blindly accepted by the general population.

My brows rose along my forehead, and my hands jutted into the surrounding air. "Like, why even train us for war if no one can even get to us at all?"

The pause between my statement and Ryana's response was just long enough to be considered awkward. She regarded me with some unnamed emotions, those marbled brown eyes sweeping my face for several pregnant moments before she spoke again. "There is so much about this kingdom that is a mystery to me." It sounded like a conclusion, although the sentence didn't feel complete.

Regardless, something like excitement shimmied its way through my body. Ryana was the first person I could recall who had been so forthright about the inconsistencies of Demetros, and I felt the unfurling bud of eagerness blooming within my chest. Finally, someone who wouldn't look at me like I was the problem when I thought to question the very basics of our history.

A cleared throat and a hand on my shoulder interrupted my strangely acquired mirth, halting me in my tracks.

"Hey, Ashton." It was Cade's voice I heard from behind my back. His palm applied just enough pressure to turn me around, my gaze meeting his sheepish expression all at once.

"Hi?" I said, more question than statement.

He released his grip on my shoulder and made no move to shorten the gap between us. "Can we talk?"

When I glanced at Ryana, I found her waiting patiently, several paces away. "I'll just be a minute," I offered her, knowing she was eager to set up for our study session.

The one thing I had learned with certainty about my new friend in the last few days was that she took her studies seriously, perhaps more so than anyone else in this place. Except maybe Nielsen, who still intimidated me with his sterile approach to our interactions in Helga's weapons session.

Ryana's warm ochre eyes sliced the air to Cade before trailing slowly back to me. She gave me a single nod in response, then turned on her heel, and only then did I allow myself to bring my gaze back to the Wyvern House leader. "You wanted to talk?"

He stuffed his hands in his pockets. A casual tan linen today. Unfortunately, no less fitted than the navy pants he wore in class. "About the next lesson in my course."

Warmth gathered in the peaks of my cheeks, but I held his stare regardless. "Yeah?"

Cade's palm clasped the back of his neck as he tugged lightly. "I was wondering when you had some free time to work on that?"

This was absolutely not a date, but my heart leapt into my throat as if it was, and even my conscious reminder that nothing could come of this didn't aid in slowing down my pulse. "I'm about to study with Ryana." I motioned in the general direction of the library.

The admission seemed to make him smile. "I don't want to take away from your study time, so whenever you are free works for me."

For a long moment, I stared into those indigo eyes, trying and failing to find anything within them that pointed to his motives. It wasn't as if I knew him well enough to gauge his intentions here, and for now, I would have to trust that he was being honest and only wanted to have me work on demonstrations with him, even if something about that deflated me a little. "I should have some free time Monday," I conceded. "After sessions."

His smile broadened, and I thought I caught authentic delight. "I'll come find you before dinner, and we can work on it then."

His expression was contagious, and I felt myself returning the expression. "That sounds great."

"See you around, Ashton," he added before turning in the opposite direction of the library and leaving me behind on long, fluid strides.

In order to keep that smile from turning into a full-blown grin, I bit down on my lower lip. "See you around, Mr. Hudson," I muttered to the empty hallway. With an all too bubbly feeling floating light and airy in my chest, I made my way to the library to focus on the only thing that I should care about within these four walls: working towards solidifying my future as a member of the Select Guard.

Jemma slid into her usual seat that night in the dining hall, eyes trained on me. "What's got your face all scrunched up, Ash?"

The answer was more complicated than the simple response I gave, posed as a question. "Why does everyone here want to be the heir?"

Jemma snorted a halfhearted laugh. "I certainly don't. I have no interest in having that much responsibility, and I'd like to get as far away from Fulgrande as possible when this is all over."

Before I could ask her to elaborate on that, Connally spoke up. "I want to know their secrets. Clearly, there is so much going on behind the scenes that we don't know." She looked around at each of our widened eyes before adding, "And I bet the wardrobe budget is extraordinary."

I wasn't sure if I was more astonished that Connally also questioned the history of Demetros, or if I was annoyed that part of her consideration for being a monarch was the closet.

Jemma huffed loudly at the same time her fork clattered against her plate. "Can we talk about anything else?"

Knowing just the topic to turn her mood around, I asked. "How goes the quest with Dante?"

Jemma's grin turned wolfish, feral in a way that told me all I needed to know. There were few seconds between my inquiry and her response.

Her brows bounced along her forehead. "I was correct in my original assumption; he definitely knows how to wield his weapon and had no problems providing me with private tutoring."

My palms pressed against my ears. A different kind of regret swirled in my mind. "Great," I called over the sound of her voice filtering through my fingertips. "Happy for you!" There was no part of me that wanted to hear the explicit details of Jemma's conquest. She was my sister, and that was not something I needed to know with the level of intimate detail she loved to offer.

Jemma threw her head back and cackled like a braying donkey. When her mirth had ebbed, her bright green eyes locked with mine. "One of these days, a boy is going to come along and show you a good time, and maybe then you will finally understand."

Heat licked along my neck and face, and I loathed the fact that the first image that appeared in my mind was of Cade. It didn't matter how many times since our conversation I had reminded myself that he was strictly off-limits. "Understand what?"

Jemma shot an incredulous look at Connally, nodding her head in my direction as if to ask for verbal backup. The curls that framed Jemma's face bounced as she shifted her gaze back to me. "That it's okay to just have fun and let loose sometimes. Honestly, you should try it."

My scoff released as a shaky exhale, a fragile mask to my sudden hurt. She wasn't aiming for malicious, but the statement cut all the same. "And entering into a prohibited relationship with an instructor is fun to you? Some of us have goals here."

If she had taken my comment as retaliation, her expression did not reveal it. "Yes, and it's called *forbidden romance*," she deadpanned, ignoring the second statement altogether. "Highly popular trope in those books you're always reading. I expected you to know that."

Against my own violation, my gaze caught on the instructors' table where Cade and Dante were chatting with each other. I had the sudden urge to tell them about my new role helping with demonstrations for my hand-to-hand combat, but as I looked to Jemma, something held me back. Her and Connally were sharing a glance, communicating in a silent language that made my heart constrict.

"I heard it's just a suggestion anyway," Connally muttered like she was offering a way out of Jemma's predicament. "That the house leaders aren't technically instructors yet, or something."

Jemma scoffed through an exaggerated pout. "I don't want to know if that's true. It ruins some of the appeal."

Leave it to Jemma to turn the mood with one of her ridiculous comments. Of course, she would prefer Dante more if he was supposed to be off-limits.

Connally's brow scrunched, but I piped up, knowing exactly what to say to my friend to lighten the mood. "Then it's awful that you're doing it. He should be ashamed of himself for taking advantage of his position."

Jemma's lips curled back into the smile I knew and recognized. "He takes advantage of many positions." Her green eyes lit up with the memory of such things before her gaze landed on me. "That's better, thank you." A breathy chuckle racked my body, and I closed my eyes as I leaned into the sensation for a moment. When I opened them, they immediately landed on a pair of indigo eyes across the room. Cade lifted his head in acknowledgment, his grin widening.

For the second time in less than ten hours, I had to tuck my lower lip between my teeth to keep from beaming, averting my gaze from him before anyone could take notice. Instead, I opted to pick up my previously abandoned fork and bring a mouthful of salad greens to my lips. My teeth ground together as I chewed, not even bothering to register the flavor because the entire time, I was wondering if I could be more like Jemma.

Maybe an escape from the stresses of my predicament wouldn't hurt me, but help me relax? While I didn't let my focus drift back to that table, my mind remained stuck on the not-date Cade and I had planned for Monday night, telling myself it was only about gaining his favor for Select Guard recommendations while simultaneously cramming down the butterflies that flapped violently in my stomach.

Nineteen

On Monday, my classes went by in a weird bend of time and motion. Some moments whizzed by so fast I hardly noticed them, while others—namely my time in Viggo Wood's class —seemed to drag out like I was moving through pools of amber just before it hardened.

Connally's statement about buying loyalties from the instructors had weighed heavily on me since she had imparted that opinion, and I found myself making a more conscious effort to keep my head down in the battle study class, lest I find myself on the wrong end of sabotage. Which was why this particular lesson on the various defensive strategies for meeting an opposing army approaching by sea threatened to undo my resolve.

No one could cross the treacherous ocean that surrounded Demetros, not even the Elemental Queen. I had seen the evidence of this myself in the graveyard of ships that collected along the northern shore, a side effect of all of those that sailed too close to the massive whirlpools that both protected and trapped our people within the borders of the continent.

Not that I had a desire to come across anything like Berit had in hand-to-hand combat, but I couldn't see how a largely fictitious scenario was going to help us unless the faculty truly thought that another civil war might break out and an armada would sail from the south to attack the north. Instead of raising my hand and putting a voice to my opinions on the matter, I doodled drawings at the edge of my paper to focus on anything but the topic Viggo had posed.

When the bells began to toll to release us, I looked down to find a tiny little wyvern curling over one corner of my paper with its wings spread wide. Hastily, I dumped the notebook into my bag, hoping no one around me saw enough to put together where my mind had drifted.

My thoughts were still halfway stuck on a certain house leader when I left the classroom, and I all but jumped out of my skin when I heard my name.

"Hey, Ashton." Cade was leaning against the wall to the right of the doorway, obviously waiting for me. Catching the surprised look on my face, his brows lowered. "I told you I'd come find you. For our demonstration?"

A few other students glanced our way, but I ignored their attentions and the thrum of my pulse in a mostly useless attempt to put myself back together. "I remembered," I blurted out before realizing it sounded kind of rude, so I pushed a smile to my face. "You just startled me."

He glanced down at my attire, my academy-issued navy skirt and a crisp button-up top, before returning his stare to my eyes. "Do you want to change before we start?"

Dipping my chin, I hazarded a glance at my outfit as well as if I wasn't perfectly aware of what I'd find there. It seemed even my skin was against me because a furious blush overtook my face, like it was somehow embarrassing that I was wearing a skirt. "Probably." My grip tightened around my bag straps, looking for anywhere to expel this nervous energy. "Wouldn't want to take you out with my awkwardness by tangling you up in my skirt and breaking a leg or something."

Cade barked a laugh. "Yeah, that would be awful," he deadpanned when his mirth had receded. "Let me walk you to the dorms. I'll wait outside while you change."

Choosing to chalk his comment up to a joke and not an attempt at letting me know he might want to be wrapped up in my clothing, I

nodded my agreement, and we both started heading towards the residence wing at the same time.

Awkward silences weren't really my thing, and I heard myself
blurting out a question before I could consider it. "I don't really know
anything about you. Where are you from?"

He regarded me with a bit of curiosity before he replied. "I'm from
Manteno." His gaze snagged on a nearby window, showing the view of
the lake. "I know there is water here, but I find myself really missing the
salt air."

Something about that loosened the tangle of apprehension that had
balled in my stomach. "I'm from Elmhaven, so I completely understand.
Nothing compares to the coast."

We took a turn down the next hallway, and Cade's hand fell to the
small of my back as he stepped behind me to let another student pass.

"What is it like in Manteno?" I asked, rather than focus on the heat
of his hand. Manteno was one of the port towns that was too large and
too wealthy for anyone there to need my father's aid. We had passed
through it from time to time but had never truly stopped.

My gaze fell to Cade as he grimaced. "My parents operate the largest
fishing fleet in Manteno, so most of my time at home is centered
around working for them. They want me and my siblings to take over
one day."

Where pride might have rested on another person's features at the
admission, his expression only seemed despondent. So, rather than push
about his family's business, I asked about his siblings. "How many
brothers and sisters do you have?"

The hint of depression washed from the edges of his downturned
lips as he smiled a little brighter, although nothing as broad as I had
witnessed in the past. "I have two older brothers and two younger ones.
No sisters. You?"

My shoulders lifted and fell. "I just have Jemma, and she's not really
my sister. We are just really close."

His brows seemed to rise in recognition. "Dante has mentioned that
a time or two."

That was an intriguing segue that I had intended to ask more about,
but before I could get to it, Cade had already lobbed another question

at me. "Tell me about your hometown. Elmhaven is the one with the creeks, right?"

Thinking about those creeks, about a childhood spent exploring those shores, had my cheeks rounding with a grin. "I work for my dad too. It's just us on account of my mom." I glanced at him, finding understanding there instead of confusion, grateful I didn't have to explain that again. "He runs a construction company, and we travel all over Demetros together. Or we used to."

Cade's face lit up. "Maybe we've crossed paths before? What jobs have you done in Manteno?"

At his question, I found myself frowning. I wanted to come up with some clever response that didn't make me sound like I was vying for sympathy, but I was damn proud of my dad and what he did for the kingdom, and that surge of confidence gave me the momentum I needed to speak plainly. "We wouldn't have stopped in Manteno."

"Why not?"

"My father helps those who are less fortunate. Most of the time, he trades goods for his services and..." My words trailed off because I also didn't want to come off as offensive by telling him that no one in his town would lower themselves to hire an unknown company whose portfolio consisted of stream diversion and roof repairs for towns so small they likely weren't even noticed by most of them.

"That's really admirable," Cade said. Only when I heard the authenticity in his voice did I glance over at him.

We came to a stop just outside the entrance to the girls' dormitory, and Cade brushed a shoulder against the wall before leaning into it.

The conversation could have been over then, but I felt like I had more to say. "My dad is a very powerful Flumen wielder," I offered. "He could have been employed anywhere, but he chose to do something that gives back to this kingdom, and I am honored to be a part of it."

My gaze fell to the opulence that surrounded us in the hall. Sumptuous rugs and gilded framed oil paintings that likely cost more than all the belongings in my room back in Elmhaven. "It's not like it is here. There isn't a mass of wealth everywhere, but my dad helps them anyway."

It was starting to sound like I was defending my father's choices, and

I worried that maybe by being too forward, Cade had changed his mind about our plans, but he reached a hand out to me and gingerly rested it on my forearm. Only after a shuddering breath did I let my gaze lift to meet his.

"I meant what I said." His voice was calm but held an edge to it. "I admire what your family is doing."

He retracted his hold on me and nodded towards the door. "Go get changed, and you can tell me all about your dad while we work on our lesson."

Relief spilled out of me in the form of a sigh, and I slipped into the doorway and headed to my room to find those same academy-issued leggings and tops that I wore for the other physical education courses. My fingers moved quickly to tie my hair into a loose braid, and I tugged my boots back on, lacing them just in time to catch Jemma and Connally entering the space.

"Where are you going?" Jemma asked, taking in the look of my exercise attire with confusion.

Time suspended in the air between us, and although I probably would have told her my plans, considering I had no reason to hide them, when my gaze slipped to Connally, I opted to keep them to myself for a little longer. I didn't want the girl who had threatened to fight me over Cade—even if it was in jest—to know that I was meeting with him after class. It seemed like the kind of thing that could be used against me if she became my competition later in the semester.

Shrugging, I continued to advance on the doorway. "Just getting in a little extra training before dinner." The lie rolled off my tongue as easily as if it were the whole truth, and as I let my focus fall on Jemma, she only rolled her eyes.

"My little overachiever, always choosing work over fun." Jemma clucked her tongue. "Let me know when the pressure of that gets to be too much. I promise I'll show you a good time."

A breathy laugh escaped me as I made it into the hall. "Bye!" I called over my shoulder, letting my legs carry me quickly to the instructor who was waiting for me.

I practically ran into two girls, giggling to each other as they walked arm-in-arm down the hallway. "Who do you think he's waiting for?" one of them asked.

"The instructors have their own suites, so it's definitely a student," the other answered. Clearly referencing Cade. My pulse skittered in my chest.

The first girl's eyes widened, showing off bright blue irises right as I crossed their path. "I hope she's willing to get expelled over it. My cousin told me that in her year, one of the girls had an affair with an instructor, and they both got banished from school grounds."

The severity of their words hit me like a tidal wave, and for a fraction of a second, I lingered beneath the swell of fear. Then, I reminded myself that we were doing nothing wrong. I was simply helping my instructor in demonstrations and nothing more.

As I pushed through the door to meet Cade in the spot that I had left him in, his grin stopped me in my tracks. Was he truly just eager to get our lesson underway, or was there something more behind that heart-shaking smile?

Brushing all thoughts of it being anything more than platonic to the dark corner in my mind—where I was already storing more than a few daydreams about him—I greeted him as professionally as possible.

There was no consideration about things like possibilities as we walked down the hallways, so close to one another that I could feel warmth seeping from his arm that brushed against mine with our movements.

We slipped into an abandoned classroom and Cade gave me an apprehensive smile as he asked, "Okay, how do you want to do this?"

A breathy laugh tumbled from my lips. "I thought that was your job to know what to do here."

Cade's palm slid to the back of his neck where he rubbed out obvious tension. He looked almost sheepish as he took a step towards me. "I'd like to compound on self defense for one more class. See if we can teach the students to get out of trickier positions."

My face flushed at the mere mention of the word *positions*. It was going to be nearly impossible to be around this man without letting my mind drift to the inappropriate. "That sounds good," I squeaked out. "Where do you want me?"

If it wasn't for the blush overtaking Cade's cheeks, I might have felt more ashamed of my reaction. He cleared his throat, averting his attention momentarily to his feet. "Um, the floor is good." A heavy sigh fell from his mouth. "On your back."

He almost grimaced as he said that last bit and without my explicit permission, a laugh busted out of my chest.

Cade slid his attention to the ceiling, the pink tint to his skin spreading to his throat. "I genuinely did not think this through. This really makes me look like a creep."

"It's fine," I pushed out between a series of laughs. "It's obvious that you're trying to get me in a position where I can't attempt to break your nose again."

"Definitely," he agreed, a little too quickly, drawing his attention back to me. His palm cupped the back of his neck again. "We can scratch this idea if it's too uncomfortable. I am usually not this..."

My nose wrinkled as I failed to come up with a word to help him finish his sentence. Instead, I lifted my shoulders in a quick jerking motion.

"Awkward," he blurted out. "I don't know that I've ever felt so weird in my entire life."

I chuckled at his admission. "It's fine. I personally think it's only fair that you embarrass yourself after our first meeting. You owed me some sliver of mortification on your behalf after the way I acted."

At this, he laughed, letting his hand fall from his spine and hang by his side. "Thanks."

"No worries," I said, feeling the twisting in my stomach as I asked, "So, the floor?"

"Yep," he replied, still somewhat stiff. "I'm going to teach you how to throw off an assailant if you're on the ground."

"Okay." My voice sounded more level than I expected as I lowered myself to the floor and got into place.

"I'm going to get you into a compromised position," he muttered, avoiding eye contact again. "Hands above your head."

My body heated, but it wasn't entirely due to the embarrassment of it all.

His hands gripped my wrists and I hardly heard a word he said as he instructed me in the best way to gain leverage from that position.

We tried a few more moves that he wished to show the class before he said, "Lift your hips," and all I could do was stare at him in astonishment. He rolled off of me, coming to a seated position beside me.

His eyes closed again as he winced, although I surmised that the expression had little to do with pain. "I don't think we are going to be able to do our demonstrations in class."

"No, probably not," I agreed, chewing on the inside of my mouth to keep from grinning. The entire thing was just so comical. "Do you have any other situations you think would be better suited for demonstrations?"

Our eyes locked in the space between us and we simultaneously burst into fits of laughter.

When the mirth ebbed to a reasonable level, our gazes met again. "I did not foresee it being so..." Cade paused his words, neither of us willing to fill in the gap.

It had been intense and charged and I was finding it harder and harder to convince myself that I didn't want his hands all over me, pinning me to the floor of this abandoned classroom except for a different reason.

"I'll give it some thought, and let you know when we can meet again to try something more appropriate for public," he said with a huff of a laugh.

I lifted a single brow. "You want to do this again?"

"Yeah, I do," he replied, quickly but softly.

"Good," I responded, wondering if I had just made a mistake. I had no indication that he was attracted to me or that he would even want to act on it if he was, but something about the look in his eyes as he reached his hand out to help me up told me that one way or another, I was going to be in trouble.

Twenty

My breath came in sharp bursts as I pushed the muscles in my legs to work harder, carrying me down the trail that wound through the woods on the edge of the academy's border. Ryana and I had been running together almost every morning for the last few weeks before breakfast, and despite my severe lack of enthusiasm at waking up even earlier than I already had to, I could tell that our hard work was paying off. With the added cardio, I was faster now, winded less often, and could even carry on conversations despite my heavy panting.

"Want to meet at the library after classes to go over something I found for the challenge?" She asked, keeping pace beside me with all the grace of a horse who had been bred to race.

Offering her a puzzled look, I asked, "What did you find?"

An announcement had been made at the start of September, letting us know that the first challenge would focus heavily on the skills we had been taught in the survival sessions by Mr. Higgins and Katarina Evans. Exact details hadn't been given, but whispers in the girls' dormitory common room suggested some sort of hunt for edible plants, which aligned with Katarina and Mr. Higgins' previous hints. It wouldn't be the first time that the challenge had revolved around a scavenger hunt, so it wasn't exactly surprising.

Ryana's arms continued to pump as the gravel crunched beneath our boots, her gaze cast on the trail before us rather than on me. "I was searching through the tomes in the back corner of the library—you know that dark area where no one goes?" It was obviously rhetorical because she didn't wait for an answer for even a heartbeat. "Anyway, I found a text called *Unusual Species of Demetros*. I thought it was just going to contain animals, but there is a lot about plants in there. The diagrams include most common regions for each species."

Mentally, I filed through my plans for the evening, considering if I had told Cade we could meet up for hand-to-hand combat-demonstration work. "I can go to the library after battle studies," I replied, although my mind was already straying to the indigo-eyed instructor I had been secretly consulting with.

He had been nothing but professional in his sessions, even while we demonstrated complicated stances and moves. No boundaries had been crossed, but our relationship had shifted as we talked about our lives before the academy, our interests and hobbies, and even our food preferences.

I learned that he wanted to do the demonstrations as a way to prove his eligibility as a full-time instructor next year, even though he was skeptical his parents would allow him to accept such an offer. Which is why it made sense that he had chosen me, of all the students, to work with.

"Where were you?" Ryana asked, slowing her pace a bit to match mine. I hadn't even realized I had drifted away from her until she had spoken.

"Wh-what?" No one had asked where I was on the random evenings I had chosen to work with Cade in an empty classroom in the main hall. It seemed that Jemma was content to assume I was with Ryana and vice versa. Connally had obviously been occupying my oldest friend's time, but I wasn't entirely sure what Ryana had been distracted by.

Ryana came to a full stop as we reached the outer perimeter of the academy, marked by towering stone walls. She scrunched her nose at me as I followed her lead, turning back the way we had come to make our return to the building. "Just then, you seemed lost in thought. Where did you go?"

Masking my relieved sigh with a deep inhale, I held my hand to my chest to convey that I needed a minute to catch my breath. "I'm just worried about the challenge," I stated. It wasn't exactly a lie, just not the entire truth, which was pretty much the theme with me these days.

There wasn't anyone I could confide in completely, and although my anonymous donor hadn't sent me any more correspondence since the announcement of the Queen's heir selection, the idea that a letter could turn up at any moment haunted the back of my mind like a ghost lurking in the window. Just enough out of reach not to be an immediate threat, but visually present enough to slice me with fear any time I considered it.

"Look, I'm making little cheat sheets for our team," she stated, "that's what I was going to show you. I found a ton of useful plants in that book that haven't been mentioned by Higgins or Katarina."

My eyebrows knotted together on my forehead, no doubt creating deep slashes between them. "Cheat sheet? I don't know…"

Ryana shook her head, gathering instantly where I was going. "It's not against the rules, I checked."

My gaze lingered on the path ahead of us, although neither one of us made a move to head back to the academy just yet. "Why are you helping your competition?"

It wasn't that I didn't trust Ryana, I just didn't understand. In the not-so-distant future, I was going to be her competition for a coveted spot in the Heir Trials—as they had been unimaginatively named like everything else around here—and it didn't make sense to aid the people who would strike her down without a second thought when it came down to it.

She shrugged, pulling her knee to her chest in a stretch that told me we were about to head back, whether I was ready to or not. "We get points as a group for the Ice Trophy, and I really want to see it."

The instructors had reiterated that while we could score individual points for the challenges, we should be focusing more on our group's points because the entire purpose of the academy training was to get us to work as a unit.

"*Ad Maius Bonum*, I suppose," I supplied with a slight twitch of my shoulders.

A hand curved around the edge of my upper arm, and I looked down to find Ryana's eyes shining with some unnamed emotion as she took me in. "You've told me that you wanted to be Select Guard and that it was to honor your mom," she paused as if she was treading lightly on the topic. "Is there another reason this is important to you? You seem really worried about it, and I wanted you to know if you need to talk to me about *anything*, I'm here."

Sucking in what I hoped was an indiscernible breath, I felt the weight of all of my secrets crushing down on me. A longing spread over me, unlike anything I had ever felt before, urging me to tell her about the donor and my father. Instead, my fists tightened by my side as I was only able to release one of my secrets.

"My father is really sick," I admitted. "He just keeps getting worse, and I've always wanted to be in the Select Guard, but it's the reason I need to make it now." More fractions of honesty that threatened to fracture me.

A flash of something that went beyond alarm flittered across her features, but it was gone in an instant. Her head bobbed as if she were agreeing with a question I hadn't asked. "Because of their access to specialized healer training."

It was predominantly a statement, but I acknowledged it with a dip of my own chin.

Her hand, which I hadn't realized was still on my arm, tightened in a gentle squeeze. "Oh, Ashton. I'm so sorry. I'll do everything I can to help you."

There was immense honesty in her tone, and I knew she meant it. Despite the chaos around the heir selection, and my rising concern about who could be trusted in this place, I was confident Ryana was to be counted amongst the people that I could place faith in. Even if I couldn't describe what drove me to that decision.

"This is helping," I offered her. "You are pushing me to run every morning and study on the weekends. You're making me a stronger candidate for the guard selection, and I cannot thank you enough."

That didn't seem to fully placate her, but she slipped her hand from my arm. "I just wanted you to know that after all of this, whatever happens, it has been nice to have a true friend, and I needed to tell you that I would be one for you too. Any time."

A tangle of emotions lodged heavily in my throat. It wasn't that I never made new friends, but it hadn't been since Jemma that anyone had come crashing through my barriers so quickly and made me care for them in such a way. "I know," I whispered, gratitude hanging thick in my tone. "Thank you."

Ryana smiled softly before her face shifted into something more mischievous. "Race you back to the dorms!" With that, she took off, and I didn't take her quick change in subject as a dismissal. If anything, I felt a little more understood. Ryana was incredibly competitive, sparking a love for the game in me when we interacted like this. Plus, I assumed she could tell that the heaviness of our emotions—although kind in nature—was adding to the weight on my chest. A race was just what I needed.

Taking off like a bolt of lightning, I used my height on her as an advantage as I pushed my legs to pump faster to catch up to her. "Last one there has to give the other one their dessert tonight," I called as I reached her side, striving to outpace her to the dorm.

"You're on!" She bellowed, and our conversation fell silent save for the heavy pants of our breaths and the slams of our boots as we both pushed ourselves as hard as we could.

"I want to show how you can take down an opponent that's much larger than you," Cade said as we walked into the abandoned classroom the next afternoon.

I cocked an eyebrow up at him. "Full of ourselves, are we?"

His returned smile was jovial. "What?"

My fingers bunched in gestured quotations. "Much larger? You have maybe six inches on me at best."

Cade clapped a hand to the back of his neck. "Six inches is considered a lot."

"To some," I muttered wryly, dropping my bag in an empty chair.

It was his turn to raise a brow. "What was that?"

Certain he heard me, I didn't dignify his question with a response. Instead, I smirked as I stretched my arms and rolled my neck, making my way to the practice mat. "Have you already paired people off for this particular exercise?"

Cade stood on his side of the mat in a relaxed stance. "Yeah, I've tried to match people up to give as much height disparity as I can, but..."

"It ends up mostly looking like a match of boys versus girls?" I surmised.

Cade shrugged. "It won't matter during the third challenge, but there are certain people I'm not excited about matching in such a way."

I already knew he meant Berit Murdock, the red-haired man who seemed hell bent on challenging me in every hand-to-hand combat session we had. Eventually, I knew I'd have to face him, but I wasn't aching to get that particular fight over with. It also didn't take a genius to notice his propensity to pick on students smaller than him, specifically the females.

"You could always pair with Berit yourself," I offered, crouching down into a defensive stance. Cade had done his part to shield me from most of Berit's advances by claiming he needed me for demonstrations, but I got the distinct feeling that protection was starting to come at a cost, as many of the students were beginning to notice our familiarity. At least nothing we had done thus far had crossed the line to provide anyone proof, but we had been growing significantly closer. I'd even consider Cade a friend.

"And who would I pair you with?" Cade asked, beginning to circle me on the mat.

I snorted a laugh. "I'm pretty sure the bloody nose I gave you that first day should tell you I can handle my own against someone *much larger* than myself."

Cade smirked. "Yeah?"

My chin dipped in a nod. "And the last few weeks of this."

"Good," he said. "Prove it."

So I lunged.

By the time I had almost handed him his ass, we were panting and out of breath laying shoulder to shoulder on the mat.

"You're as well trained as some of the Select Guard legacy students," Cade admitted through his choppy breaths. "You're telling me a construction worker trained you this well?"

My gaze cut over to the man beside me. My father, like so many of the people of this kingdom, was so much more than his profession. "My mother was Select Guard, and I'm sure my father picked up a thing or two from her." In all honesty, I had never questioned how he was so skilled. There had never been anyone to compare his abilities against. It had just been him working with me up until now.

"And all of this is because you want to be in the Select Guard like her? Not some family expectation, but because you *want* to honor her?"

Because I got a sense that he didn't mean anything offensive by the question, I tried not to bristle at it. "That and my father is sick." The admission cracked my voice. "He's gone from being one of the most vivacious people I've ever met to having to rest two or three days after every job."

Tears brimmed along my lashline, and I hated that I was showing such vulnerability in front of Cade, even in the safety of our newly founded friendship. "He's lost so much weight, and he won't spare the coin to see a specialist healer. Says it's a waste of time."

The skin along my pinky tingled as Cade's finger brushed tentatively against it. "I'm sorry, Ashton. About your dad and my question, I didn't mean anything by it. My family has high expectations for me, and I couldn't imagine wanting something like this for any reason other than obligation."

I don't really even want it for myself. The thought was pushed aside before I could give the idea any merit. Making it to the Select Guard was about me because it meant I got to keep my father around longer. Meant that he got to walk me down the aisle and meet his grandkids one day. Being in the guard had either been about being worthy of my mother's legacy or saving my father, but it had become such an ingrained part of me that I couldn't untangle it from my own desires anymore.

"It's okay, I know it's an unconventional goal for someone like me." The words tasted bitter on my tongue.

The hesitant pinky that slid along mine became more assured as Cade wrapped his fingers around my entire hand. His eyes remained trained on the boards running along the ceiling. "It's not a bad thing to be selfless and to consider others above oneself. That might make you different than everyone else here, but it doesn't make you less than. It makes you special. Precious. I admire that about you."

His words stoked something within me that I hadn't realized had been neglected. Not once had I expected any sort of recognition for my own sacrifices, but it felt so damn good for it to be noticed.

My hand squeezed against his for the span of two heartbeats before we both let go. It was one thing to discuss our families and food preferences, but it was another altogether to touch like that, and we both knew it.

Cade moved first, rolling himself to a standing position in the blink of an eye. The hand that had just been holding mine extended to help me up. "Come on, Ashton, you don't want to be late for dinner."

I let him pull me off the mat, and I brushed off some imaginary dust from my pants. "Yes, I'd hate to make you miss any calories. You'll need all you can get for your big match against Berit. Especially since he's practically your size."

Cade only rolled his eyes. "I'm significantly taller," he mumbled as we walked out of the classroom and headed in opposite directions down the hall.

Twenty-One

A dense fog streaked over sections of the practice field as the students gathered with blank expressions, huddled together with steaming cups of coffee that swirled into the surrounding air like apparitions.

Through the thick cloud cover, I could just make out Headmaster Dracorris standing behind some portable podium that rested along a makeshift platform. A cluster of instructors stood around him, talking idly, waiting for the bell to toll to signify the start of challenge one of the Ice Games.

Even though I knew in my heart that I was prepared, the warm liquid from my cup slid down my throat and sat heavy on my stomach. There would be no luxury of a backup plan if I didn't perform at peak today. So, instead of conversing in a hush with those around me, I kept my eyes glued to the podium, not wanting to miss a single word.

A startling gong reverberated across the field, silencing the majority of the crowd as everyone shifted their attention to Trenton Dracorris. My grip tightened along the strap of my satchel as I looked on.

The Headmaster waited until the last ring ebbed from the air before clearing his throat, addressing the students in a bright melody that spoke of exuberance and excitement. "Welcome to your first Biltons Academy Challenge!"

His greeting was met with the roar of applause and cheers, drowning out a few of his next words.

By now, we knew we would be divided into four separate groups to complete our assignment, which took place during each of the regularly scheduled sessions. We had been tasked with harvesting edible plants from within the borders of the capital, which meant we were relegated to the few patches of woods and the random parks scattered around the town to find anything useful.

"Some of you, especially those assigned to the fourth session, will have less material to scavenge from—"

Groans interrupted the headmaster's speech, but he persisted, raising his voice to continue with a palm facing the crowd in an attempt to quiet the distress. "Which is why we have randomly, but equally, distributed the houses across the four sessions."

Headmaster Dracorris plucked a timepiece from his gray wool pants, an entirely inappropriate choice for a September morning, even if the first hints of autumn had settled in the subtle changes of leaves and slightly crisper morning air. He regarded the silver clock hastily. "We have ten minutes to sort you. Please head to your house leaders to get your assignments."

The crowds dispersed, and before he lost them altogether, he screamed out. "Good luck! *Ad Maius Bonum!*"

Katarina's bright yellow flag alerted me to her location. When I approached, I almost snorted a laugh at the clipboard grasped tightly in her hands. There was no warmth in her greeting as her gaze found ours. "Ryana, session two."

Katarina's eyes roamed the parchment before her before jerking back up to meet mine. "You are session four."

I flinched as if I had been slapped, but Katarina did not try to reassure me or offer forced condolences. She simply moved on to the next person.

Ryana's hand clapped along my back as her face came into view, sporting an apologetic smile. "You are prepared for this; it will be fine."

My hand patted against the outer pocket of my satchel as I gave her the most genuine grin I could summon. Inside rested the cheat sheet she had made, which contained a drawing of a Dragonsbane berry—typically confused with a poisonous yew berry, and the Gods Hand Tree, which held plump pink fruit at its base. Neither of which had been mentioned in our survival courses. "We've got our secret weapon."

Her eyes lingered on mine for a second longer before she turned her attention to the academy buildings, and I already knew that she was eager to meet with those in House Lynx who hadn't been assigned to session one to go over strategy.

Minutes later, we crested the library doors. "Thank the gods," Ryana sputtered as we entered. I half expected to see Grethe, whom I had found chatting with her on multiple occasions, but instead I saw the hardened brown eyes of Nielsen. It was only after a few moments of confusion that I remembered Nielsen was from the capital and could provide more insight into the most fruitful locations for our search.

He was standing over one of the large tables, sketching something on an enormous piece of parchment. As we approached the drawing, I recognized it as a map of the capital. The iconic lake was in the dead center of the sheet, with Biltons Academy on one side and the Queen's castle on the other. A halo of smudged mountains circling the town marked the edges of our travel perimeter.

"I'm session three," he stated before returning to his illustrations.

Nielsen sketched out a couple of the more distinguishable buildings in town, as well as the main roads leading away from the lake, like the spokes of a wheel. With a green-tinted pencil, he began coloring in the sections of Fulgrande that were forested. When he was done, there were several larger patches of green and a few smaller spots that were so minuscule that they looked like accidental scribbles.

He took a yellow pencil and drew perpendicular lines across the entire sheet in an evenly spaced cadence.

Ryana pointed at the various people gathered around the table who were set to leave in the next wave of students, assigning them quadrants based on speed and determination. With our plan in place and knowing there was nothing more to do than wait for each round to conclude, we broke apart for the time being.

Most of the other members of House Lynx left the library, but I found myself settling into a seat. Not the leather-clad chair pushed up against the expansive tables, but a winged-back tufted sofa nestled by the crackling fire.

The cushion beside me dipped, and I peeled my eyes open to peer at my unannounced companion.

"Are you okay?" Ryana asked, her eyes searching mine. She asked me this at a frequency that made me question my ability to appear unbothered and normal.

Not that I was okay, but she already knew as much as she was allowed to know about that. "It's just nerves. Can you distract me with something else?"

Dad hadn't mentioned his health in any of his weekly letters, but I could read between the lines. He had taken fewer jobs, and more of his days had been consumed with work in the garden, which meant he had not left the house. Everything was riding on these challenges.

"What do you want to talk about? We've got until Grethe returns and gives me his update, and I'm all ears."

Grethe. At the reminder of her semi-secret companion, I blurted the first thing that came to mind. "Is there something going on with you two?" We never discussed boys. On my part, it was because my crush was forbidden, but for her...

She snorted a laugh. "I have someone already."

My eyes widened as I took in her expression. A soft smile curled the edges of her lips.

Blinks attempted to clear my surprise. "Here?"

"I met him back home," Ryana confessed. "We've been together for ages now. I'm not even sure I remember the exact timeframe anymore. We've just sort of always been."

The admission made me reflect on how little we knew about each other, almost adding to the somber mood of the day.

As if she had inferred my thoughts from my twisted features, she placed a hand on my knee. Our eyes caught. "I don't talk about him because weaknesses have a way of being exploited in competitions like this."

Ryana was far more experienced in the political layer of society than I was, and I let that provide me some relief over our lack of sharing personal information. It wasn't as if I wasn't keeping my own secrets. Being hurt by the same behavior directed at me would be more than a bit hypocritical.

A forced smile curled my lips. "Thank you for sharing it with me then."

"What else can we talk about?"

Chuckling, a more genuine grin crested my features. "We can talk about how obvious Jemma and Dante are being. Did you know I caught them kissing in the hallway outside of battle studies?"

Ryana snorted, and our conversation moved swiftly to the juicy gossip that I felt no guilt sharing, knowing full well we'd likely get another update about exactly how Dante handled his weapon later this evening.

Before long, Ryana and I had abandoned our perch by the fireplace to greet the students who had completed session one. On the outside, Ryana seemed calm, but I noted the subtleties that pointed to her growing anxiety. She shifted her weight between her feet as her eyes darted between each and every person who pushed through the doors.

There was no distinct evidence that she had been searching for an individual until Grethe came into view, and Ryana abandoned her attempts at a stoic demeanor to rush him, grabbing forcefully at the edges of his collar. "Give me the quick report. I don't have long to make it to the practice field before they release us for session two."

Grethe seemed at ease with how she was roughly handling him, only offering her his typical lopsided grin in response. "Good to see you too, Ry," he quipped. "I completed my task and scored in the top 10. Thank you so much for asking."

A low growl emitted from Ryana's throat as her eyes narrowed to near slits, like a predator about to strike.

Grethe chuckled as if he found nothing about her behavior intimidating. If anything, he looked happy. He threw his hands in the air in a mock surrender. "Okay, okay. House Irontail had a solid strategy. They—"

"They what?" Ryana barked, her grip tightening forcefully around the fabric of his tunic that she still hadn't released.

Grethe was wholly unbothered, his grin only widening. "They used speed to their advantage. Apparently, they fanned out quickly and grabbed everything close to the academy, so we didn't find a blueberry or blackberry in any of the nearby groves."

Ryana gave him a pointed look, eyes flickering with her impatience.

His amusement seemed to swell at her aggression, but he continued with his report without antagonizing her further. "From what I can tell, the forests a little farther out still have some Hawthorn berries and salmonberries. House Wyvern seemed to just go wherever House Irontail didn't, so they got good marks as well." He paused, eyes drifting up as he racked his brain for anything else of note. "Oh, and I didn't see any of the berries you mentioned on the list in my quadrant."

Ryana spent a moment calculating something in her head before she released Grethe's shirt and allowed him to back away. He performed the action slowly, as if he wasn't ready to be out of her clutches yet. Maybe he was just concerned that fast motion might attract her aggression again, much like a wild animal.

Ryana's gaze formed an arc back to me. Her face looked as serious as if someone had told her that war had broken out. Maybe for her, it had. "Stick to the plan. Stick to your grid. Tell the others."

With that, she turned on her heel and ran out of the library. One thing was certain to me: even if she was not chosen as the heir, she would make an excellent member of the Select Guard. My chest constricted pleasantly over the prospect of having a friend with me when I was inducted into the exclusive unit.

I hadn't been the only one watching her retreat because as I turned, I discovered that Grethe's focus remained on her vanishing figure. His eyes were dancing with an admiration that I mirrored.

With two sessions and lunch between me and my turn to attempt the challenge, I drifted away from the rest of my group to find somewhere quiet to cram in as much information from *Unusual Species of Demetros* as I could find.

For the majority of the people I regularly interacted with from my house, I actually enjoyed their company. Some of them, I had grown to consider friends. Even Nielsen, with his matter-of-fact attitude on our education, had grown on me. That didn't mean I wasn't going to seek out an edge up on them if I could find one. This was about more than glory for me.

Twenty-Two

The library was nearly silent and empty by the time I had almost gone through "*Unusual Species of Demetros*" again.

The librarian, Miss Bella, had offered to let me have the text. She couldn't even find it on the academy's sanctioned list, so it had been earmarked to be destroyed, given its condition. There was something comforting about its worn edges. It meant that it had belonged to someone and that it had been cherished in some ways. It had a history, even if I was not privy to the logbook of its adventures.

My quest was fruitless for the most part. I turned one of the yellowing pages to a passage about the edible petals of the blue-tipped blood roses. The author denoted that the blossom was named because of its transition from crimson red to purple to blue, almost as if the rose had been dipped in rich azure paint. The text explained that while eating the blossom directly provided minimal nutrients, the petals could be steeped like leaves of a tea. When consumed, it would alleviate pain.

A tiny handwritten scribble at the top of the page showed *Fae blood rose* with a question mark hastily scrawled next to it. The script didn't appear familiar, and there was no other inscription to indicate why it had been written, so I closed the book with a huff. Rereading the same text was not going to help me in any way.

Pushing away from the table, I stretched as my eyes fell to the shaded section of the library, the place where Ryana had found the tome in the first place.

Ryana had won her session and was at lunch with the others. Even as a pang of guilt stabbed at my guts, I had the thought that this could be my time to find my advantage over the others. Even her.

Tucking the Unusual Species of Demetros into my bag, I left it there at the table to wander to the darker stacks of books on the lower level. My eyes scanned over spine after spine, finding nothing of value for what must have been at least fifteen minutes, when I heard the faintest sound of approaching footsteps behind me.

My breath caught in my throat. This must be how Berit was choosing to find his retribution for that first class. Wheeling around, I held the closest book I could grab over my head as a makeshift weapon.

Cade's eyes widened in alarm as he raised his hands to show that he wasn't a threat. "Expecting someone else?" The corners of his mouth twitched as he held his pose.

My shoulders dropped as I lowered the book. "Competition is fierce this year, haven't you heard?" My lungs expanded on a deep breath as I turned back around to place the book on the shelf. *Fables of the Forge* was hardly a useful topic for this challenge.

"This is precisely why I was hoping to find you alone," Cade remarked, his tone neutral.

Sabotage. It was my first thought after over a month of assuming that everyone here was potentially against me. Had he just been playing a long game with our session preparation to get close to me?

With a plastered smile on my lips, I did my best to hide my swelling dread. "What did you want to talk about?"

He stepped closer to me, our bodies nearly brushing against each other, the heat radiating from his chest. He tipped his head down and, in a hushed tone, said, "I have some advice."

This piqued my curiosity but did nothing to still the organ thrashing about against my ribs. "Advice?"

Cade's head swiveled right and left as he checked that we were indeed alone in our corner of the library. "I know how important it is for you to be inducted into the Select Guard..."

He allowed himself another half-step into me so that his lips were nearly caressing the shell of my ear, his breath hot against my neck. "If you want more points, head to the castle gates. Near the mountains."

My eyes flared as I recognized what he was doing. House Leaders were not permitted to interfere in any way to help their own team, but the rules had not specified that they could not give information to another house. Probably because it was unheard of.

Without thinking of the consequences, I closed the gap between us, snaking my arms around his torso and pressing my face against the muscled wall of his chest. My voice came out as a cracked whisper. "Thank you."

With my eyes squeezed shut, I found myself hyper-fixating on the slide of his hand as he wrapped his arms around me, engulfing me in an embrace that dragged a sigh from my lips. I couldn't recall the last time I had hugged someone like this, and I hadn't been aware of just how desperately I needed the contact until I had it again.

He leaned back, regarding me cautiously as his palm slowly drifted to cup my face. "I just thought if anyone here deserved a place on that guard, it's you."

My insides melted as I stared up at him, afraid that if I let myself move this time, I'd kiss him over those words.

As if he sensed my thoughts, his gaze fell to my lips, and his head angled just enough to make me think everything between us was about to change.

The moment burst like a fragile bubble landing amongst pine straw when a throat cleared behind us. We separated as if some painful electric spark had snapped between us and, in unison, turned our attentions to the source of the interruption.

Miss Bella's typically ambivalent expression pulsed with disapproval, her lips pursed into a judgmental scowl. Her eyes were trained on Cade, ignoring me altogether.

"As I'm sure you're aware, Mr. Hudson," she snapped, "relations between house leaders and students are against employee conduct rules."

The majority of her harshness was focused on Cade, but I caught the slight flicker of her eyes in my direction as she continued to reprimand the House Wyvern leader. "I expected better behavior from you."

She stepped towards us, lowering her voice to a whisper. "Your mother is a good friend of mine, so if you can promise that this won't happen again, then I won't report it."

Cade's head bounced with his urgent agreement.

Miss Bella wasn't done with him yet, though. "I don't need to remind you that they would terminate your contract if this was discovered. The embarrassment would devastate her. And your father..." Insinuation was heavy between them, but I couldn't discern her meaning.

In an attempt to read Cade's expression, I glanced in his direction. All I found there was a clenched jaw and eyes wide with what appeared to be fear.

"Of course, Miss Bella. I'm so sorry," he muttered. Without sparing either of us another glance, he hurriedly walked away, leaving me to my own devices with the librarian.

Miss Bella watched me with a rueful expression. "Careful, Miss Blake. He's a good boy, but he has his demons."

Her gaze arced to where I knew the library doors were. "Regardless of that, you don't want to be labeled as the girl who got ahead by sleeping with an instructor." Deep brown eyes, the color of melted chocolate, met mine once more, pinning me with a sort of urgency I couldn't explain. "Believe me."

Obviously, there was more to the story, but Miss Bella had had enough of my presence because she didn't wait for a reply before she sauntered back to her desk.

Frozen in place, I allowed myself several moments to catch my breath and process all that had just happened before I abandoned the stacks and made my way back to the sofa closest to the crackling fire.

Slipping my copy of *Unusual Species of Demetros* from my bag, I dropped to my seat and began where I left off at an illustration of the blue-tipped blood rose. Or the Fae-blood rose? Anything to get my thoughts away from the bizarre situation that had just occurred and back into a headspace I'd need to compete.

Before I could linger in my regret any longer, a group of House Lynx members walked into the double doors. Which meant that it was almost my turn.

When I glanced up, I found Nielsen being dragged to our table by the collar of his shirt, which was balled in Ryana's fist. She released him and then hastily spread out the makeshift map he had drawn earlier and pointed to it.

Standing, I closed the book once more, making my way to the table. Ryana stomped her foot and crossed her arms in an uncharacteristically haughty display. "Alright, tell us where session four needs to go. Make it quick." She snapped in the air between them.

Nielsen's stare slid to mine for a heartbeat before he began drawing over his makeshift map, placing large red X's on most of the quadrants until only seven remained untouched. The unmarked squares fanned off in every direction, but they were all the farthest boxes away from the academy.

Leaning against the wooden plank of the table's edge, I scanned the map for the area that Cade had alluded to, pointing at the square that seemed to meet the Wyvern House leader's vague description. The map wasn't an exact to-scale model, so it was hard to be confident. "I'll take the square near the castle."

It didn't take accuracy in distances on the drawing to know that this was one of the farthest points out, the perimeter grazing against the outer ring of mountains that encircled the capital.

Ryana cut her eyes to me before they narrowed. "Are you sure?" There was a surprise softness to her tone.

I nodded emphatically as I handed her *Unusual Species of Demetros* for her safekeeping.

"Okay then," she replied, with no protest at all. She turned to the rest of the gathered housemates and continued reassigning quadrants. All of her words faded to a dull roar in my periphery.

Leaving them all behind, I bolted from the library, finally ready to participate in the first challenge of the Ice Games.

Twenty-Three

Everything from the moment I left the library was a blur. The worn path from the outer courtyard, the other students around me, and even Headmaster Dracorris' heartfelt speech were lost to me in an adrenaline-fueled haze.

Even with a potential leg up—if Cade's advice proved advantageous—I couldn't drown out the mind-numbing fear coursing through my veins, pulsing like its own heartbeat in my throat. A steady, forceful drumbeat to remind me of how much was on the line.

An explosion of fire magic flared high in the sky, my only indication that the last and final round of challenge one had started. The world snapped into focus with that sound, sharp and clear, as I honed my attention to my surroundings. Joining the others in the stampede through the gates along the outer wall of the practice field, I left Biltons Academy campus for the first time since my arrival.

My lungs filled with the crisp air as I tore past the others, heading south along the cobblestone streets that Nielsen had pointed out in his crude drawing. At the fork in the road, I veered left.

Picked over blackberry bushes and remnants of what might have been bountiful harvest spots in session one scraped past me as I pushed on. My heartbeat reverberated in my ears as the scenery washed away in grayscale, my singular focus on the path ahead until I reached the outer perimeter of the Queen's castle.

Only then did I slow and just enough to take in the view of the structure, wondering only briefly if the Elemental Queen was somewhere within, watching the chaos of the challenge from a balcony. I shoved the thought away, driving myself forward until I reached the base of the mountains that ringed the capital.

My face tilted to the sun, noting its location in the cloudless afternoon sky. By my best calculation, I had only wasted twenty or thirty minutes with the trek here, which gave me ample time to collect whatever harvest Cade had suspected I would find. Katarina was also owed some thanks as it had been she who had taught us the skill of determining the time through the solar position, as well as the stars in a night sky.

My gaze dipped to the surrounding foliage, scanning rapidly until I found the hints of a ruby-red berry. I wasted no time crossing the forest floor to snatch a handful when I paused, my palm hovering over the fruit. My fingertips plucked at a singular sphere, observing it with more scrutiny, only to find no evidence of a purple star marring its flesh that would denote it as the Dragonsbane berry Ryana had illustrated on our cheat sheet. A flick of my fingers launched the berry to the ground.

My head jerked with rapid movements as I took swift steps deeper into the thicket of trees. Only a few more moments of frantic hunting, and I was rewarded with a fluttering of leaves in the shape of an extended palm. There were only two of the god's hand trees, mostly shielded behind the trunk of an oak tree. But thankfully, the space around the root system appeared undisturbed. Dropping to my knees, I dug up the damp earth, finding the pale pink fruit underneath. Roughly, I wiped each piece off before placing it smoothly in my satchel.

I relocated to another patch of blackberries that had clustered nicely on the bush, folding the delicate fruit gently into the cloth I had brought after a tip from Grethe suggested that this might help preserve their shape in my bag. Points would be deducted from the overall score if the harvest was too bruised to eat. Mindfulness, not only in placing the bounty in the bag but traveling with it, was paramount.

After several more minutes examining the underbrush for plants, I all but bumped into the edge of an iron fence hidden behind curtains of leaves. Peeling back some of the dense ivy vines, I revealed a set of crumbling brick columns holding up the remnants of heavy black posts that made a wall that sliced through the middle of the forest. The ivy had long ago overtaken the iron fencing until it was almost indistinguishable from the foliage around it.

If I hadn't practically run into it, and if it wasn't for the brick, I might not have noticed it in passing at all. I wasted valuable time pacifying my curiosity by walking around its perimeter until I found a gate. A horrendous screech flittered across the tree line when I pulled its handle towards me. The rust accumulating along the hinges was almost so severe that I was shocked it had even opened for me at all, rather than disintegrating.

Tentatively, I stepped between the vine-wrapped post and an audible gasp escaped my lips as my hand scraped against one of the sharp pieces of the metal, blood instantly welling to the surface. That pain, and even the bleeding, was lost to the fray behind my astonishment as I took in the view before me. Although it had clearly not been tended to in many years, I recognized the telltale signs of a once-loved garden.

Wild, unkempt rose bushes flourished around me, with blooms in every color of the rainbow. Clementine orange and golden yellow lilies pushed their way from behind overgrown hedges. The faint outline of brick embedded into the earth outlined what must have once been a defined pathway to the center of the garden. My boots crunched against fallen leaves as I followed it.

Everything about this pocket of vegetation reminded me of home, of my dad's garden. Home was the only other place I had seen this variety of plant life growing together in one space. An overwhelming sense of belonging washed over me, and I longed to tell my dad about this hidden refuge and show it to him one day if I could. If either of us survived this.

It was as if I had been doused in ice-cold water as a shiver ran up my spine at the reminder of all I stood to lose if I did not get my head back into the game. Time was dwindling, and I had chosen to go to one of the farthest quadrants away. At this point, my satchel was light, unburdened with the bounty I knew I needed to collect.

My attention arced over the garden, this time with the purpose of completing my task. Even without the view of the sun, hiding behind the canopy of trees and thick interwoven vines, I knew my time was diminishing, so I gave myself an entire minute to collect what I could.

One, two, three, four... Nothing to the left.

Ten, eleven, twelve, thirteen... I spied another bush full of red berries to the right and made my way to it quickly, plucking a singular fruit from the plant. Relief shoved an exhale from my lungs as I spied the purple star and grabbed as much as my hand could harvest while I pawed the bush like a bear bulking up for a lengthy hibernation.

Fifty-nine. Sixty.

My time was up. With scratched and bleeding hands, I shoved my bounty into my pack and followed the hidden brick path towards the entrance. Just before I left the archway of the gate, I stopped dead in my tracks.

It was astonishing that I had missed this plant before. Sitting in a single band of sunlight—as if some all-knowing being in the universe had shed light on it specifically for me—was the most stunning flower I had ever seen. The blue-tipped blood rose.

The illustrations hadn't done it justice. The deep sapphire penciled into the edges of the bloom in *Unusual Species of Demetros* did not hold a candle to the vibrant cobalt tip of the petals before me. It looked energized, like a smoldering azure flame. The amethyst shading of the drawing had done nothing to show the richness of the eggplant purple. And while I would still describe the final color as crimson, its basic pigment assignment was only because I didn't have another word to capture anything sufficient to articulate the vivid shade before me. It was as if the darkest of rubies had been made into a carafe and then filled with the finest red wine. It was dynamic, shifting in the light like a precious stone but heavy and dense at the same time.

Sharp thorns pierced my skin as I yanked it from its stalk. Gingerly, I placed it at the top of my satchel, hoping I could protect it from the journey back to the academy, if for no other reason than to show Ryana.

Still, valuable time had been wasted with my gawking, so I didn't allow myself a farewell glance at the secret garden as I passed back through the gates, closing them behind me as if I could preserve the peace I felt inside by shutting the swinging metal door. As soon as I was in a clearing that allowed me to see the sky, my head immediately tilted upward to gauge how much time I had left.

My stomach plummeted. "Shit," I spat, tightening the straps on my bag and mentally preparing myself for the race back to the academy. One final breath filled my lungs. Then, I bolted.

The landscape around me was a distorted streak as I leaped over bramble and felled branches, hardly even slowing at the sight of the Elemental Queen's castle when it came back into view. The sun's location was not an exact science, but from the castle, I feared I only had fifteen minutes or less to reach the finish line at the academy or risk forfeiting my points and my position in the Select Guard.

Pushing myself harder than I ever had, the nerves from before washed clean with pure, unfiltered adrenaline. Sweat drenched my clothes by the time I made it to the outer perimeter of the academy grounds.

With the field in sight, my throat grew tight with unshed tears of relief.

"Hey, I've been looking for you," I heard a male voice call out.

From pure shock at not realizing anyone had been that close to me, I slowed momentarily. Consternation filled my lungs as I caught a swatch of red-orange hair and cold onyx eyes as Berit began running alongside me.

Drawing whatever energy I had left, I pushed it all into the muscles of my legs, willing them to move faster. There was nothing to indicate what he wanted, but I had no desire to find out. The glint in his eye had alarm bells chiming violently in my mind.

"Hey! I'm talking to you!" He shouted, lengthening his stride to reach me again.

I couldn't—wouldn't—spare him another glance. "Sorry, I'm on a time crunch. Aren't you?" I huffed, struggling to breathe around my words.

"I... Just... Want... To... Talk..." he called, thrusting the last words out like a growl. It seemed the effort was finally catching up to him, meaning I just had to outlast him.

My molars ground together as I gave everything I had to propel myself ahead of him and towards the table of instructors gathered just in my sights. He disappeared from my periphery, offering me a fraction of a second's reprieve.

Then, the bells started chiming.

BONG.

I forced my thoughts away from Berit's odd behavior and channeled every ounce of my strength into my aching muscles. Begging them to contract faster and my feet to pound harder.

BONG.

My backpack was being shaken so hard with my efforts that I couldn't even be sure that anything would be edible when I finally stopped.

BONG.

The faces of the instructors came into view as the finish line grew within reach.

BONG.

My hips collided with the surprisingly sturdy wooden planks of the inspection table as the last bell chimed, bringing with it the end of the first challenge.

When I glanced over my shoulder, I expected to find Berit on my heels, but he had vanished. Based on his loud boasting in hand-to-hand combat, I knew he intended to become heir, but his behavior was not indicative of someone who wanted to earn that spot. Had he even been carrying a bag for his bounty?

Then again, if his connections were as great as he bragged about, he might have the ability to bribe his way into the selection process. The idea of that turned my insides solid and heavy. Even in our limited, albeit uncomfortable interactions, I didn't gather that Berit was beyond stepping on other people to get his way. It wasn't a far reach to assume he'd extend that to the competition.

A throat cleared from across the table, and I looked up to find Mr. Higgins holding his hand out for my satchel. "Better at the very last second than never, Miss Blake."

My cheeks flamed as I pulled the rose from the bag, clutching the bloom to my chest before handing the latter over. While I waited for him to sort through my bounty, I used the hem of my tunic to wipe away the smattering of blackberry juice that had covered the petals.

My gaze flickered to the instructor, who was carefully wading through the gathered fruit, discarding the bits that had not survived my rigorous run back to the academy grounds and placing what had in several piles.

By the end, the portion of my harvest that had been considered in my total score was, thankfully, quite substantial. Mr. Higgins tallied my points on a sheet of parchment that had already been transcribed with my name and house.

"Very good, Miss Blake," he said as he made the final note on the document.

His stare drifted up to mine, a smile gathering along the corners of his mouth. That was until he saw the rose clutched between my thumb and forefinger. His eyes widened in recognition as his breath audibly caught in his throat.

"M—may I have a closer look at that?" he asked, glancing over his glasses, which were perched precariously on the tip of his nose.

Reluctantly, I passed him the blue-tipped rose, and he delicately plucked it from my grasp, finishing the removal of the blackish remnants of the berry with a simple silk handkerchief he produced from his tunic pocket.

"Trenton!" he called to his left, in the general direction of the Headmaster. "Trenton, you must see this."

Headmaster Dracorris made his way to the table, his eyes narrowing on the flower Mr. Higgins had taken from me. While his facial expression betrayed a sense of curiosity, he did not share the same level of enthusiasm that the botany instructor had.

"Oh my, indeed. What a rare find, Miss..." Trenton Dracorris relocated his stare from the bloom to me, a question lingering between us.

"My name is Ashton Blake, Headmaster," I replied nervously.

The Headmaster's brows lifted as he nodded. "Why yes, of course. I have heard your name mentioned a time or two. All good things, my dear."

Never one to take a compliment well, I cringed at the attention, covering it with a grin I was sure was unconvincing.

Not that it mattered because Mr. Dracorris had already turned his focus back to his assessment of the rose. "Mr. Higgins, please recalculate Miss Blake's score."

My focus bounced between the two men several times before I spoke. "I thought the blue blood rose was only used for pain relief and that it's not nutritional? I didn't think it would award me any marks for this challenge."

The Headmaster was lost in thought, turning the flower over in his hand with a glazed-over expression.

It was Mr. Higgins who finally saw fit to respond to my question. "Well, yes, it is traditionally used for pain relief, but it's much more than that. There is some nutritional value, but it is most sought after as a healing agent. The petals from this flower can expedite the remediation of wounds and reduce feelings of hunger. Sometimes, the feeling of starvation can affect your ability to survive mentally if it becomes all you can focus on."

Headmaster Dracorris glanced my way, an inquisitiveness blanketing his face, all but masking a hint of concern. "Where did you find it?"

Something in the back of my mind set off a flare of caution, and while I couldn't put my finger on what was driving the urgency, I listened to my gut. "I went into the woods outside of the Queen's castle, but I lost concept of where I was once I was inside the forest. I don't have an exact location." Half-truths.

The Headmaster hummed an unreadable noise in response.

"Well, you had a decent score before," Mr. Higgins said, his focus shifting from the parchment before him, "but the rarity of this particular bloom will bump you to first place across all four sessions."

The Botany instructor smiled as he extended his hand for me to shake. "Congratulations on your win."

Tears sprang into my eyes, and the center of my throat burned with the urgency to cry. It certainly wasn't the end of my plight, but I had made significant strides to be one step closer to my goal, to my freedom, and to my dad's health.

When I took Mr. Higgins' outstretched hand in mine to shake over my victory, I noted that his grip was stronger than I had expected from a man who tended to plants all day.

The relief I felt was short-lived because the moment our palms separated, a frantic commotion of noise began from further down the path towards the outer gate.

"Help us! Please, anyone! Help!"

Even in their blur of motion, I recognized two of the students as members of House Irontail, although I couldn't recall their names.

The faster of the two reached the cluster of instructors first, dropping his hands on his knees to pant out his frenzied message. "It's Sylvia," he gasped. "She's not moving... We think she's hurt."

Headmaster Dracorris sprang into action, his spine straightening him to his full height. He turned to me with a deranged sort of panic in his eyes. "Take this and follow me."

I took the flower without question as I trailed behind the headmaster and Mr. Higgins. Heading straight for whatever danger lurked beyond.

Twenty-Four

Having never seen one before, I hadn't spent much time contemplating what a dead body would look like in the initial moments after death claimed their soul. Even so, as we came upon the girl lying motionless in the dirt, I knew beyond a shadow of a doubt that there was no spark of life left within her.

Tendrils of mouse-brown hair fanned away from her greying face. Scratches collected along her cheeks, but I recognized her as the House Irontail captain that I had met on my very first night at the academy. The girl whose name I had never asked for.

Her body lay supine, almost shoved beneath the bushes that lined the section of cobblestoned road. Her clothes were rumpled and torn, skewed awkwardly in a way that suggested someone other than her had handled them. Maybe her housemates had attempted to revive her.

"We won't need that rose, Miss Blake." The headmaster's solemn whisper drew my attention to his face, but his eyes were trained on the girl before us. Sylvia, I reminded myself.

Averting my gaze to the ground, I shifted it to the rose that was still firmly clasped between my fingertips. If I could do no good, I desperately wished that they would send me away.

Mr. Dracorris kneeled beside the House Irontail captain, gingerly placing two fingers along the pulse point at the hinge of her jaw. He grimaced, then shook his head, affirming what we already knew.

The female student who had alerted us to Sylvia's position began to cry, her sobs piercing the air around us with a mournful sound.

The headmaster stood slowly. "I am deeply sorry for your loss." His tone was even but not dismissive. He turned to the second student, the one with a misty-eyed expression but, overall, the less hysterical of the two. "Do you think you can answer some questions about what happened here?"

The man nodded, and the Headmaster steered him away from the scene with an arm around his sagging shoulders.

Mr. Higgins stepped closer to me. His head was still bowed in respect, his fingers fidgeting with his shirt and pants. He seemed to be just as uncomfortable as I was. "Miss Blake, do you think you can go back to the academy and ask Tamari to hook up a carriage to the horses? We will need to take the body to the town morgue to perform the appropriate diagnostics."

Numbly, I felt my chin bob as I allowed myself one more glance at Sylvia's lifeless form. I didn't know her beyond our brief conversation, but there was something so tragic about a life lost so young. She was on the cusp of really finding herself and her place in the world, and she was snatched away before she ever got a chance.

My heart ached for this senseless loss and for her family, or whoever was waiting for her to come home. I was all too familiar with the pain of spending a lifetime missing someone who would never return.

Other than to bid farewell to Mr. Higgins, I didn't acknowledge another soul as I left the small cluster of people. My legs and feet were tender, but it felt good to run away from that scene, away from the shroud of lingering death.

It was a bit more than speculation that led me to find Tamari in what I had learned was her favorite place: the stables. The sweet scent of hay mixed with the pungent aroma of horse excrement wafted from the open double doors as I entered. Horses stomped and snorted at my sudden entrance into their space.

The House Platypus leader was towards the back of the hallway, mucking out a stall while she hummed a cheerful tune. I hated that I had to be the one to burst that bubble of happiness. Especially since I had come to think of her as something like a friend. Given the chance, outside of the academy, we probably would be just that.

Rich brown eyes and an affable smile met me as I crossed the entrance to the stall. "Hey, Ashton, did they call us all back to the hall for a final readout?" She rolled her eyes at herself, sighing softly. "I lose track of time back here, I swear. I'll be right there if you give me a minute."

My face dropped, my lips curling down. "Actually, no..." The musty air that filled my lungs did nothing to steady my racing heart. "Mr. Higgins sent me to ask you to hook up the carriage to retrieve a body."

Tamari dropped the pitchfork with a loud clattering on the floor. Her gaze widened. "A what?"

A knot of despair lodged itself in my airways, making it difficult to breathe normally. "It's Sylvia, the Irontail captain," I explained with a cracked voice. "She died during session four. I don't know why... she's just gone."

Recognition registered across Tamari's face at the mention of the name, and she began shaking her head in disbelief. "Okay." Her voice came out in a whisper. Her nostrils flared with a long inhale, and I watched as her body physically transformed with her exhalation. The shock disappeared, and a resolve coated her features. "Can you help?"

Honestly, I would have rather been anywhere else, but I nodded anyway.

Tamari pointed at a horse in the stall directly behind us. "Can you grab Cupcake?" She handed me narrow leather straps. "Here's the bridle. I'll grab Peppermint, and we can start hooking them up to the carriage around back under the shelter."

When I had first heard the horses' names, I had laughed. Even wondered if some other child had named them, the way I had named Sugar. But now, there was nothing humorous left in the atmosphere. We finished the work in tandem in record time, and Tamari climbed up into the driver's seat, staring down at me. "Will you come with me to show me where to go?"

A silent scream gathered in the back of my throat, but another part of me recognized that it was the least that I could do. Sylvia was dead, and I was not, and if all I had to endure was a moment of discomfort, it was a small price to pay to return her body to her loved ones.

Grabbing the rose from the nearby table and nearly scoffing at the fact that I had carried it all over this damned campus, I loaded myself into the seat beside Tamari.

Unintelligible words bubbled from my lips, directions to the body that the Platypus House leader was somehow able to decipher, because before I knew it, we were lurching forward, heading towards the practice field.

A crowd was already forming around the body by the time we arrived. Someone had alerted the medical steward, not the healers. Healers wore red ribbons around their arms and were brought in when something could be done. Staring at the grey armband that encircled the sleeve of the male steward's tunic, I couldn't help but think that it looked like the color of Sylvia's lifeless skin.

We dismounted from the carriage and walked up just as the steward was picking something out of Sylvia's scraped left hand. My heart sank as I took in the small piece of parchment the man unfolded. Even in the dimming evening light, I could make out Ryana's illustration of the yew berry, next to the carefully drawn rendition of the Dragonsbane. He examined the paper methodically before folding it back up and placing it into a wooden box.

A hand patted my shoulder from behind my back. "Thank you for getting Tamari for us, Miss Blake," Headmaster Dracorris stated. "You should head back to the academy before you miss dinner."

Twisting around, I moved to face him, and when our gazes locked, he dipped his chin, lowering his voice. "Please do keep any and all information about Sylvia's demise and..." his eyes flickered momentarily to Sylvia's still corpse. "...current position to yourself. I would like to address this with her family before the rumors begin."

Of course, I understood the sentiment, and I had no problem staying silent on the subject. My teeth grazed along the inside of my cheek as I slowly nodded my agreement. The headmaster shifted away from me to speak to the steward, and I recognized it for what it was: a clear dismissal.

Sighing, I shifted my gaze back to the academy and mentally prepared myself for the journey back to the dorms. It was just as my foot lifted to commit to the trek when a hand reached out and grabbed my wrist. Instinctively, my arm jerked back as my startled stare landed on the confused expression on Mr. Higgins' face.

My palm flew to my chest. "I'm so sorry," I muttered, "you surprised me."

A nervous laugh escaped the botany instructor's throat. "Forgive me. I just came to make sure that you were alright."

A shaky exhale broke from my chest as I rubbed my arm with my right hand, if for no other reason than to expel some of the rising tension in my body. "I'm fine," I lied.

Mr. Higgins hummed a noise that could be construed as agreement. "It would be a shame if a tragedy like this caused students as bright as you to leave this academy."

The sentence struck me as odd, and I couldn't find the right words to construct a response. I wasn't confident he even expected an acknowledgment, as his focus was trained on Sylvia's body.

He spoke again as he blinked slowly, never taking his eyes off the girl. "I hope they don't cancel the rest of the Games either." It sounded like the idle contemplation of a man in shock. Still, the insinuation caused the muscles in my body to go taught.

If the Games were canceled, would they call off choosing Select Guard recruits this year? Would I be in violation of my contract by default? Would the magic in the parchment recognize that I had no choice?

The movement of his shrug brought me back to the present, my vision coming into focus on his soft smile. "Better get back to the academy before it's too dark to see." His eyes flickered momentarily to the rose, still clutched in my hand. His index finger twitched in the air between us. "May I have that?"

At my clear hesitation, he added, "for a demonstration for your session."

Despite my wariness, I was almost relieved for there to be a purpose behind the bloom I had carried all over the better part of Fulgrande. A mumbled goodbye passed across my lips as I handed him the blossom.

It wasn't evident that he even heard me because he seemed too enraptured by the vibrant petals of the rose before him to even bother looking at me again.

Walking away from the chaos, I felt equally relieved and sad. Despite my victory, there was no levity in my heart as I returned to the academy.

Twenty-Five

THE NAMELESS

The nameless woman noticed a sudden shift in her body, a tingling at first that pulsed and spread across her skin and sank into her bones like the sharp teeth of a wolf.

She froze, having the briefest recollection of this feeling, like a memory soft against her fingertips or a view of a destination shrouded by dense fog. Like she knew where it should be, but couldn't materialize the visual.

She tugged against that thought, wrapping her hands around the notion and yanking forcefully until something more than an inkling of remembrance surfaced.

An image of a golden mirror came to the forefront of her mind, a reflection within of a child. A petite girl, plagued by the look of horror overtaking her features, stared back at her.

The image expanded and shifted, swirling like smoke until all at once it snapped into place. She knew two things with utmost certainty: the girl was her and the sensation plaguing the younger version of herself was the awakening of her power.

The scene played out like a moving portrait, and she was thrust into the psyche of the long-ago iteration of herself, experiencing the moment again in realistic detail. The sensation on that day had begun as a flutter and ended with an eruption of storms and chaos. Could it be that her magic was returning?

She didn't think that it was possible, but then again, as of late, there had been a certain level of awareness to her that she only now realized had been missing before. Before... whatever had put her here.

In fact, this had been the first time that she had ever dragged a memory to her consciousness, and if she could do it with one, maybe she could perform the same trick with the others. Maybe she could remember her name. Her parents and family. Who that woman in her worst nightmare was to her.

Another scene came into sharp focus, slamming into her like a mighty tidal wave. A pristine white block of solid marble, freezing cold against the skin on her back. Chanting in another language, an old language lost to time. Indescribable pain searing through her. Past skin, muscle, blood, and bone. All the way to her very soul.

The memory made her drop her gaze to the skin along her arms, although she wasn't sure why. Angular white shapes had been carved into her flesh, and although her mental block had never allowed her to recall what they were, something clicked into place. Suddenly, she just knew that they were the root cause of her loss of power.

The magical shackles spanned from her wrists to her shoulders, and the sight of them, intact and almost pulsing with her own heartbeat, told her they were still very much activated. Or whatever they needed to be to keep her from accessing her gifts.

Could flaying the skin from her muscles return her magic to her? There hadn't yet been an opportunity to try, as she had never been left alone with an object—or wits—sharp enough to test such a theory. It was impossible to know if she'd even have the stomach for it.

That didn't keep her from considering it as a viable option, if only to feel that thrumming emanating from her bones once more. Still, the tingling was a curious development, and for the first time in what she suspected to be a very long time, she found herself feeling a glimmer of hope.

Twenty-Six

My eyes opened the next morning, barely registering the light filtering through the room's singular window, when I heard someone speaking.

"Are you awake yet?" Jemma's voice was too close to my face, although I couldn't sense the weight of her body smothering me.

Blinking away the sleep in my eyes, I twisted my head to find a celery green gaze regarding me from the slat in my bunk. My lids slammed shut again as a sigh escaped my lips. "I am now."

It felt like a normal morning for that fraction of a second until images of the previous day slammed into my mind. Sylvia's already greying corpse, and Berit's almost predatory stare swam in my head until I forced my eyes to open and focus on Jemma instead.

Jemma was smiling, blissfully unaware of my thoughts. "Great."

Her cluelessness to my problems stung initially, but it truly wasn't her fault. She had been so distracted with her budding relationships with Dante and Connally that we hadn't spent much time together as of late. My own secrets and our differing goals here did a decent job at keeping her at arm's length, regardless of her other relationships.

Jemma must have said something else that I had been too preoccupied to hear because she cleared her throat with a tinge of aggravation. "Get up and tell me about your session."

There wasn't a world where I could confide in her about what had happened. Not that I thought Headmaster Dracorris would expel me for speaking about Sylvia, but I didn't think it would help me in my goal of making it to the Select Guard. That, and I truly didn't want to have to relive any bit of what I had witnessed.

Peeling back the covers, I shimmied to the edge of the bed and climbed down the ladder to meet her on the floor, surprised to find Ryana sitting on her mattress with her hand folded into her lap.

Ryana was practically vibrating when our eyes locked. "You won, didn't you? I heard the rumors, but you weren't at dinner to ask."

For a sliver of a second, I considered lying to her because I didn't want my success to take away from our comradery. Instead, I put my trust in the fact that she had helped me, even knowing that I was her competition. "I did."

Both women stared at me expectantly, prompting me to explain. "I found one of those roses," I said to Ryana specifically. "The blue and red ones. Apparently, it had enough nutritional value to bump my score considerably." I didn't elaborate further because Ryana had sworn me to secrecy about the *Unusual Species* book, where we had discovered the plant.

Ryana beamed with something I thought might be pride. "That's great, Ash! Congrats!"

"Wherever did you find such a thing?" Another voice asked, causing me to jerk my head in the speaker's direction. Connally Owens was perched on her own bunk, where she clung to a leather-bound tome that I thought I recognized as an old fairytale. Catching my attention on the book, she abruptly slipped it beneath her pillow like I, of all people, would judge someone for reading stories rather than the assigned textbooks.

Absentmindedly, I began sifting through my drawers as I responded. "I was assigned to a quadrant by the Queen's castle."

My gaze shifted over my shoulder, meeting Connally's narrowed-eyed stare. "How fortunate," she stated dryly. For the first time, I wondered if she was taking this competition more seriously than I originally suspected.

Averting my attention from her assessing amber glare, I landed my focus on Jemma, who was being uncharacteristically calm. The moment our eyes met, she crossed the space between us and wrapped her arms around me. "I'm so proud of you," she whispered into my hair. And just like that, all concerns about our dwindling friendship evaporated. Five words, and I felt our bond strengthen once again.

When I pulled away, I smiled at her despite all of the horrid events from the previous day. "I didn't think you cared about this silly competition."

Jemma snorted a laugh. "I don't." She waved her hands over my body. "I care about you, and you care about this silly competition, so I suppose I care a smidge." Her index finger and thumb pinched in the air between us, leaving the smallest gap between them.

That was the thing about Jemma. She wasn't apt to blow smoke or lie for the sake of someone else's feelings. She was the most honest person I knew—sometimes painfully so—therefore, I had every faith that when she told me she cared because I cared, it was her truth. It was impossible not to appreciate that about her. It was a strength to be that open and vulnerable with people all the time. Even if she guarded her heart from romantic love, she never kept it from me.

A motion out of my periphery caught my attention as a head popped into our dormitory. "The Headmaster is calling everyone to an early assembly in the dining hall. Rumor is some girl died yesterday." The stranger said it like it was a special breakfast treat, like the gossip was so juicy she could actually sink her teeth into it, and my stomach roiled at the sight.

"Oh fuck," Jemma remarked, thankfully more shocked than excited. Her nose scrunched. "I thought this was supposed to be safe. Just a fun little way to test our skills."

This wasn't an incorrect assessment. Outside of the random injuries during the hand-to-hand combat portion of the Ice Games, I wasn't aware of anyone being egregiously hurt, much less dying. "Accidents happen, I suppose." I muttered the words more to myself than anyone in particular.

The unfamiliar girl had already disappeared from our doorway, and I scrambled to get ready so that I could walk with the others to our table. Within minutes, we had slipped into our usual seats, foregoing the line of food altogether as we waited for the Headmaster's announcement.

I caught a glimpse of Cade before he spotted me. His eyes were scanning the crowd as if he were looking for someone, and it wasn't until they landed on me, and his chest heaved with a relieved sigh, that it struck me that I might have been his target.

Are you okay? He mouthed from across the room.

Clenching my jaw so I wouldn't immediately mouth no, I offered him the lamest thumbs up.

His face softened, but his lips drooped into a frown as if maybe he suspected my answer was not completely honest. Without another word, he inclined his chin, then made his way to his own seat with the other house leaders.

Moments later, a hammering sounded from the same direction. Headmaster Dracorris stood at the center of the mostly empty instructor table, beating a gavel against the wooden planks like he was holding some sort of court. There were purple smudges streaked beneath his eyes like he hadn't slept at all the previous night.

Silence fell across the hall. We had never been summoned early, and the rumors of a death had clearly already made their rounds amongst the students. Some people held their somber attention firmly on the Headmaster while others watched with an eagerness that made me sick to my stomach.

"It is with deepest regret that I must inform you of the death of your fellow cadet, Sylvia Lemmons." The way he enunciated her name felt like a blow to my chest. "She unfortunately made a grave error in her collection of berries during the challenge and succumbed to the poisoning."

Shock and confusion rippled across the gathered students. Katarina's expression caught my attention first, something between anger and surprise. There was no time to linger on that as Mr. Dracorris continued.

"Due to the grievous nature of this situation, all classes will be suspended for the remainder of the week." He tucked the curtain of his gray hair behind his ear, a nervous tick I had picked up on.

Regret flooded his features. "I have been instructed to inform you that a new captain has been appointed for House Irontail. Please join me in congratulating Berit Murdock on his new position."

Legs of a chair screeched against the stone floors of the hall, drawing everyone's eyes to the red-haired figure who stood proudly.

My body clenched with dread at seeing him again. His gaze swept across the crowds, waiting for cheers or signs of exuberance. A couple of students clapped, but otherwise, the room was eerily quiet. I pocketed this as resounding proof that my reservations about him were not misplaced, or at least not unique to our interactions.

His onyx eyes slithered to mine, and he pursed his lips together in a mock kiss. My attention fell to my lap, and not for the first time, I considered that he might end up being more of a problem than I had originally thought.

The Headmaster had not appeared ready to announce Berit's promotion to captain, and I was reminded of Connally's comment about bribing instructors. I'd have to discern if speaking against him would affect my ability to be in the Select Guard. If the price of remaining here was mildly uncomfortable, rather than losing ten years of my life, I would just deal with it.

The Headmaster cleared his throat. "Moving on..." He stared down at the table as if he had some prompt he was reading from, even though the space was bare. "The winning house for the first challenge is House Lynx."

Cheers of elation broke me out of my thoughts. Ryana's hand clapped on my back. "You did it! We won!"

Her exuberance only furthered my soured mood, but I plastered a smile across my face, nodding enthusiastically with her. "One step closer to that Ice Trophy."

My awkwardness was lost on her as her focus shifted to another table, to a swatch of bright blonde curly hair and a lopsided grin staring back at her. The moment seemed intimate somehow, so I pulled my gaze back to the Headmaster.

Trenton Dracorris pounded his gavel against the table in another attempt to quiet the room. It had only barely worked when he started speaking again. "We will be going over the points for every team and the harvest items of note in your survival and botany classes. The next challenge will build on this one, and just because you have won this round..." He gave a pointed look to Ryana. "It doesn't mean you will win the Ice Trophy."

There was no formal dismissal. He just scurried off the instructor platform, practically running to the hallway, where a hooded figure stood in the doorway. Both were too far away to study any interactions between them, and the moment the figure began to turn, the heavy double doors to the dining hall closed.

With a scrunched brow, my attention returned to those around me and the bustling of a busy morning. The chattering of excitement exploded in the room as all thoughts of Sylvia Lemmons and her cold, lifeless body drained from everyone's mind. Everyone except mine.

My thoughts snagged on what might have happened to her in those last moments because I certainly didn't believe for a second that it was the consumption of poisonous berries. If the mistake Syvlia had made was consuming yew berries, rather than the Dragonsbane illustrated on the cheat sheet she had somehow gotten her hands on, the quantity of fruit she would have ingested would have been astronomical. Almost impossible given the nature of the challenge, which was to turn in as much bounty as we could.

As I glanced around at our table and beyond, it was clear I was the only one who shared the sentiment, and since I wasn't supposed to relay the fact that I had walked upon her body to anyone, I couldn't exactly voice any explanation of my suspicion.

Instead, I sauntered to the line, grabbing a single muffin before returning to my chair to consume it. It had been nearly a day since I had eaten last, and although it tasted like ash on my tongue, I knew I needed the nourishment.

My teeth ground in instinctual movements as I chewed mindlessly, my thoughts still stuck on that girl left for dead on the trail. It was a senseless death, but not an accidental one. What was happening at this school?

I mumbled some excuse for needing to go back to my room before the others got there, just to have a few minutes alone. The hallway went by in a blur as I made my way to Suite C and just when I thought I might get a reprieve from the stressors of the day, tucked away in a moment of silence, I found an envelope on my bed with my name in the recognizable scroll of my donor on top.

Tearing it open without a care to keeping the integrity of the paper intact, I unfolded it quickly to read the message. There was one word on the center of the page, not even a sign off.

Congratulations

The word, while celebratory in nature, taunted me from the otherwise blank sheet. Relief and fear coursed through my veins in equal measure because while I was very much on my way to achieving my goals, the letter served as a stark reminder that I was still being observed, and yet again, someone had made their way to my bed without being seen.

Crumpling the letter into a tight ball, I waltzed directly to the bathroom and tossed it into the rubbish bin there, wishing that I had my fire magic so I could incinerate it. Instead, I stripped my clothing and stepped inside the shower stall.

The shower was an invention that was specific to my experience at the capital. At home, I had only ever taken baths. There was something so therapeutic about standing under the nozzle, which spouted a mist of heated rain over my skin, and I stood there, letting the water run over my body until my fingers pruned and my mind was clear again.

<h1 style="text-align:center">Twenty-Seven</h1>

Classes resumed without a hitch, as if our free days had never happened. Like Sylvia Lemmons was not dead. Like absolutely nothing would stop the world from continuing to turn on its axis.

Everyone else seemed to accept the explanation given for Sylvia's demise, but images of her body continued to assault me in random bursts, even taking over my dreams on some nights. Flashes of her graying complexion and scratched skin on repeat. Her body haphazardly tucked under a bush. Her lifeless, glassy eyes.

My body revolted at the return to normalcy, but my brain welcomed the distraction my courses offered.

As I walked into that first survival class, I was unsurprised to find Mr. Higgins standing beside Katrina, clutching the blue-tipped blood rose. Or the Fae blood rose, if the scribbling that I had yet to ask about held any validity.

Katarina's class was taught in a mixture of a classroom setting and the outdoors, but on this October morning, we had gathered inside. Taking my seat towards the front of the room, I watched intently as the botany instructor twirled the bloom between his thumb and forefinger.

"Welcome to a very special session of your survival course," Mr.

Higgins said once everyone had gotten settled. Even Katarina slid into a chair to watch his lecture.

"This rose," Mr. Higgins stated as he held the flower aloft for all to see. "Is very rare indeed. In fact, a bloom hasn't been spotted in the kingdom in years. Perhaps even decades."

Because the blue-tipped blood rose had been listed in *Unusual Species of Demetros* as having origins in Fulgrande, I hadn't considered that it was spectacularly rare. The God's Hand tree that the book mentioned hadn't been an uncommon find during the challenge for those of us who knew to look for it.

Knowing I was in a safer space than battle studies, I raised my hand. "Why is it so rare if it originated here in the capital?"

Mr. Higgins' brows furrowed as he studied the vibrant petals. "The origin of the plant has been argued with those of us in the field. Some believe it is native to the capital, while others think it may have been transported from the barrier islands."

"Interestingly enough," he continued without sweeping the room for any additional raised hands, "the majority of the surviving plants are in the north now."

Another student lifted their palm, asking the question that was already forming on the tip of my tongue. "Then why is it so rare?"

The botany instructor placed the delicate flower on the nearby podium. "Let me give you a brief history of the flower, and then maybe you can help us figure that out."

He drew in a deep breath, but there was genuine mirth in his eyes, like he was excited to tell this tale. "While the rose is most often associated with Fulgrande, it is my belief that the flower did not originate here but rather was brought in as it was highly favored by the royal family."

This at least explained why I found the rose in an abandoned garden along the walls of the Elemental Queen's castle. Maybe her parents had tended to them once upon a time.

"Evidence shows this species naturally growing on the northern border islands. As none of those have ever been inhabited, to our knowledge, it stands to reason that this was where they had been originally discovered." He picked up the flower once more, rotating the stem again as he stared wistfully at the spiraling colors.

"Because the petals have medicinal properties, they were propagated and grown in abundance all over Demetros. However, some time ago, the blooms decreased, and whatever triggered the flowering of the plant ceased. No one knows the root cause."

Again, his stare fell over the students, and I found myself hanging on the edge of my seat. "When the plants were no longer of use, most of them were destroyed or relocated, with the majority of the replanted bushes moved to the north, where the kingdom has a higher area of uninhabited forests and grasslands."

"Do they have any idea why the blooms stopped?" I asked, not even raising my hand.

Mr. Higgins smiled fondly at my question, so unlike Viggo Wood that I nearly sighed in relief. "Not a clue," he admitted. "The climate has not significantly shifted, and neither have soil conditions or nutrients. It is almost as if the plants went dormant, although no one knows why."

I found myself staring at the flower in his grip, wondering what made that garden special enough to allow the plant to finally bloom after so many years. Perhaps I could have offered Mr. Higgins the exact location where I found it, but something was still holding me back. A gut reaction that made no sense, but I chose to trust anyway.

"So," the botany instructor continued when he sensed that I was done with my line of questioning. "While this may not be of much use to you in your future endeavors, I would love the opportunity to show you how to brew the leaves for the healing remedy. Although they can be chewed to some effect, preparation makes the healing properties more potent."

He turned the rose between his fingers, studying it like it was truly the last bloom of its kind on the planet. "For all we know, the roses may be waking up again."

With that, Mr. Higgins drew himself from his trance and began to tinker around on a setup towards the edge of the space. Glass vials and flame burners he lit with flint were arranged in multiple stages that allowed us to see the entire process, and when he was done, he produced several small vials of vibrant violet liquid.

He held one up to the class to show off its beauty. "This is the proper dosage for someone of an average build and height, but can be adjusted for someone larger or smaller. While it is not harmful to give excess, it is wasteful."

His attention moved momentarily to the vial clutched between his fingers. "These might very well be the only blue-tipped blood rose remedies in existence right now, so they are very valuable."

With one last longing look at the purple liquid, he pocketed the vials, patting the place where he had put them on his vest. "Now, are there any further questions about the species or what we have learned today?"

No one raised their hands, and I kept my attention on the discarded stem of the once beautiful rose. There was a part of me that hated that I hadn't gotten to enjoy it longer, but perhaps the bloom marked the return of the flowers. Maybe I would see it again, one day.

Mr. Higgins cleared his throat. "Well, then, congratulations are in order for Miss Blake, who found this bloom. It awarded her first place in the challenge, and overall in the competition for now," he said with a wink in my direction, "for its rarity and medicinal use. " He began to clap, obviously expecting others to do the same, but the sounds of celebration were far and few between.

It was only then that I realized that my classmates might not be receptive to my accomplishment, and I was reminded of how stiff the competition was this year.

Katarina stood from her desk, quickly making her way to the front of the room. "Thank you, Mr. Higgins, for that lovely demonstration."

The botany instructor nodded at his dismissal and waltzed out the door while Katarina continued to address the class. "This is an excellent end to the botanical portion of our sessions. From now on, you will see a bit less of Mr. Higgins, but you might notice that my instruction will overlap with your weapons courses."

There were some looks of confusion, but most of us understood that the second challenge would take us beyond the borders of Fulgrande. If rumors were to be believed, which they typically were about this, we'd be expected to use those acquired skills to do much more than locate fruit amongst the patches of capital woods. Apparently, last year, someone killed a bear as part of their challenge, although it was unclear how that related to their task.

"We will be learning the various ways to hunt and prepare wild game, and therefore, most of our sessions will occur outside from here on out." Katarina's glare fell on me, and although I wasn't as intimidated by her as I had been on that first day, my body grew tight with tension. "Make sure to wear appropriate clothing."

And that was it. No inkling as to what would be appropriate for hunting or whatever *preparing* meant.

It was going to have to remain a mystery because I wasn't about to lean over to my fellow classmates and ask them what they thought when so many of them were still staring at me with that guarded apprehension. Like I had come here to take something from them, and the only way for them to get what they wanted was to eliminate me. At least, that's how it was starting to feel.

"See you next session," Katarina said to all of us, but no one in particular, again before walking from the room.

Rather than stick around and find out if anyone planned to make good on the promise their eyes conveyed, I stood abruptly, grabbing my bags and hurrying from the room.

If this was how poorly my survival course was going, I hated to see how much worse the other sessions were going to be. Especially the one that already held my biggest fan: Viggo Wood. I could only hope that news of my first-place position would not reach the rest of the student body before I could figure out how I was going to manage the glares.

Twenty-Eight

For the first week after challenge one, battle studies had been transformed into geography lessons, and I seriously struggled to determine what the purpose of the class actually was.

"This information is crucial for the remainder of the semester," Mr. Wood had said as he slid his focus right over me. Given the animosity in the room, directed at me after my domination of the challenge had been more formally announced, I had no plans to question his curriculum. Plus, there was a decent chance that the information would be pertinent to the second challenge, so I planned to listen with rapt attention, even if the fundamentals he was explaining made it all too obvious how wildly varied our basic educations had been.

Then again, most of my knowledge had been gleaned from years of traveling Demetros with my father.

Despite my honorable plans, the moment I heard the battle studies instructor say, "Fulgrande is surrounded by a mountain range with openings to the north, south, west, and east via tunnels that allow access to that respective region," I zoned out.

On the list of things I already knew, that was at the top. I didn't need someone telling me that the South was comprised of fishermen and farmers and was equally famous for the specialized healing training that occurred at Chapelstone Academy. Or that the North held Wythe Academy and the majority of the mines.

Naturally, most of the class's questions surrounded the western and eastern regions, as those were smaller, less affluent settlements.

"The eastern shore is dominated by small barrier islands and many shoals, which make large boat navigation nearly impossible," Viggo Wood had told the class.

"What do people even do for a living in the East?" A girl asked, her tone almost sneering.

My fists balled by my sides. Neither the eastern nor western regions were known for having large cities or bustling markets but, they were a splattering of business that locally run markets that supported its citizens. People like my father and me. Like Marjorie and Jemma. An entire subsect of people who were content to live life with less opulence.

It was sheer will and the grinding of my molars that kept my mouth shut when Viggo Wood replied, "Many in those areas do odds-and-ends jobs, living off the land or living minimally to survive."

It was such an oversimplification of the rich network of people who lived and thrived in the area that my heart physically hurt to hear it. We didn't just work to survive. We lived meaningful lives.

Luckily, I didn't have to suffer in the basics of the regions, or Viggo's demeaning comments, for long. Somewhere in the second week away from the challenge, battle studies began to show promise of adhering to its namesake.

While none of the battles were real, our instructor read out fictional scenarios about made-up kingdoms warring across Demetros. In some stories, the nations used terrain to their advantage to find optimal locations for battle that would be advantageous for their army, while others leveraged their control over roads to starve out opposing realms in a siege.

This way of teaching almost felt like Viggo was just narrating a series of mini-stories, and I loved to read. It allowed me to escape into fantastical scenarios that almost made me forget what was on the line or the dangers that lurked in the shadows.

At some point, we had been sorted into four groups, one for every region of the kingdom, where each team was tasked with battling the others in made-up scenarios in an attempt to gain control of the continent. Somehow, I relished the strategy required to complete the tasks, making it possible for me to ignore the other student's attitudes towards me.

With each newly invented plot and fresh pairings, we had to collectively determine how we would defend our region and also launch an attack against the others. Each quadrant of the island nation had its own strengths and weaknesses, and Viggo surprisingly did a decent job of giving us feedback in real time so that we could learn from our pitfalls and adapt.

It wasn't until the final pairing that I realized that our assigned region, ironically, the Eastern quadrant, was in the last round of the game. We won easily due to my intimate knowledge of the streams and rivers that cut across the east, giving us a vantage point the Southern quadrant did not anticipate.

"Congratulations, Miss Blake. It seems that you have led yet another team to victory." Viggo stated his compliment in a way that was so opposite from Mr. Higgins that I hoped that some of my classmates would take pity on me and quit staring at me like I was a blight on the picturesque lives they had imagined for themselves.

That, of course, did not happen. But at least my own group offered me muttered thanks as we departed the class that evening.

The problem was that everything I feared was coming to fruition. My accomplishments within the classroom were garnering more and more negative attention, and it wasn't like I could simply stop performing well, or I wouldn't be considered for the Select Guard.

It made me constantly on edge as I wondered when the ire would shift from petty glares to something more dangerous.

My stomach was in knots as I walked to the practice field the following day. We were well within the second week of October, and hand-to-hand combat had shifted away from self-defense and straight into fighting.

Cade, for his part, had remained perfectly professional since our encounter in the library with Miss Bella, but he hadn't asked me to aid him with demonstrations since. Although I understood completely, the removal of our time together stung all the same. He had been a source of something positive in my life, and after the first challenge, I was sorely lacking in good things.

Regardless, the logical part of me agreed with his choice. Neither of us wanted to be expelled or suspended from the academy. I, of all people, needed to keep my wits about me, and that was something that had been becoming increasingly difficult in his presence.

So, my nerves had nothing to do with seeing Cade as much as having to deal with another day of Berit's senseless taunts. Threats that I wasn't sure were entirely benign.

I gave the redhead a wide berth, standing opposite the group from him as Cade showed us the next set of moves we needed to practice with a partner.

He looked good today. The same navy pants and grey top seemed to fit him even better somehow. Maybe it was because the grey shirt was sleeved now, because of the transition into autumn, and the sleeves were rolled up to show off the black ink of his Ignus brand.

Cade walked over to another group to help them get into their stances as I watched, distracted to the point that I didn't realize that I had been approached.

Startling at my sudden proximity to another body, I flinched backwards, looking up to find Berit's toothy grin.

His soulless black eyes were pinned to mine. "I think it's about time we go at it, eh?"

My pulse picked up as I considered yet another taunt, but I had been taught that sometimes you have to face a bully head-on. Not all conflicts could be resolved by talking, and I was sick and tired of evading his words and ducking from everyone's stares. "Let's do it," I agreed.

A hand clasped around my arm. "You don't have to do this." It was Ryana, and I knew that she meant well, but I was done hiding from my problems. At least this one, I could do something about.

Squaring my shoulders, I lifted my chin in his direction. "I'd be happy to hand your ass to you," I goaded, knowing full well I was playing with fire. It just felt so good to let out some of the tension roiling within me.

His tongue darted out to wet his lips as he approached me, getting close enough that I could smell the bacon on his breath from breakfast. "I love it when you talk back. It will just make the reward so much sweeter."

My palms made contact with his chest as I shoved him away from me, holding the fear back in my voice with sheer willpower alone. "Get in your stance," I demanded. Crouching into position, I focused all my attention squarely on Berit, letting the rest of the world fade to nothing around me.

We circled each other for a moment, neither appearing inclined to make the first move, and after what felt like minutes, I realized I would have to be the one to strike. With a quick surge, I lunged at him, and he evaded, spinning out in the opposite direction. It was then that I noticed a slight limp on his left side that could be advantageous.

Several of my follow-up movements were only to test my theory, and when I confirmed that he was favoring his left ankle, I made my move. Launching myself at him, pretending to go one way and then changing it up at the last position, forced him to put his weight on his injured side to counter me. At the very last second, I dropped to the ground, swinging my leg wide and letting my heel make sharp contact with the left ankle.

He cried out as he fell to the ground with a loud thud, a small dust cloud forming around him as he crumpled in the dirt.

Inching closer, I glanced down at him as if he were nothing, and this time, I let my emotions flood my features, making sure he saw the disgust there. "You can leave me—"

The sentence hadn't even fully left my mouth before his hand gripped around my ankle, yanking me to the ground beside him. Pain radiated across my skull as it made sharp contact with the dirt.

Berit was over me in an instant. Pinning me against the gravel that pierced through the thin academy top. I didn't need to look behind me to know that I'd find blood seeping through the fabric.

Instinct took over as I twisted from his grasp, knocking his arms out of the way and shifting our position once more until I was straddling him. There was no moment when I considered I was defending myself or even registered the voices around me. My fists collided with the delicate bones of his face as I channeled every ounce of fear and rage I had felt since I stepped foot on this campus into Berit's face.

The crunch of bone cracked like a whip in the air. Either his nose or my knuckles, I didn't care. My fists wailed on him in a steady rhythm until firm hands gripped my shoulders and pulled me away.

My eyes remained trained on the redhead on the ground, my lips twitching as I noted the blood pouring from his face, splattered across his shirt in an almost artful display. His nose was bent to the side, and I couldn't bring myself to feel anything but satisfaction at the sight.

"That's enough," Cade said sharply. When I wheeled around on him, his focus was on Berit and not me.

The Irontail captain stood, spitting a wad of blood into the upturned soil at his feet. He wiped the back of his hand against his mouth, only serving to smear a crimson streak from his busted lip to the hinge of his jaw, making him look like some sort of deranged character from a horror novel.

"You'll regret that," he seethed, but his focus slipped between Cade and me with equal fervor. He stomped off the practice field in the direction of the school, never once looking back.

"Everyone's dismissed," Cade called. "Take your free afternoon to work on those stances."

Cade's fingers tightened around my arm as I began to pull away and join the crowd retreating from the fields.

"Not you."

Although his voice wasn't inherently aggressive, I froze in place while the rest of the students emptied from the field.

Twenty-Nine

"What were you thinking?" Cade asked, searching my face for some answer that I knew he couldn't even begin to understand.

He released me, but he didn't step away from my position. We were alone on the practice field, and in a bizarre moment of overwhelming weakness, I relinquished a sliver of the truth that I had intended to keep to myself.

"He found me in my session, and I think he was trying to sabotage me, but I outran him." My chest sank with my admission, along with my gaze, which fell to the gravel by my boots. "Ever since, he's just been more and more aggressive, and I thought if I showed him that he couldn't intimidate me, he would leave me alone."

The silence between us grew taught. Enough so that I raised my focus back to Cade's face. His expression was that of confusion, his brows drawn together, nearly connecting in the center of his forehead. When he finally spoke, his words were breathy. "He wasn't in your session."

My pointer finger jabbed in the general vicinity of where I had seen him. "He was out there. I saw him."

Cade sawed in a breath. "Come, sit with me." He motioned to a nearby bench as he guided me with his hand at the small of my back. The feel of his touch on me for the first time in weeks sent a shiver racing across my limbs.

We sat on the worn boards, washed nearly gray by the elements, our knees almost touching in the space between us.

His eyes shone more violet than usual as he took me in. "I thought you were the one who had died in challenge one."

The confession surprised me. I recalled the look of panic as his eyes swept the dining hall the next morning, even the hint of relief that washed over him as he found me, but I had forgotten all about the notion in the wake of everything else. Especially considering we had barely spoken outside of sessions.

My fingernails picked at the skin along my thumb as I waited for him to continue.

"They wouldn't tell us anything about her. Most of the House Leaders didn't even find out details until Trenton announced them to the entire student body."

A crease of discomfort formed between my eyebrows. "I saw her," I whispered. "Right after."

Cade's palm came to rest on my knee. "That must have been horrible. I'm so sorry."

A breath whooshed from my lips, one I hadn't even realized was being held captive in my lungs. The relief at finally opening up cracked something within my chest, and before I could stop them, I felt warm tears gliding down my cheeks. There was no room for shame amongst the other heavy emotions weighing down my chest.

Cade looked to me with determination in his eyes, his jaw set tight. "I want you to stay away from Berit." The shift in topic back to the current Irontail captain was enough to startle me, but the magnitude of the seriousness that blanketed his face told me this wasn't some jealous outburst.

With the sleeve of my shirt, I wiped away the salty stream from my face. "I'll try, but he's certainly been making that impossible."

The hand on my leg squeezed tightly, not a flickering pulse but a firm grip. "I'll do everything I can to help."

He leaned slightly against the back of the bench, almost forward, as he took in my appearance again, undeterred by my display of emotion but concerned all the same. "Besides that, is everything okay? How have you been?"

A laugh bubbled from my chest. "I was beginning to think you didn't care," I admitted somewhat harshly.

Cade's jaw clenched, but he didn't back away from me or make to leave. "It's not fair to you, but after Miss Bella caught us…" His gaze fell to his hand on my knee before he glanced over his shoulder to ensure we were alone. From this far away from the main buildings, it would be impossible to know that he was touching me, but I supposed I couldn't blame him for wanting to be cautious.

"I understand," I clipped, "you don't want to lose your position over a misunderstanding." I hadn't intended for my words to come out so icily, but it seemed that some of my hurt was bleeding through regardless. Truly, I didn't blame him, but it did sting a little that he had pulled back from our friendship.

A defeated breath filtered through Cade's pursed lips, and I shifted my attention from his mouth back to his eyes. "Ashton, I want you to know it's more than my position here. My family…" He dispensed another sigh. "They are serious about image, and I can't do anything to embarrass them."

For all that we had in common, this was one thing I simply couldn't understand. He had spoken randomly about his family and their fishing empire, had even touched on the fact that they had been strict in his youth—only allowing him to play with other kids of equal social standing—but this was more than he had divulged about his current predicament with them.

My hand came to rest in my lap, itching to grab his instead. "What would happen if you embarrassed them?" The odd way Miss Bella had phrased her mention of his father returned to the forefront of my mind.

Cade's grip tightened on my leg, and for a heartbeat, I wondered if he'd answer me until I heard him clear his throat again in preparation for his response. "I have two older brothers and two younger ones, but my father has high expectations of us all. We are each expected to work on the fleets that we will one day take over. I was only allowed to stay here because being asked to return as a house leader at Biltons was considered to be a high honor for them."

"For them?" My brows pinched. "You aren't allowed to take whatever job you want? You're grown!"

He shook his head, his brunette strands forming a half curtain over his eyes as he dipped his chin. "No. My life is pretty much planned out for me. This was a detour, one they would pull me from in an instant if they thought I was tarnishing their good name. If Miss Bella had told them..."

"You would have lost your position even if the academy never found out?" I offered, finishing his statement for him.

The nod he gave me was almost sheepish, like he was embarrassed.

"I get it," I replied, even if I couldn't fathom my father acting in the same way. "It's just odd because they're treating you like some heir to a throne rather than a business. Couldn't you choose something more for yourself?"

His expression was solemn, but I gathered that he had considered this option before. "They do see it as the inheritance of an empire, and they have treated me as such my entire life. It's the whole reason I never considered dating. No one ever lived up to their standards of wealth or power."

"But your career?" I added, pushing past the whole dating thing with a slight hint of color staining my cheeks. "Isn't that the whole reason we were doing demonstrations in the first place? So you could come back next year as a permanent instructor?"

Cade released his hold on my leg to run his hand through his hair, pushing it back from his face. "It's my hope that if I were offered a position, they'd let me take it, but it's not that simple. They'd disown me if I went against their wishes, and even if their rules are a bit much, they're my family. They're all I have."

Frowning, I let my gaze fall to my own hand, resting limply in my lap where I had left it. I was struggling to understand his decision, even if it made a little more sense that his real fear came from the worry that he would lose his family. That I could empathize with.

Cade's hand slid along my leg again, coming to rest over mine. "It doesn't mean I want to stop doing our demonstration work. I—I look forward to those afternoons more than you could ever know."

It was everything I could do not to beam at those words, so I continued to stare at the hand in my lap. This was the first time I had an inkling that he felt the same way about our friendship, or whatever it was, that I did.

"We just have to be more careful. Cut back on the hours. Especially if you're already getting such negative attention over winning challenge one."

My eyes lifted to his, and there was a twinkle of something there that had been missing while we spoke of his family. "Congratulations, by the way. That's a great accomplishment."

Disappointment must have filtered across my features because Cade twisted his hand around to intertwine our fingers together. His grip pulsed, sending a shockwave to my heart. "I don't want to stop spending time with you, though. Even if it's selfish."

The breath left my lungs as if Berit had landed a hit to my chest. "You want to keep doing demonstrations?" His words needed clarification, but that was as close as I could come to asking outright.

He nodded slowly. "Yes."

"Why?"

His head tilted as he lanced me with a pointed look. "It might be a quiet rebellion, but there's something about being with you that makes me feel like myself. You make me want to be braver and do something for myself."

I snorted a laugh. "Like secretly apply for an instructor position at a highly prestigious academy to really stick it to your parents?"

Cade's smile was delighted, if not a bit sheepish. "Like continue to work towards those goals while spending time with a girl who pushes me to be a better person."

My cheeks heated at his comment, but I kept eye contact. "What changed?" I was elated, but I couldn't help but remember how we had barely spoken the last few weeks after being caught almost kissing.

The movement of his shrug was sluggish as he raised his free hand to the back of his neck. "I don't know. Before, you didn't know why I would be standoffish, and now it feels like I'm not hiding this shameful secret from you."

"But we'd still be meeting in secret?"

His nod was borderline non-committal. "I mean, yeah. We'd still need to meet somewhere private." I thought he was going to leave it at that, but the muscle in his jaw worked, and he opened his mouth again to speak. "I'm trying to tell you that I'd like to get to know you more. Then maybe, after graduation, we can..." This time, he did leave his words unspoken.

Graduation was so far away, but there was a level of relief flooding my veins. I couldn't afford to do anything to be kicked out of the academy either, knowing full well that would definitely keep me from upholding my end of the deal with the sponsor. Cade was telling me he wanted me; he just needed us to be careful about it until there would be no repercussions from the academy or his family.

Then, my heart swelled at the thought that he believed in me well enough to think I would make the Select Guard. With my parents' inherited power levels and a job that was both prestigious and paid well, I might meet the requirements they had set forth for his romantic inter-ests. And that meant he was likely considering me for something more than friendship.

Much to my surprise and immense regret, Cade released my hand, and before I could sink into the letdown, he leaned in with his whole body, letting his arm rest along my shoulder. The fingers that had once been laced with mine squeezed along the edge of my upper bicep, pulling me against his body. "Thank you for being someone that I can talk to. It's been a while since I've just been able to complain about my family stuff." He sniffed another halfhearted laugh. "Most people don't get it."

Maybe I couldn't relate completely, but I did want to ensure that I was there for him the way he had been there for me. It was his tip that had pushed me to first place in the challenge, and regardless of what became of us, I'd be forever grateful. "I'm here whenever you want to talk." My head tilted back so I could glance at him beneath my lashes.

His chin dipped further as he looked down at me, and for the briefest, stupid moment, I thought he might kiss me. Our breaths mingled in the space between us, and my pulse fluttered wildly in my throat, caught between my desire for myself in this sliver of time and my want for my future. But it wasn't just me who would suffer the consequences of this if it went sour. Cade would lose something too.

So, instead of pressing my lips to his, I dropped my head to his shoulder and pushed my body against him in a way that I hoped communicated my adoration when I couldn't count on my mouth to relay the words. Not because I didn't trust him with my heart but because neither of us could afford to open that door. Not until May.

After what felt like hours but might have been mere minutes, Cade cleared his throat. "You should probably get back to the academy before people start looking for you. They're on edge since Sylvia."

Reluctantly, I peeled my face away from his warmth, extracting my limbs from his, unable to look at him for a single second for fear I might just plop back down and say to hell with it all.

"Good point," I said, promptly standing from the bench and brushing off invisible gravel from my pants. "See you next session."

"See you around," Cade clipped. I could sense he wanted to say more, too, but if I let the moment swell any further, I wouldn't be leaving this field.

"Bye," I called over my shoulder as I pushed forward to the academy, making a beeline for the dormitories.

Thirty

With a sniff under my armpits and the resulting grimace that ensued, I made a detour to head to the bathing chamber rather than go directly to my suite. It was fine with me because standing beneath that spray of water put me into a box of nothingness that could probably do me some good in the wake of Cade's almost admission of his feelings for me.

I was still reeling from the conversation—half giddy, and half nervous at the prospect of us being an us one day—when I gripped the handle of the bathroom door and ripped it open, immediately hearing soft gasping noises coming from somewhere in the tiled space. The echoes made it difficult to pinpoint exactly where they originated.

"Hello?" I called out, my voice reverberating against the damp tiles.

A sharp staccato inhale pulled my attention to the right as my head snapped in that direction. Steam still billowed around me, but I got the distinct impression we were alone, as no other noises filtered through the heated fog. "Are you okay?"

My boots splashed in some of the standing water on the floor as I padded down the line of shower stalls, checking under each for any sign of a person.

Another escaped sniffle narrowed down my search radius as I

approached the row of toilet compartments. Sure enough, two boot-clad feet were visible under the gap between the door and the floor of the furthest stall.

My palm rested gently on the wooden boards, my lips nearly grazing the material as I whispered. "You don't have to talk. I just want to make sure you are okay."

When no answer came, I rapped my knuckles lightly against the planks, intending only to get some confirmation that whoever was on the other side was fine, but the motion popped the door open.

Something told me that it wasn't deliberate, at least not on the woman's part, because two widened blue eyes stared back at me, puffy and red from crying. Based on that sight alone, I should have backed out immediately and relinquished the stall to her, but my gaze snagged on her haggard appearance.

Her face was covered in slight scratches, and the beginnings of bruises dotted her neck. More disturbingly, though, her clothes had been torn and were caked in a fine layer of mud. Her tunic had been ripped down the front, her pale hand clutching the flaps together, shielding her body from my gaze.

Shock took over my ability to regulate my expression. "What happened?" The words catapulted from my mouth, and I cringed at the accidental insensitivity of my tone.

She hiccupped in a breath, pulling my focus back to her face, where I noticed that her brown hair had been matted against her cheek with something that resembled blood.

Holding out a palm, I lowered my voice to a suitable tone that was purposefully less abrasive. "I'm sorry, that was a bit too direct of me. I'm Ashton. What is your name?"

"Ellie," she whispered, her voice cracking with the effort.

I didn't think that offering her a smile was appropriate, even if it was just to soothe her nerves, so I kept my features as plain as possible. "Hi, Ellie. I just want to make sure everything is alright with you before I leave. Are you okay?"

She seemed to somewhat keep her composure until my question, the last syllable releasing the floodgates of her emotions. Frantic sobs escaped her lips, and she crumpled forward, folding in on herself, her body heaving.

The overwhelming need to help her surged within me. "Can I get someone for you?" A friend would certainly be better company than me, but the question seemed to intensify her crying.

Her voice was shaky, and the words only managed to come out in fits between her gasps. "He... out of... I didn't... couldn't..." Another wail tore through her mouth, and she covered her face with her hands. Beneath her fingernails was a thick layer of dirt, but the skin on her hands was covered in something crimson and crusty. There was no need to speculate what the substance was. The unmistakable scent of iron filled my nose.

"I think we should take you to the healer's unit," I suggested as calmly as I could muster. Whatever had happened had been traumatizing enough, from both a mental and physical perspective, and I was not equipped to aid her with either.

Ellie shook through another gut-wrenching cry. "Okay." She seemed to have to force the words out.

This time, I held my hand out between us for her to take. She flinched from it but still took the offer, sliding her bloody palm against mine. As she stood, I noted that she was probably about an inch shorter than me at full height, which she only maintained for a second before she wobbled.

"I'd like to help you walk if that's okay?" I gestured towards her, indicating where I'd need to put my hand. It was obvious that touching her was triggering in some way.

She nodded, and I looped my arm under hers, letting her rest her weight against me as we emerged from the bathing chamber. My singular focus was on the fact that I needed to get her somewhere where someone—anyone—could help her. For her sake, I was grateful we seemed to be treading down empty hallways, evading the lingering stares and whispers I knew would come if anyone caught us.

When we reached the infirmary, my knuckles beat against the door of the healer's office, much in the same way Headmaster Dracorris' gavel banged against the instructor's wooden table at the start of an important announcement.

The healer opened the door, irritation spanning the entirety of her face until she caught sight of Ellie's appearance. She hastily ushered us into the room, which contained several chairs, a bench for examinations, and a shelf full of medical texts.

I released Ellie to crumple into a vacant seat, where she started to sob.

The healer looked to her, concern flooding her features where irritation had just been. "What happened, dear?"

"It was so dark... I..." Ellie dissolved into a puddle of fresh tears again, and it was clear that she wouldn't be saying much else for a while.

My weight shifted between my feet as I fidgeted with the fabric of my now bloodied shirt. "Well, I found her like this, Miss..."

The healer's attention snapped to mine. "You don't know her?"

A wave of embarrassment colored my cheeks as I noted her reprimanding tone. I didn't think I had done anything wrong, but the stern look I received said otherwise. "She said her name was Ellie, but I hadn't met her before today." Regrettably, I had not prioritized getting to know my classmates once my victory during challenge one proved most of them to be my rivals.

"You need to leave," the woman clipped, practically shoving me to the door. "It is a privacy issue, you understand." It was not a question.

Sparing Ellie one last glance that she did not return, I pushed through the door. The healer practically propelled me across the threshold before slamming it behind me. Metal scraped against metal as the healer locked me out of the room.

Collecting a deep breath within my lungs, I pushed myself to leave her behind and head back to the bathing chamber to finally get that shower that I needed now more than ever. The judgmental stares I received in the now not-so-empty hallway told me I probably looked even worse than I suspected, considering all I could see was the mixture of blood and mud smeared across the front of my academy-issued shirt.

Between the sweat and dirt I had already accumulated fighting Berit, and now the blood stamped in the shape of crimson handprints, I was certainly a sight for sore eyes.

Ignoring everyone, I continued my trek down the hall, letting my mind drift to Ellie for a few minutes. This could not be passed off as an accidental attack in the way Sylvia's demise had been because whatever had happened to Ellie hadn't been during a competition. She had mentioned a boy to me, and that she had been attacked in the dark. It didn't take a genius to deduce that someone had purposefully gone after her.

My assumption was that now that the rankings for our class had been published after the completion of the first challenge, people were starting to take everything more seriously. But I couldn't recall enough about the list to know where Ellie might have fallen on it, especially considering I didn't know her name before today.

Making a mental note to check that when I got some free time, I slipped back into the bathing chamber and peeled my soiled clothing from my body, wondering if I would be better off just tossing the garments into the rubbish bin rather than the one designated for academy laundry.

The warm water fell over me like fat raindrops, and I let all the thoughts of competition and sabotage eddy from my mind while my fingertips rubbed lavender-scented shampoo in my hair.

When the suds were sufficiently washed, and my body was wrapped in a fluffy towel, I stepped from the shower stall, catching sight of my muddy boot prints from earlier when I had tried to find the source of the crying.

Not that I hadn't already come to the same conclusion before, but I was surer than ever that something was going on at this academy, and part of me wondered if it had more to do with the Queen's heir selection than a simple bout of rivalry between candidates. The misinformation about Sylvia's demise had come from the headmaster. Were they trying to cover the crime up?

The sentiment was only solidified when Ellie never showed back up in the dining hall or in classes, and her absence was never acknowledged, and I didn't know enough about her or her friends to find them to ask what had happened. For all intents and purposes, she simply disappeared.

Thirty-One

Typically, I found a way to brace myself for this, but I had been so preoccupied with my courses, avoiding Berit Murdock and keeping a watchful eye on those around me, that my least favorite day of the year had somehow come upon me without my dutiful awareness. It was my birthday again, and although twenty-one brought with it a multitude of promising possibilities, I never relished wading through the emotions of the day.

Jemma knew I was not one to celebrate the occasion, but she loved birthdays, so she always commemorated the passing of October 19th without directly acknowledging it. Some years, it was as simple as a knitted scarf showing up on my bed or a homemade cake appearing wordlessly in my kitchen. This year, her gesture had materialized as a plate overflowing with chocolate croissants resting inconspicuously on our breakfast table in the dining hall.

As I approached my designated chair, I narrowed my eyes at Jemma, who was already seated and actively avoiding my attention. She did a horrible impression of feigning ignorance when our gazes finally met.

With a jerk, I pointed to the plate piled high with flaky deliciousness. "What are those?"

Jemma regarded them as if she had never seen them in her life, false surprise twisting her features. "Oh," she gasped. "They appear to be croissants. Of the chocolate variety."

My disbelief hummed from my pursed lips.

Connally slid into the chair next to Jemma, reaching excitedly toward the plate of pastries. "Oh, are these from that bakery in town? What is the occasion?"

Almost involuntarily, I flinched against her words. Not that I could fault her for asking about them. She had no way to know the significance of the day or the gesture. It was unlikely, given her nonchalance, that Jemma had warned her.

Jemma quickly swatted her hand away from the mound with a quick slap.

Connally pulled her arm back in surprise. "Ouch," she snapped. "What was that for?"

Jemma raised her chin unapologetically. "Those are for Ashton. She may share as she sees fit."

Confusion marred Connally's beautiful features, pinching her brow. "What, is it your birthday or something?"

It was such a harmless and altogether normal question to ask, but I still recoiled at the words. It was my day of birth and also my mother's day of death. One was synonymous with the other, and I hated it.

"Yes," I said flatly. "You can have a pastry."

Connally's face lit up. "Oh, well, why didn't you say so? Happy Birthday!" She practically sang the words as she successfully grabbed a pastry from the top of the pile and shoved it into her mouth before Jemma could stop her.

My eyes contracted in Jemma's direction once again.

Jemma's features turned aloof. "What? I didn't get these for... this day," she explained. "Dante just happened to be making a run into town, and he surprised me with them. And I chose to gift them to you since they are your favorite. No other reason. Swear." Jemma's palm pressed against her sternum.

A slow, deliberate exhale flowed from my nose. My head tilted in astonishment. "He just happened to go into town this morning and retrieve my favorite pastries? On this day?"

Jemma's tone betrayed only a hint of her delight. "As a matter of fact, yes. You can choose to believe me and eat the pastries or not believe me and sulk about it while your stomach growls."

As if on cue, my stomach released a garbling noise. To top it off, my mouth had been watering since I sat down and took in the aroma of butter and chocolate. "Fine." The words strained through gritted teeth, although they held no bite.

Ryana, who had taken her seat sometime during all the commotion, turned her body to face me. "May I have one of these... nonspecial day pastries, please?" Her voice conveyed caution.

I nodded, and we both reached for the pile at the same time, grabbing at different pastries without making eye contact again.

Unlike Connally, Ryana knew enough to recognize that I didn't want to celebrate the day. Still, I had never fully explained how far my discomfort went, how little I wanted it to be acknowledged. It was difficult for me to articulate my feelings to someone who did not bear the burden of grief associated with a day that should otherwise be joyful. A cloud hanging over a picnic, when all anyone else could see was the sun shining vibrantly above.

"Woah, are these from Mayte's?" I heard Cade asking as he approached our table from behind my back. We had only managed to meet in secret once since his declaration of almost feelings for me, and the sudden, unexpected sound of his voice surprised me. Slowly, I twisted towards him, my mouth, unfortunately, stuffed full of pastry as I met his sapphire stare.

My muffled response came out as an undecipherable noise around the flaky dough.

Cade's warm chuckle reverberated across my skin as he reached his thumb up to gently wipe a crumb from the edge of my cheek. It was enough physical contact to elicit a series of goosebumps across my chest and arms and a twisting of unease in my gut.

We had touched before, obviously, in our hand-to-hand combat demonstration practice. He had recently held my hand. We had even almost kissed. But none of that had felt as exposed to everyone else as his thumb brushing softly against my face.

His hand was gone in the blink of an eye as if maybe he registered that as well, and my palm wrapped around the nearest glass, tugging it to my lips and drinking half of its contents to wash down the bite before I recognized it as Ryana's. I had opted for orange juice, and my mouth puckered as the unexpected flavor of cranberries assaulted my senses.

Fighting off the grimace and ignoring Ryana's low chuckle beside me, I straightened in my chair, fully facing Cade. "You can have one if you like."

Cade's mouth twisted into a fierce grin. "These are my favorite!" He plucked a croissant from the plate, instantly taking an enormous bite. His eyes fluttered closed for several moments as if he was savoring the flavors as he chewed.

My vision snagged on his mouth, and I felt the sharp stab of an elbow in my ribs. I blinked through the haze to respond. "Mine too," I added lamely.

He grinned. "Must be for something really special if someone woke up early enough to get them."

Thankfully, Jemma interrupted before I was forced to explain it was *my* birthday. "Dante just made a run into town and grabbed them for me."

A smirk crept up Cade's face. "Dante must really like you then because he is not an early riser."

"He always rises early when I'm around," Jemma deadpanned before her lips twisted into an incorrigible grin.

The entire table, including Cade, groaned at her comment.

Cade shook his head. "I don't even know what to say to that."

"Nothing," I replied quickly. "It only encourages her."

"Thanks for the croissant then," he said to Jemma just before tossing the last bit into his mouth. "I'll see you guys later."

He paused just as he started to walk away, doubled back, then leaned low with his lips just out of reach from my earlobe, whispering so that only I could hear. "Happy birthday, Ashton." Then he left, this time without turning around again.

"So, you're not going to even tell *him* it's your birthday?" Connally asked.

My lashes blinked furiously as I pulled myself from the daze his words had caused. "My mother died on my birthday from complications of childbirth. It feels wrong to celebrate."

"Well shit, Ashton." Connally bit out. "I didn't know." She glared at Jemma. "You could have warned me."

The remorse in her tone came off as genuine, even if she didn't actually apologize, and I wasn't in the habit of blaming people for curiosity when I knew that I was the anomaly here, dreading a day that everyone else used as an excuse to jubilate.

Forcing a smile on my face, I let my gaze meet hers. "It's fine. You didn't know." I pulled away from the table, grabbing the last croissant on my way to my first session, albeit way too early. "See you at dinner," I called out as I left the dining hall.

It was Jemma's voice that followed me. "Bye! Have a great day!"

The others remained silent, and I was oddly grateful for that.

If I could have chosen, I would have lain in bed all day—possibly feigning a mysterious illness—but we were too close to the next challenge for me to miss out on any pertinent information that might apply to our task.

The last several months had seen me prove my merit, and by all accounts, I was confident that I was in the running for the Select Guard. All I had to do was maintain my trajectory.

With my goal so close to my reach and my studies going as well as they could be, I couldn't fathom a scenario where I wasn't inducted. I almost let myself feel solace in that thought, imagining a world where my father was healed of his ailment, and I was honoring my mother by serving the crown.

My father's letters continued to leave out direct communication around his failing health, but I didn't need him to spell it out. He just had to hold on for a few more months, and the minute that I got access to those healers and my new Select Guard salary, I was sending him all the best treatments my money could buy.

Lost in my own thoughts, I practically barreled into a chest, and for the briefest of moments, I let myself think it might be Cade waiting to speak to me in private.

"Oh, I'm sorry—" I started to say as my shoulders were grabbed and my body was thrown into an alcove, my back scraping against the rough stone walls. The action caused me to drop my croissant, which alone would have irritated me, but the violence of the movement had me on high alert.

A quick glance at a mop of red hair and the splattering of freckles over the bridge of his nose like blood across snow caught my breath in my throat.

"Get off of me," I seethed, raising my voice in an alarmingly futile attempt to alert anyone in the halls to my distress.

Berit's breath was hot and rancid on my face as he leaned in. "Finally, alone," he purred. "Don't act like this isn't exactly what you wanted for your birthday."

My eyes widened in both fear for my current predicament and shock that he somehow knew what day it was. I schooled my features into smug indifference. *Never reveal your weaknesses.* It's what Cade had said in our combat lessons, and it was exactly how I had been able to take Berit down in our own fight.

My voice only gave away an inkling of my anguish with the slightest tremble. "I'd rather gouge my eyes out with a dull spoon than share any of my personal space with you, Berit. But thanks for the offer." Using both of my hands, I shoved him away from me and into the open hall, quickly inserting myself into the free space before he could trap me again.

Just as I had begun to storm away with clenched fists, Berit's words struck like lightning. "You should leave."

Jerking around, I whirled to face him, fists balled by my sides. "Just leave me alone, and you won't have to worry about me being in your presence."

His eyes darkened with a sinister shadow. "Maybe you misunderstood. You need to leave this academy. You don't belong here, and everyone knows it."

Bile climbed up my throat, and I swallowed roughly to keep it down. His words played on my insecurities, and I wondered if many other students truly felt this way. I didn't hail from a wealthy, prestigious family, and I was forced to come to a reckoning that the glares I had received over the success of my win might be about more than just my first-place ranking.

"I'm not leaving," I growled. "I earned my place here and on that ranking board." My expression remained neutral even as my blood roared in my veins. Stopping only long enough to pick up my ruined croissant, I hastily made my way from the alcove and Berit's hateful glare. Since I refused to turn around, I couldn't be certain he was watching me, but my skin pricked underneath his presumed stare as I bolted down the halls, his laugh following me like a predator chasing prey.

Thirty-Two

Time slipped by me like a stream, swelling with nerves and determination, carrying me to the morning of the second challenge. It was fully autumn now. Apart from the pines, the leaves of the trees surrounding the academy had already started shifting from the vibrant green of a lush summer to the dying oranges and reds of a flame.

The air was crisp and cool against my skin, and I pulled the material of my scarf closer to my face as I crossed the courtyard to the chapel-like building where I was set to meet my house. The little lynx patch at the bottom of the knitted garment fluttered with the wind as I picked up the pace. It had been a gift from Katarina for our house winning the first challenge, and it warmed me to her a little more.

My thoughts lingered on my house leader as I recalled the way she had informed us of the changes to the next challenge. In years past, this event was performed alone, just as the first challenge had been. Considering the accident that had befallen Syliva Lemmons, the academy had modified the second task to sort us into small groups. Each group would be assigned a chaperone, one of our instructors or qualified staff, to travel with us on our journey, although they could not aid us in any way.

Then, we would be sent to various parts of the kingdom and forced to use the skills we had learned up until now in our courses to find our way back to the academy and survive several days—or more, depending on the challenges that we encountered—living off the land until our return.

My grip tightened along the straps of my bag as I approached the chapel where we were set to meet Katarina to get our group assignments. Just like for the sessions in the first task, this had been put off until the morning of the second challenge.

I pushed open the ornate doorway that led to the main chamber of the building, sighing my relief as my eyes caught with Ryana's and then dropped to her hands curled around two steaming cups of coffee. She passed me the cup with a smile, and we slipped into our seats along the third row of pews, nestling our bags at our feet.

The location of the chapel away from the other buildings made it so I rarely passed by it. Certainly, we had never been asked to meet within its walls, so it was only in this moment that I was able to fully appreciate the beauty of the structure.

Floor-to-ceiling stained-glass windows lined the entire room, all but one showing various scenes rather than people like the ones mounted at the entrance to the main building.

The closest one showed the moon, a sparkling crescent in an inky sapphire sky, while another illustrated a gorgeous sunrise with reds and yellows rippling over a stunning azure sea.

The next depicted an unfurling storm, the pane littered with iridescent bolts of lightning. Besides that, another had various types of animals dispersed between an array of flowers, intricately made with minuscule shards of glass.

The final pane depicted a young woman with flowing crimson hair and a halo of light around her crown, as if it were a tiara gifted by the heavens. In her arms, she cradled a swollen and obviously pregnant belly.

It was likely an ode to Merè, this time taking the form of a mother to symbolize the fertility she bestowed upon the lands, but it was evident that this place hadn't been used as a chapel to honor her in some time. Whatever connection she had to the other glass-hewn illustrations had likely been lost in one of the many tomes that had been rendered to ash with the fires that had claimed the majority of Demetros' history.

Katarina cleared her throat loudly, drawing my attention away from the red-haired deity and to my house leader. Grethe slid into the space beside Ryana just as Katarina began her speech. "Good morning, House Lynx." Her words held very minuscule levels of enthusiasm, per usual. "We have little time, so I'm going to make this quick. I will call out the group number, the chaperone, then the names from this group associated with that assignment. As soon as you hear your name, head to the gates to board your carriage."

Her focus shifted to a clipboard balancing along her forearm, and without further fuss, she began reading, projecting her voice to an almost yell.

Students began to stand and exit the chapel as she went, until there were only a handful of bodies still lingering with me in the room. Ryana and Grethe had already been dismissed, offering quick farewells and wishes of good luck.

When Katarina got to group thirteen, with Dante Wolfe as the chaperone, I was relieved to hear my name called alongside Ingrid's. We hadn't spoken extensively since that first day, but she had not given me the same glares as the rest of the students, which made sense considering she was one of the few in attendance who didn't long to sit on the throne.

I shouldered my bag as I stood and moved to wait for Ingrid in the aisle so that we could walk together to the front gates to find our carriage.

"Are you ready?" I asked her lamely.

Ingrid offered me a shy smile in return. "Kind of ready to get this over with, but yeah, I think I'm well prepared."

There was nothing much to say to that, so I nodded towards the door to prompt our movement. We passed through the wrought-iron gates, held wide open for the first time since we were welcomed onto the academy grounds. Hooves stomped the cobblestones as the student's nervous energy permeated to the animals connected to the transports.

A team of four horses was attached to each large windowless carriage, meant to take the groups to their destinations. Of course, we wouldn't be allowed to see outside during the journey, a tactic meant to force us to utilize our learned skills as opposed to memorizing the route back through visual cues picked up along the drive.

We made our way to the assigned carriage, and I smiled weakly at Dante as I approached him. Ingrid boarded without much more acknowledgment.

"Hey, Ashton, welcome to the coolest group around!" Dante said, and I wished that his joy was contagious. "Jemma made me promise not to let anything happen to you, so don't worry. I'll be your protector." He said the words with a wink, and my face fell at the realization that my best friend was not assigned to my group as I had hoped would be the case when I found out her boyfriend—or fuck buddy, at least—was my chaperone.

The House Irontail leader gestured to the carriage. "Go ahead and load in. We are just waiting on a couple more, and then we can go."

"Thanks," I muttered, trying to sound more hopeful than glum. Positive that I had failed in that endeavor, I resigned myself to climbing into the riding compartment rather than trying to convince him—or myself—that I was okay.

My eyes scanned the crudely cut benches, searching for familiar faces or an empty seat. Ingrid had chosen a spot further in the back and was already laughing and chatting with another student, so I plopped into the closest available bench, dropping my bag to my feet between my knees. A few more students loaded in, but they avoided the bench next to me, and I didn't mind. I was still struggling with viewing everyone around me as a potential enemy.

The lingering scent of horse manure wafted in through the open door, churning my stomach with its addition to the near-stagnant air within the compartment. I had just convinced myself to stand when another person slipped into the opening. A slash of red hair had me gripping the wooden bench.

Berit's onyx eyes slid to mine with that same predatory glare he seemed to always wear in my presence these days. While I had assumed that putting him in his place in hand-to-hand combat would get him off my back, I had been wildly mistaken. If anything, his taunts had gotten worse, and that said nothing about his threat when he had found me alone on my birthday.

He licked his lips, wiping a smirk along the corner of his mouth. "Hey, Ashton," he cooed, standing above me, blocking my exit. "It's so great that you ended up in my group. What good fortune."

My heart was beating frantically in my throat, my pulse erratic like a caged animal. For days, I'd be trapped with him in the woods. Calling it a survival challenge was now ironic in a way that turned my blood to ice in my veins.

Dante stepped into the carriage, the door closing swiftly behind him. "Move Murdock." He shoved past Berit to slip into the open space on my bench.

Berit sneered. "I was going to take that seat."

Dante hunched his shoulders. "But you didn't. Better find another one before we start moving. I'd hate for you to get hurt."

The two men stared at each other for far longer than was comfortable, but after a few tense heartbeats, Berit begrudgingly took his place at the bench across from ours. I could feel his gaze sliding across my skin, and I gritted my teeth together, staring straight ahead at nothing as the carriage lurched forward.

"Don't let him get to you," Dante whispered. "It gives him power."

It took concentrated effort to hold back my scoff because it certainly wasn't that simple. Berit clearly had power that was derived from more than just my reactions to him. It was almost as if he had orchestrated being assigned to my group, and that alarmed me more than his idle threats.

Swallowing down a fresh wave of panic, I forced my attention to the mountain of a man beside me. Because of Jemma, I knew a lot about him—a lot of the things I wished I didn't know about his preferences behind closed doors—but I thought this would be a good opportunity to get to know the person my oldest friend spent most of her time with. It had the added bonus of acting as a distraction. "So, you are with my best friend?" I whispered the words, careful not to say anything too loudly or name her specifically in case anyone was listening.

A smile split Dante's face, teeth glowing white inside the dark frame of his beard. "She's incredible."

He was gushing, and I laughed despite myself because Dante Wolfe was easily six foot six, as wide as two regular men, and instead of trying to be intimidating, he was doting over a girl.

"She is the best," I agreed with him.

He sighed, but not the exhale of irritation, the dreamy release of breath that someone usually makes when they are reminiscing on something lovely. "She's just so fun. But she's kind. And she makes me laugh. It's never a dull moment with her, you know?"

I almost felt sorry for him because I knew she was careless with hearts, even more so if she had any inclination that someone was getting too attached to her. In all the time I had known her, she had never considered herself in love with any of her conquests. In fact, she had been more apt to leave them faster if they had portrayed any evidence of the taboo emotion.

Once, a boy from our year of basic education courses at the local school told her he loved the color of her eyes. She never spoke to him again. When he saw her in public, she pretended like she didn't know him.

Perhaps more enthusiastically than necessary, I nodded as Dante continued his monologue about how breathtaking she was, and we spent the rest of the day sharing our favorite stories of my favorite girl.

Hours later, when the carriage jerked to a stop and the doors finally opened, a brittle breeze caressed my skin. A quick glance at the evergreen forest encompassing our drop-off point confirmed my suspicions that we had been taken to the northern region, although I couldn't pinpoint exactly where we had been dropped. Yet.

Gripping the edges of my thick wool coat, I pulled it tighter around my body, eyeing the sun as I stepped from the carriage. Given my best estimate of time through the rays breaching the needled branches of the trees surrounding us, it was midafternoon. We'd need to prioritize building fires when we set up camp if it was this cool before nightfall.

Dante waited patiently for us to exit the carriage and gather our bearings before he addressed the group. "Rules are a little different this year, so listen up. We will travel back to the academy as a group, so no running off and trying to get back first. You will be disqualified if you show up alone."

He let that statement settle amongst the crowd before continuing. "I will not aid you unless it is a life-or-death situation, and neither can anyone else. That means if we run across a settlement, you cannot ask anyone there for aid either. Any questions?"

Scanning the cluster of students, I noted a few of my new teammates doing the same. A look of bewilderment flashed in more than a couple of the returned stares, but no one raised a hand.

Dante knocked twice on the edge of the carriage, and within seconds, it was pulling away from us, leaving us alone in the woods.

Ingrid came to stand beside me, nervously digging through her bag. She produced a small compass. "I know how to use this," she offered the group, but no one made a move to direct the team.

Giving Dante one more look and confirming that he would not play a role in leading us, I spoke up. "Then lead the way." Despite being generally loathed within the walls of the academy, everyone seemed to agree. Or at least, no one outwardly protested.

Ingrid gathered her bearings, adjusting herself to face the southern direction. "Now what?" she whispered.

Raising my voice so that everyone could hear, I said, "I think we should walk south for a few hours or until we see anything that can orient us to our exact location. We should forage along the way and make camp before dark."

Much to my surprise, I was met with more than a few nods of agreement. A satisfied smile spread across my lips. It wasn't exactly an innovative plan, but I was grateful that—outside of Berit, who was lurking along the edges of the group—I might have been assigned to the one team that would not ignore me simply because I had won the first challenge.

Lowering my voice to speak only to Ingrid, I said, "Okay then, tell us which way to go."

We walked forty minutes or so before the tree-lined path began winding into unusual rocky crags. Instead of gradually sloping hills that transformed into mountains, these cliffs were just sheer ledges that appeared to burst straight up from the ground. The ridges themselves stood almost as tall as the Elemental Queen's castle, made from a similar shade of gray stone.

"These are the cliffs of Alamance," a boy I thought belonged to House Irontail said to someone behind me, but loud enough for us all to hear.

"Correct, Jared, good work," Dante noted with a thumbs up to the boy.

We had learned about the Cliffs of Alamance during our lessons on the northern region. They were unusual for many reasons, the most obvious being that their given location in the kingdom made the possibility of them being created naturally very low.

The cliffs had been around since before recorded history of the kingdom—or at least what remained of it—and none of the intact tomes mentioned any wielder, or a group of wielders, that had taken credit for its erection. In the same vein, none of the Saxum gifts worked on the rocky walls. All attempts to alter the rock face in any way had only ever resulted in a few stones crumbling from its edges.

It wasn't just the mysterious formation that set the hair on the back of my neck upright. The air itself was different here. Dense with something I couldn't put my finger on and yet empty at the same time, as if the oxygen that lingered here was magically pumped full of loneliness and despair.

My instincts were screaming at me to run in the opposite direction or find another way back to the academy on my own, but I shoved those thoughts down and joined the group trudging forward.

Ingrid paused, reorienting herself with her compass. "By my calculations, we are approximately fifty clicks to the academy, give or take the specific path we end up on inside the cliffs."

My nose scrunched. "How long will it take us to go through the cliffs?" My focus returned to the rocky walls themselves. I was more than a little apprehensive about the daylight we had left, and I did not want to spend any more time in this place than we had to.

Ingrid placed her compass back into her pocket. "Maybe another forty-five minutes. They're not that big."

Deciding I could live with that, I nodded. We were still several hours from dusk, so there was no need to worry. No one else seemed as disturbed by the rock formations as I was, and there was really no benefit in going around them for such a quick jaunt through them.

So, we entered the cliffs.

Thirty-Three

It had been two hours since we began our *forty-five-minute* trip through the Cliffs of Alamance, and we were rapidly losing the light of day behind the sheer rocky cliffside surrounding us. On top of that, foraging had become impossible.

If I didn't know any better, I would conclude that everything that made life possible avoided the maze of rock-lined ridges and sharp, confusing turns. Other than the short, gnarled trees at the peaks, no vegetation grew anywhere else around the cliffs. It seemed as if the area was void of wildlife as well, like the animals all collectively agreed to circumvent this spot, or something kept them away. So far, we had only seen signs of a few skittering bugs and a hawk flying overhead, off in the distance.

The cliffside was staggering, and I could only visualize four to five feet in any direction before the path curved and another ridge rose. After recognizing the same bend that hosted a nearly square-shaped rock—that I had spied several times by this point—I finally suggested that we pause our journey until the following morning.

Ingrid frowned, eyes blazing up at the evening sky. "Maybe with a fresh mind, we can figure this out tomorrow."

Given the eeriness of our surroundings, I doubted I'd be able to get any significant rest, but if we couldn't find our way in the daylight, I had reservations about continuing our journey in the darkness.

"Let's make camp," she called to the group, to the chorus of several groans.

The landmark we were trapped within wasn't only unusual for its unexplainable origins but also for the numerous waterfalls that poured from its peaks into skinny, winding waterways. I pointed roughly in the western direction. "There is a stream that way." Although some faces that turned to me were skeptical, the entire group followed my lead as I weaved through the rocky walls.

The thing about the falls was that they seemed to sprout from nowhere. In my limited knowledge of magic, I knew it would take a powerful wielder from the Flumen class to create a never-ending water-fall without a natural water source. Only the strongest amongst the class could conjure the liquid. Not only that, but continuing to fuel the magic without being in close proximity would be nearly impossible.

The site continued to baffle scholars, as the only way this would be achievable was if a group of wielders managed the magic required to upkeep the falls. Considering that the power died with the wielder, it would mean that someone was continuing to add their magic to the construct to take the place of those who passed. Even if that were feasi-ble, no one had ever been witnessed tending to the cliffs in such a way. Adding to the mysteries of Demetros.

Just as I had recalled, a glen opened up around the next corner, home to a trickling freshwater stream. I instantaneously spied a conve-nient spot to set up my dwellings for the night—towards the edge of the clearing where I would be less open to attack—and I split off from the group to claim it.

Tucking my tarp against the rocky ledge, I tied the other side down to the ground to lay my pallet within. I double-checked my remaining supplies, then abandoned my pack to retreat from my shelter to join the others. Just as I backed out of the opening, I came face to face with another person.

Obsidian eyes roamed my body, and when they reached my wide-eyed stare, Berit spoke in a whisper. "I hope you know I pulled a lot of strings to be here with you tonight." He lobbed me with a wolfish grin, but there was nothing pleasant about it.

Acid churned in my gut, but I forced my features into neutrality, trying to heed Dante's warning and not provide any entertainment through my expression of these complex emotions. "That was unnecessary. I can manage the challenge on my own." The words were pushed through the clenched-jawed smile that I tried and failed to soften.

Berit raised and lowered his shoulders in a slow, drawn-out fashion. "I'm here to ensure that you don't find a way to make first place this round."

My mouth popped open as I blinked away my surprise. "What is your problem with me? I don't even want to be named heir, so just leave me alone."

He clucked his tongue, the gesture holding none of the amusement I typically associated with the sound. "Nothing is going to get in the way of my goals. I can't fail, and you are the thing standing in my way."

"I have no interest in ruling a kingdom," I replied. Despite my best efforts, my voice was beginning to tremble. My eyes flickered around to see if anyone else was close enough to witness our exchange. I wasn't naïve enough to think that anyone would come to save me, though. For all they could tell, and because of Berit's body blocking me from view, we were just having a normal conversation.

My focus slid back to the predator in front of me, and I squared my shoulders, chin raised in his direction, a subtle warning for him to back off.

It only stoked the embers of his amusement. "One way or another, you're going to leave this academy before you have a chance to steal my spot."

His body leaned into mine; his chin dipped as if he was going in for a kiss.

My revulsion crested like a wave, ripping away all thoughts of just avoiding him from my mind. "Over my dead body, Berit," I ground out through gritted teeth, taking a long step backwards out of instinct, causing my spine to press into the stone ridge behind me.

He winked. "If you insist." Without another word, he turned away and headed back towards the small group gathered by a fledgling fire. Instinct and experience told me that was not the end of his pursuit.

The hair along my entire body was standing on end, and I wanted to scream or run back to the academy and say to hell with working with my team for this challenge. But the threat of disqualification held me back. The sight of my father lying in bed in his weakened state blazed in my memories, followed by the image of me in that emerald uniform, waltzing into the healer's building to pay for his cure.

When my focus came back, Ingrid was standing in front of me, wearing a tight-lipped smile. "He's such a creep," she said, shaking her head and glaring over her shoulder in Berit's direction. "I heard he's been harassing people all over campus, but no one will speak up for fear of ruining their chances of being named heir."

A scoff tore from my throat. "Does he even have that kind of power?"

The grimace on her face told me all I needed to know. "A few people have already left the academy to get away from him."

The image of Ellie's bloody hands popped into my mind, but I shoved it away quickly. No amount of threats was going to make me leave my one chance at saving my father. "Let him come for me. I showed him how easily I could put him on his ass in hand-to-hand, and I'll do it again out here if I have to." There was a steely determination to my voice that masked the anxiety broiling beneath the surface, a sort of dreadful anticipation that kept my heartbeat thrumming in a rapid rhythm.

Ingrid gave me a knowing smile. "I have no interest in making it to the Heir Trial either, but people are weird about this once-in-a-lifetime opportunity."

A hum sounded from the back of my throat. Weird was one way to categorize the behaviors of the students around us. "You might be the only other person I know here who doesn't care about the title besides my friend Jemma."

She shrugged as she tossed her pack to the ground with a dusty thud. "All I want is to get back to my dads with some sort of magic that can help them with their business."

The confession endeared me to her in so many ways. "What do they do?" It was surprising that a student of Biltons had no aspirations outside of returning home. Even before my desire to gain access to the royal healers, I had wanted to be inducted into the Select Guard, knowing it would separate me from my father.

"They sell tea," Ingrid admitted as she dropped into a crouch, pulling at the ties along her pack. "Do you care if I set up my tent next to yours? Maybe we can keep each other safe?"

Despite my earlier attempts at feeling brave, relief washed over me at her request. "Yes, thank you, I owe you."

Her lips twitched around the corner, not quite curling upward. "We must look out for each other. *Ad Maius Bonum* and all that."

A humorless snort clawed its way through my nose.

Without another word, Ingrid began setting up her shelter a few feet away from mine, all topics of home and parents lost to the rustling of her tarp and my own thoughts on missing that cottage along the coastline.

My eyes cautiously drifted over in the direction of Berit. He was sitting by the fire, body angled towards mine. Flames danced against his expression as if molten steel was pouring down his face, making him look even more menacing than when he was spewing his threats. With pursed lips, he blew a kiss into the air in my direction, and I quickly averted my gaze back to Ingrid's efforts.

When Ingrid was finished, we moved to the fireside to capture the last bit of warmth and go over any final changes to our strategy before we called it a night. I gave Berit a wide berth as I picked my place along a fallen tree that another student had dragged over to provide us with seating. The conversation was short, and with nothing to eat, the group quickly agreed to prioritize our hunt for food the moment we could leave behind the cliffs at the first morning's light.

As soon as the plan of action had been determined, Ingrid and I walked back to our shelters together, silently scanning the surrounding area for any sign of Berit. When it was clear that he wasn't biding his time in the shadows to attack, we parted ways and said goodnight.

I settled into my bedroll and listened for rustling for what felt like hours. The typical night sounds of chirping bugs were disturbingly absent. The air was so still I could hear all the commotion from the nearby campers.

Canvas tarps readjusted as the sound of whispers swirled in the air, but I didn't perceive any evidence of footsteps nearing my tent. I stayed awake like that, mentally scanning my surroundings for any warning that Berit was going to make a move until my body succumbed to exhaustion, and my world faded into blackness.

Sleep had claimed me for what felt like moments when a series of high-pitched noises jolted me awake. A bright light lit up the tent as shadows danced along the tarp fabric, swaying with each new ear-piercing sound.

Rolling to a crouch and peeking out of the shelter, I halfway expected to find myself in the midst of a magical skirmish. But what I was met with instead was something else altogether. Something mesmerizing and lovely.

Stepping all the way out of the awning and into the clearing, I tilted my head upward to get a better view of this nighttime spectacular. From our positions within the cliffs, my perspective was partially obstructed, but within the sliver I could see, I witnessed the heavens being sliced apart with light. Enormous bolts of purple and blue lightning streaked across the sapphire sky, carving through the atmosphere like cracks in glass.

The movement followed a pattern, always striking in the same direction, even if the cadence appeared random. In its wake, plumes of colored clouds swirled in the space the bolts had left behind, shimmering as if they were full of stardust. The only way to describe it was a kaleidoscope version of a thunderstorm, the colors too vibrant to have been born from nature.

Prying my gaze from the horizon to sweep over my surroundings, I found that most of the other campers had left their shelters to witness this event. Ensuring that Berit was nowhere to be seen, I moved to a spot more central in the clearing to get a better view.

We weren't taught about it in basic education—probably because no one knew anything about it with any certainty—but I had heard about this phenomenon before. It was called *The Lux Scaporum*, and it only occurred in the northern part of Demetros. A memory flashed in my mind, my father telling me he wanted to take me to the Cliffs one day to view them.

Those who believed in a spirit realm were of the opinion that once a year, on the last night in October, the souls of the departed all migrated to the afterlife at the same time. According to this theory, the energy of the souls crossing the dimensions caused lightning-like light emissions to streak through the sky during the process. The plumes of pastel clouds were said to be proof of their souls finally departing this plane. I wasn't sure if I believed that this was the spirits of all the dead of the kingdom, but it was still breathtaking to witness.

Others believed it was simply a natural phenomenon occurring due to the energies in the air building up over time and finding release once per year. Although none of the scholars who considered this a fact knew exactly what caused the annual display. It seemed nothing about the Cliffs followed the laws of nature.

"I'm glad everyone woke up for this," Dante said from beside me. "I wasn't sure if I was allowed to tell you guys about it or not, but it's certainly not something to miss."

My head tilted to the side so that I could look at him. His face was illuminated by the flashing starlight, and his eyes were widened in amazement. It was the same look of awe he wore when he talked about Jemma.

"Do you think it's the souls of the departed?" I asked him, turning back to the sparkling view of the sky.

Out of the corner of my eye, I could just see his lips curling into a grin. "It is a nice sentiment, but I think it's probably something less romantic than that." He pointed to a flash of light. "I always joked that it was a birthday party. One of the Guides just comes out here and throws down. They're the only ones who can wield the natural magic, and this feels like it's tied to nature."

The sparkle in Dante's eyes gave me some pause as to how much of his statement was a joke, so I only offered a light laugh in response. The idea of the ancient Guides *throwing down* was amusing but highly unlikely.

His eyes shifted from the dazzling display to meet mine, framed by bushy, scrunched eyebrows. "Why? What do you think it is?"

My gaze lifted to the heavens as I considered his question and just replied, "I don't know, but it's the most wonderful thing I've ever seen." Next year, I'd finally bring my dad to see it.

Thirty-Four

With a few hours of sleep and the first glimmer of a new day, we rose, packed up our tarps and bedrolls, and began the process of exiting the Cliffs of Alamance. We marked our travels this time, a suggestion made by Ingrid, and with surprisingly very little fuss, found our way to an opening in the rocky walls that almost appeared to be a cave. We sent a volunteer into its depths to explore it as a possible way of egress, and before long, he returned in triumph.

The tunnel led down a short pathway that opened into another forest playing host to a mixture of pine and deciduous trees. The weight and unease that hung in the air inside the stone maze were lifted as soon as we emerged into the wooded area, although my freedom from the eerie landmark did not completely shed my trepidation as I caught glimpses of Berit lurking behind other students.

My attention remained on Ingrid rather than offering the cliffs a farewell glance, and I watched as she reoriented her body south. We walked in that direction, scoping out every inch of our surroundings for anything resembling food. Between my greatly reduced and choppy sleep and our lack of fruitful foraging the afternoon before, I was feeling weak.

Just when I had given up hope, I spotted a bush dotted with a few berries. The minuscule bounty didn't stop me from rushing over to it to harvest what I could, as if it were the only thing keeping me from death's door. The fruit was oval, bumpy, and boasted an unusual burgundy color across its flesh.

Dropping my pack to the ground and crouching to rustle through its contents, I retrieved my leather-bound notebook, flipping until I got to the pages I had designated for plants. It was against the rules to bring tomes from the library, but we hadn't been specifically prohibited from making our own drawings, and I had taken advantage of that loophole.

"What is it?" Ingrid asked from over my shoulder.

My finger rested on the crude drawing that most closely resembled the dwindling fruit weighing down the bush before me. "Aleesi berry." The color in my drawing was a bit more vibrant than what was before me, leading me to believe that they had likely surpassed their optimum ripeness. "It's probably going to be tart, but it is edible."

Gathering as many as I could carry in my small satchel, I urged the others around me to do the same. Even overripe fruit on our stomachs was better than nothing.

"I'm not eating those," Berit proclaimed. His body was propped against a tree, angled perfectly to watch me. "We will burn those berries off in an hour."

He pushed himself from the trunk and sauntered towards me. His voice dropped to a whisper when he reached me. "Unless you just want us to die of starvation out here?"

When he was only inches from my body, he pulled a blade from a holster along his belt, letting the clean metal gleam in the space between us.

It took everything inside of me not to flinch at his movements, but I held his gaze as he smirked. "Be back in a few," he declared before traipsing into the forest, his bow bobbing along his back. We were allowed to bring anything that fit into our packs other than food, and it seemed that Berit had only brought weapons with him.

He returned within ten minutes, much to everyone's surprise, with a decent-sized deer slung across his back, an arrow protruding from its heart. Berit wasn't in my survival or weapons class, so I hadn't been privy to just how skilled he was at hunting. Still, thanks to class, I knew enough about the habits of deer to know finding one roaming around mid-morning was quite the feat.

He threw the doe's body to the ground in front of me with a sickening squelch and began field-dressing her as if he were putting on the show specifically for my entertainment. Joy sparked in his stare as he sliced through the skin and sinew, and I couldn't bring myself to look away, more from horror than my fascination with what he was doing.

A few of the other students had spread out throughout the forest foraging for more fruit, so I was in eyesight of other people, but the comfort of that did nothing against the waves of unease that washed over me as I watched Berit wield the knife with expert precision. These were not the movements of someone who had only recently learned to prepare wild game.

His knife stabbed at the animal, and with a sudden jerk of his free hand, he violently removed the guts with one savage pull, throwing them against a nearby trunk. He took his time removing the skin, as if this was one of his favorite pastimes, glancing up at me every so often to ensure I was still watching him work.

As much as I wanted to rip my gaze from his ministrations, I was more afraid to take my eyes away from his location. Especially while he held that blade in his bloody grip. He continued hacking away at the animal with a grin on his face, like he could tell that I was watching him.

By the time he was done, a small crowd had gathered. Their features shared the same levels of horrified admiration at his skill.

"You can thank me for this later tonight," he said, seemingly addressing the group. I couldn't help but feel a knot forming in my stomach as his gaze landed on me. He made sure my eyes were on him as he slowly licked the blood and gore off his fingers, causing my stomach to lurch as acid rose to coat the back of my throat. Nausea and hunger cramped along my abdomen.

With some effort, I tore my stare from him and skimmed the tree line to find Ingrid. It was well past a reasonable time to move south again, and I wanted desperately to leave Berit Murdock behind me. His display and descent into more and more unhinged behavior had me genuinely worrying for my safety in his presence for the first time all semester.

Telling anyone about this seemed like a risk, considering the connections that he boasted about. That didn't mean that I wanted to spend another moment in the woods with him. I was far too vulnerable out here.

Prompted more by fear than any dream of taking leadership, I addressed the group. "It's time to head out!" When I was sure I had their attention, I added, "Snack on what you've gathered so far, and we will share the rest when we make it to camp."

Dante offered me a nod that had pride gleaming in his eyes, but I knew it was only because he didn't know my true intentions.

The rest of the group gathered, chewing on various berries from our small harvests, and when Berit finally joined the cluster with a hide full of the chunks of flesh he had pilfered from the animal, we began walking again.

We traveled for hours, stopping only to relieve ourselves behind trees or gather more bounty from the pockets of bushes in the forest that still had ripe berries. At one point, I discovered a small grove of God's Hand trees and dug up the pink fruit happily. There was enough for everyone to fill their packs. We had been lucky that the northern region had not yet experienced its first frost and that there was still something to harvest.

The plains in front of us stretched out for what appeared to be miles until they reached the tree line of another small forest ahead. The landscape between was shaped by gently rolling hills and streaked with winding creeks. Previously bright green grass was starting to succumb to fall, turning a golden amber in splotches over the ground.

The terrain made for slow progressions, and we had yet to find a sign of whatever route the carriages had taken to drop us off at the cliffs, which was presumably flatter. Due to the hills and streams, we were constantly having to take breaks to check the compass or deal with waterways.

Some streams were shallow enough to walk across if we removed our shoes and socks to avoid blisters, but this still took up valuable time undressing, drying, then redressing our feet after each junction. Occasionally, deeper sections forced us to walk along the water's edge until we found an acceptable location to traverse the expanse.

The tedious nature of our passage through the plains had taken much more time than any of us had anticipated. We had barely made it out of the breadth of land and to the shelter of the next cluster of deciduous trees before the sky was streaked with orange-tinted clouds, evidence that the sun was making its final descent.

Ingrid and I found each other, wordlessly setting up our tarps under the branches of the same massive tree. We still retained some privacy, but were close enough to each other to derive some comfort from the proximity.

Once inside my own shelter, I dropped my pack and disconnected my bedroll from its strap, patting it against the ground before returning my attention to the bag. I rummaged through its contents until I found dry clothing, swapping my shirt and socks before re-lacing my boots and heading out to the campfire that had already been started.

Berit was putting his strips of meat across a spit. A cloth, laid out over a makeshift platform someone had made, boasted the excess bounty that those of us willing to place there shared.

My portion of the Alessi berries and God's Hand fruit were added to the donation, and I picked through a few of the other piles to fill my cloth with a variety of the available fruits and root vegetables.

Finding a place to sit proved a simple task when Dante gestured to the open space on the log next to him. Probably too eagerly, I took the seat, glad to have yet another shield against Berit if it came to that.

"So," I prompted, "are you ready to pull your hair out with us yet?"

Dante huffed a laugh. "Actually, it's quite fascinating to see the challenge like this. I think it embodies the values of Demetros much more than the way we had done it before. Forcing everyone to work together makes more sense. I doubt they ever go back."

The tartness of the Aleesi berry I had chosen caused my mouth to pucker as I faced him. "What was your challenge like?"

Other than Farren, I wasn't close enough with anyone who went to Biltons Academy to ask them about their time here. Since my former boyfriend had ended things so callously and then practically disappeared, I never had the chance to discuss it with him either.

Dante grinned. "Oh, I killed a bear." He was practically beaming with pride.

My mouth dropped open. Just like that, I was reminded that despite the sappy way he spoke of Jemma, he certainly wasn't harmless. Dante had become a house leader for a reason, and it wasn't his kind smile.

My lips twisted into a surprised grin. "That was you? With the hatchet?" We had all heard the story—one of the few rumors circulating the female common room that actually had to do with the competition —but I had assumed it was partially fabricated. Embellished to give an ounce of lore to the Ice Games.

Dante lifted his chin high. "It was! I got third place in that challenge!" His eyes glazed over with the memory. I wished I could have witnessed it in person, if for no other reason than to see a different side of the man before me.

"Only third place?" I chuckled.

He shrugged in response. "Yeah, I mean, I didn't get back to the academy in the first wave. If I had, I would have been top of my class."

My head slanted. "I can't believe there were scores that outranked winning against a bear attack."

"Right?" His eyes widened, and his mouth curled with his mirth. "But I still ended up being invited back here, so it definitely counted for something."

I grinned, involuntarily letting images of a certain Wyvern House leader filter into my mind. "It's almost incomprehensible to think that in a year from now, one of us could be an instructor here. Like, how can nine months of training make us skilled or confident enough to take on a role like that?"

Dante lifted his brows, swallowing down his most recent blueberry. "Well, most of us have been trained in these areas our whole lives. We were raised to attend Biltons Academy, encouraged, or sometimes forced to forego our social lives for additional preparation..." His voice trailed off.

This seemed to be a shared experience. Nielsen had indicated the same thing. It made me wonder what their lives had been like before they got here. It seemed like a very heavy weight to carry around.

My voice lowered. "Yeah, Cade told me a little about that. It wasn't like that for me, but I prepared as best as I could." Flashes of images of my father helping train me with a wooden sword sprang into my mind, and I couldn't help but smile, even if the memory dredged up my longing to return to him. "Biltons had always been a dream for me, but not a sure thing."

With an outstretched palm, I offered him the last of my Aleesi berries, which he refused with a half-smile, half-grimace. "You seem to be doing alright here. Rumor is that you're top of your class."

A dry laugh rumbled from my chest as I shook my head. "Maybe, but I've definitely had help getting there."

Dante wrinkled his nose at something that resembled a carrot, waving his hand almost methodically over the vegetable as a small vortex of water washed off the dirt.

I laughed when his face turned surprised as he realized he had just committed an act of banned magic in front of a student, but he seemed to ignore that worry in favor of biting down on the pale orange root.

He crunched on the vegetable for a few seconds before his lips curled into a smile of his own. "Speaking of, how are things with Cade?"

It was one thing for me to mention something Cade said; it was another for Dante to specifically ask me how things were between us. Dante was clearly involved in his own illicit affair with a student, and I had gathered that the two of them were friends, but it didn't feel right to offer up anything that Cade hadn't already told him about us. Not that there was an us.

"I have been helping him with hand-to-hand combat demonstrations. He's a nice guy," I replied.

Dante's eyes danced in the glowing light of the fire, brimming with skepticism that was not entirely misplaced. "If you say so," he stated evenly, but the smirk had not left his lips. Dante's voice dropped to a whisper. "For what it's worth, he's different when it comes to you. He'd kill me for saying as much, but I think he likes you."

Even though his words set butterflies loose in my stomach, I snorted a laugh. "Well, as we are all aware that student and instructor relationships are prohibited..." I offered him a pointed stare. "I don't think that much matters."

He chuckled to himself, clearly not missing my insinuation. "Well, there's not that long to wait until it doesn't matter anymore."

My gaze lifted to his, eyes squinting as if that would help me figure out what he meant by that, considering it was quite some time until May. As my mouth popped open to ask for clarification, Berit launched himself into the free space on my other side.

"Hungry yet?" he cooed, dangling a piece of cooked venison over my head. "Open wide."

My lips pursed as my head jerked back. It was everything I could do to keep my voice stern rather than tense. "No thanks, Berit."

Just as I made a move to leave the log, Berit grabbed me by the wrist and slammed me back down. The force of my abrupt return against the tree bark caused my teeth to crash together.

Berit's face had lost some of the saccharine kindness he had been emulating. "No need to be rude. I was offering some of my bounty, as protein is better than fruit. *Ad Maius Bonum*, right?"

There was nothing good about Berit in my mind, so instead of acknowledging him, I attempted to stand, only to be yanked down for a second time.

My molars ground together. "Thank you for the offer, Berit. I'm just not hungry."

Another sinister smile floated my way. "What's the hurry, *sweetie*? I just got here."

Dante leaned over my lap, putting his face between mine and Berit's. "I think Ashton has had enough, Berit. Just let her go to bed."

Shadows passed over Berit's features, but he kept his face predominantly neutral. "Calm down, Dante. I was just trying to make friends like I was told. No one's keeping anyone against their will."

Berit's lips curled into an even more menacing smile. "Plus, aren't you supposed to not interfere? I'd hate for you to get the star of the challenge disqualified... wouldn't you?" His voice was thick with warning, and when Dante didn't immediately reply, I was left to assume the threat wasn't entirely idle.

Dante's jaw rolled beneath his skin, and his bushy eyebrows bunched together in the center of his forehead. I half expected to hear growling accompanying the expression, and while he didn't verbally respond, he didn't back down either, keeping his face wedged in the space between Berit and me.

Berit's onyx eyes flickered back to me, even though he spoke to Dante. "I personally wouldn't want to be responsible for sending her home." His words were alight with the lie he told, and I knew all too well that it was his singular goal to have me flee.

His gaze slid to my mouth, and his smile widened, showing too many teeth to be innocent. "Especially since you're determined to stay here. Aren't you?"

There was something so angry in his question that had me considering my options. I wasn't going to leave the academy, no matter how much he threatened me, but it seemed that my goading had only made him more erratic and confrontational.

With a palm pressed against each of their chests, I pushed them back with equal force. "As much as I'd love to see how this ends, I'm really tired. Goodnight."

Hoping my statement hadn't landed as a taunt while refusing to look back to see how it was perceived, I pressed forward into the darkness to find Ingrid.

Just like the night before, we walked back to our shelters together and chatted for just a moment before turning in for the night.

Once I was back beneath the cover of my tarp, I removed my boots and slipped beneath my blanket immediately. Hours went by as I listened intently to the sounds around me, ears trained to any sign of an impending approach beneath the chorus of critters.

Only when the exhaustion outweighed my dread did my eyes close of their own volition, and I was dragged beneath the dense fog of sleep.

Thirty-Five

A thunderous crash jolted me from my fitful sleep. My spine went ramrod straight as I shot up, resting my hands against my mat as I oriented myself to my location. My lungs stilled as I listened intently. Other than the crickets and the typical buzzing of a nighttime forest, there was no other sound that indicated that the noise had originated outside of the nightmares that so frequently plagued me these days.

A sigh fell from my lips as I dropped back to the bedroll. My eyes closed, but instead of drifting off, adrenaline held me captive. The breeze and the wild animals taking residence in the forest could easily explain every croaking shift of the tree branches, every crunch of leaves, but I couldn't convince my brain of that. After a long while trying to force myself back to sleep, my bladder notified me that it had other plans.

Huffing at my body's inopportune time to decide to have needs, I threw the thin blanket to the side. Since my socks were already on, I only had to dump my boots before I donned them in an attempt to quell the fear that spiders had made them into a home in the dark of the night. With numb fingers, I shrugged on my coat, fastening only a few of the buttons as I emerged from the relative warmth of my shelter.

My breath unfurled like smoke in the air as I crept away from the camp and further into the woods. By the time I found a suitable location, the embers from the dying fire were far enough away that I could only see a few outlines of the tarps behind me. When I was confident that the spot was private enough, I pulled down my leggings, crouched down, and relieved myself, cringing at the echoing sounds of the liquid splatter.

After what felt like an eternity, I stood, taking several waddle-like steps away from my puddle, and I tugged my waistband over my hips. I hadn't even made it a single step fully dressed when I was thrown to the ground by something slamming into my back. My tongue caught between my teeth with the force, and the tang of blood filled my mouth in a metallic coating.

One of my hands was stuck under my body, and the other barely caught my fall as I crashed against rock and bramble, sending a jolt of pain up the arm that had taken the brunt of the impact. Gravel and pine needles pierced the skin of my palm and face, already throbbing as I attempted to push myself upright.

What should have registered immediately, had I not been in a groggy state, was the fact that the *something* that had knocked into me, and the *something* currently weighing my body down, was a *somebody*. Panic and instinct took over the second the dots connected in my sleep-addled mind, and I began flailing.

My lips parted on a scream, but the air was caught in my throat by a rough hand clamping over my mouth, blocking any sound from escaping my lungs and limiting my ability to take full breaths. Heat from rancid breath brushed against my ear. "Be still," Berit commanded, as if that would somehow calm me.

Trashing against his hold, I tried and failed to roll out of his embrace.

He shoved my face harder against the ground, his free hand tracing a line against my arm as if to showcase his dominance over me. "You aren't so brave without the instructors around, are you?"

Out of the corner of my eye, I caught the sneer on his face as he glared down at me with contempt. "Answer me, bitch," he growled, and against my own will, my body began to tremble. I hated that he was seeing me like this, but there wasn't anything I could do to stop the reaction in such a vulnerable state.

Not that I had ever imagined this exact scenario, but I had heard of such things happening to girls in dark alleyways at night when they were caught unawares at the wrong place at the wrong time. I had been so sure that, in the same situation, I would have found the gumption to be fierce. That I would fight tooth and nail to overcome my assailant, kicking them in the balls as I stood over their defeated body.

It was horrifying how wrong I had been because I hadn't anticipated being frozen with shock or being thrown into a position that would strip me of every ounce of the upper hand from the start. This scenario had gifted that advantage to my assailant.

Not even my dad's or Cade's self-defense training could help me now. Pinned on my stomach with nowhere to gain leverage from. Every attempt to get free just resulted in Berit tightening his grip on me.

As if it was the only reflex I had left, tears spilled from my eyes, plopping into the dirt like fat raindrops. "What do you want from me?" I called, hating the sound of fear that soaked my every word.

His fingers drove into the tangle of my braid, wrenching my head backwards with a sharp pain along my scalp. "I asked you a question. You don't feel so tough without the protection of your instructors, do you?"

As much as I wanted to fight back against his words, all the gusto had left me. "No," I bit out, thinking if I could just placate him, he'd be contented.

I was wrong, though. There would be no mercy in reaction to my misery. In fact, my wretched cries appeared to only entice Berit as his hand skimmed over my ribcage, and I wondered with a horrifying realization if this attack was about to take another direction.

Berit leaned away from me for a moment, and I heard the sound of fabric ripping. Shame overcame me as the only reaction I seemed to be capable of mustering was to pinch my eyes shut so I wouldn't have to watch what he would do next.

His grip against my hair tightened once more, and he used the leverage of my scalp to yank me to my back, repositioning himself to straddle my hips with my arms pinned between his thighs. My lips parted on a scream, but nothing came out as he shoved fabric into my mouth. It coated my tongue in sweat and dirt and even the tangy hints of blood as it served its purpose to muffle my calls for help.

His obsidian gaze roamed over my body, and he shifted again to retrieve the knife from the holster along his belt. Its metal blade gleamed in the moonlight, still sporting crimson smears of what I hoped was the deer's blood.

My eyes widened in fear, and the sounds released from my throat died on the dirty fabric that dried my tongue.

The sight only brought a toothy grin to Berit's face. "Now, I believe after all the trouble you've caused me, I'm due a little fun."

My gut clenched at his words. I didn't want to give any of my mental energy into trying to imagine what he meant. Not when, after his display with the deer, it appeared his particular brand of entertainment seemed to involve knives.

The sharp point of the blade slid over my tunic in shapes that I couldn't even begin to name as he perused my chest for the best place to strike.

My gaze shifted to my surroundings, wondering if anyone had heard the noise of our scuffle or if my body was going to be left to the elements and discovered in the morning. More tears spilled like a river from the corners of my eyes as I realized that my father would be left alone in this world.

I began bucking my hips wildly, one last effort to throw the man on top of me, but he only smirked, and my own pulse thudded so loudly in my ears that it drowned out whatever depraved thing he said to me next.

White hot lightning lit up my cheek as his free palm slammed against my cheek, drawing another wave of blood-soaked saliva into my mouth. "Be still, you fucking cunt," he growled as he moved the knife to my throat.

My eyelids slammed shut as I braced myself for the pain of his attack. The point of his blade pressed against the vein in my neck, and I knew without a shadow of a doubt that I was about to die. But I wouldn't open my eyes to face the gleam in his stare as he did it. He would not get that bit of satisfaction from me willingly.

My mind escaped to my morbid, intrusive thoughts. Would he do it quickly, or would he draw it out in the relative privacy that the woods offered him?

The blade caressed my jawline, making a snaking motion to my chest, just above my heart. The pinch of the sharp edge pierced my skin and slid across it, tearing away clothing and skin in its wake. It drew a muffled cry from my lips again, even as I kept my eyes firmly shut.

Just as I was sure the blade would press into my muscle and tear apart my bones, Berit's weight lifted from my body.

My eyes blew open wide as I searched for where he had gone, finding two figures before me, both rolling with each other in the dirt.

Without Berit's body holding me still, I stood, ripping the disgusting fabric from my mouth and attempting to make sense of what I was witnessing.

Flames curled from the unnamed figure, dancing around Berit as he released a yelp of surprise. It was just enough to illuminate the face of the stranger, revealing that Cade had come to my aid.

I was frozen to the spot as I watched their scuffle, Berit wielding his blade maniacally as Cade fought with his prohibited flames.

Berit laughed like this was something funny to behold. "You're going to find yourself fired over that little stunt," he taunted, pointing the knife towards the fire hovering over Cade's palms with an arrogant jab. "But of course, you can't just fight me like a man."

Cade instantly withdrew the fire, and I lost sight of his expression as darkness blanketed the clearing once more. "A real man doesn't attack a woman in the woods," he growled before adding, "But I can take you without my element if that's what you prefer."

Berit didn't hesitate, launching himself at Cade, and I shrieked as I realized only one of them held a weapon in their hands. They collided with a grunt from each of them as they tumbled back to the ground in a heap, and one of them released a cry of pain.

As much as I wanted to run to Cade and make sure he was alright, I only fell to my knees, crying out for him as I watched on in horror as one of the shadowed figures shoved a limp body away from the pile.

I should have been on my feet, running as far away from the madness as I could, but I was immobilized by fear as I watched the triumphant person push themselves to a standing position and stalk towards me.

Relief flooded my veins as the flames returned to an outstretched palm, and I realized it was Cade who had made it out of the altercation. I glanced at Berit's form, finding that he still wasn't moving, and as I returned my stare to Cade, he looked utterly haunted.

"Are you okay?" he rasped, dropping down to my position to pull me into his arms.

"We have to run," I gasped. "He's trying to kill me."

Cade spared a glance over his shoulder, a frown tugging the corners of his mouth down. "He's..." His shoulders sagged. "He's dead. He can't hurt you anymore."

Everything eddied in my mind as I sank against the warmth of his chest, and a fresh sob tore from the confines of my throat. Cade's hands stroked my hair as he whispered encouragements and rocked me against his chest. "Shhh, it's okay, I'm here now. I'm here. I'm here."

My breath stuttered as I gasped for air between my hoarse cries, which echoed into the night. I made no attempts to stifle them, I just kept shuddering and breaking in the cocoon of his arms.

Thirty-Six

At some point, I must have fallen asleep with exhaustion because when my eyes cracked open again, the forest was a fraction brighter, bathed in the inky grey-blue of an early morning. A thick blanket, smelling faintly of cedarwood and honeysuckle, was draped around my shoulders, and my face was pressed against a warm chest, but I was not being held down by arms or hands.

My eyelids fluttered closed again as I slowly took in the day's sounds, trying to forget the horror of the previous night. As if I ever would.

"You've got to get back to your group, man," I heard Dante say in a hushed tone.

"I can't just leave her like this, Wolfe." Cade's response vibrated against my cheek.

"We have a dead student. I have to send off a flare and alert the academy. And your group doesn't even know what the signal means without someone to tell them," Dante countered.

Cade sighed with evident frustration, his breath blowing against my hair. "Then you go get them. You know our campsite is close. You can bring them to yours. It will make transport easier." His arms wrapped around me protectively, and I fought off the urge to buck his embrace.

"Okay," Dante agreed with some hesitation. "But you still have to head back to my group's camp and wait for the officials."

I could feel Cade shaking his head. "Deal."

The sound of footsteps crunching through the forest floor got quieter over time until they faded away to nothing. Still, I kept my eyes closed.

Fingers gently stroked my hair away from my face, and the touch was unexpectedly more than I could handle. Flinching against the graze of his hand, I opened my eyes abruptly to the view of Cade's features, marred with concern.

The disheartened emotion morphed into something closer to fear, or maybe regret. "I'm sorry, Ashton," he blurted as he quickly retracted his hand. "I wasn't thinking."

A forced smile curled the edges of my mouth. "It's fine. Thank you for..." I swallowed down the hard lump that had formed in my throat. "...For rescuing me last night." It sounded so lame in contrast to the reality of what he had actually done. Berit was dead.

His expression fell with his shoulders, his lips drooping into a frown, and he released me so that I could stand. "I'm so sorry I wasn't here sooner."

Pushing to my knees and dusting my clothes off as best I could, I brought myself to my feet with a wince of pain as I moved. My gaze fell to his as he righted himself. "You weren't supposed to be here at all. It's a miracle you even got to me." Tears burned in my eyelashes with the effort it took to hold them in place.

He released a half-hearted laugh as he raked his hand through his hair. "Actually, when Dante and I found out that we'd both be in one of the groups dropped in the north and that you were with him, I made him promise me he'd send a signal when you settled at camp so I could come to you."

My breath caught in my throat. "What? Why?"

"I planned to come earlier," he admitted, shaking his head and ignoring my second question. "But a couple of guys in the group wanted to stay up late telling ghost stories, so I was delayed."

The tears I had been so gallantly holding back slipped through my lashes. Not because he had wanted to talk to me—about gods knew what—but because his one rogue decision might have saved my life. I was just so... grateful.

Horror filled his expression as he reached for me again, dropping his hand before it made contact. "Ash, I'm so sorry."

"There's nothing... to be... sorry... for." I pushed my words through my sniffles and made a poor attempt at halting the floodgates of my tears, wiping the snot off my nose with the back of my sleeve. "You killed someone for me." My words were breathless. Not an accusation but a shocking realization.

Cade's jaw flexed, and he took a deep breath in through his nose. His eyes did not meet mine as he spoke softly. "It wasn't my intention," he breathed. "But you were not his first attack. The kingdom is better off without him."

My mind grappled with that statement. Who else had been attacked, and what did those attacks entail?

The truth hit me all at once. *Sylvia and Ellie,* I thought, answering my own questions as fear yet again clutched my chest at how close I might have come to death.

Cade remained silent as I composed myself enough to speak again, even if the words were hardly loud enough to hear. "Still... Thank you."

Cade frowned as he looked down at me, eyes stalling on my chest. Where I was sure there was a long gash, but was too afraid to confirm. "We have to head back soon, and before we do, we should talk about last night."

Every muscle in my body went rigid as if speaking about the events of the previous evening would somehow force me to relive them. I had come so close to death. So close to... whatever else Berit had planned for me prior to my demise. There wasn't a piece of me that was ready to think, much less speak, about any of it again. Not yet, although I knew I'd have to soon enough.

He shook his head as if sensing my thoughts. "Not about that. Although I am here if you want to." He paused, and I waited with bated breath for him to finish what he was saying so that I could focus on that rather than the heap of fabric in the distance that I was certain was Berit's body. Even though I knew he couldn't hurt me anymore, I had no interest in looking at him for another second.

My gaze slid back to Cade as he drew in a deep inhale. "I hate to even ask you, but can you not tell them I was trying to find you?" Shame glossed over the purple sheen in his eyes, shifting them back to a steely blue. "Or that I used my flames before he attacked me."

"You saved me," I muttered. "It's the least I can do."

He was visibly relieved by my compliance, even though the guilt seemed to linger. His voice lowered to a whisper. "Dante and I already discussed it. The story will be that we both heard the commotion and sought to find the source." A pained sort of expression overtook his features. "The rest is basically the truth. I got here first and saw Berit attacking you and tackled him off of you. A fight ensued, and he was stabbed by his own blade."

It was a good story and harbored just enough honesty to be easy to maintain if questioned about it later, so I nodded my agreement.

"And you," he said, his voice breathy now. "You asked me to stay with you because we are friends. I think that's innocent enough that it won't draw any suspicions."

My head inclined once. "It sounds like a believable story to me," I heard myself saying.

Cade dipped his chin, then took an incremental step towards me. It was everything I could do not to flinch at his movement, but I forced the voice in my brain to remind myself that I was safe with this man.

"Once we get back to that camp, I'm going to have to follow protocol to alert the academy of an incident, and then the students are going to be really confused. I can't just hold you until they get there."

"I know," I muttered, even if the truth of it all was disappointing. Even if it was also relieving.

He took one more step, not quite close enough to touch me, but with little enough distance between us that I could feel the heat radiating off him. "Before all of that, just know I really care about you. Ash, I was so worried about you when I walked up and saw him..." his jaw clenched with barely-contained fury, and I just watched him without speaking.

"If anything had happened to you, I would have never forgiven myself." The confession pulled my focus back to his eyes. There was a pleading there, but I couldn't discern why. "I didn't realize how much you meant to me until I saw you in danger." His voice was only a whisper, but it came out cracked and shaky, as if it had wounded him to say it, or maybe it just distressed him to know it.

His feelings for me were not entirely new, but the intensity of them was news to me, and apparently to him, judging by the look on his face.

I wasn't sure what to say to that. Obviously, I cared about him too and owed him a great deal now, but it didn't change our predicament.

"You literally came crashing into my life on that first day, and you've been surprising me ever since with your humor and your kindness and your skill in session." A little laugh escaped him as he shifted his hand to the back of his neck. "I think you almost broke my nose that first day."

Despite my emotional exhaustion, my lips twitched at the reminder.

His gaze locked back onto mine. "It's more than that. No one has ever listened to me like you. No one has ever valued my opinion on what I do with my life outside of the fish empire, and it feels so damn good to be seen."

By an almost incremental amount, I leaned toward him. Not enough to bring our bodies together, but enough for him to notice all the same. "It has been nice to be seen by you too."

I had confided things to Cade that I had only ever told Jemma and Ryana in part. Cade understood my motivations to join the guard, and while I hadn't given him the entire reason, he had heard my need to save my father and even aided me in making that dream a reality. Where Jemma rolled her eyes at my seriousness, and Ryana would one day be my competition, Cade felt like the only person here who would actually have my back and support me one hundred percent. The reality of that had me closing the distance between us and pressing my face to his chest again.

"Thank you," I mumbled against the warmth of his embrace.

A twig snapped in the distance before Cade could fully get his arms around me, and we separated again, each taking two long steps backwards.

A scan of the forest around us showed no approaching students, and a heavy sigh rippled from Cade's parted lips as he bowed his head. "I..." He started to say something else but trailed off. "I need to send up the flare."

I could tell that those were not the words he had hesitated on, but I let him go regardless, walking side by side as we returned to the tent.

"Do you want me to walk you to your shelter?" he asked as we approached the collection of tarps that still contained my sleeping group members.

"No," I breathed. "It's probably better if I emerge with the rest of them."

It appeared as if it bothered him to agree, but he did with the dip of his chin. "Then I'll give you a moment to get inside. This will be loud, and no one will be asleep when I'm done."

I didn't say goodbye as I strode from where he was standing, weaving around the embers of our campfire as I made my way to my tarp to pack up.

As I dipped below the tarp, wondering what the signal would be, a giant ball of flames whizzed into the air over the canopy of trees. It exploded into the sky like the fireworks I had once seen in Demetros as a child. Except, instead of being a thing of beauty, like that display, this felt ominous.

The sounds and the flames themselves seemed to carry the threat of endings. The fire roared as it entered the atmosphere, transforming into a deep black smoke that shifted into the shape of a wyvern, menacing and dark.

Thirty-Seven

Stepping from my tent and pretending like I wasn't somehow involved in whatever occurred to elicit the smoky wyvern above our heads failed miserably as Ingrid emerged from her own shelter, eyeing my attire with skepticism. Glancing down, I found my clothing streaked in mud and still somehow peppered with pine straw and debris from the forest floor. A red and angry scar streaked across my sternum, and all I could do was avert my gaze from Ingrid's, button up the neckline of my coat to cover the evidence, and nervously step forward to join the others gathered around our abandoned campfire.

Cade flicked his hand towards the dying ember and set it ablaze once more, but no one seemed to balk at his prohibited use of magic in front of them. Most of them hadn't even noticed, with their gazes still fixated on the sky.

"There's been an incident," Cade bellowed to the crowd, turning most of their attention back to him. "It is currently against protocol to discuss the events from last night, but just know that your group, as well as mine, will be returning to the academy."

A few students let loose groans of protest. "How is this going to impact our scores?" Someone asked from my right.

"If this impacts my chances at being heir..." another said, almost threateningly.

I shrank back, finding a place to sit along the fallen tree.

Cade held his hand out in a bid to quiet them. "The academy will issue an official statement when they can, and until then, all those questions will be wasted on me. Pack your things and wait for the carriage."

His tone held a clear dismissal, but as he lowered his hands at the conclusion of his statement, several people rushed to him to ask even more questions.

"What do you think that's about?" Ingrid asked as she took a seat next to me. She was impossibly observant, if our time in this challenge had been any indication, but I couldn't bring myself to say any of it. "I couldn't say," I shrugged, gut twisting with my subtle, almost lie.

Before receiving Biltons Academy's rejection for financial aid, I had never lied so much in my life. Sure, I had omitted the depth of my grief for my father's sake, but there had never been a need for me to keep so much from the people around me until then.

The difference with this was that it was a secret I was guarding solely for myself, even if I had the excuse of whatever protocol Cade had mentioned. Because I didn't want to relive those moments, and I couldn't stand the thought of Ingrid looking at me with pity. Pity was worse than the disdain that lined my classmates' faces once they learned I had gained a first-place ranking at the school.

Dante, leading the group that must have been Cade's, sauntered into our cluster of people, and all around us, students dropped their packs to the ground, looking just as bewildered as those they joined. Most of them lowered their voices into low whispers, partnering up with each other to offer nervous glances towards the house leaders, who were now having a quiet conversation of their own.

Dante spared me a quick glance before whispering something to Cade and clapping him on the back as he turned to face the largest cluster of students. "You guys are with me until the larger carriages come, so if you have food, now is a good time to bring it out and share. We might be here a while."

It was difficult for me to say how much time had passed as I sat numbly on that log. But, quicker than should have been possible, the first carriage arrived at our campsite. It was sleek, constructed from solid black iron, and so unlike the large rectangular boxes of the vehicles that took us here that I knew instantly it was not going to be our transport back to the academy.

It came to an abrupt stop, and the door creaked open, revealing the worried expression of Headmaster Dracorris, bundled beneath a calf-length, deep gray peacoat that almost matched his hair. His eyes scanned the faces of the students around him, falling to mine for a brief moment before instantly jumping to Cade. Probably knowing that it was his magic that had marked the sky so ominously.

"Mr. Hudson, I wasn't expecting to see you with this group." His tone wasn't overtly suspicious, but I thought I caught his eyes dart back to me once more before returning to the House Wyvern leader.

Still wearing his mask with expert precision, Cade approached the man and nodded. "There's been an incident with several students. It would be best if I debriefed you in private."

Understanding flashed over Mr. Dracorris' features. "Ah, yes. No need to discuss here."

Motion out of the corner of my eye caught my attention as another figure exited the carriage. If I had called our battle studies instructor ancient, then the man standing before me predated the histories of our kingdom.

Thin, almost see-through skin covered in sunspots appeared to be loosely attached to his body. His fingernails were long and yellowed. Wiry white hair fell to his waist, tied back in a leather strap. A mustache the same color cascaded into a beard, equally long as his hair.

In all honesty, he looked a little like the stereotypical wizards illustrated in my storybooks as a child. All the way down to the ankle-length burgundy robes he wore in place of traditional garb of the times. Even amongst the Demetros elite, whose clothing styles were flashier than the practical choices made by those who resided in the smaller villages, this man would have seemed out of place.

The Headmaster swept his hand in the direction of the elderly man before us. "Mr. Hudson, I'm sure you remember Claudius from last year's final games." Deducing that they must be referring to the third challenge, which was more combat-heavy, I watched their interaction with more interest.

Cade dipped his chin, low enough that it was nearly a bow, but did not try to shake the man's hand.

It all clicked into place then. The robed man was one of the Guides. In the past, they had never attended the other events, but they always had representation at the last challenge of the Ice Games because those were the skills they found most valuable in assessing the future cadets of the Select Guard.

The Headmaster had warned that they would have a greater presence in the Ice Games this year because of the scrutiny around choosing an heir, but I had seen no hint of them at the first challenge, effectively making me forget all about them during this task.

Viggo Wood had given some information on them during battle studies. There was one Guide assigned to each elemental class, tasked with transitioning the students in their respective group into their powers, or lack thereof, if they were Operarius.

Claudius was the Ignus guide, Elvynia the Saxum, Phebous the Flumen, Theondri the Caelum, and finally, Namea oversaw the branding of the Operarius. Physical descriptions had been limited, and the painted renditions of them that lined the hallways of the academy must have been made long ago because the man before me only held a slight resemblance to the Ignus Guide's portrait, whose name matched the one Headmaster Dracorris had used.

The Ignus Guide looked feeble even though he stood upright, silently assessing everyone around him.

"You honor us with your presence," Cade said with another slight bow.

I stood there awkwardly, unsure if I should bow too, even though I wasn't the one being introduced, and I wasn't exactly close enough to be considered in their conversation from my seat several feet away.

Claudius sliced his stare over the cluster of gathered students. Searching for something that was never revealed to him because he turned to the Headmaster, speaking only in a low tone. "We should speak to Mr. Hudson with haste."

Mr. Dracorris timidly nodded to Cade, who swung his attention to me. Something passed between us. An understanding? Silent words that contained so much but remained as mysterious as Demetros' history.

Cade's indigo gaze never left mine. "Miss Blake will need to be included in the debrief." All previous hints of his feelings towards me had been stripped from his stare, evaporated before I even had a chance to decipher them.

Claudius didn't seem to care who joined as long as he got his pertinent information and loaded himself back into the carriage without another word.

"Come along, Miss Blake," the headmaster called to me.

The sensation of everyone's stares prickled the hair along the back of my neck as I followed Cade and Mr. Dracorris to the open door of the transport and loaded inside without another glance towards any of them.

I slid into the open seat across from the Ignus Guide, and Cade plopped down beside me while the headmaster took the space next to Claudius. The door slammed shut by some invisible hand and briefly made me wonder if it was the Guide's natural magic. Regardless, I refused to bring my gaze to him. There was something unsettling about his presence that I couldn't place. Maybe it was just the night I had experienced and the fact that I was about to have to relive it.

We lurched forward, and my stomach sank as all three sets of eyes turned to me at once.

"Does trouble just follow you, Miss Blake, or are you incredibly unlucky?" The headmaster's statement wasn't inherently hurtful, but tears sprang to my eyes anyway.

"She was attacked," Cade stated flatly.

Claudius watched us through beady eyes, drawing in a shallow breath before he spoke. "Tell us everything."

Cade hadn't heard any of my portion of the story, so I was forced to recount everything that had happened to me, leaving out some of the finer details of my assault for my own sake because I didn't think that it mattered how he had touched me or the fact that I worried that it might go farther than just slicing up my skin.

"When I got to them, his blade was pressed into her chest. Over her heart," Cade interjected, and I was relieved to let him take the lead on the story. I tuned out most of his words, knowing how it ended from there, but the entire time Cade spoke, the Ignus Guide watched me instead. While I didn't have any reason to suspect that he knew me before this day, there was a spark of recognition there.

"Did the boy give any indication of his motives?" Claudius asked when Cade was done, his gaze honed onto my face.

My throat was dry as I went to speak. "He thought I was his competition for becoming heir."

Claudius cocked his head to the side, regarding me as one might a wild animal, assessing me for any subtle hint of emotion. "And were you his competition?"

Now didn't seem like the best time to state my disinterest in becoming heir, but I wasn't sure what else to say. "I've always longed to be considered for the Select Guard, and Berit was intent on becoming the heir. He saw my success as a hindrance to that and was trying to get me to leave."

"You should have reported this," Mr. Dracorris stated, hand suspended just over his heart as if he were truly shocked that the competition had turned deadly. Like he didn't know that Sylvia was killed or that Ellie had left without a trace. That other students had also abandoned their education to flee Berit's wrath.

"It was very fortunate that someone came to your aid," Claudius stated, this time letting his attention fall to Cade. There was something knowing in his gaze that had my heart lurching almost as violently as the carriage shook us over the unpaved pathways.

Cade was quick to shut down any of that, though. "It's incredible that he thought he could get away with it so close to two campsites."

The Ignus Guide ignored that remark in favor of sliding his gaze back to me. "Maybe you should get some rest. You've been through an ordeal, Miss Blake," Claudius said, and although his words were kind, I felt a swell of unease inside of me every time his eyes landed on any part of me.

I nodded all the same because I would have rather leaned against the tufted walls of the transport with my eyes shut for the entire ride home than talk to any of them anymore. The severity of what I had experienced, then been forced to relive through my recounting of it, was weighing heavily on my bones.

"Thank you," I mumbled, letting my head fall against the edge of the window and forcing my lids shut so that I could block out the Ignus Guide's knowing gaze.

Even though I didn't think I was capable of it, exhaustion consumed me and pulled me under her waves, and before I knew it, the interior of the carriage and the curious stares of the Guide faded away to nothing.

Thirty-Eight

When I awoke, a pair of indigo eyes was the first sight I saw, staring at me from the confines of a now-empty carriage.

"Hi," Cade said softly as my eyes darted to our surroundings. "Are you good to walk?"

My neck was sore from sleeping at such an odd angle, and my limbs screamed in protest as I stretched, but I didn't think that I was incapable of movement. "Yeah," I whispered as if there was anyone there to see us interacting like this.

"I told the headmaster I'd get you to the healers for an examination."

A grimace twisted my features, but I let Cade pull me up, only wincing slightly at the contact of his skin upon mine.

I barely registered him leading me down the empty hallways until we were at the door to the healer's office. The same one I had taken Ellie to all those weeks ago.

The woman who opened the door held no hint of recognition as she ushered me inside and kept Cade from following. She swiftly closed and bolted the door, effectively separating me from my only source of comfort.

This time, unlike with Ellie, I was grateful that he wouldn't bear witness to this humiliation. *Had she felt the same way?*

When prompted, I slid onto the examination table, letting my eyes scan the room as the healer readied a stack of papers.

The reflective oval hanging from the far wall in her office was the first time that I had seen a mirror in days, and I was not fully prepared for what was shown to me: a distorted version of myself. My hair looked like a rat's nest, with a few stray pine needles still embedded into the knotted strands. Deep purple smudges streaked beneath my puffy red eyes. Smears of dried blood, half wiped away, coated places on my face, staining my hair in patchy crimson clumps of matted sections.

My clothes were ripped in places I hadn't realized before now, and with a sudden wave of nausea, an image of Berit's cold, onyx eyes flashed in my mind. The way he looked at me and my body, like maybe...

My arms curled around my waist as I tried to bend into myself.

"I'm going to have to take a look at you. Is that okay?" The healer's words were soft and gentle. Nothing like the woman who had shooed me from Ellie's side. But I supposed this time, I was the victim.

The healer did her best to assess my injuries without touching me and, after asking permission, cleaned up the wounds that were visible over my clothes. She wiped salve against the cuts and bruises, finishing on my cracked and still bleeding lips.

Gods, there was no way that the students left behind in the woods didn't know that something had happened to me. It shouldn't have, but the thought filled me with shame.

"I think I've tended to most of your scrapes," the healer said gently. "Shall I continue the examination?" Her tone was so passive that I didn't immediately register what she meant.

She lowered her chin and her voice. "When girls have been assaulted like this, we generally need to make sure that they don't require additional medical attention."

As the realization dawned on me, a new wave of flashbacks crested my mind. "No," I forced out, shaking my head. "He didn't..." but I didn't finish my sentence. He hadn't raped me, but there was a very real chance that he would have. Regardless, he had taken something from me all the same.

"Very well," she replied in that same tone that bordered on whispering. She wrote something down on her sheet, then gave me instructions on a supplement I should take for pain and encouraged me to spend the next several days resting. She even gave me the location of the office of the academy mind healer and urged me to talk to him when I felt up to it.

I took the paper and numbly left the room, surprised to find Cade waiting for me when I emerged.

"Can I walk you back to your dorm?" he asked, and his expression was so overwhelmed with worry that I let him guide me down the mostly empty halls.

We reached the girls' dormitory, and he turned to face me. His voice was soft as he finally spoke. "If you need me, I'm one floor up on the main stairs, first hallway to the right, third door on the left." In all the times that we had met in secret, I had never seen his suite.

I looked up into his eyes once more, unsure how to articulate the emotions I was experiencing. How could I put into words what his saving my life made me feel? How could I also, in the next breath, ask him to back away from me to make me feel safer when he had done nothing wrong? With every flashback of Berit's hands on my skin and eyes roaming my body, the more uncomfortable I became with Cade's proximity, even though I knew in my heart that Cade wasn't a danger to me.

Thoughts and words swirled in my mind, but I settled for a meager, "Thank you for everything." When it felt insufficient and awkward, I added, "See you at breakfast?"

Cade's lips twisted into a tense smile, his eyes squinting as if he was warring with himself on whether he should stay with me or go. The latter eventually won out. "Of course, see you at breakfast, Ash. Goodnight."

I receded into the girls' dormitory before he changed his mind and thought to stay. It was such a disappointing contrast to how I might have wanted this moment to go a month ago. Even a week ago. But tonight, I couldn't risk him trying to comfort me with a hug. It just felt too intrusive, my body finding it impossible to distinguish between being attacked and being cherished.

On near-silent feet, I slipped down the hall into the bathing chambers, knowing I'd have some time in solitude before any of the girls returned. Each piece of removed clothing was tossed directly into the bin designated for trash before I entered the steamy stall.

Hot water poured over my face, and without moving, I let it run down my body and soak into my skin until my fingers pruned. Then I took the lavender bath soaps and poured gobs of it into my hands and across my chest and legs, careful to avoid the deepest of the cuts. The washcloth rubbed my skin red and raw, reopening a few of the wounds that had only just started to heal.

When I was sure I had either cleaned or removed every inch of skin that had come into contact with Berit, I started on my hair. The knots took some time to work out, but eventually, my fingers could run through my strands without getting stuck, and the water beneath me no longer flowed with blood, dirt, and debris. Repeating the same motions with the conditioner, my fingers finally released the last of the tangles.

My skin was blotchy with heat when I finally emerged from the stall, wrapping a towel around myself to hide the bruises and scrapes left behind by Berit's hands.

It was unlikely anyone else had returned to the academy, but the thought of someone bearing witness to the marks on my skin—the proof of my inability to defend myself—had my stomach clenching with worry. Would others see this as a sign of weakness? As an indication that they should attack me too?

Without even lingering in front of the mirror to further assess my own wounds, I quickly padded back to the quiet of Suite C, donning my nightdress in record speed before hoisting myself to my bunk.

My heart skipped a beat, and I froze at the sight before me. Sitting on top of my covers was a little plate with a chocolate croissant. A small, folded piece of paper had been placed beneath the dish. Opening it revealed elegant script across the page.

Dear Ashton,

I thought you might be hungry after such a long day. I can't wait to see you in the morning.

Yours,

Caden Artimus Hudson

Whatever tears I had held back until now cascaded slowly across my cheeks. He remembered my favorite pastry, and not only that, but he had gone into the town square to pick them up, meaning he had to have run all the way there and back, if for no other reason but to make me feel better.

My sniffle broke the silence as I clambered the rest of the way into my bed. Greedily, I consumed the croissant, outdone with gratitude for the man who had saved my life, then gone out of his way to provide an extra kindness.

It was overwhelming. Would I ever be able to express to him what I owed him? If I had died, what would have happened to my father? Would the anonymous donor go after him next for the debt unpaid?

With a quick jerk, I pushed away those thoughts like a violent shove, forcing my focus back to the pastry in my hand.

When there was nothing left but crumbs, I placed the empty plate on the top of my armoire. Then I popped the cork from the small vial that the healer had given me, draining its contents in one swallow.

My head had barely hit the pillow before I drifted into a dreamless sleep.

Thirty-Nine

The awareness of being surrounded started with a prickling sensation along my scalp. My eyes flew open as I scrambled to sit up in the bed, glancing around the previously empty room to find that about half the beds had occupants. The others appeared haphazardly made and certainly slept in. It was enough evidence that the entire academy had been brought back from the challenge early.

A groan tried to claw its way up my throat. I had wanted another few hours of solitude before I had to face my friends. The heel of my palms rubbed along my eyes while I drew up the motivation to get out of bed.

When I made to push the coverlet from my body, the crinkling of paper caught my attention. A sliver of happiness flickered in my chest as I recalled the note that Cade had left. However, as I went to grab his note, my heart sank.

It was the same stationery that I had come to recognize as belonging to the donor. They had sent a letter at the conclusion of the last challenge, and I knew to expect one eventually, I just hadn't thought they'd leave it while I slept.

Ice coated my veins as I considered that they might have lingered in my room, watching me sleep, before they had placed the letter on my bed. The unruly organ in my chest thumped roughly as I slid my finger beneath the seal to unfold the letter inside, terrified of what I might find.

Dear Ashton Blake,

It has come to my attention that you may not be taking this competition seriously if you are meeting boys in the woods when you should be focusing on the Ice Games.

I will remind you that your induction into the Select Guard is required to fulfill your end of our bargain, and simply leaving the academy will not nullify our magically binding deal.

If ten years of your life is not sufficient collateral to motivate you, additional incentive may need to be obtained.

Your father is frequently traveling alone to remote areas of the kingdom. Surely, he might have some idea of what is valuable enough to you to encourage you to take this seriously.

I am watching, and I am close. Do not fail me, and do not utter a word of this to anyone, or I will know, and you will not like how I handle your betrayal.

Sincerely,
Your gracious donor

My eyes bounced along the page, reading and rereading the thinly veiled threats. I was painfully aware that there would be consequences for my actions if I failed, but up until now, the donor hadn't been overly aggressive. Obviously, I had known there was a risk to accepting such a bargain, but I had wrongfully assumed that the only price to pay would be the years of my life. With this letter, I was forced to admit that I was in over my head. Not that it mattered. There was nothing I could do about it if I wanted my father to remain safe.

This time, instead of shredding the correspondence, I folded it into thirds, tucking it safely under my pillow. If for no other reason than it might act as evidence if I were to meet some unfortunate fate. Now that the donor was threatening me, I couldn't be too careful.

With shaking hands, I climbed down the rungs of my bunk. Ryana's voice reached me just before my feet hit the plush carpet. "Oh good, you're up," she said from her own mattress. "I've been waiting on you for a solid hour down here. We all got pulled from the challenge, and no one knows why."

She hardly even took a breath as she continued. "I heard some other girls whispering that a guy was hurt, maybe even killed. Have you heard anything?"

It was all I could do to dampen the noise of my sharp inhale of breath. Cade and I had only agreed upon the appropriate story to tell the Headmaster. We hadn't discussed what other elements of the academy's protocol I was expected to adhere to, but I knew that telling the entire truth would risk both of our positions here.

My lip stung as my teeth clamped down on the chapped skin, trying to determine the most honest response I could give Ryana without breaking any rules. Blinking did nothing to clear my emotions. The pressure came to a head, and I felt a near-palpable snap as I crumbled under the weight of my emotional exhaustion and the secrets I was being forced to keep.

The moment my eyes met Ryana's again, I dropped to her bed, and the entire story spilled from my lips. My only omissions being the more gruesome details of my attack and the letter still resting beneath my pillow.

When I finished my intense stream of words, Ryana stared silently for a moment, mouth agape. "I don't even know what to say, Ashton." Her tone was just as serious as when she got competitive in the challenges. "Do you want a hug?" Marbled brown eyes roamed my body for any sign of injury, flicking from one scratch to another bruise as her gaze hardened.

A shudder racked my body. "No... thank you, though." I cast my attention to my hands.

"I'm here, whatever you need. A shoulder to cry on. Someone to bring you food while you hide in bed. We can run away. Anything."

Run away? My heart trembled at the notion. If I ran now, it wouldn't just be me who would be in peril. The sponsor had backed me into a corner, and I had no idea how the magically bound contract would punish me for breaking my end of the bargain, but it wasn't worth the risk to find out. There was no choice but to see this through.

My tongue was dry as I attempted to swallow down the words that I could not utter. As a result, my voice came out strained. "Let's just start with breakfast."

We only shared companionable silence as we made our way to the dining hall. Out of habit, more than hunger, given the situation, I grabbed my usual meal of toast, bacon, and mixed fruit and almost dropped every bit of it when I reached our table. There, sitting opposite Jemma and Connally, was Cade.

I couldn't recall any specific rules against fraternizing with students in off hours, but I had certainly never seen it. Even Jemma and Dante had kept their illustrious affair mostly contained to the shadows and empty rooms, never so blatantly flaunting their relationship in such a manner.

Still, I placed my tray down next to Cade, and Ryana slipped into her normal seat beside me.

"Good morning, Ashton," Cade said, cool and collected. As if this was just a normal day. As if he hadn't held me as I wept. As if he hadn't killed another human being for me, even accidentally. My heart fluttered in my chest, more so out of anxiety and guilt than any sort of romantic notion that he was choosing to sit with me. We had already established that wasn't possible until May.

Indigo eyes flickered to Ryana briefly. "Good morning, Ryana," Cade added quickly, losing only a hint of that stoic demeanor.

"Good morning, Cade," Ryana and I both said in unison. The briefest hint of a smile lifted one side of my mouth.

An exasperated huff came from across the table. "Cade was just telling us how you guys were in the group that got sent back first." Connally's eyes were already narrowing at me as she spoke. The tip of something off-putting wove its way through her tone, but I hastily ignored it.

Cade had saved my life, and if that fact bothered her in any capacity, she could fuck right off. There were more important problems to deal with than her judgment.

Cade's voice broke through my thoughts. "...And I was telling them that we cannot divulge information about any incidents until the academy releases an official report. Sorry, girls." He shrugged vaguely in the direction of Jemma and Connally.

When we had a moment alone, I needed to ask him for some pointers on how to act so normal again. After everything that transpired, it felt so weird inside my own skin. Almost as if I had shed that older version of myself and stepped inside a body that wasn't exactly fitted to my specifications. If anyone got a good enough look at me, I was sure it was obvious on my face, but glancing at Cade, there seemed to be no indication that anything was wrong with him. It was unfathomable.

Carefully, I watched as he remained in his seat for the rest of breakfast, only leaving briefly when he volunteered to make a trip to the line again to replenish our table with pastries.

At some point, Dante joined the table, also acting as if he knew nothing of the events from the previous day. Even when Jemma practically climbed in his lap, begging him to divulge his secrets, he simply shook his head.

After leaving in a carriage with a Guide, a Headmaster, and a house leader, battered and bruised as I was, I fully expected rumors surrounding me would be everywhere. However, only a handful of pointed fingers or curious stares made their way to our table. None of them were specifically targeting me, just the group as a whole. It was entirely possible that the scene—two house leaders sitting with students —was enough of a fuss to distract them from the real drama of the challenge. Especially when Jemma didn't seem as concerned with hiding her physical affection towards Dante from the prying eyes of the dining hall.

Ryana's voice filtered through my thoughts. "Do you know how they will score the groups, given that we were all pulled early?" It wasn't surprising that she had used the leader's attendance at our table to her advantage, trying to gain information from them. Or maybe she was simply trying to change the subject for my benefit. Either way, I looked on intently, awaiting their reply.

Dante shook his head, his palm scrubbing over his beard. "They haven't decided." I could tell by the way his lips briefly parted and subsequently snapped shut again that he knew more, but he didn't elaborate further.

As if on cue, Headmaster Dracorris entered the hall and climbed up the platform to stand in front of the table of dining instructors. The anticipation in the room was palpable. Rumblings of words and gasps filled the space until he raised one hand in the air, and every person fell silent.

When he spoke, his tone was somber but direct. "This has been an extraordinary year for *unusual events* occurring during challenges. During the second task of the Ice Games, a student, Berit Murdock, suffered an injury that led to his death."

My eyes narrowed at the implication. Pulse galloping in my ears.

"While the deaths of two students were both accidental in nature..."

It took great effort not to spray my sip of coffee across the table. Cade's hand reached out to comfort me, but he retracted it before it made contact, and I sliced my attention back to the Headmaster.

"It would be unwise to continue as if nothing had happened without considerations being made for the final challenge..."

Cries of outrage filled the hall, echoing off the large stone walls and amplifying the aggressive mood.

Again, the Headmaster's palm raised to silence the crowd. His sigh was heavy and long. "However, there has never been a year since the Ice Games were initiated that we have not done the weapons and combat portions of the challenge. Considering the unusual events of this year and the royal decree, we feel it would be a disservice to you, as our pupils, to miss out on the experience."

My sudden exhale was rife with bitter relief. I didn't want my attack to take one more thing away from me.

The Headmaster glared at the students, who had already started preemptively celebrating. "The administration will review the current plans to determine if changes need to be made to ensure the safety of our students while upholding the legacy of this academy and fitting the guidelines necessary to choose candidates for the trials to determine the heir."

He had left off specifically mentioning the Select Guard, and I hoped that was just an oversight, but I was quickly startled out of those thoughts when cheers erupted. The clapping reverberated like thunder in the air, and I wasn't sad to see Berit gone—especially since I knew how and why he had met his end—but I was astonished that his death had been glossed over in such a way.

Mr. Dracorris let the commentary and speculations continue for a few moments before clearing his throat, garnering the attention of the student body once more. I presumed that he was intending to bring the focus back to the dead student, but instead, he skipped right over Berit altogether. "We will obviously need some time to debrief with our chaperones to determine everyone's scores. Given that and the occurrence of yet another tragedy, you will have the next two days off from training."

More cheers drowned out the sound of his voice. He began to yell over them, eager to finish his speech. "Sessions will resume on Monday, per usual, and unless you hear otherwise, will focus on the final challenge, in whatever capacity we have that."

The Headmaster looked fatigued as he exhaled, as though he already regretted his last words. "We also plan to announce a new house captain by next week."

Oddly, he didn't even give a wave of goodbye before he hurried out of the dining hall, even though his announcement hadn't reached a conclusive end. His posture, the tired look in his eyes, everything about his demeanor made me wonder if there was still something more going on at the academy.

Personally, I had all but determined that Berit was the person responsible for the attacks against Ellie and Sylvia, so it made me wonder why the academy chose not to lead with that. They could have reassured the student body that the evil lurking in the halls had been snuffed out like a candle in the breeze. Then again, they'd have to admit that Sylvia's demise wasn't accidental and acknowledge Ellie had been a victim as well.

Perhaps this situation delved into a strategic and political realm that I simply did not understand.

"I've recently nabbed two bottles of Mr. Higgins' famous vineyard wine from his office that I've been saving for a special occasion," Dante stated proudly, pulling my thoughts away from the tragedies and towards the Irontail House leader.

His bushy eyebrows were lifted high, bordering his hairline. "What do you say, ladies? Want to hang out with a couple of grumpy old men for the day?"

Jemma's eyes lit up as her fingers slowly walked up his chest. She held no concern for whoever might be watching their exchange. "I'd be down to hang out with one grumpy old man... alone."

Their public display was enough to distract me from the questions I had surrounding the wine being stolen from an instructor.

Dante cleared his throat, but his eyes remained locked on hers. "If you insist, my lady." His growl-like timbre made the interaction entirely too intimate for the audience gathered at the table.

Not that either of them seemed to notice. Dante moved Jemma to a standing position before raising himself and taking her hand without a backwards glance or goodbye to anyone left behind.

Connally looked utterly annoyed when she said, "I need to get my beauty rest. Two days in the wilderness were enough to ruin my skincare routine. Thanks anyway." She hurriedly grabbed her empty tray and departed, which left just the three of us at the table.

My gaze fell on Ryana, who only offered me a sly smile in response. "I think I'm supposed to meet Grethe to discuss our tactics for the final challenge. I'll catch you around later, Ash." It was not lost on me that I had not been invited to this meeting.

My stomach twisted with the assortment of mixed emotions settling there. Nerves, anxiety, and dread all clamored to be the victor of my thoughts. Although there was something else there, too. Some tiny kernel of anticipation, something almost akin to excitement. Even though it was deeply sullied by the other warring emotions.

I fought to focus on the kernel, scratched against my mental walls to obliterate the image of onyx eyes and blood-stained knives.

"It's just you and me, then," Cade said. His tone was considerate, but his smile was entirely too hopeful for me to decline. "We can do anything you want."

Forty

In half an hour, I was standing outside Cade's suite. My thumb pushed my mother's ring around my finger as I held my other fist to the door. For a moment, I stalled, finding myself incapable of knocking even if I couldn't understand why.

My lungs expanded on a lengthy inhale as I mentally prepared myself for our interaction. Only when the air had fully expelled from my chest did I bring my knuckles against the wood in three quick beats.

Instantly, Cade's door creaked open, and his face appeared in the crack, wearing a beaming smile. My eyes darted nervously to the space behind him, and he cleared his throat. "I'm ready to go if you are," he said, stepping into the hall beside me and closing his door behind him.

A basket rested in the crook of his arm, but I held onto my silence instead of questioning it.

We meandered through the narrow stone hallways on a path I hadn't seen before.

"This is how the staff moves about the academy," Cade stated, as if responding to my unspoken curiosity.

"Oh," was all I managed to reply.

We wound through another couple of turns, back into larger, more decorated passageways, until we came to an unassuming piece of artwork—almost as tall as me—hanging on the wall at the back of a dimly lit alcove. It was a simple painting of the capital city of Fulgrande, but with only the Queen's castle nestled around the lake. The rendition was void of the buildings and structures that made up the town itself. Even the academy was absent in this rendering.

An ornate oval-shaped golden frame, likely carved from wood, surrounded the scene, bringing out the yellows in the warm sunlight that was depicted shining down on the castle spires in thick streaks of paint. The beams were reflected across the still waters, painted so lifelike that it appeared that if I reached out to touch it, my fingertip would come back wet.

Of course, I could appreciate art in its many forms, but novels were my preferred medium. "It's really pretty," I stated, unsure what else I was supposed to say about it.

As if in response, Cade tilted the painting to the side to expose a stone with a jumping white rabbit painted in the center. He pushed against it with his hand, and a loud click echoed down the corridor. He pressed his palms next to the painting, and the entire wall shifted, opening to reveal a stairwell drenched in shadow.

Cade chuckled to himself. "I'm glad you liked the painting, but I'm more interested in showing you this." He produced a ball of flame in his upturned open palm and smiled. "Follow me."

As soon as we had stepped fully inside the opening in the wall, the rough sound of stone on stone screeched behind us as the entrance sealed once more. I blinked a few times while my eyes adjusted to the dimmed light.

Just past the landing where we entered was a set of steep steps that only headed in one direction: down. It was musty and slightly damp in the dark stairwell. I couldn't imagine that anyone had found these tunnels by accident, and it appeared, based on the layers of dust gathering along the crevices in the rock, that they had remained undisturbed for quite some time.

"How did you find this place?" My words bounced around us.

Cade continued to descend the steps without seeming overly concerned with my line of questioning. "I'm a naturally curious person."

I lobbed an incredulous look in his direction, and he sniffed a laugh. "It was actually an accident. I was planning to steal that painting."

It was difficult to imagine any version of Cade that would steal from the academy. My brows scrunched with my confusion.

He shook his head as if I had misunderstood. "It was going to be a prank. I was going to put it up over Dante's bed." Even in the soft glow of his flames, I could tell that he flushed a little at his confession. "It was stupid," he added quickly. "But when I saw the rabbit, I just kind of had the urge to push it, and then this happened."

For several long seconds, only the sound of our steps reverberated against stone. My head tilted towards him as we continued to descend. "Did you ever tell anyone what you found?"

"No," he replied. "The academy can be loud and overwhelming at times, you know. There are people everywhere, and sometimes it's nice to find a quiet space."

There was no way for him to see the knowing smile that I gave him from behind his back, but it didn't stop my lips from curling upwards ever so slightly. "I do know. It's why I like the library."

Cade glanced at me from over his shoulder. "Yeah, well, Miss Bella tends to like to bombard me with stories of my mother as a teenager, and... well, I kept this place to myself. First, because I wanted the silence, and then because it felt like something that shouldn't be revealed to just anyone."

I understood that, too, because I had yet to tell a soul about the secret garden I had found in the first challenge. The home of the rarest rose blossom in the kingdom.

At the bottom of the stairs, the tunnelways opened into a large, cavernous room with three darkened passages sprouting off in different directions. Cade confidently moved towards the tunnel in the middle.

Pausing in the center, I glanced between the options. "Where do these even lead?"

Cade pointed to our left. "That one is a dead end. It just leads to a brick wall."

His finger slid across the air to the opening on the far right. "This one leads to the pantry in the back of the kitchens, but it's evident that it's been long forgotten."

Edging towards the flame to avoid being left behind in the darkness, I pointed to the final passageway. "And where does this one go?"

He stepped closer to me as we resumed our walk, and our shoulders brushed. Just enough for me to flinch, instantaneously loathing myself for that reaction.

You are safe, I chanted within the confines of my mind.

When I turned back to him, there was an enthusiastic gleam in his eyes. "That's a surprise."

The forgotten passage seemed to go on for an eternity. I was starting to question my blind faith in following this man down a dark tunnel when the slightest hint of sunlight radiated through a crack in the wall ahead.

As we approached, I could hear the sounds of running water. Cade pushed on the wall, and a seam formed in the shape of a door, opening into a lush meadow.

A turbulent stream flowed somewhere behind a thick band of trees whose leaves were all deep shades of orange and red. Patches of the grass remained green, but it was slowly losing the fight to stay alive this far into fall.

In the spaces between the tree line and the open spots of grass, a multitude of flowers were blooming. I recognized them easily from my dad's garden. Festive red chrysanthemums, bright yellow goldenrods, and pink Dahlias littered the edges of the tree line. The colors surrounding us looked like the fiery sunsets I had seen on the coast.

Unabashedly, I gawked at the scene before me. "Where are we?" My voice was a meek whisper. As if there was anyone here to hear me speak. As if we were about to be caught.

Cade's face contorted in a way that told me even he wasn't sure. "Outside the walls of the academy, I suppose. But somewhere only accessible from within... somehow?" There was more question than statement in his words. "I've tried to find it from the outside, but I've never been able to."

My lungs expanded to take in the crisp fall air. "I'd like to stay here forever," I said, only halfway joking. "I can see why you kept this to yourself."

His returned grin was sheepish. "Well, I brought enough supplies that we can stay the rest of the day, if you'd like."

My chin jerked in an instinctual nod. "I would." Some of the nerves from earlier washed away like the stream of water flowing through this oasis.

Cade pulled out a green quilt from his pack and laid it on a spot dappled in sunlight in the clearing before placing the woven basket on top. He pulled out a set of wooden cups and plates and various containers and spread them about. Lastly, he removed a bottle of what I had to assume was Mr. Higgins' famous wine.

My head cocked to the side as I stared at the red liquid within. "How does Mr. Higgins still have so many bottles of wine if you and Dante are always stealing them from him?"

Cade huffed a bemused laugh. "Apparently, he owns a vineyard. He's only working at the academy because he enjoys botany."

Laughing, despite myself, I recalled that look of wonder on the instructor's face when he took the blue-tipped blood rose from me. "So, how does he not notice how many are missing?"

Bracing himself on his hand, Cade leaned closer. "If I tell you a secret, do you promise not to tell a soul?"

There was no shortage of secrets that I was guarding, but something told me that this one would be harmless. My head inclined in a silent agreement.

"He sells them to us," Cade stated. "It's a secret passed down from house leader to house leader at the exchange of duties."

A barking laugh ripped from my chest at the idea of mild-tempered Mr. Higgins running an illegal operation out of the halls of the academy.

Cade's expression turned more serious then. "I was able to bribe Dante to let me have one of them. Given everything…" His voice trailed off. Clearly, he had not meant to brush up against that topic.

Pushing past it, I snorted a laugh. "Something tells me Jemma doesn't need any loosening up after two days away from him."

Cade blew out a breath at my remark, grinning from ear to ear. His almost mention of the incident with Berit already forgotten. "Those two are intense."

A genuine chuckle shook my chest. "That is an understatement."

"We share a wall," Cade deadpanned, releasing a deep belly laugh from me that I hadn't thought possible.

I couldn't fathom why I would want to burst the bubble of happiness that the two of us had cultivated in the meadow over the last few hours, but something was gnawing at my insides. It was the same way it always had been with me, once a thought entered my mind—even just the tingling of an idea—I couldn't just let it go until it was resolved.

It was the same reason I had spent entirely too much time bothering Viggo Wood with my curiosity about the actual history of the kingdom at the start of his battle studies session.

My gaze lifted to where Cade sat, picking at a nearby blade of yellowing grass. "Can I ask you a question?"

His indigo eyes shifted from the dying vegetation to my face. "Of course."

My lips pinched, unsure if this was the best route for me to take. "And you promise to answer honestly? Even if it's weird."

Confusion filtered across his features, notching two lines between his brows, but he nodded all the same, abandoning the scrap of grass and giving me his full attention.

Dragging a deep breath through my nose, my muscles tensed with nerves. And a bit of aggravation with myself that I was the one bringing up *the other night*. "Why were you looking for me in the woods?"

Cade blew a raspberry through his lips, drawing his palm to meet the back of his neck as he rubbed out the tension there. "There was something I wanted to talk to you about."

My head cocked to the side, heart thrumming nervously in my chest. "And it couldn't have waited until we returned?" Not that I wasn't grateful, but it wasn't as if we hadn't had any opportunities to speak.

He didn't respond, his expression pained.

"Do you still need to talk to me about it?" I prodded. Obviously, if it had been a warning about Berit, it was fruitless now.

"No." His answer came too abruptly to confirm my suspicions.

Dipping my chin to catch his attention, our eyes locked once more. "Do you still *want* to talk to me about it?"

A pregnant pause grew between us while Cade considered my question. I could tell he was combating something in his own mind because his features had twisted into a blend of concern and resolve. "I don't think it's appropriate any longer."

"Because Berit is no longer a threat?"

Cade's jaw clenched, making indents along the point where it hinged. "I wasn't going to warn you about Berit. I already told you to stay away from him, and I thought Dante would watch out for you..."

My voice was pleading then, fully ignoring any role Dante might have played in saving me. That wasn't something I could change now. But this... "Please tell me." My weight rested on my palm as I leaned into the space between us.

He shook his head vehemently. "It's not appropriate."

"Why?" I snapped.

Cade looked unsure for the first time I could ever remember. His hands were wringing together in his lap.

"Please," I begged, one more time. "I can't stand the not knowing."

Iridescent eyes swept across my features, searching for something he must have found because, with his next exhale, he seemed to sigh away the rest of his resolve. "I wanted to tell you we didn't have to wait so long, but after..." He stopped himself from saying it out loud. "I don't think that's appropriate any longer. I just want to be there for you in any way I can."

My thoughts snagged on those words like a hangnail caught in a knitted sweater. "What do you mean?"

His palms pressed into his eyes as another deep huff rustled from his chest. "Technically, at the solstice, I'm no longer your instructor, and I thought we might..." He growled, and his hands dropped so he could look me in the eye. "After everything you've been through, I don't think this is the time."

"He doesn't get to take this from me too," I barked, and I wasn't angry at Cade for trying to be a good guy, but I was furious with Berit for somehow stealing away one more joyous thing from me.

"He's not," Cade countered, voice even. "You just need time—"

"I need you to let me make that decision for myself," I interjected.

Cade's lips slammed shut, and his chin jerked down once. "Okay."

My shoulders squared, and my spine straightened as I drew in a steadying breath. "Pretend this is just us meeting that night. Pretend nothing else happened. What were you going to say to me?"

Again, the silence stretched on as Cade's gaze roamed my face for fear or regret that he would not find. "I was going to tell you that—"

My palm jutted out to the space between us as I cut off his words. "Don't tell me what you were going to say. Just tell me."

There was worry behind his stare, but he obeyed. "I have already told you that I care about you, and I was reading over my contract, and technically it ends on the last day of courses for the semester. I was going to tell you we only had to wait until the ball."

"The solstice ball?" I questioned. "Not after the solstice ceremony? Or the year?"

I knew there was a chance he'd stay on as an instructor, and since his elemental affinity was fire and my mother had been Ignus, there was a reasonable likelihood we would continue to be in the same situation.

"If my parents allow me to stay past the solstice and you get your mother's element, then I would be your instructor again," he replied, but that same uncertainty from his expression had already bled into his tone. "But we don't know for certain you will get fire or that I'll even get it and—"

"I want that," I interrupted, my head bouncing with an enthusiastic nod. "I want to give us a chance, even if it's for a short time." The words rang true, not just a spiteful reaction to Berit's actions but simply because it stemmed from a genuine desire.

Cade shook his head. "I don't know that now is the best time."

"Because of what Berit did?" Tears sprang into my eyes. "I obviously liked you before, and I just didn't think we would find a way until..." My fists curled into tight balls as a sob racked through my chest.

Cade looked panic-stricken at the sight of me. He leaned forward to draw me into his embrace, and I flinched.

He returned to his side of the blanket, folding his hands in his lap where he sat cross-legged, facing me. "I feel like I'm fucking up by just trying to comfort you because I don't know how to help you through this. You need to talk to a mind healer."

The tension in my jaw crested as I shook my head. It wasn't that there was no merit to his suggestion; it was that, without being able to open up about everything, I wasn't sure I could be honest with the healer in a way that would help me. "I know you're not going to hurt me; I just need to remind my body."

There was a defeated look in his returned stare. "You're one of the strongest people I know, but I can't contribute to the thing that breaks you."

My throat burned, then bobbed as I attempted to push down the rising sob. Resolve replaced my panic as I realized I knew how to I could prove to him that I could do this. I rolled to my knees, crawling awkwardly over to his side of the quilt. "I'm fine," I reiterated as I brought my face closer to his.

With so little distance between us, I could make out the flecks of violet embedded into the bright blue of his irises. He sat stock still as my palms braced against his shoulders, and I closed my eyes, pressing our mouths together before I could back down.

"Ashton," he warned against my lips, and I took the opening to slip my tongue against the seam of his mouth.

Internally, I told myself that I needed this. More than just proving it to Cade, I needed to prove to myself that I was the master of my own body. Not some trauma that happened to me. Even if his proximity had caused a sinking feeling to enter my stomach, and the overwhelming desire to pull away flooded me.

Stubbornly, I fought against the instinct to run, forcing my attention to Cade's mouth on mine. His kiss was tentative and unsure, but he kissed me back. Slow and patient. He kept his hands to himself, and although a small part of me longed to feel his palms sliding against my skin, an even larger segment was silently grateful.

He broke the kiss first, pulling back to sweep his gaze across my features for the hundredth time since he found me in the woods. "Thank you for trusting me with this," he said instead of the letdown I had been expecting. "I need you to know that I don't expect anything from you in regard to..." His eyes trailed over my body before reaching mine again.

"I expect something from you, though," I stated, leaning back on my heels.

His eyebrows raised as if he was bracing himself for another tongue-lashing.

A sigh tumbled from my lips. "I expect you to treat me no differently than before. I'm not some wilting flower, and I can't stand the sight of your pity."

Cade lifted his hand in the air, pausing just above my thigh. "May I?"

With my nod, he let his palm rest on my quad. His touch was as light as a feather. To my credit, I did not recoil from the contact, even if my breath hitched incrementally in my throat.

Maybe he recognized my discomfort or my genuine need for something good to come out of this because his features softened. "Will you go to the solstice ball with me?" There was so much emotion in his expression that I couldn't pinpoint a singular one.

It sounded so juvenile, being asked to a dance, but it was so much more than that. It was the promise that after everything I had endured this year, I would have something to look forward to.

At the prospect, a smile curled my lips. "I will."

Forty-One

W ith the same bruised smears above his cheekbones and haunted expression in his stare, Headmaster Dracorris addressed the student body the following Monday morning at breakfast. "As you are well aware, we have had to come up with creative ways to award points for the second challenge, especially for those who had not yet returned to the academy."

To my knowledge, no one had beaten me to the school, but then again, I hadn't exactly had enough wherewithal to notice anything past my empty suite and lack of other presence in the bathing chambers. Clearly, I had slept through the placement of my donor's threatening letter, so it was possible I had missed much more.

Mr. Dracorris cleared his throat, and although silence didn't abruptly follow, the mutterings reduced significantly. "Final scores have been given to your house leader, as we will no longer be posting the rankings." So, they did realize that the ranked list might have contributed to the attacks, even if they weren't admitting it.

"Please gather at your designated meeting areas following the breakfast hour to retrieve your individual ranking. First session will be delayed by thirty minutes."

The man started to step away from his spot at the table, but then added, "House Irontail has won this round," almost as if it were a second thought. "Their new captain is Marsha Cosgrove."

The name was wholly unfamiliar to me, and the Headmaster made no move to introduce her either. As he typically did after relaying hurried news, he scurried from the dining hall before he could be bombarded with questions.

In a daze, I finished my meal, although I couldn't distinguish the flavors any longer, and before I knew it, Ryana and I had separated from Connally and Jemma to meet with Katarina in the chapel.

My palms were drenched in sweat as I approached the building, thankful that Ryana had gone first to open the doors.

"Are you okay?" she asked as I walked over the threshold and made my way to an empty pew.

Over the last few days, she had repeated the question over and over as if she expected a different result. It wasn't as if I could tell her the truth about the donors' most recent correspondence, though. Every time I longed to be honest, images of my father wasting away to nothing in my absence always held me back. "I'm worried that what happened during challenge two will hurt my score. I need this."

She nodded as if she understood, even though she couldn't possibly get what I meant, not in its entirety. "Talk to Katarina. I'm sure she could give you some pointers."

It felt like a brush-off, but that wasn't really like Ryana at all, so I considered her advice. Katarina had obviously done well enough during her year at Biltons to be named a House Leader, so it stood to reason that she would know a thing or two about holding the upper hand.

So, when she waltzed into the chapel, blue ponytail swishing behind her, demanding that we line up to receive our scores, I put myself at the end of the line purposefully to catch her alone.

When I approached her, clipboard in hand, something pitying flashed across her hazel eyes. She let them fall to the paper in her grip, flashing her attention back to me with a more neutral expression. "You did okay this time around, but your score wasn't enough to place you in the top ten."

She gave me the number, which meant very little in the context of my overall ranking until she said, "This puts you roughly twenty-third across the academy."

My heart sank. At most, only a handful of students were selected for induction into the guard. Had I truly done so poorly on the challenge that I had fallen down the ranks so dramatically? Was this Berit haunting me from the grave with whatever connections he claimed to have made in his life? Had I said "gods damn it" one too many times?

The image of the red-haired deity over Katarina's shoulder mocked me from her window pane, and I willed myself not to cry as I forced my gaze to meet my house leader's stare once more. "What can I do to make up the difference? I need to be inducted into the guard."

She studied me, much in the same way that Cade and Ryana had done since discovering what happened to me in the woods, and I wanted to shrink against the perceptive look flooding her attention. "You'll need to pick up a weapon," she said matter-of-factly. "It's not advertised, but if you win the weapons portion of the challenge, they will award you additional points. Not just for your house but as the individual."

The third and final segment of the Ice Games was perhaps the least secretive portion. In the last challenge, students battled in hand-to-hand combat for top marks. Finding yourself in the final round, the Select Sixteen, as it was commonly referred to, all but solidified your chances of being invited into the Select Guard initiation. For those who wanted it.

"The weapons portion is voluntary," Katarina stated, "so you won't be forced to do it unless you want to, but it's the only opportunity left to add to your score outside of the hand-to-hand rounds."

"What are my options?"

Katarina sighed, glancing towards the door to make sure we were alone, and although her aid wasn't quite as obvious as Cade's had been for challenge one, I wondered if this was somehow against the rules. "This year? Swordplay, Jousting, and Archery."

"I'm best with a sword," I said quickly, feeling the creeping edges of hope blossom within my chest. My dad had done an excellent job training me in swordplay, and now that I had gotten a feel for the iron version in my hand, I thought this would be my greatest strength. I had even bested Nielsen a time or two, much to his dismay.

"I think archery would be your best bet. You are good with a sword," she added hastily, "but there are others here who are better. I've seen you. You have the highest chances with the bow."

The stakes were too high for me to give up now, even though I doubted my skill was up to par with some of the others for that particular choice. "If I wanted to get better with a bow, who could help me outside of sessions?"

Katarina smiled, and it wasn't the grim approximation that she had shown before. "Helga."

There was nothing I could do to mask the cringe that followed. She was so intimidating that I wasn't sure that she could provide the help that I needed to achieve dominance in the field.

"Blake, I'm going to be honest with you." Katarina's voice was firm but not harsh. "If you are going to make it, you have to be willing to do things that put you out of your comfort zone."

I could have snorted because everything I had done since I signed that gods-damned agreement had put me directly out of alignment with the things that brought me comfort.

Katarina clearly wasn't done with me, though. "You can either go to her and ask for help, or you can lose sight of your goals. Just know that if you fail from here, it is because you didn't want it enough to even try, not because some entitled asshole attacked you in the woods."

My mouth fell open as I blanched. There had been suspicions that some of the staff had been informed of my ordeal, but having it thrown right out there between us was enough to drain the blood from my body. Her words were bordering on cruel, but they held some truth if I chose to listen to them.

Either let what Berit did define me, or persevere despite the setback.

"Thank you," I mumbled, genuinely, because I had needed that kick in the ass.

Katarina clutched her clipboard to her chest. "I am only harsh with you because I see how great you can be, and I want you to get there."

It was perhaps the nicest thing that the house leader had ever said to me. "I'll make you proud then."

"No," Katarina said, pursing her lips. "Make yourself proud."

It took days for me to gather the courage necessary to approach Helga, driven fully by Katarina's words ringing in my ears and the unsettling, persistent fear of what I would lose if I failed.

The woman had glanced down at me with an expression I had never seen on her face. Pity. Obviously, word of my situation had gotten around the faculty table, but I held my head high as I explained I needed the extra points to meet my lifetime goal of being inducted into the Select Guard.

"I will help you, but I expect discipline and dedication." That was the only thing she ever asked of me in exchange for her aid.

Discipline and dedication came in the form of meetings every Tuesday and Thursday afternoons after session four and on Saturday mornings just before lunch. She never deigned to go easy on me, but she wasn't mean. In the same way that Katarina had given me the ugly truth of my predicament, Helga pushed me to greatness.

I hadn't been unskilled in archery before the additional lessons, but with her guidance, my ability became exemplary. It was almost as if Katarina had known something I didn't about my propensity to take up the weapon with ease.

Helga started me with stationary targets, elongated the distances until we reached the limits of the bow that she had lent me. When I had mastered hitting still targets, she brought the contraptions out that caused the animal-shaped boards to traverse the practice field with strange, jerky motions. It took no time to master that, too.

Today, it was obvious that I had graduated from being on the ground for my lessons when Tamari walked to the training field leading a fully saddled gelding from the stalls. She offered me a conspiratorial smile as she approached. "We had an idea."

We? Had the instructors been conversing about my extracurricular training? My gaze darted between Helga and Tamari. "And it has to do with the horse?"

Tamari laughed. "Yep. Mount up."

My boot hit the stirrup, and I threw my other leg over the saddle, looking down at Tamari for further instruction.

Helga handed me the practice bow, which I accepted with a quizzical look.

"You will shoot targets while on horseback," Helga stated as if it made the most logical sense. Catching my prolonged confusion, she added, "It will help with accuracy."

Not entirely convinced, I slung the quiver over my shoulder. "Will there be horses as part of the third challenge?"

"Maybe," Helga replied flatly. "Maybe not. This is about skill improvement."

"It's unconventional," Tamari added, "but it will help you focus your aim while moving so it's second nature, even when you're the one running."

That was all I needed to hear, the reason behind it. "Okay, tell me what to shoot."

The instructors led me to a portion of the wooded area where, once again, those strangely moving wooden animals had been set up along the path.

Helga adjusted her stance, folding her hands behind her back. "I will time you. One minute. Go."

With that, she smacked the back of the horse's rear, and he took off down the trail before I could gather my wits completely. Scrambling, I got the bow in the correct hand, knocking an arrow into place and letting it fly at the first target I saw. Over and over again until Helga yelled, "Time!"

Pulling gently on the reins, I turned the horse around to return to where the instructors were standing. I hadn't even glanced at the targets, but when I reached Helga, she offered me a rare nod of approval. "You hit almost every target."

Tamari beamed at me from beside Helga. "I knew this would work. You're a natural with the horses."

Remembering our horse, Sugar's disdainful stares in my direction, I snorted a laugh. He would probably disagree with that statement, but I did feel more confident on the Biltons Academy horse's back.

"Fetch the arrows and then we will go again," Helga stated, but her stern voice did nothing to dampen my mood because I caught the small hint of a smile on her face.

The expression was contagious, and I found myself grinning as I plucked each arrow from the wooden animals. Most of them were dangerously close to where we had been taught to aim in Katarina's course, giving me empirical evidence that I was improving. Things were finally starting to turn around after that night in the woods, and I could feel myself leaning into my determination and growth.

I would come out triumphant.

Forty-Two

The rules against leaving the academy were still being strictly enforced, especially in the wake of two student's untimely deaths. So, when Ryana's birthday rolled around, I made a request for the kitchen staff to grab her favorite treat: macarons.

It was absurd to think that a few pastries could pay her back for the way that she had been there for me in the weeks following the challenge, but I liked to show my love with food, specifically sweets. As much as I loathed even acknowledging my own birthday, I truly enjoyed celebrating my friends on their special day.

The morning that the macarons were to be completed, I snuck down to the kitchens before Ryana even woke, tiptoeing around discarded clothes and trunks on my way out the door. There was something so peaceful about the hallways of the academy in the early morning. They were empty but not lonely. There was a sense of warmth and connectedness here that went past the bodies currently resting in their beds. Maybe this place would never feel like *home*, but I felt a certain familiar comfort here.

My footsteps scuffled against the stone floors of the kitchen as the greasy scent of bacon and eggs wafted past my nose. My stomach growled in a quiet rebellion as I made my way to see Maude, the kitchen manager.

Maude was short in stature, but what she lacked in height, she made up for in kindness. "So great to see you this morning, Ashton!" she called out to me as I approached her cubby near the center of the kitchens. Her brown eyes crinkled in genuine happiness.

"Good morning, Maude," I replied, returning her smile with one of my own. I had met Maude earlier in the year when I had been having a particularly stressful evening prepping for the first challenge and had come to the kitchens to see what I had to trade to get some chocolate cake.

Maude had given me a hug, which barely wrapped around my hips, thanks to her shortened stature, and passed me an apron. We had spent the afternoon baking a cake together, and while I wasn't sure I could call her a friend, given our age difference, I did enjoy a certain comradery with her.

Maude was likely in her late sixties; her once brown hair had almost turned white as proof. She kept it in a low bun at the nape of her neck. At one point in her life, she might have been considered petite, but now she bore the curves of a woman who not only was an exceptional cook but also preferred to devour her creations regularly. She wore her shapeliness well, sauntering through the kitchen with all the grace of a slinking leopard.

"Sorry, I couldn't make it in to help you with these... I've been a little preoccupied," I admitted to her as she tightened her stained linen apron around her hips, smoothing out the edges with her hands.

"That's alright, deary. These Ice Games always keep the students busy. Especially this year with all this heir talk." Maude talked with her hands, and they flailed wildly with the inflection in her tone.

A breath released from my lungs in a slow exhale. She had no idea how much the *heir talk* had impacted my time here. "I almost wish I had come a different year," I mumbled, knowing that if I could talk freely to anyone, it would probably be the woman before me.

"Psshh," Maude replied, waving her hands in the air in front of us, her wrinkled mouth pursing in disapproval. "In case you can't tell, I've been around a few years, and in all my time, they've never once even hinted at an heir. She doesn't need one," Maude said matter-of-factly. "She's immortal."

My eyes narrowed as I leaned against the nearby wooden island, crossing my arms against my stomach. Both eyebrows were raised as I took her in. "She's not immortal. She just has special abilities that let her live a long time. Like the Guides."

Maude tutted. "Those old dirtbags are barely alive. They're like walking skeletons that just wear skin-like clothing."

The snort that left my lips might have rivaled a pig. Her description of Claudius was not far off, and despite his intimidating presence, he wasn't exactly wearing his age with glowing health. "Maybe she needs to name an heir to replace them?" As soon as I offered the suggestion, my brow furrowed. There was so much about the timing of her naming an heir and even the strange way she was going about it that made very little sense to me.

The face Maude made at my statement conveyed her lack of confidence in my hypothesis on the matter. "The crowns have always passed by blood. I'm not sure how pointing at a random person will matter."

Shaking my head, I pushed away from the island. "She has no children, and... how do you know the crowns have always passed by blood? No one was alive to see her coronation."

Maude hummed a note of disapproval, tapping her temple with a single fingertip. "That's what they want us to think. But there will be no way to name an heir who isn't a blood relative. It's the way of the throne."

I laughed off the comment because I was starting to be concerned that I had broached a topic that highlighted some mental instability. For all my theories on the Elemental Queen and her Guides, Maude's comments were starting to sound fantastical, even to my ears.

"You make it sound like there's magic ruling the crown," I whispered, not wanting to be dragged into a conspiracy but still curious as to what she meant. "The Guides are the only humans with natural magic, so if that was the case, they could clearly undo it."

Maude shrugged, ignoring my questioning statements. "Whatever is going on, I hope to stay out of it. Nothing good can come of this." She shook her head as if shuddering off an invisible layer of snow. "Anyway, that's not why you came here, is it?"

Seeing as I was on a time crunch, I crossed the small space to stand by her side. "No, and if I spend any longer surrounded by the smells in here, I'm going to eat it all, and there won't be anything left for the students."

The warmth lit Maude's face again as she motioned for me to follow her to the other side of the kitchen. She produced a wooden box, no wider than a sheet of parchment, and handed it to me. As I took the box from her hands, I noted the brand on her forearm: the kingdom's flower rested in the middle of a halo of leaves. Maude was Operarius.

I subdued my shock, thankfully, before her eyes met mine again. If she had noticed me staring at her brand, she spared me the embarrassment of bringing it to my attention.

"Thank you," I muttered awkwardly, "I'll return soon for more baking lessons."

Struggling to mask the cringe on my face, I exited the double doors that led out into the dining hall. It was easy to discern that the emotions that Maude's brand elicited were a byproduct of my own fears of inadequacy, but seeing that mark made me feel sorry for her. She was surrounded by the magically gifted in a school whose purpose was to transition its citizens into power, and she had nothing.

She never seemed unhappy, though, in fact, she appeared to love her job, a feat that was hardly universal, even within the magical world. Still, I couldn't stop the pang of sorrow in my heart for her as I made my way to my usual table in the hall.

Ryana was giving me a strange look as I approached the table, but Jemma and Connally seemed preoccupied with each other, per usual, and I tried not to bristle at the sight.

"Where have you been?" Ryana asked me, inspecting the box as I laid it on the table in front of her.

Beaming, I pointed to the offering. "Happy birthday!"

The look of confusion morphed into something more ecstatic as she opened the box and discovered her pastries.

"Happy birthday!" Jemma called from across the table, startling Connally with her voice.

"Yeah, happy birthday!" Connally added, eyes flickering over to me with the smallest hint of uncertainty.

Ryana passed the box around, having it come back to her at just the moment Grethe approached our table.

"It sounds like the birthday festivities have continued," Grethe said offhandedly.

My gaze snapped to Grethe, sure I would get nowhere with Ryana. "Continued?"

Grethe sifted through the box of macarons before landing on a chocolate one. "Yeah! We—"

Ryana smacked him in the chest, cutting off the rest of his words. "We celebrated last night by studying for the next challenge and going over strategy."

Grethe grinned, suddenly looking so much more boyish as his green eyes glittered with amusement. "Yeah, we talked a LOT about strategy. All sorts of strategies..."

Ryana's icy glower caused him to end his rambling early. He cleared his throat and stuffed the pastry into his mouth, giving his farewell through several chews. "Well, happy birthday... again, Ryana." He swallowed, already retreating from the table. "See you later."

There was something questioning about his statement, and Ryana nodded as if confirming that she would see him later before her gaze returned to the table, and she rapidly changed the subject. "These are amazing, Ash, where did you get them?"

"Did Cade get them for you?" Jemma teased, making a show of wiggling her eyebrows. We had continued our meetings in secret, but I had thought we had been sneaky enough to avoid being noticed.

Ignoring Jemma completely, I opted to face Ryana to give my answer. "No, I got them from Maude." I selected a pink pastry that I hoped was raspberry and plopped it into my mouth, letting the sugary delicacy melt onto my tongue with a satisfying moan.

"If you say so..." Jemma snarked. "But it's not like I would be the one to judge you, you know."

Catching the hint of hurt in her voice, I turned to face her finally. Her bright green eyes were narrowed, but something solemn hung from her lips. For once, I wasn't lying, but I could gather that she wasn't particularly asking me about the pastries as much as she was trying to get me to open up about the Wyvern House leader.

We had always shared everything between us and although I knew she had Connally and Dante to keep her occupied, it seemed that maybe she was noticing this divide between us as well.

Not that I planned to share my feelings and upcoming date with Cade in front of the others. "Seriously, Maude helped me make them." I pointed towards the kitchen. "You can go ask her yourself."

Jemma shook it off with a laugh. "Well, you might not be willing to admit your feelings for your house leader, but I have plans with mine before session starts." She pushed back from the table, looking down at me as she stood over us. "And he isn't hiding our relationship under the guise of rules. In fact," she lobbed us all with a conspiratorial grin. "We are planning to share a certain Platypus captain in a bit."

Her eyebrows bounced along her forehead as if any of us needed hints as to what she meant.

Ryana snapped the lid of her box shut, drawing my attention back to the table with a sharp jerk of my head. "I have to head off too," she stated, providing no further details of her plans before she practically ran from the table. "Bye! Thank you for the treats!"

Jemma threw her thumb over in Ryana's direction. "That girl is going to get laid, too. Mark my words."

Scoffing, I remembered how fondly she talked about the love she had back home and brushed off Jemma's comment as projection. Ryana was likely cramming in more study sessions or perhaps some personalized training as the final challenge loomed over us.

Jemma didn't seem to care one bit what Ryana was actually doing. "See you guys later," she stated over her shoulder, already walking away. "Or not," she added with a smirk before picking up her pace.

"What is she just going to skip classes to screw her boyfriend?" I asked offhandedly before I realized that I was alone at the table with Connally Owens.

"Probably," Connally responded with an almost defensive look in her eyes as they roamed over my face before our gazes connected again. The amber in her eyes shone like gold, and for a sliver of time, I almost forgot how much she annoyed me on a regular basis. Although if I was honest with myself—apparently the only person I could be completely truthful with if I chose to,—my irritation with Connally stemmed more from her closeness to Jemma than anything the girl had actually done to me.

"So, how are your courses going?" I asked, willing myself to be a little nicer to her out of guilt, more than anything.

She shrugged, the glimmer of amusement flashing across her golden irises. "Fine, I'm ranked higher than you are right now."

And just like that, I was reminded why I didn't spend any time with this girl alone. A smile curled my lips, and I didn't care if it looked fake or not. "Congrats, hope you have a great day."

I stood abruptly, gathering my tray and leaving the room as quickly as I could without even a backwards glance at Connally fucking Owens.

Forty-Three

Cade had been so understanding and patient with me—and so utterly platonic within the halls of the academy—that I was filled with anticipation when he asked me to meet him at the painting that led to the secret tunnel one late November evening.

"Can I blindfold you?" he asked as we reached the cavernous room that split into the three different passageways. Pride blossomed in my chest as I realized that the idea of that didn't make me cringe. There was no recoil from my muscles as he rested his hands on my shoulders and guided me along the now-familiar channel.

Through our time together, I had gained so much confidence in him, even if our intimacy was confined to professional touch during hand-to-hand combat and the rare stolen kiss within the hidden boundary of our meadow.

With all that progress, I was beginning to want more from him, from us, in a way that did not strictly stem from my desire to prove that my body was my own and that my choices belonged to me alone. I just wanted him.

The squeal of the rusty hinges of the outer door reverberated against stone as he nudged me further, guiding me into the clearing, which filled my lungs with the crisp autumn air immediately.

With a gentle prod, he shifted my body again, pointing me toward what I believed to be the tree line.

"Keep your eyes closed," he whispered into my ear. Weeks ago, this would have been too much, but we had slowly worked up to this level of trust through his unwavering friendship and ability to consistently give me exactly what I needed. Even when I hadn't been sure how to identify, much less articulate, those needs.

The blindfold fell from my face just as his lips grazed my ear. "Okay, open."

Slowly, my eyelids peeled apart, and I came face to face with a wooden circle propped upright by three legs. Inside the circle, a hand-painted trio of rings sat one inside the other like nesting dolls.

Disappointment crested in my chest as I forced a smile to my lips. "Thank you," I offered politely.

Cade huffed a laugh. "This is not the surprise," he mused. "You've been doing so well with Helga, but I think you could be even greater with a weapon that generations of students have not mishandled."

Confusion marred my already crumbling smile just as Cade bent at the waist and produced a dark wooden bow in his hands. He passed it to me, and I studied the golden inlay with fascination. The shapes mirrored the golden wheat that decorated my mother's ring. The ones that adorned the kingdom's flag.

Weighing the instrument in one hand, I found it was lightweight and easy to maneuver. It was single-handedly the nicest weapon I had ever had the honor of holding. "You're lending me your bow?"

"I'm giving you a bow," Cade corrected, passing me a hardened leather quill full of arrows that was attached to an ornate strap that matched the regal design of the bow.

My gaze slid from the extravagant gift to his indigo stare. "This is way too much, Cade. It must have cost you a fortune." My words hinted at my reluctant rejection of the gift, but I couldn't bring myself to hand it back.

He offered me a tight-lipped smile, acting as though the notion was nothing to him, even though it was everything to me. A bow might just secure my freedom and my father's life as well. It was more than just symbolic.

He waved off my words. "A weapons master owed my family a favor, and I called it in. It's yours. What do you think?"

My throat burned, and without further evaluation, in perhaps one of my first normal reactions since challenge two, I leaped into his arms, pressing my face against the crook of his neck and placing a firm kiss against the column of his throat.

His muscles moved as I sensed a grin forming against my hairline. "So, you like it?"

Still beaming, I extracted my arms from his waist. "I love it, Cade, thank you! The inlay even reminds me of my mom's ring."

He flashed me another handsome smile. "I know, that's why I added it."

I waffled between kissing him again and testing out my new bow as my eyes fell to the weapon, revealing which won out.

An amused chuckle bounced around the space between us. "Go ahead," he prodded. "I know you are dying to test it out. It's why I brought the target."

Glee filled my veins. It was the only way to describe the emotion that bounded through my body when I lined my arrow up in that bow, made specifically for me, and released it directly into the bullseye.

Minutes, or perhaps hours, passed while I practiced with the weapon, only abandoning it when the rumble of my stomach reminded me that neither of us had eaten in a while.

Cade spread out the green quilt again, producing a bag of meats and cheeses with a handful of grapes. He was making us a picnic, and it was hard not to feel almost giddy about it when I was finally feeling healthy enough to do more than simply drag myself out of bed and survive the day.

Slipping from my side of the quilt, I stole a handful of grapes from Cade's hand before plopping back down.

"Hey," he called, leaning across the invisible barrier in the middle of us to snatch them back. With his face so close to mine and the bow no longer stealing my attention, I used the proximity to my advantage, tossing the grapes to an empty spot on the blanket and fitting my palm to his cheek instead.

With a firm touch, I pulled his body on top of me, pressing my lips against his as my back came to rest against the ground. There was something unspoken about being here in this meadow, where the rules that applied to us and our relationship no longer held any weight. The meadow was the only place we touched like this.

The kiss deepened for a few heartbeats before Cade pulled away like he always did. "Are you sure that this is okay?" He asked in the same tone he used each time our sweet kisses turned more sensual.

My assured fingers pulled against the ties of my tunic, revealing the lace of the bralette underneath. "I'm good," I replied, a bit too harshly. "I want this."

There was a pause before he moved, a fragment of time where I was certain that he was going to deny me going any further—as he had so many times before—but I watched as the indecision and doubt in his eyes washed away, giving rise to heat and longing. "You don't owe me anything for the bow," he commented, like he was already changing his mind, although his hips remained wedged between my legs as he hovered over me.

This was about so much more than the unpaid life debt between us. "I want this," I repeated, keeping my stare locked with his. "I don't know how far I can go, but I'm not doing it because I owe you."

The rest of his conjecture abandoned his features as he looked down at me. "Your pace then, Ash." He dropped his weight over me, and his mouth collided with mine once more.

These were not the timid kisses from our past, these were filled with a passion I had yet to see from him. His hands slid beneath the hem of my shirt, sliding up my bare skin in a way that was far too gentle to overtly remind me of Berit, even if those hands had been the last to blaze that trail.

Tightening my grip on Cade's shoulders, I pushed through the shame of the fact that I had let the redhead enter my thoughts during such a pivotal moment between us. Shaking the images away, I turned my focus on the heat emanating from Cade's palms as they came to rest along the fabric that did very little to separate his skin from my breast. His thumb grazed along the lace edge, and I moaned into his mouth as my nipples peaked in response.

Again, he pulled back, and I growled in frustration as my eyes blew open wide to glare at him. There was a look of desperation tarnishing his otherwise longing expression.

"Cade," I whined, hearing the petulance in my own tone. "Touch me anywhere you want. I promise I want this."

Cade's eyes flickered across my features, scanning my face for any hint that this wasn't what I wanted, despite my words and my bleeding desperation. I slid my hand through his hair, resting my palm on the back of his neck, pulling him to me again.

I sensed the moment he lost this round as his hand flexed, his fingertips pinching my now-exposed nipple between his fingers.

Despite my cries of pleasure, he refused to linger there. His hand roamed from my chest, sliding down to the dip in my waist and meandering to my hipbone, where his thumb began taunting the lacy band of my underwear beneath my leggings.

Heat rushed between my thighs as I thrust them forward, silently urging him to give me more. To let me, and him, reclaim my body as mine.

He lifted his hips, and before he could ask me if anything else was okay, I abandoned the handful of his hair that I had been gripping to shove my leggings and underthings down my legs all the way to my knees so that he wouldn't have to question my intentions.

He paused, and this time, I broke our kiss. "Hands on me now, Mr. Hudson."

A low rumble escaped his chest as his lips hovered just above mine, giving me those precious moments to take it back.

I didn't. I couldn't.

When he moved again, it was to sit back on his heels to take me in. His gaze locked on mine for several elongated heartbeats before moving across my lips, my cheeks, down my neck, and to the opening in my tunic. Across my exposed breast and down my stomach until he reached the apex of my thighs.

His hands gripped the band of my leggings, and he slowly, torturously, pulled them down the rest of the way until I was completely bare from the waist down. He sighed heavily as his focus centered on my most intimate flesh. Appreciation and lust danced in the depths of his blown-out pupils. "Gods, you are magnificent," he whispered.

It was then that I noticed the sensation of a fingertip circling one ankle and then the other, the pressure increasing until his hands were cuffing my leg, gently urging them apart. In a testament to the trust we had built, I let him move me and allowed him to spread me until he was satisfied.

A fingertip trailed along my ankle bone, wandering up my calf and down my inner thigh until the sensation tingled just outside of my core.

My hips wiggled enough to get the point across, and with the most delicate touch I thought was possible for a man of his stature, he traced the edges of my folds.

A shiver crawled across my body at the contact, but I didn't flinch. There was no recoil from this touch because I wanted it so desperately. Instead, I let my knees fall open, shifting my center until his finger brushed against my clit.

A moan erupted from my lips, all the encouragement he needed to press his thumb against the bundle of nerves between my thighs as he lowered his face to mine to take my mouth.

He moved his hand in tight circles, the pressure at my core mounting at an alarming rate, considering he hadn't even entered me yet. He paused, only long enough to garner another pitiful whimper from me, before he slowly pressed a finger inside me, watching me for any hint of a retreat. When he found nothing but longing, he returned his thumb to that glorious spot that filled me with ecstasy.

Even in the privacy of my bedchamber, it had never felt like this. Certainly, nothing Farren, or any of the other now forgettable boys, had ever done compared to the euphoria I was experiencing now.

My moans transformed into muffled groans as his movement quickened and his finger curled to hit an even more sensitive spot within me. He moved in and out at a frustratingly slow pace, and my hips bucked against the building tension. I might have been embarrassed by my neediness if I hadn't been so overcome by my own pleasure, reduced to a writhing mess of instinct and primal desire.

My hands grasped at his arm, grip tightening with each thrust of his fingertips until he slowed and pulled out of me completely.

Another growl loosened from my chest, a wordless demand to

return his hand to me. He listened, and this time, as he pushed into me, I felt myself stretch around two fingers.

When my body relaxed around him, he began pumping his hand again, harder and faster than before. *Gods, this was heaven. I was going to die right here, and I was okay with that.*

His face dropped down again, our open mouths meeting in a fury of desire. He began swirling his tongue against mine with the same rhythm as his fingers, coiling me tighter in response.

Warmth gushed from where his hand worshiped my body. Desire glistened along my thighs and was probably pooling on the quilt beneath me, but I couldn't find any ounce of shame over something that felt so right.

With the next curl of his fingers, I released another moan into his mouth, which he ate up with the hungry motion of his tongue.

Then, just when I thought this was the peak of pleasure, he picked up the pace. The slickness from my core dousing his hand and making obscene noises in the space between us.

He broke our kiss once more, dropping his face into the crook of my neck and nuzzling his nose against my gathering hair. "Gods, you're so wet."

His words sent me spiraling further. I liked that he could feel how much I wanted him. Loved that he praised me for it. While he was exploring my body, I was discovering new things about myself as well.

He sucked along the skin just under the hinge of my jaw. The pressure winding tighter in my center was almost unmanageable.

"Don't stop," I begged him, thrusting my hips into his hand repeatedly to match the cadence of his fingers. His thumb began quickening the circles against my clit, and he pressed his mouth against mine, pushing through my lips with his tongue.

Wild with need, I rocked against him, frantically kissing him with a frenzy that I knew would be unflattering outside of the safety of his adoration. When my knuckles went white with my iron grip around his arm, he pulled his fingers all the way out.

I released another strangled whimper against his mouth, but he wasn't gone for long. He rubbed the slick on his hand against my swollen bud, swiping his fingertips through the mess he had made before pressing back into me again.

Something about the pause in his attentions made everything hypersensitive when he returned. A bead of sweat formed along my brow as my muscles strained to spread my legs wider, take more of him into me.

"Come for me," he whispered into my hair. His command toppled me over the cliffs, and I felt like I was falling and then flying as I shattered around him, shaking with the intensity of my release. He took my mouth once more before a sound could escape my lips, my muffled moans releasing on his tongue.

He slowed his pace while the waves of my pleasure dissipated, only removing himself from my center when the tremors had stopped. My chest heaved, but my bones were limp as I all but melted into a satisfied heap against the quilt, staring up at the evening sky with as much contentment as I had ever felt here.

A soft kiss landed on my forehead. "I could watch you come undone like that forever," he whispered before taking his place on the quilt next to me.

Even in the haze that followed the most intense pleasure I had ever experienced, I became painfully aware that he was still fully clothed, and I was missing my pants.

Abruptly, I shot up. But before I could panic about where he had thrown them, Cade was already moving, a grin on his face as he slipped my feet into the holes of both my undergarments and my leggings.

He moved the band up my legs with the same sensual prowess he had shown when removing them, and something about him dressing me was just as erotic as what we had just done.

A wave of embarrassment washed over me as I was forced to reckon with the fact that I had just lain there and taken from him. "I can do stuff to you next?" I offered, cringing at the way I had worded that. It wasn't like I was some inexperienced teenager. Why had I called it *stuff* instead of just offering in a more sensual and organic way?

Cade, ignoring my awkwardness, prompted me to lift my hips so he could pull the bands of my clothing back to my waist. He settled on his side so that he could face me. "This relationship isn't transactional," he replied. "I have been wanting to do that for a *very* long time."

The heels of my palms pressed against my eyes. "I just feel like maybe the scales aren't very balanced between us. You saved my life and then gave me this mind-altering orgasm and—"

The fingertip against my lips caused me to remove my hands from my eyes and look at him. He was grinning from ear to ear. "You calling it a mind-altering orgasm is payment enough."

My cheeks flamed, but he simply lifted his hand in the air and motioned for me to join him. "Come here."

Obliging him, I turned so that my spine pressed into his chest, his body molding to mine, and his warmth seeping through the fabric that separated us. His arms wrapped around my waist, and I relished when they squeezed me against him.

"Did you put in your application for the instructor position yet?" I asked him, eyes already shutting.

"I finished it," he admitted in a whisper. "I just need to talk to my parents before I turn it in." His arm squeezed again. "Don't worry, Ashton. This will all work itself out."

There was no panicked or trapped feeling as he held me, or any of the other vast emotions that seemed to complicate my normal interactions since that night in the woods. I simply felt adored. Safe.

This will work out.

Instead of letting my mind run around a thousand miles per hour, I sighed and let myself bask in the moment.

Forty-Four

The last Monday in November was dreary and cold, but despite the morose weather, I was ready for the third challenge. Helga, Tamari, and even Cade had prepared me to the best of my abilities.

Thick grey clouds hung low in the sky, and the biting wind whipped through my hair, causing me to wrap my arms around my waist in search of warmth. I trudged behind the other students who had signed up for the archery competition, following Tamari down a well-worn path to the designated pocket of trees.

The instructors had already explained the general premise of the challenge to us in each section of the weapons class, so no further instructions were given when we reached our destination. I already knew that the roving course would consist of various targets, some stationary, while others moved. Our scores would be derived from the number of targets we hit—as well as the accuracy of those strikes—within the time limit set for the course.

Tamari offered me a wink as she headed to the table of judges, and I nodded slightly in response, hoping it didn't garner too much attention from my competition.

Reluctantly, I joined the line forming in front of a table where

Viggo Wood sat, handing out quills of color-coded arrows. My grip tightened on the bow, the one Cade had commissioned for me, slung over my shoulder. Thankfully, the rules had not barred me from bringing my own weapon to the challenge, as I had grown quite fond of Cade's gift.

When it was my turn, Viggo shoved the collection of arrows towards me, denoting the markings and color combination in a notebook resting on the table.

"Thank you," I muttered to the man who barely gave me the time of day before heading to an empty space to the side to inspect my arrows.

Berit had been the only one so forthright in his disdain, but I could sense that he wasn't the only person who had held ill will against me. Even with my lowering in rank after the second challenge, I hadn't been given much reprieve from the glares in the hallway. This challenge was no different, so I tucked myself at the base of a tree, making sure to steer clear of everyone else.

Gingerly, I pried a single arrow from the quill. The shaft was long and stiff and perfectly straight, made from a light yellowish white wood. Each one had been left unstained and was equipped with a head made of some type of charcoal colored stone, likely manufactured by Saxum wielders.

On mine, a single painted band of indigo wrapped around the place where the wood met the arrow.

My gaze traveled to the fletching, which had been taken from an enormous bird and was dyed a deep shade of blue, almost the color of a polished sapphire. Nearly the color of Cade's eyes if the tone hadn't been missing his unique threads of amethyst.

Sighing, I placed the arrow back into the quill, glancing around me to ensure I wasn't missing some pertinent instruction. Students were still lining up in front of Viggo to retrieve their own quills. More than a few of them were giving me dirty looks and whispering amongst themselves.

Wrenching my focus from their attention, I pulled my bow into my lap to check the string, still uncertain why my fall from grace via my plummeting ranking in the Ice Games had not quelled some of their hatred. Was there more merit to what Berit had said in the woods? That others believed I didn't belong here...

My fingertips ran the length of the bowstring as I battled with the urge to turn to them all and scream at the top of my lungs for them to leave me alone. Instead, I kept my gaze trained to the dark wood of my weapon, admiring the golden inlays along the limbs yet again. Knocking an arrow into position, I drew the string back, barely grazing my cheek and aiming at the empty forest away from the growing crowd.

There was something different about the feel of this arrow with my bow. Maybe it was a slightly longer shaft than the ones I had practiced with? It was nothing I couldn't quickly adjust to.

"Stand at the line!" Viggo called out, causing me to abruptly push to my feet.

Returning my arrow to its container, I threw the quill over my shoulder and made my way to the streak in the dirt that signified the boundary of the course. Whispers ignited around me, but I stared out into the woods beyond, shutting out everything but Viggo's command, which came seconds later.

There was no buildup. No countdown. Just a simple, "Go!" shrieked into the general vicinity of the starting line. His voice ricocheted off the trunks surrounding us.

With my boots scraping against the gravel beneath them, I tore from my position and bolted into the forest. Before I had a chance to second-guess my own abilities, I let the first arrow fly, only pausing long enough to hear the triumphant *thunk* before I hurriedly moved on.

Over and over again, I repeated the motions, leaning on the skills I had honed with Helga. I only missed the bullseye on a few attempts, and I didn't even let that bother me, knowing quantity would be on my side if I could combine my accuracy with speed.

Further into the course, I spotted the outline of a deer, its wooden antlers catching my attention first. An arrow with red feathered fletching already protruded from its neck. My lungs expanded in a steadying inhale as I aimed my arrow right at the location its heart would be if it had been a living creature.

Just as I was releasing my fingertip, something hard crashed into me, knocking me to the ground. My arrow whizzed through the trees, missing the deer altogether, and a seizing panic took over me.

Not again.

I bucked and flailed, but the body covering mine simply stood up, the face of a House Lynx girl grinning down at me with a predatory glint in her eye. She shrugged. "Oops." Her tone was taunting, but before I could make a comment about her not-so-accidental exchange, she was on her feet, grabbing a handful of my arrows and running off into the forest.

What. The. Fuck.

Confusion stole my attention from the reminder of Berit's attack, but I willed my focus to return to the task at hand, even though my heart continued its relentless pounding in my chest.

Bewildered, I pulled myself up and dusted off the debris lingering on my academy-issued pants. I counted five arrows remaining and threw the quiver over my shoulder.

There wouldn't be time to dwell on what had just happened until this competition was over, so I scanned the surrounding forest in search of the deer that my arrow had missed. It never showed, having somehow disappeared into the abyss of the evergreen trees on its strange mechanical legs.

My feet stomped against the dirt as I followed the path to finish out the course, stopping a few times to release arrows into some remaining moving targets I knew would give me more points than the stationary ones.

The sound of crunching leaves told me that everyone was converging on the trail now, the noise echoing against the thick pockets of trees, even if I couldn't see any of them yet.

Blocking out everything but my task, I caught sight of a wooden squirrel swinging by a chain from a small pine. With a new arrow, I took aim once more, but just as I released it, a shoulder slammed into my arm. Salvaging the arrow before it could whiz away, I held it over my head like a blade, whirling on my assailant.

A guy that I thought I recognized from House Platypus stood a few feet away. Watching me.

My eyes narrowed. "What the hell was that?"

He sneered in return, a loose shrug lifting his shoulders. "My bad."

One mistaken collision I could count as bad luck. Two? My glare hardened. "It's a friendly competition. What is your problem?"

He snorted a humorless laugh. "We will not let someone like you hurt our chances for consideration as heir. You don't even want this." His voice had transformed into a shout.

"Us?" I asked, brows raised. Berit had been deranged, but apparently, he hadn't been lying.

"We don't even know why you're trying so hard. Do you know many of us have been preparing for this honor our whole lives?" He spat at the ground between us. "Who are you to show up and take it away from us?" His voice bounced off the surrounding woods, turning into a sort of warped beat as the sound returned to my ears.

The unnamed, brown-haired boy started approaching me, and I tensed, my gaze roaming his body for any hint of a weapon other than the bow slung across his back. His quill was full of arrows. Had he even been trying to compete, or had he just been sent here to thwart me?

My voice settled into a false calm. "I can just turn it down," I replied while slowly backing away from him.

What was meant to be disarming only served to redden the boy's face more, turning it into an otherwise lovely shade of crimson. "Was your backwoods upbringing really so terrible that you don't know how this monarchy works? You can't refuse the Queen!"

The pounding in my ears drowned out whatever else he said to me as I was overcome with a sudden urgency to run. This time, I didn't give it a second thought because fighting back had done nothing to deter Berit.

Turning towards the direction I hoped the finish line was in, I sprang forward. My lungs burned in my chest as I pushed my legs to pump faster and harder, nearing me to the edge of the course. Even in the spaces that seemed void of others, I didn't pause to shoot another target.

The Platypus boy had said *we*, and I couldn't trust that more people hadn't signed up for the archery challenge with the sole purpose of coming to thwart me. Just because I believed that Berit had been the cause of both Sylvia and Ellie's attacks didn't mean that no one else was capable of the same level of violence. For all I knew, there was a group of them acting together, a thought that sent chills racing down my spine.

What I had already shot would have to be enough points to push me ahead because I couldn't bring myself to stay in this forest for a minute longer.

My panting increased as I ran across bramble and rocks, not stopping until I reached the cluster of people that signified the end of the course. Even then, I only paused behind a group of students, thinking that if another attack came, it would be more difficult to hit me behind the bodies acting unwittingly as human shields.

With everything else that had happened during the Ice Games, and with the increasing intensity over the race to be named heir, I didn't even feel relief in the presence of the instructors. Not even Tamari's gentle smile could drag me from the feeling of helpless panic.

My chest heaved, not only with the exertion of running but of the fear, stuttering my heart rate and tightening my sore muscles.

We weren't required to stay until everyone had crossed the finish line, so I handed my mostly empty quill to Viggo Wood and practically raced back to the academy, even if I would find no safety there either.

Forty-Five

The atmosphere was ripe with anxious energy as the students clustered at their tables in the dining hall the next morning. We all fell nearly silent as Headmaster Dracorris stood from his table. He clutched a piece of parchment in his hand, eyes shifting over the page as he read. "The winners of the archery competition, and an additional one hundred points for their team, are as follows..." He drew in a breath as I held mine.

His words droned on like a chant in another language. My name never left his lips, and my brain didn't quite catch on that he had moved on from archery until his voice grew louder over the claps that echoed in the room to list the winners of the final two portions of the weapons challenge.

"For these, we only award additional points to the first-place winner, so please join me in congratulating Nielsen Bell and Grethe Alexander in their respective victories in sword fighting and jousting."

I didn't need to look at Nielsen to know his chest was likely peacocked out with pride, but I clapped for him and Grethe all the same, chasing down my disappointment with another swig of my coffee.

Headmaster Dracorris raised a palm to silence the rowdy crowd.

"With those victories, House Wyvern and House Lynx are tied for first place."

Although this was good news for my team, it couldn't erase the dread bubbling in my stomach. There hadn't been a word from my sponsor since the conclusion of the second challenge, but with the evidence of my failure called out to the academy, I knew to be expecting one any day now. Perhaps the messenger was already placing the folded parchment on my pillow as I sat here waiting to be released to the first day of the hand-to-hand combat competition.

There was a hollowness in my chest as I followed Ryana to the practice field. It had been divided into four quadrants that would play host to each house's matchups for today and tomorrow. The rules had been relatively simple. The pair-ups were scheduled to last until one person pinned their opponent to the ground for more than ten seconds or until someone yielded.

Nothing was off limits, but weapons were banned, and serious injury was frowned upon, although not strictly prohibited. This meant that the people aiming to sabotage me would get a slap on the wrist if they chose to employ more sinister moves.

Even though I attempted not to let the terror win, I found myself reverting back to that girl I had been in early November, glancing over my shoulder for the next attack. It was why I currently had a small dagger strapped to a holster I had fashioned with a reconfigured belt around my thigh. Steadying myself with an elongated inhale, I trudged forward with my hand flexed over the handle of the weapon. Now, more than ever, I needed to be one of the last four people standing at the end of this segment of the competition if I had any hope of being inducted into the Select Guard.

Because it was so common for the Guides to choose students who made it to the final day of the challenge for the guard, the four people from each house who moved on to compete in this last round were known as the Select Sixteen. My last chance hung in the balance of my making it into that group.

Ryana, Grethe, Ingrid, Nielsen, and I clustered on the edge of the sparring mat, huddled under our blankets in an attempt to block out the frigid gusts that remained even after the cloudy haze from Monday had been chased from the sky. My teeth were chattering loudly, and my hands were numb by the time the matches started.

The day was a blur as we took turns sparring, rarely getting the opportunity to meet back up and discuss our individual matches. A few of my pairings had been an easy win, either because the students weren't taking the match seriously or I was simply more well-equipped.

The first truly intense match came when I was partnered with a boy several inches taller than me, with dark wavy hair and cinnamon skin. Matches had been truly randomized, neither a coupling of size nor abilities, but this was the first time I got a sense that the height difference would be an issue for me.

While I already planned to lean into the strategy that Cade had taught me to use with someone larger than me, I had not been prepared for the taunts spewing from his lips.

"What is a poor girl like you doing here at Biltons?" He asked, circling me like a buzzard would a dying animal, waiting for its demise with hungry eyes.

My expression remained neutral, my footwork light. "I got in, same as you, and I didn't even need my dad to pull any strings. Can you say the same, Jeffery?" I was pretty sure his name was Jonathan, but I didn't care. Goading him helped distract me from my fear, and it was a safe bet that plenty of the people here were admitted on a favor.

His face turned a ruddy shade of red. "Yeah, and whose strings did you pull to get in? You seem pretty cozy with a few of the instructors."

Ignoring his pointed remark, because it was impossible he knew about my meetings with Cade, I replied calmly. "Obviously, my merit. Which seems to be enough to beat you at everything else we've done."

His jaw locked into place, and his movements became more erratic. "They don't admit people without social standing here, so I know you're lying. Your parents either had strings to pull, or someone pulled on the strings of your mom's corset before they fucked a Biltons Academy admission out of her."

He was wrong on so many accounts. Jemma wasn't wealthy, although her mom was more well off than my dad, but she had gotten in just like me. Farren had been admitted the previous year, and I was certain we were not the only three people from Elmhaven to walk these halls.

He was also an idiot for bringing my mother into this. Wrath pulsed through me.

His satisfied smirk was soon wiped from his face as I ducked low, using momentum to slam into him, catching him off guard and throwing him to his back. I pinned him to the mat, putting my entire body weight into holding his flailing body down until I heard Helga yell, "Time!"

Before I released him from my hold, I leaned down so that only he could hear me. "My mother's dead, but glad to know how your mom got you admitted here. I was starting to wonder, myself."

He shoved me off him and scrambled to his feet. Instead of giving him the satisfaction of engaging further, I sauntered away back to the edge of the field where I stood, reattaching the holster to my thigh while I waited for my next pairing.

He stormed towards the academy too quickly to notice my hands balled into fists at my side or my palms bleeding from the nails digging into the flesh there. I would never let him see that he got to me.

By the time the sun was setting, my housemates and I had finally regrouped. Ryana, Grethe, Nielsen, Ingrid, and I had won all our matches and would fight again tomorrow in the second round of inter-house pair-offs.

The next morning brought about a shift in the air. Those competing today were more intense, more determined to make it to the select sixteen, either for the crown or the honor, I wasn't sure. Hardly anyone spoke as we split off to our various assigned rings for day two.

By the time my final pairing came around, Grethe and Ryana had all secured their positions in the select sixteen, with far fewer theatrics than I had expected. Neither of their opponents got carted off to the infirmary today. Yesterday's adversaries had not been so lucky with either of them. I counted myself fortunate that I hadn't been forced to face my friends, but that luck died the moment I stepped into the ring to face my last opponent.

Nielsen stood across from me with his arms folded and dark eyebrows raised as I got into position.

Today, Katarina had been given the responsibility of starting each match. She eyed us both with that same lackluster assessing glare she always gave. "I'm not going to go over the rules again. You are both part of my group, so you already know. And if you don't, that's your problem."

Oddly enough, her words brought a smile to my lips. I was sure that I looked unhinged, and I hoped that it would serve to intimidate Nielsen.

"Go!" Katarina called into the sky.

The sound of her voice catapulted my feet into motion.

Nielsen lunged, and I swerved away. I pounced to the right, and he stepped to the left. We occasionally landed taps on each other's shoulders or legs, but nothing to end the round. We were evenly matched, thanks to all those extra lessons with Cade.

Tiring of simply circling him and eager to have this behind me, I jumped towards him, dropping to swipe my leg into the back of his calves. For all of his preparation, that was where his weakness was.

Before I could adjust to his counterattack, Nielsen bent, his grip tightening around my ankle, flipping me to my back. He jumped on top of me, straddling my hips, slamming my hands over my head, pinning me to the ground.

Instantly, a feral panic took over my body. I was no longer in a competition. I was in the woods, alone, underneath a different body. Coal-black eyes were staring down at my skin hungrily, and a knife glistened over my head.

Screaming out, I thrashed wildly. The only thing that brought me back to reality was the sound of Ryana's frantic yelling. "Yield, Ashton!"

A gurgled "yield" left my throat, and the weight of Berit's body left mine. Except when I opened my eyes, it was Nielsen, and I was back on school grounds with a dozen wide-eyed, confused people staring at me.

My cheeks heated, and tears filled my lash line. "I, uh... I'm sorry."

Nielsen offered me a hand, but I refused to touch him. Pushing myself up off the ground, I rose to my feet, then ran down the well-worn path towards the academy buildings and the solitude of my bed.

There was nothing left for me on the field anyway. I had just forfeited my last chance at getting into the Select Guard.

Forty-Six

It was Jemma who found me the next morning, sulking beneath the quilt in my bed as if I could block out my new reality with a layer of navy-hued cotton.

"Get up," she demanded.

My face burrowed into my pillow as I released a deep groan. "No."

"Ashton, we have been friends a very long time," she reminded me. "So, I know what this meant to you, but I am here to tell you it isn't over."

I lifted my head to glare at her as her weight dipped the mattress at the foot of my bed.

She frowned at me, and I was struck by the notion that I couldn't recall the last time I had seen her expression so void of amusement. "You know, my mother has said that you are powerful."

A huff escaped my lips as I let my cheek fall back against the pillow-case, still damp with my tears.

"And she's never wrong," Jemma added.

My eyes fluttered closed, unable to look at her even if all she was doing was trying to help. "They only look to the Select Sixteen or winners of multiple challenges. Jemma, I am neither of those." It took the entirety of my willpower to rein in the fresh wave of tears threatening to crest my lashes, knowing that if I allowed myself to start again, I might not be able to stop.

Jemma's hand came to rest on my leg, gripping it loosely from atop the coverlet. "That's not true. They look at overall performance and power levels."

The sniffle that came from me was neither ladylike nor subtle. "How do you even know that? You don't care about the competition at all."

She scoffed. "I already told you I care about you." Annoyance laced her tone. "Plus, Connally told me. She's into this whole heir thing, too."

I tilted my chin and opened my eyes to get a better look at my friend. The friend I had accidentally neglected over the last month while I attempted to pursue a goal I might never reach.

Her emerald eyes pinched as she took me in. "I can't tell you that everything is going to be okay, but I can't sit by and watch you mope away your last chance at achieving your lifelong desires." There was pity lingering in her stare, but I found a contagious hope there, too, so I ignored it.

Jemma removed her hand from my leg and reached for me. "Come with Connally and me to the lake today. It's a free day, and I think it would be good for you to take your mind off this."

The academy had given everyone a day off from the challenge before the final matches took place on Friday, and while the desire to wallow was intense, I found myself grasping onto the hope she offered instead.

Marjorie had never been wrong about a reading, and I had done well in the Ice Games and in my sessions, despite my failure to breach the Select Sixteen or win more than one first-place ranking in the challenges.

Reluctantly, I took her hand in my own. "Okay."

Thirty minutes later, I was sitting by the lake on a patch of rocky sand that had warmed beneath the sun. This far into autumn, the air was consistently cool, but I basked in the toasty rays as I tied my scarf tighter around my neck.

To my surprise, Grethe and Ryana joined us as well, stating that Jemma had given them no choice.

When I glared at her with narrow eyes, Jemma's expression shifted to feigned innocence. "I figured you could use some more friends right now."

A heavy sigh fell from my lips, and I let them curl into a smile at yet another of her small gestures that meant so much to me.

Sensing her victory, she clapped her hands together before dropping to the space beside me. "Okay, you all know the drill. We don't talk about the competition, and we give Ashton all the wine she wants."

Connally gave her a sideways glance with those mesmerizing amber eyes. "You just brought it up."

A prideful expression filtered over Jemma's features, one I had seen many times. "I simply reminded the rest of you of the rules. Now, we need to move on to something more fun."

If there was something I knew I was good at, it was evasion. Speaking to no one in particular, I asked, "Is everyone excited about the break we are getting after the ceremony?"

Jemma pouted, but she obliged me for no other reason than she could sense that I needed the distraction. "Obviously, I can't wait to see my mom and maybe more of you."

My eyes rolled at the dig. If Jemma had been truly upset by my absence, she would have just told me. "I think you've been fairly preoccupied as well."

She wiggled her eyebrows. "At least I have been occupied with orgasms." She snapped her fingers in the air. "That's what you need. A good orgasm."

My face flamed at her words, not just from the embarrassment of her being so forward but also at the mental images of Cade's hand between my legs.

"Oh, my gods!" she shrieked. "Have you been getting orgasms? Have you finally admitted your feelings about a certain dark-haired —"

"I am dying to go back home," Ryana, thankfully, interjected before Jemma's line of questioning went too much further.

Whether or not it was intentional, I was thankful for the shift in topic. I turned to my savior, grinning. "To see the guy that you left behind?"

Instantaneously, I regretted the words as Grethe's brows bunched in confusion, and I realized that whatever had been going on between them had not been fully fleshed out.

"I'm ready to get back home as well," Grethe admitted, although the awkwardness of my question seemed to taint his response.

Connally pushed herself upright. Her long platinum hair shone like pure silver under the scrutiny of the sun's unfiltered rays. "I'm not ready for break. I don't have anywhere to go back to."

We all swiveled our heads to look at her.

She hummed some noncommittal noise. "I'm an orphan. My parents died a long time ago. I have no other living family here. My aunt has been raising me out of obligation mostly, so once the school year is over, I am no longer welcome back there."

She said the words as if she were simply stating her favorite color, devoid of the heavy emotion that should have accompanied them. It had probably taken years of practice to be that nonchalant about something so devastating.

"That's awful, Connally," I whispered. "I'm sor—"

"You guys are supposed to be making Ashton feel better, not bringing her down with all of your drama," Jemma chastised the group, only making things even more uncomfortable between us all. "Let's revisit those orgasms," she suggested with glee in her eyes.

"No!" we all shouted at the same time.

"Let's get drunk," Grethe offered, pulling a set of cups from his own bag.

Jemma's eyes narrowed in my direction, but a smile tugged along her lips. "Fine," she conceded, producing a bottle of wine from her own stash. I snickered as I pictured Mr. Higgins making some deal with Dante in a darkened alcove for the alcohol.

"Pass me a cup," I said to Grethe, reaching my hand between us and resolving myself to block out the rest of the day to dissociation.

Later that evening, I staggered with the girls back into our dormitory to find a vase full of purple roses sitting on top of my armoire.

"Someone got you flowers!" Jemma shrieked; a bit too loud even beneath the haze of the wine that made everything but Jemma's outburst softer. Flinching against the noise, I cupped my hands over my ears to dampen the shrill volume of her voice.

Stumbling slightly, I giggled as I approached the flowers, finding a crisp envelope resting against the glass container.

"Tell us who it's from!" Jemma squealed, pushing herself against me in an effort to get closer to the letter.

It was only after a few blinks that cleared the fog from my vision that I recognized the handwriting. The blood drained from my face in a sobering retreat from my careless drunkenness. My mouth was too dry to even swallow. "It's a secret," I said, wondering if I could get away from her long enough to read the note in private.

Shoving it into the waistband of my leggings, I pulled my fist to my face, knowing I didn't have to fake the nausea now churning my gut. "I think I'm going to be sick," I exclaimed, racing to the bathing chamber.

"I bet it's from Cade," I heard Jemma whisper-yell to either Connally or Ryana, but I had very little interest in their suspicions of my relationship with the House Wyvern leader.

The sponsor had written me again, and I had no doubts that they were planning on calling in their debt early, considering I had already lost my place in the Select Sixteen.

Slipping into an empty stall, I sat on the lid of the toilet as I ripped apart the seal on the letter, unfolding the parchment with shaking hands.

Dear Miss Blake,

I have been informed that you failed in your attempt to garner extra points at the archery competition. In addition, you did not secure a position in the select sixteen. It is of utmost importance that you finish out the year with top marks in order to have any chance of reaching our goals.

I will be watching.

P.S. I hope you enjoyed the flowers from your father's garden.

The paper fell from my hands, fluttering like a fallen leaf to the tiled floor of the bathing chamber. Whoever this was had recently been to my father's cottage. They, or someone they employed, had traveled for the majority of a full day to pluck the blooms from his gardens as a warning to me. How did they know that the purple ones were my favorite? How long had they been watching me?

Fear blazed a frosted trail in my veins, but something else was there, too. If the sponsor thought that I stood a chance, maybe there was some validity in Jemma's earlier statement. All I had to do was make it to the ceremony and prove myself powerful, and then I could still save the man who had dedicated his life to caring for me.

The only thing I wanted was to go home and wrap my arms around my dad, just to be sure that he was alright and that nothing had happened to him in my absence. But the image I conjured would have to suffice because I couldn't go home yet. The only way to save him was to stick this out.

On shaky legs, I stood from the toilet, sucking in a deep breath that did nothing to slow the harsh rhythm of my heartbeats.

There were three weeks left until the solstice ceremonies, a handful of days to endure before my bind was removed and my power released.

Three weeks until this was over, and I could breathe again.

$$\mathcal{F}orty\text{-}\mathcal{S}even$$

By the time breakfast was over on Friday morning, I had shoved my disappointment so far deep within myself that all I had left was excitement for the day and a goal to cheer on my friends in the last competition of the Combat Games.

It wasn't until I found a spot on the edge of the sparring ring and scanned the crowd that I remembered that at least a few of the Guides always observed the last day. They were impossible to miss. The ancient man that I recognized from challenge two as Claudius, sat in his outdated apparel next to two other equally elderly beings that I assumed were other Guides.

The Guide to Claudius' right was a woman with pale skin almost the same color as her icy white hair. From this distance, it was hard to tell her eye color exactly, but they were dark, almost black. Her bony hands were mangled with knobs, several fingers misshapen like the wiry branches of a tree. Like her companion, she also wore strange robes, hers in a deep green. She most closely resembled the oil paintings that depicted Elvynia, the Guide who represented the Saxum powers. I wondered if she wore green to signify her association with the land.

To the left of Claudius sat a man with dark brown skin. Deep lines etched along his cheeks and forehead. His eyes drooped like the scrunched face of a hound. His hands were hidden under the sleeves of his enormous black robe, but a worn wooden cane was propped against his chair. I knew from the cane alone that this was likely Phoebus, the Guide in charge of Flumen powers, as the walking aid was actually painted into the official portrait. Nothing about his appearance screamed water to me, though.

The Guides in front of me were so still that I began to worry if they were even breathing until one of them spoke softly to the other, words I could not hear. Their presence felt so out of place, surrounded by all this youth. Their stoicism was a stark contrast to the clashing of bodies they were sent here to bear witness to.

The other two, Theondri and Namea, who presided over the Caelum and Operarius classes, were nowhere to be found. It was uncommon for all five of them to leave the Queen at once, with the exception of the transition ceremonies. Biltons was the only academy whose ceremony occurred on the solstice. Wythe's rituals were performed the day before, and Chapelstone's the day after.

Some said it was why Biltons' graduates were always more powerful since their unbinding occurred when the magic of nature was at its peak. I had assumed, especially after all of my conversations on the subject with Cade, that the power levels had more to do with the wealthy families being selective on who would marry into their bloodlines. Essentially, they were breeding magic within these families like they were prized horses rather than people.

Headmaster Dracorris stood from his chair next to Elvynia, facing the students before them and pulling me from those thoughts. "Welcome, students and esteemed guests, to the last day of the Ice Games!"

The Headmaster summarized the rules, which we had already been given countless times in both battle strategy and hand-to-hand combat sessions. When he finished, his eyes raked over the gathering students. "Let the games begin!"

Clapping and whooping echoed along the stone perimeter of the field, but my gaze remained on the Guides seated with the Headmaster. Their presence filled me with a sense of looming dread. Had I already missed my shot to stand out to them? To be part of the exclusive guardians of the Elemental Queen?

With regret pulsing in my chest, I tore my gaze from them and shifted it to the field.

There was too much to keep track of once the matches started. Bodies darting within their circles. Punches were landed, and grunts reverberated down the field. I caught Cade's attention once, his indigo eyes only meeting mine for a moment as he stood on the sidelines with the other house leaders.

These matches weren't over as quickly as the house matches had been. Every one of the sixteen students deserved their spot in this elite portion of the competition. Even Grethe was breaking a heavy sweat when he pinned his opponent to the ground, ending the round.

The next eight students took their places within the four designated circles. This time, I made my way closer to the ring that Ryana was in, standing next to Grethe as he watched, panting from his exertion. The next few rounds were going to be rough because the minute two people were triumphant, they were reshuffled in rapid rematches.

Ryana circled her opponent. Her violet-tinted hair had grown enough since August that I was able to braid it for her this morning into a sleek plait that fell to her shoulders.

Ryana shifted back and forth on the balls of her feet, dancing around the other student as if this were a choreographed duet between them. She popped the other girl on the shoulder, bounced back, then came forward to smack her face.

My friend was taunting the other woman, trying to get a reaction. Her opponent took the bait, and I watched as the woman clenched her fists together, infuriated. The opponent charged, and Ryana reached out her arm, hitting the woman against her chest and throwing her to her back.

Ryana pinned her opponent easily and glanced over at Grethe. I watched as his eyes shifted to the observation table and back to her. He made a gesture with his hands that I didn't study well enough to comprehend.

Whatever it meant, it distracted Ryana enough to cause her to loosen her grip on her opponent. This gave the woman enough time to flip Ryana on her back and pin her for the ten seconds it took to win the match.

Before I had any time to contemplate what I had just seen, Cade called out to the group again. "Alright, last assignments before we move onto rapid rounds." A line formed in front of him as he waved each person to their respective field marker. Moments later, his loud whistle signified the start of round three.

Ryana found me on the sidelines of Grethe's next fight. In the final eight, the stakes were higher, and the opponents would be more determined. With the Guides observing from their raised platform, the intensity of the competition had already seen a swift increase in injuries as the students scrambled to prove their worth. Grethe was sporting a freshly busted lip, blood flowing from his mouth.

"He's just being dramatic," Ryana said with slight irritation as Grethe spit a wad of blood off to the side.

Keeping my gaze on the fighting, I spoke softly. "What happened back there, Ry?"

There was movement out of the corner of my eye where I caught Ryana's shrug. "Rookie mistake." Her voice was not as carefree as her words suggested.

Something about her demeanor bothered me. She was irritated that she had lost her match, but I had expected her to be outraged. Her competitiveness was unmatched, her reactions unbridled. This relatively calm version of her once again flipped the script of the person I thought I knew.

SNNNNNNAP!

A sharp sound, almost like a tree limb breaking echoed across the field, followed by a howling wail. I shifted my gaze from Ryana to the source of the noise, only to find the rust-haired boy that Grethe had been fighting cradling a bloody arm and screaming at the top of his lungs.

White bone pierced the skin halfway between his elbow and wrist, and the splintered edges protruded out, catching on ribbons of flesh. The unexpected image made my stomach roil, but I held it together, suppressing the rising urge to vomit.

"Yield!" the rust-haired boy cried out between his body-shaking sobs.

Grethe was gloating over his win until he met Ryana's stare, and his face fell. No other communication transpired between them, but Grethe remained stoic as he walked to Cade to get his next match assignment.

"I think I'm done here. Are you ready to go back?" Ryana's tone was full of feigned indifference.

As much as I wanted to watch Grethe and maybe even catch Nielsen's match, I could sense Ryana's need to get away from the field, and I, of all people, empathized with her desires.

"Yeah," I replied in the lightest tone I could wield.

Had we both seen our chances of reaching our goals dashed on a chilly day in November?

The silence crackled between us as we made our way back to the academy's main building, ignoring the eruption of cheers behind us.

For a split second, I considered looking back to see if I could glean who had come out victorious, but Ryana didn't even spare the field a passing glance, and I scurried to keep up with her quick pace on her mute but swift march back to our room.

Forty-Eight

It turned out that Grethe had won his last match with a body slam that left his opponent, Nielsen, yielding almost immediately to the wave of pain caused by broken ribs. This quick and efficient win in the last round of the challenge, as well as having two of our people in the final round, gave House Lynx enough points to be named the winners of the Ice Games.

This was how I ended up standing in a courtyard at the Elemental Queen's castle on a frigid day in early December.

The building itself looked much like the academy but smaller. Gray and sand-colored stones piled high into cylindrical towers, green tarnished copper roofs adorning each one. The flag of Demetros sat atop the tallest spire, fluttering in the gentle gusts of wind. A set of heavy, wooden, arched double doors marked the main entrance. For once, they were open, inviting me and my curiosity further into the depths of the Queen's residence.

Two of the Select Guard walked in front of our group, and several more flanked our sides. They wore emerald colored uniform jackets with pine green caps at their shoulders, which also boasted the golden embroidered wheat shapes I had come to associate with Demetros. Complementary golden straps buckled down the front of their jackets.

Their hair was all tucked neatly in braids or ties and hidden underneath matching green hats, with the flower of Demetros embroidered above a dark emerald rim. Thick black leather belts were strapped around their waist, matching their onyx pants and boots. They all wore white gloves that stopped halfway between their elbows and wrists.

Each soldier had a few daggers fastened along their waists, but I knew that only the most elite wielders made the Select Guard, so these people were dangerous even without a weapon. Standing here, where my mother must have stood many years ago in that green uniform, my heart ached even more with the need to be one of them.

We were ushered into a spacious receiving room. Curved wooden beams lined three-story ceilings. Large plush burgundy carpets blanketed the floors, bringing a softness to the space in contrast to all the wood and stone features.

An ornate brass chandelier hung in the center of the room with what must have been thousands of candles illuminating the chamber, glittering with red and pink gemstones that cast brilliant spots of light around the space.

We were clustered in the entry until we were permitted into the viewing room in smaller waves. Once again, I found myself at the tail end of the line with Ryana and Grethe, who were deep in their own hushed conversation. When it was our turn, we were escorted by one of the Select Guard members, who introduced herself as Leilani.

The room she brought us to was full of art and tapestries, but my attention was drawn to the center of the space where the Ice Trophy stood, its power a gentle hum against my skin.

The trophy was resting on a wooden stand with a brass plaque that, according to the chief guard, had been engraved with the winning team's house name every year. After the brass was full of victors, it was then retired to the enormous wooden slabs that hung on the walls surrounding the prize. There were so many of them.

My focus drifted back to the guard, Leilani, and her recount of the rules we had already been told numerous times before even leaving the academy grounds. Her voice was monotone as if she were reading from a script in her head. "You may touch the trophy for no more than five seconds, at which point we will ask you to leave the room. A member of the Select Guard will be waiting outside to escort you back to your carriages."

Everyone formed a line, and from my spot, admiring a tapestry in the far corner of the room, I ended up at the back of it. With only five seconds to touch the trophy itself, the group moved out quickly, and before I knew it, I was alone with the guard.

"Go ahead, miss," Leilani said, gesturing at the trophy before folding her hands neatly in front of her.

My hand stilled as I took precious moments to admire it instead. It was far more intricate up close. The two reindeer that made up the base were so lifelike that it appeared they had been frozen while lurching into the air on their hind legs, their hooves curling into handles for the cup. Together, their antlers tangled into a holster for the bowl that rested atop their heads.

Those details were where their realistic features ended because the entire trophy was comprised of the same glittering blue material as if it had been carved out of the kingdom's largest aquamarine. As I inched closer, my breath formed huffs of curling smoke as the heat of my exhale collided with the frigid air surrounding the prize.

Slowly, I reached my hand out towards the closest little hoof, letting my fingertip graze it like it was a fragile glass figurine, even though I doubted they'd let us near it if it was so delicate. A chill shot up my finger, a level of cold I had never experienced before. It climbed over my forearm and up my shoulder, leaving painful goosebumps in its wake. My skin tingled like the pins-and-needles feeling of getting into a too-hot bath, except I was shivering.

There was a tinge of sadness that followed the wave of cold, almost an emptiness, like the trophy was not only void of temperature but also life. Similar to the eerie feeling I had felt at the Cliffs of Alamance.

"That's enough," the guard said sternly, placing her hand on my shoulder in a gentle warning. But when she touched me, we both jolted backwards.

Leilani rubbed her hands together, a grimace twisting her features. "Are you alright?"

"I think so," I replied. "I just got cold."

A line of confusion formed between her brows, and I wasn't sure what to make of it.

A nervous laugh bubbled from my chest. "I guess that's why we can't touch it for more than five seconds."

Ignoring my comment, the guard pulled off her gloves to inspect the fingertips of the hand that touched me. They were the lightest shade of purple, like frostbite had claimed them, although the color was quickly returning to them as we watched.

Leilani's focus shifted from her hand back to me. "Yes, the Queen's magic is rare and extraordinary. You never know how it will affect people."

She looked as if she was about to say more, but she put her glove back on and gestured toward the door. "Our time is up. Let us join the others."

I walked out of the room, sparing only one more glance at the trophy. At this angle, I could have sworn it was shimmering in the distinct motion of a wave goodbye.

As I crossed the threshold, I found myself back in the receiving room, except instead of being full of my classmates, there were just two other people. Even the rest of the guard had vacated the space, likely escorting the students back to their carriages.

Leilani didn't stiffen in the presence of the two figures, but her demeanor changed into something more guarded. As she guided me past them, holding onto my elbow to steer me, I got a better look at them.

One was a man, older than almost anyone I had seen. He had somehow retained kohl black hair, despite his age, which was cut close to his head. His almond eyes were dark brown, covered partially by the sagging skin of his eyebrows. With his apparent age and his strange sapphire robes, I deduced that this must be the Caelum Guide, Theondri.

Which meant that the equally ancient being beside him must be the only other Guide I had not seen in person before, Namea. The one who oversaw the branding of the Operarius.

They were ambiguous, neither male nor female, but something both masculine and feminine in between. Their tanned skin was weathered like leather that had been left out too long, and green eyes shone through chin-length, mousy brown hair covered in streaks of gray.

I tried not to stare, but it was impossible. There was something so wrong about the Guides. Like the magic that kept them unnaturally alive, well past the normal human lifespan, was stealing happiness and warmth through their pores, chilling the air surrounding their bodies.

Both of them met my gaze with little more than curious contemplation, like an adult assessing an unrelated child's artwork, obliged to consider it but wholly unimpressed. It still sent a shiver running down my spine as I let Leilani pull me from the hall and into the sunshine of the castle's vast courtyard.

Forty-Nine

THE NAMELESS

So much had changed since that first tingle of her magic. The trickle of her power had transformed into a steady beat, thrumming inside her body, knocking along the magical wards and demanding to be set free.

It wasn't just the sensation of her power that had returned to her. That very evening, her memories had begun to flood her with an intensity that stole her breath.

She could recall her father's emerald green eyes and her mother's icy blues.

Her father had a mustache, and she knew this because she could remember the way it tickled her cheeks when he kissed her goodnight.

Her mother wore her hair in a bun, low on her neck. She loved the color burgundy, and she wore it often.

Most of the memories were mundane flashes of a simple life that she had taken for granted. Horseback riding in the woods. Ice skating on a frozen lake. Sneaking chocolate from the kitchens.

Some were horrible, even in their lack of completion. She could recall that her parents had been forced to travel beyond the kingdom's borders to find something important. They had never been seen again, presumed dead.

In her memories of those dark days, she had been so young, saddled with the responsibility of a household. Too young to make funeral arrangements for the people who had raised her.

Unfortunately, she knew now that this was the weakness that her captors had exploited back when they had wormed their way into her life.

She also remembered that stranger, from a time before the woman's body had been frozen and obliterated.

In these recollections, the woman's face was split into a wide grin, her hair unbound and blowing in an autumn breeze. Sometimes, there were snippets of a barking laugh or images of their fingers intertwined.

Flashbacks came in jagged spurts of these renderings, laced with heavy emotions that clawed at her chest. The memories were rarely together or in chronological order, but they were returning.

Still, she couldn't recount her name or how she ended up here, but she knew that once her memories belonged to her again, she would know how to free herself.

She would know where to run and who to run to.

She just had to wait it out.

Fifty

The official end of the Ice Games brought with it the conclusion to anyone taking their courses seriously. Final exams had been administered, and all the students had left to do was prepare for the solstice ball and the subsequent ceremony.

At this point, there was no obstacle remaining for me to fret over, no additional work I could do to prove my worthiness here, so I let Jemma convince me that dress shopping was the best use of my time. She steered me to a carriage parked in front of the academy, and I boarded to find Ryana, Connally, and even Ingrid already seated in the velvet-lined transport.

Connally was the only one amongst us who had any experience attending more formal events and was ecstatic to use us as real-life dolls in her game of dress up.

"Presentation matters," she had chided when I told her during our journey to the capital markets that I was planning to wear something simple without all the extra accessories.

What I didn't say was that I wasn't sure I could afford anything new, but I didn't want to be left out or left alone with my thoughts, so I figured I could try some things on without purchasing anything.

Being around Connally when she was like this made it difficult to fathom that the woman before me, comfortable with extravagant parties and the finer things in life, was the very same person who had admitted to us that she would be homeless at the conclusion of the academic year. Technically, her exile from her familial home started after the ceremonies occurred in a few short days.

It troubled me for numerous reasons, mostly because I couldn't comprehend a family member being so callous, even if Connally was known to make a snide comment or two. Why would an aunt who had the means to expose her niece to such frivolous affairs be so eager to abandon the girl the moment her powers came in?

Just as I was allowing myself to feel bad for Connally, I glanced over at her only to find her eyes narrowed in on my mother's ring with a sort of disgusted confusion. Her sneer mocked me, as if she couldn't puzzle how someone as low-born as myself would own something that screamed affluence. My eyes rolled as I averted my gaze to the window of the carriage, reminding myself that we had to get along for Jemma's sake.

When I eagerly departed the carriage, I noted that the streets of Fulgrande were more crowded than I had ever seen them, a testament to the sheer number of people who had procrastinated their solstice shopping. All of them braving the bustling capital markets to check the last few items from their lists.

The solstice was a popular time for celebration, not just for the transition into power for those of us at the academies, but also as a time when gifts were exchanged. It marked the longest night, a sign that the hardships of the winter would fade with every day growing longer from there.

In Elmhaven, it was not uncommon to receive new seeds to be planted in the spring, wreaths constructed of evergreen branches, candles made from beeswax, and any number of still-blooming floral arrangements.

Because of his love of all things plant-related, it was my dad's favorite holiday. Our cottage had always been decorated with ropes of evergreens woven together into a garland. He'd pull out what felt like a thousand tiny candles, placing them all about the home and making it look like a rendition of the night sky had been transposed into the décor of our small cottage.

The reminder that I would be missing the setup for the solstice this year sent a jolt of pain to my chest at the same time my excitement bubbled up at the knowledge that I was days away from seeing it for myself. Dad usually left it all up until the pine needles turned brown and fell off the branches, littering the floor with tiny dustings of itchy debris.

"This place is perfect," Connally stated as she approached an unsuspecting building that looked more like a house than a business. The front was plain in architecture but painted in a light pink, an unusual color for a home in the capital. Fuchsia flower boxes hung from each window that contained purple and yellow pansies. An average-sized frosted glass window was nestled into the confines of the blood-red door.

If it hadn't been for the small silver plaque that read *Madame Luthane's Apparel Shop*, in elaborate cursive script, I would have assumed that this was the entrance to an eccentric residence rather than a place of business.

My eyes squinted suspiciously at the unusual building. "I'm not sure we should go in there."

Jemma released a huffy breath. "Why not? We need a dress, and it's a dress shop..." She pointed at the last two words on the plaque as she enunciated them.

My teeth grazed the inside of my cheek as I fought the urge to clamp down. "Don't you think it might be a special kind of dress shop?"

Ingrid stepped towards the plaque, read it for herself, then faced me to ask, "What kind of dress shop would it be?"

Clearing my throat, I lowered my voice. "For the ladies that work..." My words cut off as I struggled to find a less offensive way to articulate what I meant.

Jemma's eyes rolled so hard I thought they might fall from her head. "Even if it is a shop meant to create garments for the skin trade, then it would stand to reason that the dresses will make me look irresistible. So, I'm in."

With her palms cupped next to her temples, she attempted to peer inside the frosted glass. Either having seen what she was looking for or out of sheer impulsivity, Jemma opened the door without knocking. The rest of us waited a few beats before Connally followed her within the shop, and we were given no choice but to reluctantly do the same. Or stay in the cold while they shopped.

As unusual as the shop had been from the outside, it was even more eccentric and extravagant on the inside, a fact which didn't soothe my fears that we had entered an establishment that supplied gowns for more *adventurous* patrons.

The dark wooden floors were covered in plush ruby and magenta patterned rugs. Two deep crimson velvet settees faced each other in the center of the space. Along the outer perimeter, racks of jeweled-toned garments in every color lined the walls. A pale pink floral wallpaper peeked out from behind the dresses, and various oil paintings boasted a litany of flowers illustrated within ornate golden frames.

Thanks mostly to the trio of frosted glass windows at the front of the shop, the room was blanketed in only the soft glow of the flickering oil lamps that hung in equal spacing between the artworks. It made the shop feel cozy and sensual at the same time.

A thick accent rolled across the room from behind an extravagantly painted dressing screen that was covered in lifelike painted flowers. "Welcome to my shop. How may I help you ladies today?"

Connally stepped forward. "We need dresses *and accessories* for the academy ball at the end of the week."

The woman who slipped from behind the screen, presumably Madame Luthane, was likely only a few years older than my dad. However, it was difficult to tell exactly as she had polished her face with a cacophony of products and was wearing the latest and boldest fashion trends.

A single thick strap curled around a milky white shoulder. Ample breasts were lifted from a hidden bustier, expertly fashioned into her pink taffeta gown that complemented the floral wallpaper behind her. The fabric cascaded from her waist, spilling over the slope of her hips as she sashayed across the room.

A smile curved her full lips, the color of ripe cherries, and her eyelashes fluttered as she took us in with warm brown eyes. "Of course, dears," she said, gesturing towards the settees. "Have a seat, and I will find something that will work for each of you."

We took our places on the designated furniture while she rummaged through the racks, revealing dark auburn curls that fell in ringlets to the middle of her back. She threw out the occasional hum or scoff as she worked diligently, scurrying down a hallway as she pulled pieces that I couldn't see from my spot on the settee.

Finally, she returned to the seating area. "You will come back one at a time, as I call you." She stretched a delicate finger in Connally's direction. "You. Come."

Connally followed without hesitation, and fifteen minutes later, she reemerged in a deep periwinkle silk gown that looked like it had just melted across her body. It had thin straps, a modest V-neck, and fabric that crisscrossed at her waist. It boasted a slit up one side that showed off her long legs.

Madame Luthane had outfitted Connally in the accessories she had requested, pinning her hair halfway back in a twisting silver clip that revealed dangling teardrop-shaped stones that perfectly matched her dress, swinging from her earlobes. As Connally adjusted her position in the mirror, strappy silver sandals peeked out from beneath the shimmering purple skirts of her gown.

Either from years of knowing that she was a master at her craft or a complete lack of caring what her customers thought, the shop owner didn't even wait for Connally's reaction, spitting out a quick, "This will do. Next," before turning to Ingrid.

In much the same manner that she had summoned Connally, she gestured for Ingrid into the narrow hallway that presumably led to the dressing room. Approximately five minutes later, Ingrid emerged wearing a simple pink taffeta gown that was the exact same hue and sheen as Madame Luthane's garb. This version had a sweetheart neckline and was missing the slit that Connally's dress had.

Ingrid was adorned with simple silk slippers and a pearl necklace and earrings. Her raven black hair was braided down her back and it appeared the Madame had added some makeup that caused her face to glow. Ingrid looked incredible.

"You are happy," Madame Luthane stated. "Next."

The shop owner gestured at Ryana, and they disappeared into the back.

Minutes later, Ryana rounded the corner in a bold amethyst gown that highlighted the violet streaks in her dark tresses. It also had a sweetheart neckline with capped sleeves. The top resembled a bustier with boning down the line of her body, which ended at her waist. Fluffy tulle in the same shade as the top billowed out from the end of the corset. As she walked, strappy black-heeled shoes darted out from beneath the soft fabric.

Ryana's hair rested in a braided coil like a crown atop her head. Flower-shaped earrings made entirely of amethyst stones hung from her ears, and a dainty black chain with a matching flower pendant fell from her neck. Kohl lined her reflective brown eyes. She was feminine but in a boldly intense way that suited her.

The shop owner didn't even need to say anything further, her face dripping with smug satisfaction as she jabbed a finger in Jemma's direction, prompting her to take her turn in the dressing room.

When Jemma emerged, my breath caught in my throat. Vibrant red silk hugged the dips and flares of Jemma's curves, held up only by a pair of thin, jewel-encrusted straps. A deep v in the neckline dipped to the very top of her belly button, showing off her full and perky breasts. As she twisted to catch her own reflection in the floor-length mirror, she revealed the dip in the back, the fabric curving to a point just at the base of her exposed spine. The silk was smooth and taught over her hips and ass, flaring only as it reached mid-thigh into a flowing flared skirt that reminded me of a mermaid tail.

Jemma grinned at her image in the mirror, spreading stained lips that matched the tone of her dress, crinkling the corners of her kohl-lined eyes.

"There is a release string here if you have to relieve yourself," Madame Luthane said as she showed Jemma the hidden string in the front of her dress. Jemma beamed, and I already saw the beginnings of her plot to use the release for other activities.

My original position had not changed as I still fully believed that the target clientele for this shop were those who willingly sold their pleasure, but Jemma had been correct in her assessment too: these dresses were perfect.

When Madam Luthane nodded to me, I followed her down the short hallway before she ushered me into a small, curtained room. It was decorated in the same floor coverings and wallpaper as the rest of the shop, with one small burgundy footstool in the corner.

The woman's eyes roamed over me for a moment, and whatever she saw there caused her to shake her head and leave the dressing room in a flurry of pink fabric. When she returned, she had two dresses. One a deep, shiny emerald, and the other a sparkling gold.

"Choose," she said sternly. Nothing about her other interactions insinuated we'd get any sort of choice on the matter. It made me wonder if the others had this same experience. Connally had been gone the longest, presumably the pickiest out of the group. I scoffed at the thought that I was anything like Connally, and yet, as I stared at the two dresses that the shop owner held in her outstretched hands, I couldn't bring myself to pick between them with any sort of haste.

My teeth gnawed on the edges of my lower lip. "May I try them both on?"

Her eyes narrowed slightly, but her words were kind. "Of course."

Because it reminded me so much of the lush greens of my father's gardens, I reached for the emerald dress first. Madame Luthane placed the golden dress on a nearby hook, but she didn't leave the room as I stripped down to my undergarments, and I had to remind myself that she saw unclothed bodies all the time to keep the blush from covering my face and extremities.

The woman fastened me into the dress with nimble fingers, twisting me until I faced the mirror within the suite, and I blinked back as my image stole my breath.

This dress was elegance personified. The curved neckline was modest, and fabric draped across my body in a way that reminded me of flowing water. A lovely chiffon cape cascaded down my back from capped jeweled sleeves.

Seeing myself in the rich color of the Select Guard had me squeezing my eyelids shut, picturing a different image in my mind. Madame

Luthane cleared her throat, and I blinked away the vision, letting my focus fall upon my reflection once more.

"Is this the one?" the shop owner asked me, eyebrows lifted.

My gaze darted over my shoulder to the golden dress, and although I loved the emerald gown for so many reasons, my heart clenched at the sight of the other. It took a few minutes to switch out the gowns, but the moment the golden fabric slid over my shoulders, I knew it was the one.

Jemma's gasp was the first thing to greet me as I returned to the main part of the shop.

Turning to face the mirror next to the settee, I finally had enough space to really take it in. The dress was so tight it left little to the imagination. The entire garment was constructed from a thin champagne colored material that clung to my curves. A subtle v in the neckline should have been demure, but the tightness of the dress pushed up my already full breasts, making it border on sensual.

A thin mesh connected from the edge of the top of each strap, creating a see-through capped sleeve silhouette. Diamond-like gems and beads were sewn into the mesh, giving the appearance of jeweled shoulders, a twinkling necklace, and vines snaking up across my chest toward my collar.

From my hipbones, sparkling neutral gemstones had been painstakingly sewn to appear to drape across my thighs and around my backside like the regal curtains one might find in a theater. Below these beaded drapes, the billowing fabric was completely sheer to the floor, with only a few of the jewel-encrusted vines curling their way up my legs. My intimate areas were covered, but I felt utterly naked, and it was strangely empowering, given everything I had been through.

Madame Luthane handed me simple studded gold earrings. A champagne-colored stone with a diamond halo. Then she placed champagne-hued shoes on my feet, pointed at the front where they covered my toes, one strap wound across my ankle connecting me to about four inches of heel. The woman braided a crown across the top of my head but left the rest cascading down my back.

"Excellent choice," Madame Luthane said as she smiled, assessing my body like I was nothing more than a completed work of her own art. In a way, I supposed that I was.

"Holy shit, Ash, you look so fuckable right now," Jemma exclaimed from her perch on the settee. My cheeks heated at the crude comment, but my lips parted on a wide grin regardless. No one, including Cade, knew it yet, but that was exactly what I had planned for the night of the solstice-eve ball.

Madame Luthane nodded her agreement, mouth twisted into a smirk. "One more thing, ladies," she stated suspiciously as she sashayed back behind the screen once more with a twinkle in her eyes. When she returned, she was fisting a bunch of lacy scraps of fabric that matched our gowns.

She passed them out, some complete sets of underthings, but when she got to me, all she handed me was some strappy approximation of undergarments that didn't appear to have enough material to cover anything of note.

I grimaced as I held the bits up by a narrow string that I suspected was intended to wrap around my backside.

"That strap fits into your ass crack," Jemma said, pointing at the lacy thing in my hand. She stifled a laugh. "It'll make it easier for Cade to get to everything."

My face burned, shifting to a shade of scarlet that I knew complemented the room's décor, and I tucked the garment into my balled-up fist. This was not the first time she had called out Cade specifically, but it felt wrong to deny it when I knew we would be going public in a matter of days.

"Thanks," I muttered instead of addressing the comment further.

Jemma gripped my waist and pulled me into a side hug. "I'm glad we got to go out together to do this today."

The rest of the girls piled into our hug, Connally and Ingrid holding onto Jemma's back and Ryana tucking herself under my left arm.

My forehead came to rest on Jemma's as I sank into the warmth of the embrace. "Me too."

My stomach soured when I took in the image in the reflection, knowing that I wouldn't be leaving here with this gown. I extracted myself from the pile-up, hurrying back to the room so I could remove the dress and offer it a proper goodbye.

The curtain peeled back just as I stretched and contorted my spine in an attempt to unclasp the buttons. Madame Luthane entered without a word, and I offered her my back. She unhooked me slowly in a painful, drawn-out removal of the most beautiful garment I had ever worn.

"Your dress is paid for," she remarked as she released the last jewel-toned bauble from its loop down my spine. The gown sagged off my shoulders, and I gripped it against my chest as I whirled to ask the shop owner more. Except, she was already gone.

By the time I got dressed and exited the dressing room, the shop owner had disappeared from the establishment altogether, leaving instructions for the girls to close the locked door on our way out. I supposed the mystery of my dress would stay that way a bit longer.

Fifty-One

The entire day of the solstice-eve ball was consumed by elemental testing. Procedures and moments that I now had no recollection of. Just as we had been warned, our memories were wiped clean, although whatever magic had done that hadn't been able to erase the unease that coiled and tightened in my gut as I got ready for the ball.

It was more than the nerves over my elemental power, which would be revealed within the next twenty-four hours, but also a hint of anxious anticipation over tonight. The night Cade and I might finally give ourselves a real shot at being together outside of the confines of our meadow. The night I had decided to push my physical boundaries with him and relinquish the last of my reservations about our intimacy.

We had discussed it at length, and even if I was found to be Ignus tomorrow, we would allow ourselves this one evening where none of that mattered. A space in limbo reserved just for hearts and delicate touches. Technically, he wouldn't be my instructor again until his new contract went into effect in January, if he even got the position, so we weren't breaking any rules that could get him fired or me expelled.

Jemma brushed the final touch of powder against my nose as I stared at my reflection in the bathing chamber, surrounded by so many others doing the same. Connally had been the one to help with my hair, but she, Ryana, and Ingrid had already vacated to collect their jewelry and meet up with their dates.

"Promise me you'll let yourself have some fun tonight," Jemma stated. Where I thought I'd find a mocking sort of amusement, I only saw a hardened glint in her bright green eyes.

Absentmindedly, I spun my mother's ring on my finger and smiled. "You too, Jem."

She snorted. "As if that was even going to be a problem."

Shaking my head, I made to turn away from her, but she stopped me with a firm grip on my elbow. "I know you don't want to tell me about it..." Her words were so solemn that my eyes flew to hers, catching the sincerity there. "But for what it's worth, I am happy for you. I want you to get everything you deserve and more, Ash. I love you."

"Love you too, Jem," I muttered, but when I went in for a hug, she backed away laughing.

"Oh no, all those beads," she said, waving her hand over me, "will snag my dress."

With that exchange, I rolled my eyes at her, offering a quick goodbye so that we could part ways. Her to find Dante and me to meet with Cade at his suite.

This felt like a turning point, not just for us, but for my life in general. It all seemed so monumental. In a haze of nerves and giddy anticipation, I approached Cade's door and knocked lightly. The sound seemed to echo around in the empty halls, and even though it opened almost immediately, my heart raced in between that first rap of my knuckles and the moment Cade's face came into view.

The door widened just enough for Cade to slip his body through, and he shut it swiftly behind him. His bashful grin only set the pace of my pulse higher as an almost tingly warmth washed over my body in waves.

"Hi," he whispered.

My face heated as if he could read my thoughts. "Hi," I replied, allowing my gaze to drift over the length of him, admiring the way his black tuxedo fit his form with expertly tailored elegance.

I sniffed a lighthearted laugh. Men's fashion was so much less hassle than what was expected from women, and yet he was no less dashing than if he had been covered head to toe in diamonds.

"You are stunning, Ashton." Cade's voice dragged my attention away from his body to stare back at his indigo eyes. He stepped forward, just grazing my chest with his, as he cupped my face in his hands, pressing his mouth against mine.

My lips curved against his. "You too, Mr. Hudson," I mumbled, pulling away and wiping the bits of my lip stain that had transferred onto his cupid's bow.

Cade's hand curled itself around my wrist, and his deep indigo eyes met mine as he planted a firm kiss against the inside of my palm, trailing pecks up the line of my arm, pebbling my flesh as he went. Heat poured to my center when he reached my neck, and I twisted in a failed attempt to join our mouths again.

Cade pulled away. "Ah, ah, ah," he teased, waving his finger at me. "Not yet, Miss Blake."

My teeth scraped against my bottom lip as I attempted to hide my grin. "We don't really need to go right away, do we?"

His eyes darkened, but a soft laugh shook from his chest. "If we start that again, I won't go at all. And it would be a shame to waste such beauty only for my eyes." Those eyes slithered down my form, eliciting another full-body shiver that felt like the cool graze of fingertips across my flesh.

My words came out embarrassingly breathy. "Fine."

He swirled his palm in the air, letting it rest between us in a silent offering. "Let us go then before I change my mind."

I knew beyond a shadow of a doubt that if I said no, he would whirl me into his room and descend upon me with every ounce of the passion I had come to expect from him. Except, I did really want to dance with him. In the open for everyone to see.

My palm fit itself to his, and he twisted his hand so that our fingertips could weave together like an ornate tapestry that was never meant to unravel.

He led me to the dining hall, where members of the staff had transformed the space from a cold, echoey room to a grand and magical dance floor.

The large wooden tables and matching chairs had been removed or repurposed for trays laden with all kinds of food. Velvet curtains, the color of midnight, blocked the entrances to the kitchens from view. Miniature candles had been woven throughout evergreen garlands that draped from the crown molding like the elegant ribbons along a lady's skirts.

Along with the scent of sugary cakes and rich salty meats, the air was alight with the melody of stringed instruments that a quartet played from one corner of the vast room.

Some couples were already dancing, swaying to the euphonic strum of chords, and without a modicum of hesitation, Cade guided me to the center of the dance floor.

It was an odd feeling being with him here, where everyone could bear witness to our joined hands after months of being relegated to the shadows. My jaw clenched around the notion before I could remind myself that—at least for tonight—there were no rules being broken. Ignoring the possibility of that changing if he got the instructor position was easy when his fingers were laced with mine.

Still, with all eyes on us, it was nearly impossible not to note the look of shock and even anger I saw filtering through many of the unrelenting stares. Miss Bella had done her best to warn me that some people might determine that our relationship had given me an unfair advantage in class, but I had dismissed the librarian's advice as projection of her own situation at the time. Now, with all those judgmental glares lobbed in my direction, I had a hard time ignoring her words.

"It's just you and me," Cade whispered, bringing my attention back to him. Back to us.

Cognitively, I forced my jaw to loosen, reminding myself that none of their ire mattered, even as my fingers flexed against the place where my dagger might have been if I had strapped it on tonight. I made my hand fall limp at my side, reminding myself that I didn't need it tonight. Disparaging glances couldn't strip away everything I had worked for, and no one here was going to hurt me in the open like this.

Cade snaked his hand across my hips, resting his flat palm against the small of my back as we began moving in tandem with the change in song. We glided along the dance floor, and I only stumbled over my own feet a few times as I agonized over getting the steps that we had learned earlier in the week just right.

When the music slowed, I rested my cheek against his shoulder. "I'm sorry, I'm not better at this."

He huffed a laugh. "You're perfect, Ashton. And there is plenty of time to get used to dancing. One day, it will be second nature for us."

I peered up at him through heavy lashes. "You see yourself dancing with me a lot, Mr. Hudson?"

With his palm splayed across my back, he pulled me closer. "All the time, Miss Blake. I plan to show you off at every chance I get." His lips brushed lightly on the top of my head as his words ended.

My cheeks warmed, but not from embarrassment, from happiness. *We* had a future together. That was not something we had ever really discussed, being too preoccupied with the most pressing timeline that clustered around this night. Hearing him admit that he had already considered us beyond the confines of the academic year sent butterflies swarming in my stomach.

Daydreams swirled in my mind like the plumes of iridescent dust that billowed over The Cliffs of Alamance during the *Lux Scaporum*, glittering with the prospect of what life could be like.

Me, coming home to him every evening in my emerald uniform.

Him, on his day off from teaching at Biltons Academy, already cooking a meal in our small but comfortable townhome near the square.

My dad, healthy and happy, would visit often, bringing Marjorie with him when he came so Jemma could join us for dinner and reunite our families once more.

The images flashed like slashes of lightning as we moved and spun until the pads of my feet were sore from my too-tall shoes. We might have stayed in that moment forever had a loud commotion not erupted from somewhere over Cade's shoulder.

Cheers and applause reverberated across the dance floor, drawing my attention to the tight cluster of students gathering in a darkened corner. We stopped swaying as I inspected the mass further.

Ingrid approached me with Nielsen by her side, their hands intertwined. A wide smile split her face. "Someone found a list of students with their assigned class, and I'm Caelum, like my dads!"

My guts twisted like a rung-out dish towel. "Congratulations, Ingrid. That's great news."

Cade squeezed a palm along my shoulder as my gaze flickered to Nielsen, fully prepared to give him the same forced exuberance. His scowl told me all I needed to know about the outcome of his results. Clearly, he was not Saxum as he had so casually boasted on that first day.

"Do you want to check it out?" Cade asked, a whisper against my throat.

Apologetically, I waved to Nielsen and Ingrid as I turned to face the growing crowd. Logically, I knew that the class assignment wouldn't inherently reveal power levels, so finding out this piece of the puzzle wouldn't give me any indication of whether or not I was still in the running for the Select Guard.

With a deep breath and my fingers laced tightly around Cade's, I stepped into the chaos of frantic students and reached for the first sheet of paper. It took several more disorganized hand-offs before I found my name.

I unlatched my hand from Cade's to skim the page, and in my haste, I read from the wrong row.

This time, I aligned my finger more intentionally as I slid it across the page.

My breath caught in my throat.

It couldn't be possible.

I folded the paper, so the straight edge made a line across the row and there it was again: *Operarius*.

Working class.

Powerless.

Someone snatched the page from my grip before I could confirm for a third time.

Blood flooded my ears so that the only sound I could hear was the throbbing of my own pulse, its beat erratic and heavy.

I didn't think; I didn't even look around to find a familiar face for comfort.

With my skirts bunched in my hands and my shoes kicked to the side, I ran from the ball.

I could just make out the sound of Cade yelling my name as I retreated down the abandoned hallways of the academy.

"Ashton, stop!" Cade called out, catching my wrist and turning me around in one swift, jerky motion. Giving me no time to flee again, he pulled me into a darkened alcove. I briefly registered that my shoes were gripped in his right hand.

His face was drowned in shock, his deep blue eyes widened as they caught on the track of tears that had already escaped my face, probably making streaks of kohl all the way to my chin.

His stare returned to mine, frantic and full of concern. "What's wrong?" He whispered, but it felt like he screamed the words.

Flinching against the volume and the truth, I choked back a sob that threatened to claw its way out of my throat. "I'm not magical." Maybe if I didn't say the class designation out loud, it wouldn't be true.

Cade's face fell. His disappointment for me was palpable in his frown and the notch that formed between his eyebrows. His grip tightened along the straps of my shoes that he held in his grasp. "What?"

My hand swiped against my cheeks, wiping away the salty stream as I took a steadying breath. "I'm sure it's a mistake. I'll talk to the Headmaster tomorrow. Let's not let this ruin our night."

Denial.

Solemnly, he nodded, putting his arm around my shoulder as we walked towards his room. The now-familiar scent of cedarwood and honeysuckle was a balm against my shredded nerves. It did nothing to stop my racing thoughts, though.

It was just a mistake.

It had to be a mistake.

I chanted the words in my head like a mantra.

He was silent as we meandered the halls, letting me process in the way I needed. When we reached his suite, he motioned for me to wait outside. The hinges creaked as the wooden door slowly swung open, allowing him to enter just slightly ahead of me.

A flash of yellow light illuminated the crevice, and for a moment, I worried something had gone wrong. My palm pushed against the door as I peered around the threshold. The sight nearly erased my trepidation completely.

Hundreds of candles clustered along every flat surface in the room. The warm, flickering light bounced off the gemstones on my dress, spraying glittering, fragmented sparkles across the walls and ceiling. Red rose petals had been laid out in a pathway leading from the door all the way to the bed.

My heart rate climbed from an equal mixture of excitement and anxiety. There had been so much leading up to this moment, and I was desperate to cling to the effervescent feeling I had held mere minutes earlier. The door clicked shut behind me.

You're lucky he still wants you when you are magic-less. The thought entered my head before I reined it in.

More intrusive sentiments slammed into me.

He won't want to be with you when he realizes he has to wait ten years for you to earn your freedom.

My fists clenched into tight balls as I repeated my mantra.

It was just a mistake.

It was just a mistake.

Gods, it had to be a mistake. If it wasn't... I had just witnessed the final nail in the coffin of that life I had envisioned. The one where my father was healed, and I was free. The Operarius class couldn't be in the Select Guard.

My palms stung with biting pressure as fingernails dug deep grooves into my skin.

It was just a mistake.

My spine straightened, and I sauntered across the room to Cade. He was quiet and stoic, letting me come to him, always letting me be in charge of how this went.

When I had closed the distance between us, I ran my hand up his chest, weaving my shaking fingers through his hair and pulling him into me so that our bodies were sealed together.

So that I could shut out all the thoughts.

So that I could pretend for just a little longer that I wasn't powerless.

Cade wrapped his arms around me, dragging me deeper into the embrace. He traced the line of my spine until one hand found my hair, threading through the curly strands still cascading down my back.

His chin dipped, lips meeting mine with slow, hesitant movements as he gave me the space to set the pace.

It was just a mistake.

With my hand fastened around his cheek, I pulled back, tilting his jaw so that he was looking down at me. So that he could see how much I meant it when I made my confession.

"I love you," I blurted out, neither low nor sultry like I had always planned. It was as if I was using the sentiment like hooks on a mountainside as my body clung to him for dear life. But surely this was love?

The corners of his mouth drooped, and his hands stilled in my hair.

Instantly, I released him, taking one long step backwards as my eyes darted along his features for any hint of what he was thinking.

Had I missed the signs? Was it too early?

He sighed, the longest sigh in existence, or maybe it just felt that way in the wake of my unreciprocated admission.

When I gasped the beginning of a sob, he closed his eyes and shook his head. "Ashton, no. I didn't mean that. I'm so sorry, it's just..." When he opened them again, his focus was on his shoes, his hands wringing in front of his hips.

My eyes enlarged with my horror. "You don't have to say it back," I stammered. "I... I'm sorry."

His brows pinched together. His reply was sharp as a blade sliding between my ribs. "Gods damn it... You don't have to say you're sorry."

My attention moved to my attire, glancing down at my body in the skintight dress. The intrusive thoughts barreled through my head again like a raging river after a storm, dragging every positive notion I had ever held about myself under its depths and drowning them.

You hadn't been enough for Farren or anyone else. Why would you think you'd be enough for this man?

It sounded like my voice asking, "Is it me? Is this all too much? Too soon?" We weren't even officially together. Of course, it was too fast to make such a confession.

This question seemed to break him more. His brow remained scrunched, but there was pain lancing his expression now. He was quick to respond, but his words fell flat. "Of course not. You are the most beautiful girl I've ever met. Inside and out."

The salty stream had resumed its trail from the corner of my eyes down my face, dripping slowly off my chin. "I don't understand," I whispered. A confession. A plea.

Cade shook his head. "It's not your fault, Ashton. It's me." His shoulders slumped as he averted his gaze, like I was something too painful to look at. "As soon as I found out you were Operarius... I haven't been able to get it out of my mind that my parents won't accept you. I just..."

Indigo eyes flickered back to mine, held me in place as he kept going. "Damn it, I do love you, and I can't stand the thought of them not letting us be together. It's not fair to you for me to even say that to you. I just..."

Cade lifted a hand like he might reach out to touch me, but dropped it just as quickly as it had risen. "I need some time to think. Before we make this official. If we even can..."

The air left my lungs in a sudden whoosh. Icy realization coated my veins, freezing me in place for a split second. This sudden change in his feelings for me was about my class. He wasn't even willing to go against his parents to find passion in his own life, much less love.

But that was a mistake.

It had to be a mistake.

My breathing became erratic, matching my strange and painful heartbeat. The glittering light reflecting off my dress into the room suddenly became blurry, smearing into white streaks as tears spilled from my eyes and took over my vision completely.

With a shaky inhale, I looked around for somewhere to sit, but all I could find was the bed, covered in rose petals in the shape of a gods-damned heart. My focus lingered there for just a fraction of a second too long.

The voice in my mind sprang to life once more. *He would have you there already if you weren't powerless. Worthless.*

The words were ruthless, cutting me down like the heavy slam of an axe, but they were right. All of my hard work had amounted to nothing.

I had lost my freedom, my father would succumb to his illness, and the last thread of hope I had left, the one stringing me to the man before me, had just been severed.

Cade couldn't bring himself to choose me if I was nothing.

With a pleading determination, Cade stretched his hand between us. I recoiled from his touch as a strangled sob escaped my throat. Before I knew it, my feet were shuffling backwards as I made my retreat from his room.

Cade's eyes remained locked on mine, a rich sapphire blue, ringed in red. Try as I might, I couldn't decipher the emotions shining there. Was it fear or regret? Longing?

It didn't matter. The result was the same: I wasn't enough, and I never would be.

I snatched up my shoes from the floor in my retreat, not wanting to leave a single piece of myself behind in this room.

My spine knocked up against the wooden boards of his door, and I fumbled around with the hand behind my back until it creaked open. With the shift, I all but fell into the hallway, grateful for the lone reprieve that it was empty. Collecting whatever scraps of strength I had left, I slammed the door right in Cade's shocked face, severing the connection of our stares for good.

You will never be worthy, the voice cooed.

In the fog of my retreat, I thought I heard Cade yelling my name. Maybe I just imagined it, allowing myself to foolishly hope for it.

Still, I ran as fast as I could, legs and arms pumping wildly to get as far away from that room as possible as the reality of my new life settled in.

I had risked everything to come here, and now I was leaving with nothing. Not even my freedom.

Fifty-Three

It was either instinct or lack of any other option that led me to the girls' dormitory. Suite C was probably the safest place to wallow in my misery, considering that most of the student body was still at the ball or coupling with their partners in the dark and private alcoves of the academy.

My heels flung across the room as I wasted no time throwing them towards my bunk from the open door. Twisting and turning, I attempted to unlatch the clasps and buttons holding the dress up, ready to shed that, too. Ryana had helped fasten them, and I hadn't counted on being alone tonight when I took my clothes off.

A growl of frustration vibrated my chest when I discovered that I couldn't reach a single clasp. Resigning myself to remain in the dress forever, I scaled the ladder to my bed and threw myself on top of the covers, not even bothering to burrow into its warmth.

But the tears didn't fall, even in the privacy of my own bed, as I had suspected. Maybe it was shock, or maybe I just had nothing left.

You are nothing.

Nothing could help me fully comprehend what had happened to skew our night so far off course. Rationally, I knew Cade put a lot of weight on his parents' acceptance, but I always thought he was working to distance himself from them and their impossibly high standards. There was never a scenario that I imagined I'd be something that wouldn't meet those criteria. With Cade, I had always felt worthy.

You are worthless to him like this, that voice reminded me.

My head shook as I mentally argued with myself. My designation had to be a mistake. Maybe it was an effect of whatever happened to me when I touched the Ice Trophy.

The voice retreated as if it recognized defeat.

It seemed logical, anyway. The Elemental Queen's magic was rare and unusual. If I were Flumen, maybe it just froze my water powers, making them undetectable throughout whatever tests I had been subjected to. A simple conversation with Headmaster Dracorris could sort it all out.

My lungs filled with an inhale so deep that it burned until I released it in an equally long count, repeating the process until the voice disappeared completely, and all I was left with was my resolve. This would not be how my story ended.

With any luck, the sponsor would never learn of what was on that document before I had a chance to right this wrong. In fact, I couldn't wait until morning to act, just in case the unnamed stranger came to claim me early.

Hastily, I pushed myself from the bed and dropped down the ladder, quickly donning socks, lacing my boots, and throwing on my thick wool coat to cover my sparkling attire. I didn't care if I had to wake the Headmaster up from his bed. Nothing would stop me from finding him and discussing the oversight in my testing. Some bizarre interference from the Ice Trophy or a clerical error—which I had not ruled out—would not be the reason I lost my freedom and my father.

Stomping, I left Suite C, emboldened by my new determination. It wasn't until I reached the level that led to the faculty living quarters that my mind drifted back to Cade.

What if I showed this was all a misunderstanding? Could I go back to the man who had just proven that his love for me was conditional?

Admittedly, this was an aspect of affluent society that I could not comprehend enough to empathize with. I would have never cast him aside for something like this. True love could not do such a thing.

My jaw clenched again as I shook my head, tossing away the dilemma for another day. Tonight, I needed to focus on waking the headmaster and forcing him to hear my pleas for a retest. Surely, he would take pity on me in such extreme circumstances.

Finding Mr. Dracorris' suite was more an act in educated guessing than any experience on the matter. Starting with the room that I assumed would be the nicest of the spaces, I held my fist to the door, hovering over the wood with a beat of hesitation.

That fraction of a second was enough to cause me to waver in my plans. What if he ignored my pleas and nothing changed? Would I be forced to leave Biltons, no more than a slave?

"Miss Blake, what are you doing in the faculty wing?" a familiar voice asked.

I turned to see the curious stare of Mr. Higgins, a sight which caused me to sigh in relief. Kind and gentle Mr. Higgins would help me find the headmaster.

"I was looking for Mr. Dracorris," I confessed.

Instead of empathy, the botany instructor's usually soft features hardened. His brown eyes darkening with something akin to anger. "And why would you need to find the Headmaster at this hour?"

His gray brows furrowed, and I found myself suddenly gripped with fear. Something I had never even considered feeling around this man, who, by all accounts, had been patient with his students at every interaction.

"I think there's been a mistake," I answered with a shaky voice. My eyes darted around the hallway to see if anyone was close enough to witness this exchange, but I was, unfortunately, utterly alone with him.

My focus returned to the instructor's glare, his eyes dancing with menace. "A mistake?" He slid his foot forward, moving incrementally in my direction.

As a counter, I took a long step back, quickly finding my shoulder blades pressed against the door behind me with nowhere else to retreat. "Y-yes," I stuttered. "They released the list of class assignments." I decided that my best bet was to remain honest with the man.

"And you believe you should not be Operarius?" he asked, his tone an uncharacteristic taunt.

My head shook fervently. "No. My friend's mom read my energy; she said I have power." The sentiment had sounded so reassuring in my own mind, but here in the space between us, it felt like the ramblings of a desperate woman.

Mr. Higgins' cold brown eyes trailed over my face. "There is no mistake on your designation."

"You don't understand," I interjected. "I touched the Ice Trophy, and it hurt me. I think it messed with the results of the testing."

The instructor released a shallow, breathy laugh. "Did you know that for some of you, we are aware of your class designation well before the actual ceremony occurs?"

I blinked back my confusion, and when I didn't answer, he shook his head in disapproval as if that had been a test I had just failed.

"Your file, in particular, had you flagged as Operarius before you even stepped foot on this campus."

My heart constricted with the rest of my muscles as my body locked into place. Every cell within me came to a screeching halt. "That's not possible," I choked out. It couldn't be true. That would mean that I had given up my freedom the moment I signed that parchment.

Mr. Higgins took another step towards me. There wasn't even a sliver of an inch for me to move away, and my heart slammed against the cage of my ribs.

His lips curled back to reveal another menacing grin. "Why do you think some stranger offered to pay your tuition after you were tragically denied aid?"

For the third time tonight, my world flipped on its axis. "What are you talking about?" There was no way he could know about the deal unless...

His brows arched to his forehead. "I think you know, Miss Blake. Now is not the time to play coy with me."

A gasp of air collected at the back of my throat. Bewilderment overwhelmed my system. "It's you?"

This educator had marveled at the sight of the blue-tipped blood rose as if the plant were some precious thing. He had been comforting when I left the scene of Sylvia Lemmon's demise. He had been nothing but compassionate until this moment.

My brain, wrapped up in shock, wanted to buck at the thought that he was somehow the person who had been threatening me and my dad.

His grin turned feral, a bit more than simply unhinged. "It was me, Miss Blake. And now, it is time to pay the price."

My lungs stuttered with a trapped breath. If he had known I was going to be labeled Operarius the entire time, that meant that he had sought me out to trap me in his servitude. A sourness plagued my stomach. "You tricked me."

Mr. Higgins sniffed an amused laugh. "I merely saw an investment opportunity."

The door behind my back grew warm with my prolonged position pressed against the rough boards. Mr. Higgins was still far enough away from me that there was a shred of hope for my escape. If only I could distract him.

"What do you mean?" I asked, as my eyes darted in the direction I would need to run, praying that the motion didn't betray my thoughts.

The man shrugged lazily. "You are not the first person from the lower rungs of society who wished to make their dreams come true here." He laughed again, and despite his obvious joy at my terror, it was mirthless. "You'd be surprised to learn how many students from even high society can no longer afford the tuition here."

"So, you prey on those less fortunate?" I asked. Even my dismay could not extract the accusation from my tone.

He gestured in a swirling motion in the air. "Only those that have already been tagged Operarius," he replied. "I am not from a wealthy house, and I dislike taking risks."

As much as I wanted to ask more about why some of us had already been *flagged* with an Operarius designation, I couldn't bring myself to question him further because, at that moment, a noise distracted him from down the hall, and I was forced to abandon curiosity and take my chance.

My palms slammed against his chest as I pushed him away with every ounce of strength I had left. He stumbled backwards, and I didn't watch as he righted himself. I refused to spare him even a sideways glance as I bolted down the hallway.

Fifty-Four

My vision blurred with the collection of gathering tears as I raced down the passages of the academy, praying for once that I'd meet a staff member during my journey. No one was there, and I couldn't count on Cade to be looking for me this time, nor did I truly want to endanger him by going to his suite.

After a heartbeat of contemplation, I took the stairs down because if I got trapped on an upper floor, I'd have nowhere to go. On the ground level, my modes of escape—or at the very least finding another human with elemental power—were higher.

The heavy footfalls of my botany instructor sounded behind me, indicating some physical prowess that had not been obvious during any of his sessions. Resisting the temptation to look backwards, I trained my eyes forward, knowing any distraction on my part could give him an advantage I could not afford.

My chest heaved as I reached the next landing, taking the steps two at a time to gain some momentum, my legs nearly tangling in the delicate fabric of my gown. Flashes of light bounced around me as the flames from the sconces reflected the sparkles of the stones woven into the skirts.

My blood muffled my hearing, tearing its way through my veins like the sound of a thousand wingbeats. My movements were born from instinct alone, following some invisible pathway as I pushed through the enormous double doors at the entry to the academy. I practically threw myself into the chilly night air, traversing the courtyard with a desperate plea on my lips.

On I went, my boots pounding against stone. Past the spray of the copper fountains. The water illuminated beneath a pale crescent moon. Farther and farther away from the academy to the one place, I knew there would be a person with magic: the stables.

The ballroom was full of powerless, unsupervised students, so I couldn't go there, but the House Platypus' leader was almost always in the stalls. It wouldn't have been surprising to me to learn that she slept there some nights, as she typically smelled faintly of the sweet aroma of hay.

Light flickered from the edge of the building's cracked doorway, and I could have cried with relief if I hadn't heard a growl from far too close behind me.

My hands shoved against the opening so hard that I felt splinters from the wood biting into my palm. My mouth was already open, ready to explain to Tamari that we needed to defend ourselves, but the stables were completely empty. The only living things that stared back at me were the beady eyes of the horses.

Frantically, my eyes scanned the space for anything I could use as a weapon, but fell short when the door was practically blasted off its hinges behind me with an unnatural gust of air.

Mr. Higgins stood, panting in the doorway, eyes locked on my location, wide and feral. He was practically frothing at the mouth, but when he found me, that grimace turned to a predatory grin. "Did you really think that you could run from me?" he seethed. "I know where you live. I know where your *father* lives. And that parchment you signed was imbued with magic. There is no escaping our deal. You will die if you run."

Backing away from him slowly, I raised my hands as if I could calm him like Tamari would a startled horse. "What do you want from me?"

Naively, I had assumed that the sponsor wanted some inside influence within the Select Guard and that our goals aligned for that fact alone. There had not been a single consideration that the person granting my tuition had counted on me failing.

Mr. Higgins bared his teeth as he stalked across the space, eyes always pinned to my location.

My back hit the rough, unfinished boards at the same time an iron hook pressed into my skull, the reins hanging from it knocking against my arm.

The instructors snorted. "I don't think it's necessary to concern yourself with what I do with my investments. But if you must know, I utilize my free labor on my vineyard."

My mind was mush as it tried to decipher what was happening. "Berit was part of this, wasn't he?" I couldn't shake the feeling of Déjà vu, recalling with unsettling clarity a similar frantic look on Berit's face when he cornered me in the woods.

The question seemed to take the instructor aback. His eyes narrowed. "He was another unfortunate investment that couldn't handle the pressure put upon him."

A gasp filtered from my lips. "You were blackmailing him to join the guard too?"

Mr. Higgins supplied me with a sadistic chuckle, although his eyes still held the irritation that clung to him like smoke at a campfire. "His goal was to be named heir. I thought to change it up for the sake of the entertainment."

Entertainment?

My lungs froze in disbelief, and I had to force myself to suck in another breath. "So, he tried to kill me because you were blackmailing him to win, knowing that he was going to be named Operarius too?"

The botany instructor shrugged. "If he hadn't gotten so serious about it, he might be alive to join you at the vineyard. But since I've already lost out on one investment, I can't afford to lose you too." He made to take a step towards me, and the horses around us stomped and brayed as if they, too, sensed the danger I was in.

My palm slid against the rough boards behind me. I had seen a pitchfork leaning against the wall somewhere to my left. If I could reach it, I'd have a fighting chance. It had been my own petrified reaction, not my abilities, that had kept me from winning that last round of the hand-to-hand combat challenge. Ryana had called it a panic attack, and I would not let myself succumb to that fear now.

My fingertips crept towards the handle as I spoke. "They will know I'm gone when I don't show up for the branding ceremony."

Amusement danced in his cold, lifeless eyes. "I have no intention of letting you miss out on the branding ceremony. That's the deal here: I get access to the pre-labeled students, and they don't ask any questions as long as the brand is placed on your arm. It's a win-win for all of us."

There he was again with that word. *Us.* Were the other instructors in on it? Did Mr. Dracorris know? Were the Guides aware of what this man was doing to the people of Demetros?

With the threat of a magical death looming over my head, I knew I probably wouldn't run. But that didn't mean that my absence would go unnoticed. "And afterwards? My dad will expect me home for the solstice break."

Mr. Higgins' laugh grated against my insides. His shoulders raised and dipped in quick succession as if that was no bother. As if he had planned this all out. "There are ways to ensure that no one expects you back for some time. Ways to assure them that you don't want to return."

Tears streamed down my face, not for myself, but for my father, who would spend the rest of his shortened life wondering where I was. "My dad won't stop looking for me."

He hummed some annoyed sound as if he was growing bored with our entire interaction. "No one has ever suspected me, and my operation has been successful for many years."

My blood transformed into a frozen river, my breath catching at the fringes of my throat. He wasn't just going to take me for a decade; he was going to kill me. How else had this never gotten out?

My hand curled around the wooden shaft of the pitchfork, and I yanked it forward, shoving the pointy end toward him with a violent thrust. I would not go down without a fight. "And after the ten years? Surely some of your victims have gone back to their lives?"

He shook his head. "Why would they? You're all powerless. What other life could you expect for yourself with the shame of that truth resting on your shoulders?" His chest expanded with pride. "I provide you a place to live, a task of value, and a living wage... after those ten years, of course. Why would you want to leave when you'll have no options waiting for you at the back end of your contractual obligation? When all ties to your loved ones have been so completely severed…"

Warmth and salt coated my face, dripping onto my chest, but I ignored it, hoping that my rage would fuel me through this. "There's no way I'd choose to stay with you," I spat out.

The instructor laughed as he stepped closer, summoning the strength of the wind all around us. Hay began to lift and swirl in the air, flying directly towards my face. I tried to shield myself with my arm, but it was no use. The debris pelted me with the cadence of rain in a thunderstorm.

"Get away from her," a familiar voice growled. It wasn't Cade who came to rescue me this time. It was Ryana.

The bluster momentarily paused as the botany instructor wheeled around to face my friend, her marbled brown eyes practically glowing with indignation.

I used the gap in his windy assault to spring into action, lunging towards Mr. Higgins with all the force I could muster. Iron tines pressed into the skin along his thigh, drawing blood and a whelp of pain from his lips.

"Go get help, Ryana!" My command came just as the instructor blew us both back with gusts from his outstretched palms, the pitchfork flying from my grip and landing, handle down, embedded deeply into a bale of hay.

"Better listen to her, Miss Vance. You are no match for me without your brand," he taunted.

With my only weapon so far away from me and Ryana having brought nothing with her to defend us, I knew he was right. My shaking hands lifted into the air. "Let her go and take me." At least now, someone would know what happened to me. Someone could tell my father that I was gone. There was no hope for me left.

My vision blurred with my tears, and my eyes stung beneath their weight as my defeat gathered on my lash line.

"You know nothing of this place or those brands," Ryana said, lifting her palm to the sky and producing a ball of blue flame. I could feel the heat lapping against my skin, even from this distance, and that was the only way I knew that this wasn't my mind breaking.

Mr. Higgins' eyes widened, and his skin lightened several shades with his shock. "H – how?"

Ryana cocked her head to the side, her glare menacing in the flickering blue light. "I wouldn't concern yourself with that now," she cooed, mirroring his earlier words to me and making me wonder how long she had been following us.

Mr. Higgins backed away, nearly scrambling to find another exit to the stables that wouldn't involve passing Ryana.

A mirthless cackle climbed its way up Ryana's throat. "I don't think so," she called, launching the fireball at him with such force that smoldering air blew my hair back from my face.

The impact threw the man across the stables and directly into the opposite wall, knocking him out cold. The subtle movement of his chest told me that he was still alive, though, and I couldn't allow myself to focus on the fact that the sight left me disappointed.

Ryana's marbled brown eyes appeared right in my line of vision, hands gripping my upper arms with a ferocity that I had come to recognize in her. "You need to breathe."

I hadn't realized I was even hyperventilating until she spoke her command, and it took everything I had in me to steady my breaths. "What... do... I... do?"

"Leave this place," Ryana all but snarled. "We cannot let you get branded tomorrow, and you need to be long gone before they start looking for you.

There was no way I heard Ryana correctly. I shook my head, breaths still coming in uneven spurts. "What?"

"You need to leave," she reiterated, face slack and void of any humor that would have indicated this was a poorly executed joke. "It's not safe for you at Biltons Academy."

My lashes fluttered to the beat of my heart, wild and frantic. "Mr. Higgins made me sign a magical contract. I'll die if I..."

Ryana shook me with her grip on my shoulders. "No, you won't. There is no magic binding you to that man," she seethed. "But you need to leave before he wakes up."

I shook my head, knowing that even if what Ryana said was true—and I so desperately wanted it to be—that he'd know exactly what had transpired here and go after my father. He had delivered me those purple roses from the edges of my cottage garden, he knew exactly where to go to find the motivation I needed to stay.

"He knows that I know now. And he knows where my father lives. He brought me those purple roses with a threat..." Another sob hiccupped from my throat.

A worried expression filtered over Ryana's features, and her eyes closed for a heartbeat before opening again with a new resolve. "Do you trust me?"

It was absurd to even consider trusting her. She had just used magic in front of me without a brand. She clearly knew something I didn't and had lied to me in the process of hiding these things, and yet... "I do."

Her chin inclined once. "Then you need to listen to me." She shucked a pack that I hadn't noticed before from her shoulders, and I recognized it as my own. She handed it to me before slipping the scarf from her body and passing that to me, too.

"Put that on," she demanded.

Awkwardly, I managed to loop the scarf around my neck and toss it on the bag. "Do you remember how to get to Eden?"

My eyebrows pinched together again. "Your hometown?"

Ryana grimaced. "I'll explain everything when we meet up again after the solstice. Do you know how to get there?"

"Yes, but you're not coming?" Terrified exasperation pooled in my tone.

She spared a glance over her shoulder at Mr. Higgins' still body. "I need to take care of him so that he doesn't remember the events from this night. I think we can convince him and the student body that you ran, but I need you to leave before he wakes up. It won't work if he comes to before I can give him the potion."

A potion? That would make him forget?

Still, that was the least of my pressing questions. "Why can't I be branded?"

Ryana's stare continued to dart around the space, and I could feel her anxiety rising, my own swelling to meet it. "Those brands don't do what the monarchy says they do, and I was sent here to figure it out. Regardless, you are not powerless, and we cannot let them put those marks on your skin because I don't know what they would do to you, and we cannot risk it."

Despite not having fully answered a single question, she didn't give me another moment to ask anything further. "Ashton, I need you to listen. Take a horse and ride to Eden. There, you will find the Barker Inn. Ask for Skylar and tell her it's a code *dragonfire*. She will know what to do."

It took several heavy blinks before my brain caught up to the request. "Skylar. Dragonfire," I reiterated in a daze.

"Go," she urged. "You need to leave now."

My feet carried me forward even as my mind lingered behind. I paused when I had only made it several steps away. "I can't leave my dad. He's sick... I..." My voice cracked. I would rather risk my life than leave him to succumb to his illness or Mr. Higgins' wrath.

Ryana pursed her lips together as if she were arguing with herself over something, waging some internal war within her own mind. Then, the concern lifted. "I know your father," she stated. "He always knew that this day might come, and we have contingencies in place to protect you."

We?

She placed her hand on my forearm, squeezing comfortingly, and I so desperately wanted to lean into it. "He knows where you are going, and he will meet you there the minute he learns we've had to enact the plan."

"What?" I huffed. It was all too much. This was like being in a nightmare I couldn't wake up from, and the mysterious reassurance that my father would be okay felt like a trap.

The silence seemed to stretch on for an eternity before Ryana's expression turned grave. "Your mother's boots are beneath the chair next to your front door." The words and their implication exploded between us like fireworks.

I froze. Anyone could know there were boots next to the door to our cottage, but so few would know who they had belonged to. I was confident that I had never mentioned it to her before, or anyone, for that matter. "How?" I stammered, the wind knocked from my lungs by shock alone.

Ryana's stare was pleading as she spoke, pushing her desperation through her words. "The how isn't important right now, but I need you to listen to me and get out of here."

My heart longed to believe her, and with nothing good left to cling to but her promise, I felt my head jerk in a single nod.

"I'll help you saddle the horse," she said, already pacing to the rack that held the saddles. She did all the work while I watched on with numb observation.

"It's time," Ryana called, patting the horse's hindquarters.

I slipped a well-worn boot in the stirrup and swung my leg over, mounting the horse and ripping the bottom of my dress in the process. There wasn't time to mourn the loss of the beautiful gown, it had already been stripped of the hope it had carried anyway.

Just before I dug my heel into the steed's side, my gaze caught on Ryana's stare. On the person whom I had come to call a friend, even if I was realizing with a sudden pang in my chest that I never knew her at all.

With a twist of my wrist, the reins wound around my hand, and I steered the horse towards the back exit of the stables. "Goodbye," I mumbled over my shoulder.

"It's *see you later,* Ashton," she called. "We are friends, and I promise when we meet again, I will tell you everything that I can."

Her reassurance did little to quell my despondency, hardly a salve to the wounds the night had inflicted.

"Your dad will meet you there soon," she promised, knowing that it was the final push that I needed to leave.

The column of my throat burned as I swallowed down my reservations. Exhaustion weighed heavily in my muscles, and I wasn't sure how I was going to make it so far north when I already felt like collapsing. But I knew I had to try. The urgency in Ryana's tone was enough to spur me along, knowing that staying would mean further danger.

Mr. Higgins had been right about one thing: there was nothing left for me here, anyway.

I kicked against the horse's flank, and he bolted through the gap in the hall, out into the chilly December air. It took no time to find the gate that Tamari had driven the cart through that day when I had to show her the way to Sylvia's body. With a galloping run, the horse sailed clear over it, not even bothering to slow for me to unlock it. We landed with a jarring thud that rattled my teeth.

Again, my heel tapped against the horse's side, giving neither of us a reprieve as we lurched into the night. Before long, we were meandering down the formal streets of Fulgrande.

My grip tightened on the reins as we launched down the cobblestone pathways, the beating of hooves clapping against the buildings as we passed. I cringed at the sound, a not-so-subtle announcement of my departure, but it didn't seem to matter. Most of the people were asleep, their fires and candlelight extinguished. There was nothing but darkness and shadows to greet me.

Our pace was grueling, like I was running from some physical entity and not just the notion of whatever else was after me. Before long, the buildings of the capital city blurred into the geography of the land, and the only evidence of the town left was a tiny speck of flickering light on the horizon, giving the mountain range surrounding Fulgrande a faint glow, like a halo.

I allowed myself one last look, then I turned my back on Fulgrande. On Biltons Academy. On every single hope and dream I had made for myself. On the thoughts of proving my worth. On the idea that I would be powerful. On the prospect of a love that was not truly reciprocated.

I turned my back on everything, and I kept riding.

Fifty-Six

THE NAMELESS

She remembered so much now.

It was all coming back, striking down like lightning, slashing across her mind, and thunder rumbling in her heart. Each fresh surge brought her to her knees, but with it came new clarity and understanding.

She knew the details of her childhood home; of the bedroom she had grown up in. Enough to finally recognize that very room as the prison she was currently being held within.

Even though she couldn't recall everything, memories danced along her consciousness of that mystery woman as a small girl in this room, too.

She had always suspected that the woman had been more to her than an adversary on a battlefield, but now she had proof: unlocked moments of their time together from a collection of years before adulthood.

There were flashbacks of games and stories.

Songs and laughter.

She knew exactly what she had lost in that combat zone now, and it caved in the very structure of her chest every time she was sucked into a memory of that woman's death.

She wanted to believe that it was that love that finally broke her from the spell that stole her memories, but she wasn't sure because, as powerful as love was, it had never saved her before.

Uncertain eyes glanced down at those runes that held her from speaking, much less screaming, reminding her that there was still a final barrier between her and her powers. One that even love could not overcome. The shapes symbolized a deal she had struck and a debt that had not yet been paid. She knew that now.

With every released memory, her resolve was renewed.

With every new revelation of yet another person whom she had loved and lost, she grew more determined in her goal.

Depending on how much time had passed, there were people who could help her break these chains. She just had to find an opening to escape.

With entirely too much optimism, she thought of what it would be like to feel that static energy racing through her veins again, imagining a world where she looked out at her captors and destroyed them for everything that they had done to her and the people of this kingdom.

She clenched her jaw as her anger boiled over from within her, her magic flaring frantically for a release at the surface of her skin. Instead, she was simply met with a dull ache in her bones as the buildup reached a crest that could not be broken. A wave that would not collapse.

A knock sounded at the door. *A fucking knock.* As if anyone ever waited for a response to enter. As if she even had the capability of calling out to consent to their request.

She braced herself as the door swung open, but instead of letting her anger rise to her expression, she buried it deep within her. The last thing she needed was for her captors to realize that she was one misstep away from taking back her powers and seeking her revenge.

A smile curved her lips in that placating way that she always had; before she remembered who they were and what they had done.

"We need to talk," the man said before lowering himself to her favorite settee.

She kept her smile in place, even as it longed to lift further because she couldn't agree more.

Even though he didn't regard her with any of the respect he should have, given her newly recalled position, she didn't balk at his tone. She remained the simpering woman he expected her to be, clinging to the knowledge that she was so much more.

After all, she wasn't some weak-minded girl, terrified of her powers anymore like she had been in the memory of when they had first awakened.

Knowledge was power, and she had just remembered that she was Estella the first of her name and the Elemental Queen of Demetros.

THE END

Author's Notes

Thank you so much for reading The Lonely Kingdom. This story came about because I was in such a low spot after having my second kid (and formally quitting my high-stress process engineering job) that I was having a bit of an identity crisis. My father, who passed away in 2020, always taught me that I could be whatever I wanted to be and so I took that to heart.

I began typing away at the computer during nap times as a way to blow off steam and do something creative. At first, I only intended to write for myself but the longer I went, the more books I wrote and the more I thought "maybe I can just put it out there." It took several years (and several rounds with the editor) to build up the courage to release this out in the world so I cannot express how appreciative that I am that it made it to your hands.

Fun fact: Ashton was the name I had picked for a daughter. In my mind this series is my baby, and I had two boys, so the main character of The Lonely Kingdom got the name instead. Seems rather fitting in my opinion.

If you enjoyed this book, I would love if you would consider leaving a review on Amazon or GoodReads. Reviews can be a big deal, especially in an indie space, so they are much appreciated.

If you'd like to be the first to know about the next release, the behind the scenes of my writing, and pictures of my cat, sign up for my newsletter on KathrynOscar.com, or following me on Instagram @KathrynOscarWrites.

Acknowledgments

First of all, thank you to my husband, R, for supporting me in this insane hobby turned side (and currently non-paying) job. For listening to me drone on about plot ideas and for reading four thousand drafts of this book (and most of the others) in an attempt to keep up with the current storyline. Thank you for providing feedback and for giving me the space to write, even if that meant that you had to sleep on the top bunk so that I could take over the computer in our bedroom until late into the night. I don't think I would have ever gotten this far if you hadn't pushed me into taking it more seriously and I cannot express how grateful I am for that. I love you, always.

Thank you to my friends who didn't immediately laugh in my face when I said I wasn't going back to my job but was instead writing fantasy novels in my room. Jennifer, Caitlyn, Katelyn, and Hayley you all have been so supportive from the moment I reluctantly blurted it out. I was an idiot for ever doubting that. Thanks for still being part of my tribe even when I'm a recluse and drop off the face of the planet for months (except for the occasional meme).

Thank you to my sons, M+E, who kind of broke me a little but helped rebuild me into the woman I am today. You may never read this (because let's be honest, ew, mom wrote it) but you both were so instrumental in me getting this far, even if it was in a passive way. You inspire me every day to do things I'm afraid of because it's what I want you to do. I never want you to be held back from something wonderful because of fear and what better way to tech that than to show you. I love you both more than life itself.

Thank you to my editor Cynthia for not just whipping this book into tip top shape, but for encouraging me to be proud of what I had already done. For having five hour conversations with me that just felt like gabbing with a girlfriend. I needed that more than I can ever say (and probably didn't because I'm not good with mush despite how this acknowledgement section looks). The Lonely Kingdom became a story I was willing to share because of your aid and I am immensely thankful.

Thank you to my discord group of ragtag authors, A.M. Aurelia, Amber, Frank, Cleo, and Rachel. We mostly use the group to chat about life (and occasionally our books) but it's been so nice to have someone who gets it that I can just blabber on to at all hours of the night. You guys are awesome.

To you, the reader, thank you again for taking a chance on an indie book. I hope that you got something from this, even if it was just an escape from the world for a moment in time, because let's be honest, we could all really use one right about now.

About the Author

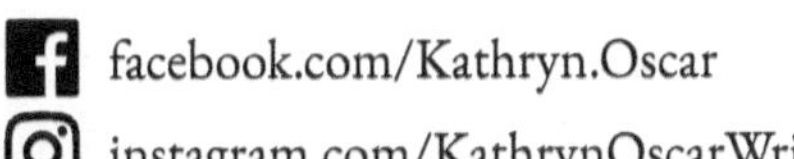

Kathryn Oscar is a self appointed "recovering engineer" who decided to spend time utilizing a different part of her brain to write fantasy stories in her bedroom. She lives on the coast of North Carolina with her husband and three kids—if you count the cat, which everyone including the cat, does.

When she's not writing, Kathryn can be found reading, training for RunDisney races, curating playlists for books she hasn't written, plotting books she will never have time to write, and taking care of her feral boys.

facebook.com/Kathryn.Oscar

instagram.com/KathrynOscarWrites